A LIGHT FROM THE ASHES

RACHEL ANNE COX

Sandie~

Thanks so much for reading.

Live free and join the revolution!

Published by Glass Spider Publishing
www.glassspiderpublishing.com

ISBN 9781076445872
Library of Congress Control Number: 2019908915

Cover design by Judith S. Design & Creativity
www.judithsdesign.com

GLASSSPIDERPUBLISHING

*For Gibs, who showed me the light
when all I saw were the ashes.
And for Jen and Steven, who helped
me keep the fire going.*

PART I

1

BEFORE

Somewhere in Virginia
The Year of 42

The scarred land and verdant forest looked brighter to Sam through the lens of freedom, even in the pre-storm gray light. Silver-backed leaves flipped their personalities with the waves of the wind. Now green, now silver. And his eyes danced to follow them. The monotony of the last seven years had blended his days into beige sawdust. Still, seven years wasn't too long to work for the woman he loved and earn the right to put his mother's ring on her finger. That kind of joy demanded a sacrifice.

Patches of sun were torn out of the shade. From the tangled jumble of trees and vines as he made his way home, Sam saw a flash of white out of the corner of his eye. Two skeletons lay out in the open, entwined and held in strange poses by creeping blackberry vines thick with thorns. They lay across the edge of the forest, partially in the adjacent meadow as if they were trying to run away from something but had fallen just short of escape. He approached them slowly, blanched bones of broken lives and interrupted dreams. He wondered, as he always did when he came across similar remains, what their story had been. He could not rest until he'd taken care of them. This was as good a place as any for a burial.

He pulled the small shovel from his pack to dig the two graves. The clean hiss of the spade in the dirt sounded and felt as if the earth would swallow the shovel up, and him along with it. Hiss. Lift. A clump of earth and roots thudded and thwapped on the ground. Sam felt and heard the rhythm, willing himself not to break it. The rhythm, the pattern, they held him in check, but the sounds didn't quite drown out the echoes of war still ringing in Sam's ears, sounds he was never quite free of.

Rifle fire in the trees beyond the meadow splits the air. Sam no longer jumps at the sound. It peppers his consciousness just as the crickets used to. He listens closely as the cracking sounds fall away, farther and farther from his hidden spot in the alders. Sweet vernal grass tickles his legs, the dew sticking the leaves to his torn shins. He loses track of how long he is crouched over the body of his friend. The blood and muck where he'd fallen now pasting his clothes in stiff swaths of torn fabric. As the air becomes thick and quiet around them, Sam pulls out his knife to begin digging a grave. He grips the leather handle, blackened with sweat, until his knuckles are white. In the trackless forest, he searches to find a spot clear of trees and roots. The sky becomes gray with rain, and he tries to quell the sickness rising in his throat. He can't look at the lifeless body of his friend taken down by a bullet. He keeps thinking the boy will rise as if he'd been sleeping and take off running into the trees as he used to. Sam hunkers over the hole he's forming, tearing the carpet of leaves and grasses from the earth with one hand, fiercely wiping the tears from his cheeks with the other.

Sam couldn't remember the name of his young friend, another child soldier—he was only the first of many Sam would see fall around him. And he didn't know the names of the bodies he was now burying. The task struck him as strangely intimate for strangers. Touching the bones of bodies that had been actual people, determining their final resting place. What made him worthy of such a task? Maybe it wasn't about worthiness. Maybe it was about availability. Within a half hour, the job was done, a shallow grave being sufficient for the bones left behind. He reached in his small pack for *Great Expectations*, where he'd scribbled some words in the front cover in his own hand.

Ashes to ashes, dust to dust. The Lord is my shepherd, I shall not want. He maketh me to lie down in green pastures: He leadeth me beside the still waters. He restoreth my soul. Yea, though I walk through the valley of the shadow of death, I will fear no evil. Blessed are You, Lord our God, King of the universe, the True Judge. This is also for the good. May all be free from sorrow and the causes of sorrow; may all never be separated from the sacred happiness which is sorrowless. From untruth lead us to Truth. From darkness lead us to Light. From death lead us to Immortality. Amen.

Sam didn't understand fully what the words meant. They were abstractions to him, unrelated to anything he could see or touch, but still they gave him comfort. He knew that the people of Before had found great comfort in these words. He'd read their religious texts and knew their deeply held beliefs had even led to wars. Somehow for him, pulling the words together from their different religions made him feel he was helping them find peace, and in doing so, he found his own. Maybe this was what they called God—this peace and space between.

Kneeling by the grave, he kissed his hand and touched the stone he'd found to mark the grave. "Rest well, my friends. I thank you for your sacrifice." He'd lost count of how many he had buried through his travels. But he'd promised himself long ago that every lost soul he encountered would receive a proper burial and his thanks.

As his final day at the lumber work camp had ended that afternoon, he was left with a strange sense of emptiness and anticipation. His days had been filled with other people's needs and orders for too long. He knew within a day he'd be seeing Gemma again—he had worked and waited for nothing else every day for seven years. So why then was he now almost frightened of the reunion? True, he hadn't actually received any response to his letters throughout the seven years, but with the haphazard carrier system being what it was, there could be a thousand reasons for that.

Sam had left the lumber camp near the Border to go on one last scavenging trip before heading home. He needed another book and thought he might find something for Gemma as well. He was lucky to still have his treasured copy of *Great Expectations*. When the Corsair sergeant had found him the night before retrieving his books from the hidden box under the third tree from his tent, Sam had been sure he would lose everything.

He'd been so careful. Everyone was in the mess tent, eating dinner. He'd looked over his shoulder a hundred times to make sure he wasn't followed. The small wooden box was in a shallow hole nestled among the tangled roots of an alder. He'd covered the hole with a large patch of soft green mold so no one would see the earth disturbed. The hinges had creaked and protested as he opened the box to reveal his few linen-packed books. He had tucked *Great Expectations* between his jacket and tunic. He breathed a little easier, feeling the worn cover and heft of it close to him.

He tenuously fingered the pages of the other two volumes—a book of Irish poetry from the 1900s and Hemingway's *A Farewell to Arms*. The familiar smell of musty paper and ancient binding overcame his senses as he sat breathing them in. Moon-cast shadows danced over the words as the wind rustled the pages.

"Samuel Erikson!" The grating of the Corsair's voice had shot through his spine like a steel rod, and the two books in his hands fell to the ground.

"What's this?" The soldier strained his tight blue uniform as he bent to retrieve what Sam had dropped. "The day before you are to leave, and we find this contraband."

"Sir, I can explain . . ."

"Silence!"

Sam felt the bulge of *Great Expectations* under his coat and hoped the soldier didn't see it. He knew this sergeant as one of the more fair Corsairs, as Corsairs went. Perhaps his punishment wouldn't be so bad.

"It seems we have a choice to make, Erikson. If I bring you to the commandant, you'll likely serve another six months here."

Sam's jaw tightened, and he felt beads of sweat breaking out on his forehead.

"You were in this camp before I arrived. Remind me how long your service has been."

"Seven years, sir. It started out as two."

"Bad behavior?"

"I wasn't given a reason, sir."

The sergeant looked around as if he wished someone else were there to tell him what to do. He was used to following orders.

"Right, then, Erikson. Either we take you to the commandant, or you throw these books on the fire. Which is it to be?"

Sam's shoulders relaxed without him thinking about it. "You're giving me a choice?"

"Only if you make it in the next five seconds. One . . ."

The sergeant stood before him, pistol in one hand, books in the other. Sam couldn't see his face clearly in the dark but sensed he wasn't enjoying his task.

"Two . . ."

Trying to strain to see the books in the soldier's hands, Sam wished he could have read them one last time before being faced with this choice. But he knew what his answer had to be.

"Three . . ."

"I'll throw them on the fire."

"Follow me, then."

They'd walked in single file to the fire just outside Sam's tent. It was beginning to smolder into coals. The sergeant took a large stick and stoked the fire into life. Tiny bits of burning ash rising up into the blackened night.

"Here you go, Erikson. Now, throw them in."

Sam held them in his hands for a brief second. Relishing the feel of the hard covers beneath his fingers. Any longer than a second, and he would have started to question his decision. In one swift movement, the books were out of his hands, being swallowed up in the burning embers.

As he thought back to the night before, he felt a hole in the pit of his stomach, an ache for the words and ideas lost in the flames. His skin itched with a layer of the fine sawdust. He ran his hand through his thick mop of sandy curls, then along his rough cheek. He tried to think of Gemma, his reason for every decision he'd made for as long as he could remember.

He thought of the creek which he would pass on his way home. Though he'd had some leaves of absence from the lumber camp—most of them spent on scavenging trips in the Forbidden Grounds—he had not been allowed in his own village until his seven years were up. He wondered if the creek still followed the same path.

Vines of memories as thick as the underbrush at his feet followed him through the forest. He thought of Gemma's long brown hair falling around her shoulders, her skin darkened by the sunlight as they played in the creek together, hiding from the kind but watchful eyes of Zacharias. She was the only bright spot in his life then and now. They had clung to each other in those first few years after Zacharias took them in after finding them stealing food in the town square. Gemma was the only beauty he'd ever seen in this world.

She would be changed some, he was sure, as he was changed, his thin arms now bulky with muscle hard-earned in the Virginia forest cutting an average of two cords of wood per day, hands calloused and worn. But she would be lovely still, and more importantly, she would be his. They would hold each other in a warmth protecting them from the descending winter. He would love her in the breathing in and the breathing out, sharing the same air and all else. He would smile at her over breakfast in the mornings, the coffee steam from their two cups blending between them.

And now he was on his way back to her. It used to be easy enough to slip past the Border guards. Although their stations weren't far apart, Sam remembered how often he had found the guards napping. The days of revolutionary armies and border raiders were long gone. He'd found a few of the guards easy to feign friendship with and bribe with alcohol he found in demolished bars in the Forbidden Grounds.

The roads outside the Border still showed remnants of the past before the Disaster and lay as crumbled and broken reminders of things that no longer existed. Within Virginia, the Triumvirate had ordered that roads be cleared and reverted back to dirt paths, easier on the feet of men and horses. But outside the Border, the asphalt roads looked like black icebergs among the encroaching trees. Sam usually found it easier to walk beside the decrepit roads than on them.

On this particular day, he had walked toward the ocean. Ancient rusted-out cars littered the roadway, tires and all useful pieces of them long since removed. He'd taken this road enough times to know he'd find nothing of value until he reached the place he called New Beach. Sam had breathed in the freedom in the crisp autumn air. No more schedules, no more assigned days off. Day after day of freedom stretched out before him, and he reveled in the luxury of it. Feet crunching in the fallen leaves the only sound, no other person for miles.

The road had turned southeast through the forest, which for years had been left unchecked. There he'd found the bodies as he took in the sights around him, the trees tall and untouched by man, the underbrush encircling his feet like a pool of green dappled with orange and red. The edge of the woods had receded. Others had been here and cut some of the trees down. Saws, not axes. He was used to seeing trees with axe-cut notches from other scavengers in need of wood for their fires or shelter. A tree here or there, hewn down awkwardly and dragged through the brush. But a group had done this, not an individual.

Sam took another look at the shallow grave he was leaving behind, then made his way down the hill to the waves lapping around the buildings in New Beach. The signs were long since destroyed, so he could only guess what the city used to be called whose streets now flowed with seawater. He scanned the horizon, finding the city library just above the waves, only the top floor untouched by water. Sam picked his way over fallen walls, bricks, and chunks of cement in piles. He saw the waves flowing in and out around the buildings. Were they farther inland since his last visit?

Sam thought of a line he'd read from Emerson and played over in his thoughts every time he saw the Forbidden Grounds, like a song that ran in his mind unbidden. . . . *universal essence, which is not wisdom, or love, or beauty, or power, but all in one, and each entirely, is that for which all things exist, and that by which they are; that spirit creates; that behind nature, throughout nature, spirit is present.*

He wondered if that was true, and wondered again about the nature of the world, the nature of creativity. He couldn't quite grasp it. What creativity rested beneath the waves around his feet? What glories and forgotten dreams of those gone before him? Sam wondered just how many lives had passed in the streets beneath him *en masse*, how many had intersected, combined, created, grown, and multiplied before the final rush of water washed them from the earth and all became still, silent, separated again.

He was able to reach the library via a high wall which reached from the dry land, then through the seawater like a tightrope. From the wall, he climbed into an open window on the fourth floor of the withered library. Rows of books in the dusty rays of what was left of the sunlight stretched before him. He wouldn't have time to really search as he would like to. He passed the shelves he'd already been through. Here and there a gull perched on a copy of Keats or commiserated with Lee's mockingbird. These were books he'd read often in his travels, but he only brought back his absolute favorites, as hiding places had been scarce at the lumber camp. Now perhaps he could bring home a few more. He passed by King's *Salem's Lot* and Salinger's *Catcher in the Rye*. Although he had read them, he couldn't count himself as fond of them. Gemma would like *To Kill a Mockingbird*, he was sure. He'd written to her about it the first time he read it. She reminded him of the young, precocious Scout, though with a protective armor which the naive Scout never needed.

He scanned the shelves, trying to find volumes with the least amount of damage. Whole sections were pasted with white salt deposits. The choking stench of mold almost overwhelmed his senses. Books stood swathed in the black, creeping growths. Some without mold simply fell apart in his hands. As he reached for what appeared to be the last copy of

To Kill a Mockingbird, several shiny black beetles and silverfish scurried from beneath it. On the shelf in its space, insects and two brown salamanders writhed in liberation. He held his breath, hoping they had not devoured the inside of the book. As it began to come apart in his hands, Sam sighed with disappointment. He would have to find another. Lists of books Zacharias had told him about scrolled through his head. He tried to think of one Gemma would like. Was *Little Women* one Z had mentioned? Yes, he was sure that it was, so he quickly went to find it.

Sam ached to stay longer, to be able to linger over the books he loved. But he kept looking over his shoulder to make sure he wouldn't be caught by a Corsair patrol or other scavengers. Something in Sam always wanted to believe the best of people, but he never trusted anyone he met in the Forbidden Grounds, and there were more patrols in the Forbidden Grounds in the past months than there had ever been before. He quickly placed the book in his knapsack, first wiping the pages free of salt and dust. He paused longingly in front of the shelf of Steinbeck before forcing himself back to the window and his wall of escape.

Standing just at the water's edge, Sam turned the ring on his little finger absentmindedly, a gold ring which seemed to hold the fire of the noonday sun. The ring his father had given his mother, and before that his grandfather to his grandmother. It was the only small connection he felt to any happiness in the past, and soon it would be a connection to Gemma and the happiness of the future. His heart was starting to beat faster every time he thought about returning home and seeing Gemma's face, her blue eyes filled with tears. He wondered if it was anticipation or fear of finding her gone. Shadows of clouds crawled slowly up the mountainside while cold came down to wash over him like his fear. He tried to squelch the nervousness that was growing like a weed in his stomach. By tomorrow at sunset, he'd be there. Tomorrow.

For tonight, he had to find a place to make camp. Looking skyward, he saw the clouds blowing inland, a fall storm looking for a place to land. All of the living things were scurrying for cover ahead of the approaching storm. A raccoon ducked under a sea of elephant ears. Sam just glimpsed the end of his tail before he disappeared. A turtle moved slowly across his path, stopping, listening, changing course, going as fast as he could go. Sam would have to build a lean-to of branches and leaves quickly if he hoped to stay dry.

A LIGHT FROM THE ASHES

* * * * *

Sophie woke in darkness, hearing a scream and recognizing it as her own. She lay still for several moments, jaw clenched, back rigid. She imagined the muscles in her body from top to bottom, willing them to relax and release her piece by piece, trying to calm her breathing. Her fingers found their way to a lock of hair at her forehead, twirling it as she often did to still her mind. She felt like a hot coal thrown out of a fire into the freezing night. Long minutes passed, and her heart continued to race.

The dream was the same—it was always the same. A man holds her by the throat against a tree, his face merely an inch from hers. She struggles for breath, his hands squeezing tighter, fingers bruising her skin. Suddenly a knife is sheathed under his ribs as the darkness closes in. Gulping in the lost air, she falls next to him, her hand on the ground in his blood when he grabs her by the hair, pulling her head down hard upon the ground. She always hoped the dream would end differently, hoped to redirect the actions in her brain. But every night she was helpless to the tide of dreamed events.

Knowing it would be at least an hour before she'd find sleep again, Sophie climbed out of the bed and pulled on her threadbare robe, which had lost its lavender luster years before, now a matted gray. Still chilled, she went down the hall to check on her daughter. She tried to tiptoe lightly, but the wood floor creaked under her bare feet, the sound shocking her as much as the cold floor, just as she reached her daughter's door. She listened first, and hearing no stirrings within, opened the door. Bridget's breathing was slow and steady. The child held tightly to her scrap of a blanket she'd carried for the four years since she was a baby but had flung herself out of the covers in her sleep. Sophie pulled the several quilts over her, tucking them under her chin. Moving as slowly as possible, she buried her face in her daughter's curls on the pillow, breathing in her scent slowly. Ending her nightly ritual, she softly kissed each eyelid as Bridget took in one quick breath and then settled into the arms of sleep again.

Sophie's feet found their own way to the kitchen through the darkened house. She stopped at the kitchen sink and looked absently out the window to the softly glowing fires along the benches below the mountain, tiny points of light in the looming darkness. Her own dying fire was a mix of

15

orange and black embers in the kitchen fireplace before she stirred them back to life. The full moon cast its light through the thin curtains, making the white sink almost glow before her. She pulled the ladle from the water bucket to fill her glass. Her fingers found the charm of the butterfly necklace—a remnant from her sister and a past life—twisting and playing with its wings absently. Often in her midnight wanderings, she would wish for her sister's company, a comfort she would never have again. The images of her dream started to fade as she gulped the water, washing down the fear. The process both a cleansing and a redemption.

Sounds of tiny scratches and scurrying from the corner assaulted her ears, quickening her heartbeat again. Sophie turned quickly to see the firelight reflected in two tiny glowing eyes under the edge of the china cabinet. She set her glass down silently before eyeing the culprit—a crouching gray rat. She grabbed the first thing she could get her hands on, a kitchen knife resting near the sink. Though her throw was swift and her aim was true, the squeaking rodent evaded her attempt on his life. She took up the knife from the floor in frustration but cut her hand by grabbing too quickly in the dark.

"Damn!" she whispered under her breath. A resentment filled her for having to clean up the blood dripping from her palm. She wished she wasn't so used to the sight and smell of blood. At times it had seemed to pervade too much of her life—blood flowing to swim beneath the garden symphony of moonlight, heaving whispers languid with red screams, revealing her thousand frantic dreams. Sophie found herself trying to remember when blood had still frightened her. Perhaps that time had never existed. Too young, she'd learned to fight for her survival. Too young, her parents' blood had been spilled.

After wrapping her hand with a clean bandage she pulled from the first-aid cabinet, she walked outside. She was tired but restless. The cold air coming down from the mountains was refreshing in her lungs while also making Sophie want to retreat back to the comfort of her quilted bed. She took several deep breaths, wrapping her arms and robe more tightly around herself. She thought of her family again, as she always did after waking from nightmares. She thought of them slumbering beneath the sod somewhere to the west. Did the moonlight wash over their graves as it now washed over her? How would her life be different now if Laurie had survived? She wondered if they would sit on a porch swing somewhere

16

together, watching their children play together in a garden. Bridget had never had other children to play with. Sophie mourned a future that had never been allowed to take its first breath.

The sharp smell of smoke in the air was often a comfort during her late-night rambles. It reminded her she was not alone in the world. But her own arms around her waist were a poor substitute for the arms of another.

* * * * *

A little boy sat shivering in his damp clothes as he hid in the bushes out of the line of sight of the border guards. He knew he'd be able to get back across the Border farther down away from the guard station, but he hadn't found much food in the last few days, and his legs were feeling weak. He struggled to stay awake, knowing he needed to get to the creek for water. More than anything, he needed water. He still couldn't believe he'd knocked over the cup he set out to catch the rainwater the night before. Now he'd not be able to get a drink until he reached the creek. Not unless . . . He turned his face upwards, catching the first few raindrops falling into his mouth. They offered him little relief from his thirst. He was just about to make a run for it when he saw the man with the knapsack approaching the guard station. The boy instinctively crouched lower in the bushes.

"Hold up there, sir," the guard called out, holding his rifle across his chest. "What's your business here?"

"Well, Harry, I'll tell ya. A little of this, a little of that." The man reached in his pack, pulling out an amber-colored bottle. "More this than that." He handed the bottle to the guard.

"Sam! It's been awhile. Too long, I'd say." The guard gratefully took the bottle from his friend as he set his gun down. "Missed you around here. But mostly I've missed this," he chuckled.

"Now you pace yourself with that one, Harry. I've picked the bar clean and don't know when I'll find another one."

"But you will, though. Join me for a drink?"

"Nah, I've got to get back. Haven't seen Gemma in a while."

"Your seven years up already?"

"Yeah. Gotta get back and surprise her, unless she's been counting the days like I have."

"Good luck, my friend. And thanks for this!"

Sam forced himself to shake hands with the guard before passing through the gates. "Remember, take it slow," he called over his shoulder. As he rounded a curve in the road, he wiped his hand on his pants.

The boy waited for the guard to take his bottle inside the guard shack and snuck quietly through the gates. The man called Sam interested him. He had supplies and ways of moving in and out of the Border he hadn't witnessed before. Surely, he'd have food as well. Dinner would come for the boy in the middle of the night while Sam slept.

* * * * *

The walking wind wandered into the stone night with hardly a rustle after the earlier storm. Sam sat in front of the fire, flipping the fish he'd caught an hour before. He was only hours away from home but had to stop for the night. The wet branches smoked more than he would have liked, but then he'd always liked the taste of smoked fish anyway.

"Be sure to give the line enough slack," his father used to say. "Don't pull at it too quickly. Gotta let the little devil think he's gotten away with something." Then his dad would pat his shoulder. "This is the good stuff, son. Remember that."

Sam had heard the boy following him for the past few miles. The first time he'd heard the movement behind him, his heart had jumped into his chest, thinking a patrol was after him, or, maybe that he'd be pulled back into working in the lumber camp. It wasn't unheard of for Corsairs to allow someone to hope for escape, only to drag them back. But whoever it was seemed to stumble every few steps. Not likely a Corsair. After a few miles, Sam had trudged up a rise in the land where he could glance back behind him unnoticed. A small boy, maybe ten in ragged clothes, with dark hair matted on his forehead. Sam had slowed his gait to let him keep up. He heard and saw him drinking from the creek where he'd caught the fish. Sam wanted to help him but figured the boy would speak to him when he was ready. He now looked down at the fish in the fire. Just about done. The boy had still not made his presence known.

"There's plenty here for two," he called out, still staring into the fire. No answer.

"You must be hungry. We've walked quite a ways today."

18

The boy stepped tentatively into the firelight.

"Come get some fish, boy. Pretty good, if I do say so myself."

The boy held his hands out. Sam took his own plate and handed it to him. Within a minute or two, the boy had polished off the fish, breathing quickly between bites as if he thought the food would disappear before him.

"What's your name?"

He continued to chew and breathe heavily. His eyes closed, enjoying every hurried bite.

"You have one?"

"Ethan," he finally responded.

"Ethan, I'm Sam. Where you from?"

Ethan looked puzzled.

"Where do you live?"

"Around. Woods, mostly. Sometimes cabins."

"Family?"

"Hard to remember. Mom and Dad have been gone a long time. The Corsairs took them. I was maybe four or five, I think." It was a common enough story that Sam had heard too often.

"You must be at least ten now. Who's been taking care of you all this time?"

"There were others like me. We traveled together for a while. But they started stealing things—not food—fighting, using weapons on people. I tried to stop them. Then one morning, I woke up, and they were gone. Been on my own since."

"When was that?"

"Two, three weeks maybe?"

"Well come and sit down at least. You look worn out."

Ethan hesitated. He wondered if he could trust this man who was so friendly with the border guards.

"Come on now, boy. You've nothing to fear from me."

There was something behind Sam's green eyes, some kind of knowing and kindness that softened Ethan's defenses. His worn out limbs forced him to soften the rest.

"Pretty tired, I guess." The boy sat on a large rock near the fire.

"You can share my camp tonight if you like, that is if you promise not to steal from me."

"I don't steal things." The boy seemed offended by the comment.

"Oh yeah, that's right." Sam chuckled. "Well, come on now. Here's some bread to go with the fish. A few days old, but still good."

Ethan practically inhaled that as well.

"You're a regular Lost Boy, aren't you?"

"I'm not lost." Another bite. "I know where I am."

"No, it's from an old story," Sam explained. "The Lost Boys lived in Neverland and followed around another boy named Peter Pan who could never grow up. They fought Captain Hook and the pirates."

"What are pirates?"

"Long ago they roamed the seas, pillaging and stealing from any vessel they encountered. In the story of Peter Pan, he's the cause of Captain Hook losing his hand, so the captain is always seeking vengeance."

Ethan's eyes lit up with wonder and renewed energy from the nourishment as he listened to the pirate stories.

"If you're going to follow me, I guess that makes me Peter Pan." Sam smiled to himself. "I kind of like that."

As the evening wore on, with their bellies full of fish, the two new friends looked out over the darkened valley toward the mountains not far to the west. Tiny points of orange light dotted the landscape, fires like stars draped across the valley.

"Sam?"

"Hmm?"

"Do you ever wonder what it was like Before?"

"Sometimes."

"What do you think it was like?"

"I've talked to some of the Old Ones about it. My adopted father, Zacharias, lived Before. He's told me a few things."

"Will you tell me?"

The fire popped and hissed between them. Sam squinted to see the boy through the flames.

"Many people died in the Disaster. We can't say precisely how many. All means of calculating the loss or communicating it were destroyed. Only a surge of sound, a blinding light, and then immediate darkness, as if some giant switch were flipped that turned off the world."

"What's a switch?"

"They used to have buttons that could turn a light on and off by just flipping it."

"Like lighting a match?"

"Not exactly. The Old Ones talk of how it was before the darkness. Before the switch was flipped. They remember times when the electricity in their houses would temporarily go out. There was a silence that would come over a house when it didn't have electricity coursing through it like blood, making the machines run like a pumping heart."

"I wish I could see a machine. And hear one. What else happened?"

"Before the final silence, the storms had grown in number and intensity with only days in between, then hours, then seconds, blending into one great storm with no foreseeable ending. Animals had stopped exhibiting their signs of warning before the storms, they were so overwhelmed."

"And after?"

"After the Disaster, everything just stopped as if the whole earth had stopped spinning on its axis. People and animals alike walked more quietly for a time. Those who had to speak only spoke in whispers, afraid to be the first to crack the eerie silence. It was more silent than any they had ever heard before, and the darkness blacker than the night sky. This greater darkness that covered the land was more than the absence of light. People became like children stumbling with no points of reference. So they started building fires. Eventually, it came to be that every household would light a fire either in their houses or outside, for cooking, heating water, staying warm. And then the darkness was lighted only by the fires of survival in those left alive as it is now."

Ethan saw Sam looking intently at the valley. He appeared to be searching for something. "What are you looking at?" the boy asked.

"I'm watching for her fire."

"Whose?"

"Gemma's, the girl I'm going back to meet."

"How can you tell which one is hers? There are so many fires in the valley."

"Hers is different." Sam took a deep breath, and Ethan waited for him to finish his thought.

"Ever since we were children, she always started her fire before anyone else—before it was even dusk. And her fire always seemed to be larger and brighter than it needed to be."

"So you just look for the bigger fire? Still, it must be hard to spot it from this distance."

"Any time I'm out in the woods like this, I can't sleep until I see her fire. Even when I was at the lumber camp, sometimes I'd climb up in a tree after dinner and look over the valley to see it. There's solace in it, I suppose."

"Have you ever had a sleepless night, Sam?"

"Many, boy. But never for lack of finding her fire."

2
HOMECOMING

Another sunrise pierced Sophie's tired eyes, her sleepless night blending into an early morning. She'd seen too many sunrises lately. Standing at her bedroom window, she gazed at the fog rising from the fields, a blanket colder than the bed she'd left behind. In the glint of early morning, a ray of sunlight caught the faded red flag raised from the side of the old mailbox at the end of the drive. Another message.

Her heart beat faster, wondering what her task would be this time. She had been a member of the Watch since she'd come to Boswell. Just as their name implied, the small band of people from the surrounding villages watched government officials and activities, reporting to each other on Corsair army troop movements, changes of guard stations, or any other matters of interest or concern. But in recent months, as more Corsairs arrived in the villages and an added strictness to the law started to prevail, the Watch captains had decided it was time to increase their subversive activity. Sabotage became the order of the day. Though their efforts were small and merely a nuisance at first, with each successive attack they gained confidence and momentum.

As children of revolutionaries, the blood of rebellion ran hot in their veins even more than a decade after the end of the Second Revolution. Each had lost someone to the Triumvirate's harsh punishments after the war, and some had lost everything. Sophie was no different. It was the memory of those she'd lost which fueled her actions and stilled her nerves.

No matter what her captain would ask of her, she knew she'd comply willingly.

Listening carefully at Bridget's door to make sure she was still asleep, Sophie walked barefoot in the cool, dewy grass out to the edge of the road to retrieve her orders from the mailbox. Pulling the paper from the box, she read the old printed words on one side: *In a sweeping passion, she seized a glass vase from the table and flung it upon the tiles of the hearth. She wanted to destroy something. The clash and clatter were what she wanted to hear.*

Paper being scarce, sometimes her messages came on the backs of pages from old books, sometimes written in the margins. Sometimes the messages were just circled words within the text.

Sophie's orders usually came from Foxglove. They'd only met a few times over the years when absolutely necessary, yet Sophie felt a connection with her. She'd imbued her with certain traits by analyzing the firmness of her handwriting and wondering about her choices of quotes and song lyrics to convey her messages. She'd met her not long after joining the Watch. Knowing that Foxglove was from a village outside of her own Boswell, they didn't have occasion to meet often. Sophie also wondered about the code name, Foxglove, and how she'd chosen it. Sophie herself was accustomed to having two names, remembering the old Romany custom her adoptive parents had continued with her. Hers, Aishe, had been given to her the day she arrived in the Romany *kumpania* when they'd taken her in along with her younger sister, Laurie. Though no one called her that since their deaths; only those she loved had ever used that name. There was something intimate about sharing that hidden part of herself with Foxglove, even just on paper.

She flipped the message over to see the handwritten note on the bottom of the page:

Aishe~
Abide with me; 'tis eventide, and long will be the night if I cannot commune with thee nor find in thee my light. ~Foxglove

They would meet that evening at the lighthouse. Sophie thought again of her adoptive parents who'd brought her to this remote place, named her, and given her the chance for rebirth.

"My Aishe, you and your sister have not been with us long. We've tried to teach you the ways of the ancient Romanies here in the kumpania."

"Yes, Daj." Sophie helps her new mother wash the clothes in the small stream outside of town with the other women.

A great yellow Monarch butterfly lands on a rock in the middle of the stream, moving so slowly that Sophie wonders if time has stopped in this new quiet place, more quiet than any other place she'd been. In the night, the sound of guns and screams still stab her dreams, bleeding out the fear and loss.

The butterfly flits its wings, restarting time.

"Do you see those young trees across the stream?" Her Daj points to a stand of saplings in almost a complete circle. Her arm is thin and graceful as the trees she points to. "Your Dadu and I planted those trees but may not see them grown tall as you will."

"What do you mean, Daj?"

"The same time is not granted to all. We have and love you now. We are thankful for this time. But later moments may not be granted to us. So you must always remember those things we've taught you. Help your sister remember. The wind may bear us away as that butterfly on the breeze. Will you try to remember our ways?"

Sophie wraps her arms, dripping wet, around her Daj's waist. The scent of wild raspberries wraps around them both. She breathes in the raspberries, the stream, her Daj, and the moment, holding them suspended in her lungs as long as she can before breathing out. "I'll always remember."

Still standing by the mailbox, Sophie turned back to look out to the bay behind her house. Her farm on the hill rolled down toward the beach, waves singing to the morning. Between the gray, salt-blasted wall of her house and the stand of trees at the edge of the woods, she could see the lighthouse in miniature, like a darkened lantern just barely rising out of the water. It hadn't been used for many years since the waves had taken over the island on which it stood and creeped toward the mainland, gaining ground without retreat. The cold Atlantic now swirled just beneath the gallery of the old lighthouse where once stood the keepers, on the lookout for ships which would never again grace the seas.

It was a dangerous endeavor to reach the old light, so the message was infused with importance. Sophie turned the paper over and over, the words crinkling beneath her fingers, enduring yet fragile. She traced the words, soaking them in, willing them to lift from the page, enter her body, and fill her with some kind of strength for what lay ahead.

"Mommy!" Bridget called from the porch, rubbing her eyes, still sleepy. Her strawberry-blonde curls a bright contrast to the faded gray house behind.

Even with frightening feats to be performed, she remembered that belonged to the night. In the day, there was still breakfast to be made, the child bathed, wood chopped, and clothes washed.

"Coming, honey."

* * * * *

Sam woke shivering in the cool morning damp. The fire was out. But something else seemed strange. His ears registered the morning sounds: birds out for their breakfast, other creatures starting to stir among the trees and underbrush, crickets chirping. What was missing? Rubbing his eyes, adjusting to the light, he sat up, looking to where the boy had slept on his extra blanket nearer where the fire was. But the boy was not there. Sam's blanket was folded neatly near his feet where the boy had left it, but there was no other sign of him around the small campsite. Sam thought maybe he'd gone into the woods a ways to relieve himself, but when he didn't return after a few minutes, Sam was concerned. He packed up quickly, pulling the last of the bread from his pack to eat on the road. He wondered which way the boy would have taken and why he'd run off so early. Sam looked both directions down the road through the dispersing fog. He thought he saw movement toward the east, so quickened his steps in that direction.

"Ethan! Ethan, boy! Hold up!"

The figure stopped and waited.

Sam ran to catch up with him. "Why did you leave so early, son? Didn't you at least want to have some breakfast?"

Ethan shrugged. "I didn't want to wake you, I guess."

"Well, why did you leave at all? I thought maybe I'd take you with me back to my village, and then we could figure out what to do with you from there."

"No need to bother. I'll be alright." Ethan started to turn and walk away.

"Now, hold on there. Just wait a minute, will you?"

Ethan stopped walking, but his eyes stayed on the ground.

"I have no doubt you can take care of yourself. But the thing is, you don't have to. I know a little of what your life is like. I was out on my own when I was a boy too."

Ethan looked up at this remark, wondering if it could be possible there were grown people who had survived a life like his.

Sam continued, "Even though I had friends with me, we were fairly starved. There wasn't much in the way of food after the war. Now, I'm not saying you have to stay with me permanently if you don't want to. I'll leave that to you. But just know I'd like to take you with me, at least help to make sure you get a decent meal from time to time. What do you say?"

Ethan straightened his shoulders, wiping his sleeve across his nose. "I guess that'd be alright."

"Peter Pan and the Lost Boy, right?" Sam grinned.

"Right."

"Now, let's see what we can do about breakfast."

* * * * *

The smells of sun-ripened apples, burning leaves, baking pies, and a hint of gardenia met Sam almost like a kiss. This is what he had remembered, just the welcome he'd hoped for. He led Ethan down the hill toward the village, Jesse's Hollow. The aromas reminded Sam it was Market Day in the town. All were preparing their trades of harvested vegetables, baked goods, hand-crafted jewelry, and the like. The sound of a guitar strumming came from the distance. Yellow birch and red maples formed a kind of tunnel over the path, obscuring the view of the town square until they were right upon it. A wave of memories of Market Days past washed over Sam as the fragrance borne on the breeze. Helping Zacharias set up the photography equipment and samples of his work, carting a basket of necklaces and bracelets for Gemma which she'd made of the stones found along the creek bed. And always the hunger in the pit of his stomach as he was accosted by all the smells of food and treats to be had for barter.

Two small tied canvas sacks hung from Sam's belt carrying raspberries and hickory nuts he'd gathered on the trail to trade for bread and honey. All other necessities could be retrieved from the Government Office. No private farms were allowed to have animals other than chickens. So every

Market Day once a week, the people could present themselves at the Government Office with their identification cards and be given a ration of meat and milk. They could also request clothes, soap, medicines, and other necessities if needed.

A shock of deep-blue uniforms stood out against the rust-colored backdrop. Sam was somewhat shocked to see at least ten Corsairs standing guard at the edge of the town square, rifles in hand. In fact, there were more groups of them spread out along the border of the square. Sam hadn't seen the Corsairs in such abundant number for many years. Ethan instinctively began walking more closely and slightly behind Sam as they neared the soldiers. Sam reached an arm around the boy's shoulders.

"Not to worry, son. This is my home. All will be well," he reassured, having to somewhat force the words out in a normal timbre. He found himself wondering if it were true.

"Halt," a sergeant spoke up harshly, stepping forward. "Identification cards."

Sam pulled his card from his pack, trying to make conversation with the soldier. "It's good to finally be home after so long. I've been at the lumber camp for the past few years. Smells like someone's got a pot of Brunswick stew on. That'll be nice for a change."

The guard looked suspiciously at the card, then Sam, then Ethan. "Sam Erikson released from civilian service two days ago. It shouldn't have taken you so long to return and report. Where did you go?"

"I was caught in a rainstorm just after leaving camp."

"Who is the boy? There are no children listed on your card. No wife or family."

Ethan shrank back.

"Stumbled upon him in the woods. He was starving. Parents are dead. So I brought him with me."

"You must register him as your adopted son at the G.O. immediately before you will be allowed any trade privileges."

Sam looked around for a moment, somewhat confused, and beginning to bristle at the sergeant's accusatory attitude. The other soldiers stepped slightly forward as he hesitated to respond. He knelt down at Ethan's level to address the boy. "I saw some more berries in the underbrush over there. I think we could use some more to trade. Can you go and pick some?"

Ethan nodded and ran off to the side of the path, happy to be away from the soldiers.

"Sergeant, I have only just met this boy. I had planned to help him find a permanent home with a family. But I'm not sure I'm the best choice of adopted father for him just now. As you say, I'm not yet married. Besides, I don't even know if he wants to stay with me permanently. Couldn't we just get him his own identification card and then go from there?"

"That is not permitted."

"Has there been a new law instituted?"

"'No child shall be allowed in any town nor to receive government rations without an accompanying parent or guardian with corresponding identification card.' This has always been the law, even if you townspeople never followed it." He almost spit the word "townspeople" as if it were distasteful in his mouth.

"Now, calm down, Sergeant. I have no intention of breaking the law. I'm just trying to get some clarification and do what's best for the boy. He's obviously been through a lot, having already lost his real parents."

"He wouldn't have lost them if they weren't revolutionaries. The Triumvirate must make sure there are no more rebels on the loose in the form of young brats."

Sam felt as if he'd been slapped in the face. The sting began to well in his eyes as he thought of his own parents long gone.

"Now, you *will* bring the boy to be adopted, identified, and recorded, or you will not be allowed to enter this village. Understood?"

"Yes." Sam tried to keep the edge out of his voice.

The sergeant raised an eyebrow, waiting for something before he returned Sam's identification card.

"Yes, sir," Sam added.

The sergeant thrust Sam's card back in his hand before standing aside. "Let them pass. Make sure he goes straight to the G.O."

Sam turned to find Ethan, who was not picking berries after all but sitting and observing the scene play out from his hiding place in the brush. "Come on, son. Let's go." Sam placed an almost imperceptible emphasis on the word "son."

* * * * *

At the Government Office, Ethan was duly registered as Sam's son.

29

Two rations of meat and milk, two sets of winter clothes, each including gray work shirts, work boots, gray winter coats, and brimmed canvas hats. Ethan felt the luxury of having his own things and enough food not to worry his stomach. He carried his clothes neatly folded in front of him, almost reverently.

Sam found a stand of fruit and autumn vegetables, trading for a small basketful. "Here's an apple, boy."

A grin appeared over the stack of clothes.

"Here, give me those. I'll carry them." Then, turning to the keeper of the fruit stand: "Do you know Zacharias?"

"Yes, of course," the kindly woman responded. "Our senator and leader of the Old Ones," she whispered.

So he'd become the oldest living citizen, Sam mused.

"I've not seen him here today. Does he still keep the same farmhouse outside of town?"

"Yes. He doesn't come every Market Day anymore. So often tired."

"Thank you, ma'am." Sam smiled and began the walk toward his old home, Ethan following behind.

His feet knew well the way, always turning toward Gemma. He wondered too why she was not in the town square on Market Day. Everything seemed odd on this day. Everything just a little off, not quite as he remembered home. There was an air of nervousness among the people he encountered. Everyone seemed to be looking over their shoulders. But Sam would let nothing ruin this day. He was within a ten-minute walk of seeing Gemma. Everything would be better when he could see her face again.

He'd played the scene out a thousand different ways in his mind. She would be outside, Zacharias on the porch behind her. Sam would run to her, spinning her around as she laughed. Or he'd walk slowly, kneeling before her to offer the ring without a word. Maybe she'd see him first and run down the drive to meet him at the gate. But every iteration of the dream ended the same way, with her in his arms and tears on their faces.

"Is Zacharias your adopted father?" Ethan asked, pulling Sam from his daydreaming.

"Yes, he is. He took me and Gemma in when he found us living in the woods behind his house. A scrawny and angry lad I was, too."

"Where were your parents?" Ethan looked at the dirt path, kicking up rocks as he shuffled forward.

Nor could Sam look at him when he answered, "Killed by the Corsairs after the Second Revolution."

Ethan nodded. Then he knew that Sam knew. He just knew. Ethan slowly reached his hand out to take Sam's as they walked on.

"Does Zacharias have a wife?"

"No, boy. She died not long after the Disaster. Things were very different back then. People weren't used to things we take for granted. Many couldn't find food for themselves and starved. Others got sick from contaminated water. Then there were the attacks that happened. You know, Zacharias never actually told me how she died. I didn't ask. But this town is named for her. Jesse's Hollow."

As Sam and the boy came around a bend in the road, he saw the white farmhouse at the end of the drive, peeking out from a stand of yellow birch trees, making the house look like it was lit from behind. The old man sat on the front porch, facing a small field of corn not yet harvested. He rocked slowly back and forth in a faded gray rocking chair. His eyes were closed, so he didn't see the two travelers walking up the drive.

Creaking steps on the front porch alerted Zacharias to their presence. His eyes opened slowly and registered recognition more slowly. "Sam." The word seemed to fill his whole being. He had to take several deep breaths before continuing, trying to sound nonchalant about Sam's return. "You've changed, son. Time was you couldn't even grow a beard. And now look at you, mountain man that you are," he chuckled.

Sam extended a hand to help his friend from the chair, pulling him into an embrace almost too much for their manly pride to withstand. "It's so good to see you, Z," Sam said into his shoulder, which seemed to have shrunk since they last saw each other.

Stepping back, Zacharias surveyed his foster son. "So, it's been seven years. It feels longer."

"So it does. So it does." Sam quickly looked toward the fields to wipe his eyes without detection.

"And who's this you've brought with you?"

"Z, this is Ethan. New member of the family."

"Nice to meet you, Ethan. Looks half-starved. Just like you were. Why didn't you feed him?"

"I would have, Z, if he'd been with me. We just met yesterday," Sam responded. "I smell your Brunswick stew. Maybe that will start to remedy his nutrition. Is it on the fire out back?"

"Of course."

Walking through the house to the back yard, Sam took mental note of the changes. Dusty furniture, some pieces missing, unfinished repair jobs here and there. Gemma wouldn't have left things like this. She couldn't be living here with the house in this state. Sam and Ethan dropped their things in the front room, then pulled dishes from the kitchen cabinets, a few of the doors nearly coming off the hinges.

"Where is she?" Sam asked, almost under his breath.

"Gemma? She hasn't lived here in quite some time, Sam."

A fear gripped Sam's heart that he hadn't felt since the war. That sinking sickness, twisting every organ, dried his mouth and made his head pound. He turned quickly to survey the eyes of his old friend.

"No, she's alright, boy. She still lives in the village, just on another farm. Calm down. I should have said that first."

Sam took a deep breath in. Then another. His hands on the counter for balance. He stood up straighter, feeling a sense of urgency he couldn't explain. He needed to see her now.

"Well, if you'll point me in the right direction, I'll go see her. Can Ethan stay here for a while? He needs dinner and could use a bath." He tousled the boy's grimy hair.

"Sam, I should tell you . . ."

"Can it wait, Z? I just need to get to Gemma for now."

"Maybe it's best this way." Zacharias placed a hand on Sam's shoulder. "The old Tucker place on the other side of the bridge. Remember?"

"Sure. Hunted squirrels on their place often enough."

"The Tuckers left a few years back. Tucker himself was called up for army duty, so they moved the family closer to the Wash District."

"That's too bad. He liked farming." Sam pulled the books for Gemma out of his pack. "I'm not sure how long I'll be. But I'll be back before dark."

"Did you notice the lantern poles along the road? Makes it easier to travel than before. One good thing the Corsairs did."

"So I did. So I did. Well, I'll be back in a while."

* * * * *

The old bridge had been fixed and patched in places, so Sam didn't have to cross it as gingerly as he used to. He remembered jumping on the boards to scare Gemma. Or the time they fell off the railing into the stream below, soaked to the skin, running in the sun to keep warm, falling in the grass out of breath.

"I'd like to be a writer one day to write about days like this," Sam panted.

"Writers don't exist anymore, silly," Gemma responded, ever the practical one.

"They could, one day. Maybe by the time I'm old enough."

"The Triumvirate will choose your profession, and you know it. They'll probably put you in the army."

"Because I'm so brave?"

"To teach you to follow orders," she laughed. "Now come on. I'll beat you home!" Her wet brown hair streaming in twisted locks behind her.

* * * * *

Gemma knelt in the front garden, pulling the weeds away from the tomatoes warmed by the sun. Sitting back on her heels, she wiped the sweat from her face with her handkerchief, hard work warming her despite the crisp weather. She looked around the garden, trying to calculate how much longer it would take to pull the weeds. She saw a movement over the rise at the fence. A man was passing through her gate. Not quite able to make out the figure, she squinted against the sun. He walked somewhat quickly but seemed to be checking his speed and purposely slowing himself down. He looked down, mumbling slightly to himself. Gemma stood, wiping her hands on her apron before removing it. Her pants showed signs of her interrupted job, despite the apron.

When the man was a few yards away from her, she thought she recognized something in his face beneath the beard. The man removed his hat, revealing shining green eyes brightened with tears. And as if the tears were contagious, corresponding drops formed in Gemma's own eyes.

"Sam," she whispered. "Oh, it can't be."

As he neared, Sam thought he saw pain in the face of his love. Too many emotions played through her eyes, too quickly for him to register them all. Her hair was pulled back under a handkerchief rather than down around her shoulders as he'd often imagined in this moment. But it didn't matter. Nothing mattered. Gemma was standing directly in front of him. She was a picture, with the wisps of hair around her face lit by the sun. But no photograph could capture that brilliance. She was a poem, though no words could describe her. She was his, but he couldn't make himself reach out to hold her. So he just stared for a few glorious moments, taking it all in but feeling that he could never get enough.

Gemma looked down, playing with the apron in her hand, breaking the moment that held them both in stasis. "You've changed." She said the words quietly and matter-of-factly, no judgment, just observation.

"Seems like a lot's changed around here," Sam responded. He noticed a tightness creeping into his shoulders and a knot growing in his stomach. He was more nervous than he had expected to be.

"Where have you been?" she asked.

Sam laughed out loud then. "No matter where I went or how long I was gone, you always asked me that question when I came home. I'd forgotten."

"It's a valid question this time," she responded quietly.

"I wish I could describe to you the places I've been, what I've seen. I wrote you letters. But I guess you didn't get them."

"Never did."

"Not even the first one I left with Z?"

"Dear Gemma. Turns out I have to go to the lumber camp for a while before they'll give me the marriage license. Two years won't be too bad. I'll write you every day. I guess you can keep the oak chest for now. When we're married, it will be both of ours anyway. Write me."

"You memorized it?" Sam was a little surprised at this. Gemma wasn't one for sentimentality.

"It's the only letter I ever received from you. The only word for seven years, Sam. I had started to believe . . . I did believe that you . . ." Her voice broke off. She had one arm around her waist, one hand to her throat, holding herself in.

"Did you think I wasn't coming back? That I'd left you?"

"I thought you were dead!" She almost screamed the words, then took a deep breath in, trying to steady her breathing, stay in control.

Sam took a step forward, forcing her eyes to meet his. He reached out to touch her arm, but she pulled back.

"Gemma, sweetheart. I'm here now. I know it's been a long time. They made me work a full seven years and wouldn't let me back in the village until my time was served. It seemed strange at the time, but a lot of things seem strange around here. I'm back now, though. That's all that matters."

"I waited the two years. Z and I kept hoping for word from you. Then I waited two more."

"Nothing's changed between us, Gemma. We can . . ."

"Everything's changed, Sam," she whispered. "I'm married."

The knot that had been growing in his gut suddenly exploded inside him. The books he'd been clutching tumbled to the ground at their feet. His vision went black for a moment, as surely as if he'd been struck a physical blow.

"Why?"

"I thought you were dead. Z was sick and getting more run down. I couldn't bear the thought of being alone forever. Then after you'd been gone for about two years, Kyle came back."

"Kyle?! I thought he was . . ."

"Yes, the army took him. But he's been released."

"Kyle." Sam spoke the word that tasted of frightened and hungry days in the woods, harking back to the past before this was his home, before Zacharias. Kyle, his friend turned Corsair.

"He didn't have a choice about the army. You know that. Then when he came back, he was kind and helpful."

"That's no reason to marry someone!"

"I fell in love with him, Sam. I truly did." Her hands fidgeted with the apron in her hand as she looked at the ground. "It wasn't the same, though. He wasn't you." Taking a deep breath, she looked up with her only defense. "I thought you were dead."

Sam stood silently for a few minutes, trying to process the new world he was thrown into. One second and two words had changed his entire existence. He had to force his body to breathe. A pair of birds flew out of a nearby tree, creating a shower of leaves underneath, which the breeze picked up and carried to another part of the yard. The acrid smell of smoke in the air pierced his nose and his consciousness.

When he could finally form words again, he spoke slowly. "You are the only person I've ever loved. And now . . . to marry Kyle when he left us the way he did. It's like I don't even know you."

"Maybe we never really knew each other, Sam. A lot can happen in seven years. I was starving on a diet of hope."

Sam couldn't meet Gemma's eyes. There was something foreign there now. He continued, almost talking to himself. "I can't look at you. When I look at you, I see him, and I feel nauseous. Everything, every move I made, was always for you. Every blow, every insult from the managers taken happily because every day brought me closer to you if I could just hold out." Sam breathed heavily, unsuccessful in staving off his tears. "I would have walked through fire for you." His voice cracked.

Gemma's protective coldness broke under the warmth of his ardor. She took him in her arms, holding the man so changed from the boy who had left. But burying her face in his neck, she noticed his scent was still the same, and she breathed him in as if she'd been underwater deprived of air. "I think you already have." Her words came out in a sob. Her world now shifted like sand under a wave.

After a few moments, they stood apart from each other, questions in both their eyes, no answers to be found. "I can't say goodbye to you, Gemma."

Looking past Sam, she saw Kyle coming up the drive and knew she had to end this here. "You aren't saying it. I am. Goodbye, Sam." With that, she turned and walked into the house, leaving Sam in the void behind her.

He picked up the books he'd dropped on the ground and walked dazedly toward the gate, brushing shoulders with Kyle as he passed him. They each turned to look at one another, recognition playing across both their faces. The years had changed Kyle. He wore a short beard now, some gray in what used to be strawberry-blond hair. He was thinner. But he was still Kyle. Turning again, they walked in opposite directions, Kyle toward Gemma, Sam away from her.

3

LAST DANCE OF COLOR

*M*y *Dear Gemma,*

When I'm writing you these letters, I like to pretend we're out here in the woods together just like we used to be. Remember how we used to count the stars at night? You could always see farther and better than I could, so you always counted higher. I've tried to train my eyes to look deeper and farther into the night, tried to learn to see as you see. I'm not sure that will ever happen, though. Perhaps that's what leads people to marry, each bringing something the other lacks, fitting together like puzzle pieces.

The days run together sometimes. It's hard to tell one from the other when they aren't accented by messages and stories from home. I hope you are well, and Z too. I haven't heard from him either. My friends here in the lumber camp tell me it's normal for the mail to be inconsistent. So I'm hopeful that one day I'll get a stack of letters. It will feel like the Christmases I've read about in books, the anticipation of gifts and the satisfaction of wishes. I've managed to get my hands on some paper. Don't ask me how, but after all, I'm in a lumber camp. So I send it to you as my gift. Hopefully, I'll receive it back with part of you.

The work here is hard, but pleasant at times. It was pretty tough going at first, but I'm getting used to it. You'll have to get used to the calluses I'm working up on my hands. The managers tell me they've gotten some news about me. It looks like I might have to stay here a little longer than the two years. The demand for lumber has increased, and there aren't enough workers. So we may be looking at three years instead. It's disappointing, I know, love. We just have to push through and be strong.

Please try to write soon. I miss your stories, your jokes. I miss kissing you, breathing you in. At night, I try to imagine your lips on mine, imagine you lying beside me. But it's not even close to the same as the nights we filled up with our love. My chest feels empty, since my heart resides with you. Be well, my Gemma.

All my love,
Sam

* * * * *

Gemma knelt on the hardwood floor in front of the old oak chest, her hands running lightly over the wooden surface of the once dark finish of the oak now faded with age. The white midday sunshine filtered through golden aspen leaves outside her window onto the chest, holding it in a rich and regal glow, the dust in the air giving definition to the rays of light. Her fingers found and rested in Sam's carvings on the top of trees, birds, and foxglove flowers now filled with the dust of the last seven years. Gemma loved and hated the chest in equal measure, as it had held so many of her dreams built and broken within its dimensions. It had first been a kind of joke with the foxglove carving, a reminder of the time Sam had saved her from the poisonous flowers. Then it was a promise, a covenant between them that they would share their futures as surely as their pasts. It was her anchor in the first few years of Sam's absence. Then a millstone around her neck when she was sure he was dead. She had closed and locked the cover along with a part of her heart the day she marked as his death date. And now here it stood, unmoved, unchanged, pronouncing judgment on her wayward heart for moving on. She found herself wishing she'd left the chest with Zacharias.

How Gemma had longed and prayed to whatever gods there were for Sam's return. But not like this, not now. She wondered if prayers were ever answered according to the desires of mere mortals. She hadn't allowed herself to open the chest in several years. And though it belonged to both of them, she'd insisted on bringing it with her to her new home when she married Kyle. She told him it was part of their shared past, a part of her, but assured him her feelings for Sam were buried, and she would never again open it. She had lied.

38

Now with her husband downstairs, she brought out the key to unlock and unbury the past now resurrected. She held the only letter she had ever received from Sam, the one she'd read so often she'd memorized the words. The paper was soft in her hands, its folds worn, almost separating it into three sections. Beneath that were the final letters she had written to Sam when she had stopped sending them finally but couldn't bring herself to stop talking to him about her life, her dreams, her fears.

. . . On these cold winter nights, I think of you, hoping you are warm, and build my fire bigger than all the rest so maybe a bit of its warmth will reach you. Although no fire can warm me enough to make me need your arms less . . .

. . . When I was watching the sunset yesterday, it reminded me of one of the photographs you took that hangs in the dining room at Z's house. He told me you left your camera behind. That saddens me. I wish you'd taken it with you, Sam. I'm sure you will see many things inspiring enough to photograph. But maybe when you return . . .

. . . Sam, Kyle came back to the village today. It's been so long since we last saw him, I never thought we would. I was surprised to find out the Corsairs had released him. Medical reasons, apparently. He will be working as a medic with the Council of Doctors. He has changed a great deal. He's lost that fire and anger that used to fuel his every move. He's much quieter and gentler, if you can believe it. Strangely, having him here makes me feel a little closer to you. I wish we could all three be together again like we used to be, all taking care of each other, depending on each other. Despite the hardness of those days, I somehow miss them. And as always, I miss you . . .

. . . I've met a young girl named Daisy, maybe five or six. A blonde and clever little urchin. She lives out in the forest outside of town with a group of children, larger than our group was. They seem to take care of her. I wish I could bring her to stay here with me, but I don't think they fully trust me yet. And I'm not even sure it would be the safest thing. The Corsairs have increased their guard for some reason. I worry about changes that may be coming. They are watching us more closely. So I let her stay in our old cabin. Remember? The one beneath the pines. I try to go out there every few days to bring her and her band of children whatever supplies they need. Maybe one day it will be safe enough that she could become my daughter. Maybe our daughter. My heart counts the days . . .

With a deep breath, Gemma pulled herself back to the present. She tried to ground herself in the physical things around her, the smell of the wood in the chest, the light from the window, her knees hurting from kneeling on the wood floor of her bedroom. She closed her eyes for a moment, pinching the bridge of her nose. These letters were her past. Thinking of time made her glance at the wind-up clock on her nightstand, noting the time. That's why Kyle had come home. It was lunchtime. He'd be waiting for her in the kitchen. Gemma wondered if she should send the chest back to Z's house. It would only torment her here. Why think now of what might have been when what *was* looked in her eyes daily, slept beside her at night, and gave her what little comfort she could expect from this life?

"Gemma, I'm home," Kyle called from the kitchen. This was her life now. This was what she had to build from. She closed and locked the lid to the chest and went downstairs.

As Gemma entered the kitchen, Kyle's broad back was facing her as he washed his hands in the cold water from the pump over the sink.

"What are you hungry for?" she asked. "We've got this week's rations in the root cellar. The hens laid plenty of eggs today. Plenty of vegetables from the garden."

"Let's save the rations for dinner. Maybe a couple of eggs and a salad? I can fix it if you're busy."

"I'll fix it. I'm hungry myself."

Kyle turned to face his wife to find she'd turned away from him and was now setting about the task of preparing lunch. He wished he could see her face but didn't want to appear awkward or make her stop what she was doing. So he spoke to the air between them. "He's back, then."

"Yes, it was kind of a shock to me for a minute."

"Thought he was dead or gone for good."

"Did you want him to be?" Gemma asked between cracking the eggs.

"You know better than that. I guess I'm just asking if I should be worried. I know what you two were to each other. At least, I know what you've told me."

"I buried Sam a long time ago."

"Doesn't mean you won't have feelings when he pops back up."

"Nothing is sure or permanent in the kind of lives we lead, I suppose."

"Meaning us?"

Gemma placed her hands on the counter to steady them before she turned to face her husband. "Meaning him, Kyle. It was strange for me to see him today. He's different. I'm different. Our entire lives are different."

Kyle stepped toward her but stopped just shy of touching her. "Are you happy? Happier than you would have been with him?"

"How do I explain this? The life he had planned for us was never going to happen. It was a dream. Sam was always idealistic. He always put me up on this pedestal, wanted to worship me. I don't think I was ever a real person to him. It was always about what I could have been."

"Unlike me, is that it?"

"I think you and I recognize the humanness in each other."

"Is that a disappointment to you?"

"On the contrary, it's a relief." Gemma reached for Kyle's hand, wanting to reassure him and herself.

The door of the kitchen from the back of the house burst open, and four townspeople stumbled in, one being carried between the other three. All were talking at once, so it took a moment to make sense of what was happening. Gemma gripped the counter behind her with one hand and reached for a knife with the other while her mind quickly ascertained whether the people in her kitchen were a threat or not. Kyle immediately ran to them to aid in carrying the one injured.

"Here, bring him to the table," Kyle commanded. "Gemma, hurry and clear it off. We'll need bandages, cold water and hot. The fire's already going outside. You there, Stanley, run out and set some water to boil."

Gemma calmed her breathing and followed Kyle's efficient orders. As her fear departed, she recognized her neighbors Stanley, Ruth, Jerry, and the injured man, Ruth's husband, Jordan. "Ruth, what happened?" she queried as they cleared the table, laying him gently on an old cloth.

"Bullet or saber?" Kyle was more concerned with relevant information.

"Saber," Ruth's brother Jerry offered.

"We weren't doing anything," Ruth cried. "He'd just gotten home after the lunch bell. We were just settin' down to eat when they burst in the door. No knockin'. No warnin'. Say they had proof my man was inciting a revolution. He's to be arrested. Course he ain't done nothin', Gemma, I swear. You gotta believe me. We don't get involved in none of that."

Kyle had ripped Jordan's shirt and was trying to determine the damage to the man's torso. The cut looked clean enough, and seemed to have missed the vital organs. Blood loss was the concern. "Focus, Ruth! Tear some of those bandages or we're going to lose him. How did the wound happen?"

"Well, all Jordan did was stand to tell the soldiers they had the wrong man. Before I knew it, one of them knocked him across the face at the same time another one had pulled out his sword. Jordan fell across it before he hit the floor. Then Stanley and Jerry heard me scream and came runnin' in from the field. I guess the Corsairs thought they'd killed him so arrestin' him was no use. And they left."

Jordan lay unconscious on the table from both the blood loss and the blow to the head. So he would feel none of the stitching which was to come.

"Jerry, help me hold him down in case he wakes up. These deep stitches will hurt him," Kyle spoke firmly but quietly.

"I suppose they're more stupid than we thought. That's in our favor, I guess," Gemma mused.

"Really, Gemma?" Kyle never liked to hear the Corsairs run down, even if he wasn't one of them anymore. "Maybe they did exactly what they'd planned. Ruth, why would they think Jordan was a revolutionary?" Kyle continued to work over her husband. "Stanley, bring in the hot water!"

"I don't have any idea. He works at their stables and in our own fields. That's it. He ain't got time for nothin' else. They seem to be makin' a lot more phony arrests these days, if you ask me."

"Why would that be?" Jerry asked.

"We don't know that's what they're doing. Let's try to keep ourselves calm now and focus on getting Jordan back to health, eh?" Kyle gave his final word on the matter.

Gemma put her arm around Ruth. "He's right, honey. Let's just try to stay calm and help Jordan. Come on outside now and let Kyle finish up with him. You don't want to see all this."

* * * * *

Sophie's village of Boswell was always a coastal town even before the coast moved inland. But it was a tiny town when fully inhabited. Now the village consisted of those few families who had stumbled upon it near the end of the Second Revolution, after the raids had forced thousands from their homes. Swaths of land miles wide, burned off the earth, paths of ash led the refugees to the sea. The days of home recovery returned when the citizens roamed from village to village, looking for habitable dwellings.

Here Sophie's flight ended. Here her body landed while her heart remained with her Romany parents and sister buried in the ash. She never thought she'd suffer such a loss again as the death of her birth parents. She now sometimes found herself wondering which of her many losses was worse.

Her home was an old farmhouse, the fields now fallow and overgrown, falling off into the encroaching ocean. She would sit on the porch with the drowning sound of waves in her ears, pushing out all thought save the in and out of each wave, like the earth taking a breath, in and out, in and out. She reminded herself that this was all she had to do as well. Just breathe. In and out. The pain of those days was now anesthetized by the passage of time—more than a decade.

As Sophie walked into town with Bridget for the required town meeting, she noticed more signs painted across the town buildings than had been there even a week before. One on the side of the blacksmith's shop was painted right on the baked brick. The words *Stay the course with the Corsairs* were painted in bold white letters across the puffed-out blue chest of a soldier, a smile painted on his face but unable to reach his eyes.

Holding Bridget's tiny hand, standing in the courtyard of the village with the rest of her friends and neighbors, she listened to the troop captain drone on in an endless stream of admonitions, reading from the prepared speech from the country's governing body, the Triumvirate. "Citizens are reminded that all public meetings are prohibited, except those called by the Triumvirate. All are urged to make accommodations for the new ration portion sizes. Each citizen will receive one quarter portion less per day, effective immediately." As the captain spoke, the other Corsairs walked through the crowd to ensure a peaceful response, which was no response at all. "And as always," he concluded, "we must remember to stay the course."

"Stay the course," came the monotone expected response from the crowd in unison. One or two people were quietly pulled out of the group for failing to parrot the response. It jarred Sophie's ears to hear her tiny daughter repeat the same words as the rest of the crowd without thinking about it. The child knew nothing of what it meant but had learned from her mother to do what was expected and not to draw attention to herself. Sophie recognized this as a sifting process, the soldiers shaking up the crowd to see who would and would not comply with orders and expectations, regardless of the stimulus. It seemed to be happening more frequently than in past years. With more soldiers came more speeches, more sifting, and more arrests. No doubt it was why Foxglove would soon be giving her a new mission.

* * * * *

Walking back from Gemma's house, Sam's head felt hot. He saw pieces of his life with Gemma passing before his eyes as surely as the leaves passed before his feet, and he wondered if he was dying. She was his compass, his navigation leading to the only place he'd ever wanted to be. He had never imagined a life without Gemma in it. He'd never had to. Yet here it was, staring him in the face, and he felt suddenly unmoored.

He had worked for her, yet not with her, for seven years. Even still, she was his every thought. He knew that was where the real battle would play out—in his mind. He began to wonder how it would be possible to extract a thought, a hundred thoughts, a thousand thoughts from the stage of his mind, a place, he was discovering, where he wasn't truly master. Eyes on the ground, shuffling back toward his old home, Sam made the startling discovery that he was gone. All the things which had made him Sam had been erased. There were no traces of memory. All of his thoughts were in his lost letters to Gemma. No bits of photos, journals, or even a line of the life he had lived. It was not as if he had died, but as if he had never existed. And into the exquisiteness of the void, he fell, not knowing where he would land or into what world this non-existence would take hold.

Walking back through the door to Zacharias' house, Sam thought he was moving more slowly than usual; everything seemed to have slowed. Zacharias sat in the rocker, gray as his hair, with Ethan at his feet, reading to him from the aged copy of *The Wonderful Wizard of Oz* he'd kept hidden from the book burners years before.

"'You have plenty of courage I'm sure,' answered Oz. 'All you need is confidence in yourself. There is no living thing that is not afraid when it faces danger. The true courage is in facing danger when you are afraid, and that kind of courage you have in plenty.'"

Sam found himself being drawn into the story for a moment, remembering how much he and Gemma had longed to travel to a place like Oz together, how they had gloried in the different creatures, shivered at the thought of the Wicked Witch catching them, and joined with Dorothy, the Scarecrow, the Tin Man, and the Lion to defeat her. His tears felt hot on his cheeks after the walk in the cold autumn air.

"Why didn't you tell me?" Sam's question interrupted the reading.

Zacharias looked at his son with pain in his eyes. He had known Sam would be hurt this day but knew there was nothing for it but to let things run their natural course. He placed the book on the floor beside him. "Ethan, boy, why don't you run out back and see if you can find any munchkins lurking in the yard."

"There's no such thing." Ethan still took everything literally and had not yet learned how to use his imagination. The need for survival left no time for play.

"Are you sure?" Zacharias grinned at him. "I'm pretty sure I've seen a munchkin or two in the grove. This is just the right time to find them. Run along now. I'll call you in a little while."

Sam waited for the boy to leave before throwing his barb, "You lead him around with fairy stories just like you did with me, letting me believe I'd find my happily ever after today. Why in the world would you let me walk into that unprepared?"

"You weren't really listening to me earlier."

"I mean before. You could have written me. All these years, not a word from either of you."

"You know the mail is unpredictable. We did write. Both of us, for years. And we heard nothing from you."

"The Watch could have found me. There are ways to get messages through when it's important."

"They can't use their limited resources for personal messages, you know that."

"Seven years, Zacharias! Seven years I worked for her, only for her. And now this betrayal. And with Kyle! I can't get those years back." Sam was pacing, unable to contain his anger or his energy as his emotions overtook him.

"None of us can get the past back." Zacharias remained calm. "We can only continue to move forward."

"You can't know what it's like to have survived what we survived together. To have no one but each other to depend on for safety, comfort, and your very life."

Zacharias took a moment to heave himself out of the rocker, a harder task in the biting chill. He brought the book back to its hiding place, giving him time to consider before speaking. "No, I didn't survive in the woods with my Jesse as you two did. But I know what it is to put your life in someone else's hands. I know what it is to lose the witness to your life. You know I understand that, son. Take time to mourn her, to feel your pain. But then you must move on. If nothing else, for this boy."

"With life as uncertain as it is, how can I possibly take care of him?"

"Precisely because life is so uncertain. I asked those same questions once."

"It's all just too much to take in. She hardly spoke to me. I need more answers than the few she gave me."

"Remember when I taught you to read from song lyrics in old CDs we found? You always wanted more. You didn't want to read between the lines, to fill in the blanks with your own meaning. You wanted more words, more explanation. You are the same now."

Sam was wandering around the room aimlessly as they'd been talking. He stopped to look out the window, musing almost to himself, "Have you ever really looked at the last leaves of autumn? They're always brightest just before they fall, a last dance of color, making you think the glory will last forever until nothing is left but the crunch of death under your feet." He breathed deeply, wiping the tears from his eyes.

"You never really knew her, Sam. You created her in your mind. You *loved her against reason, against promise, against peace, against hope, against happiness, against all discouragement that could be.*"

"Don't throw Dickens in my face!" Sam snapped but felt the pain and the truth of those words. "Z, what's going on around here? Ge—" he couldn't bring himself to say the name that had played on his lips and in his mind for as long as he could remember. "She was so thin."

"They've lessened the rations, among other things. I want to show you something." He walked to the hidden door beneath the stairs. Within that closet, there was another hidden door to a cabinet deeper underneath the stairs. On the outside of it were hooks and coats. No one who didn't know the door was there would think to look twice at it. From behind the door, Zacharias pulled out a rifle, illegal for regular citizens to possess.

"What the hell are you doing with this? You could be arrested!" Sam looked over his shoulder instinctively, expecting someone to be spying, as they inevitably always were.

"Tell me what you notice about it." Zacharias was perpetually teaching, could never just say something outright.

"It looks brand new. Not quite the same model as the ones they usually carry. What's this here?" Sam ran his finger along an extra piece at the end of the barrel.

"That's a silencer."

"They've only had the guns as a show of force since the Second Revolution. We rarely even hear a gunshot anymore. Why would they even need silencers?"

"Maybe for precisely that reason."

"How and where are they making new guns, anyway?"

"Now you're asking the right questions."

Sam handed the gun back to Zacharias as if it were a snake he couldn't get far enough away from him. "I don't want to get involved in this, Z. And I won't have Ethan involved in the Watch activities. Why couldn't we just accept the peace that was offered us?"

"A peace that isn't really peace? They give us rules supposedly to stay safe, but safe from what and at what cost?"

"I can't do this with you right now. I'm paying costs of my own for the crime of being too loyal. I have to take some time to adjust to the new way things are. I have to go away for a while, Z."

"Are you sure that's the best idea, son? It might be best to stay here and take care of this boy."

"I can't right now. I can't take care of anyone. Can you please just look after him for a little while and let me heal in my own way? You know where I'll be if you need me."

"You don't mean that run-down cabin where I found you and Gemma freezing? It doesn't even have a roof anymore."

"I'll fix it. Maybe it will give me something to do. I've gotten used to working with my hands. Things won't seem so foreign to me. It'll be fine. Look after the boy for me until I return."

* * * * *

Ruth lay next to Jordan on the pallet Gemma had prepared in front of the dining room fireplace. She listened to his breathing and periodically checked his forehead for fever, waiting for any change in his condition. Kyle had said he would be fine with time, but she still feared for her husband's life and contemplated the fragility of mortality, how it all could change or be lost in a matter of seconds.

Gemma and Kyle whispered together in the kitchen, trying not to disturb their unexpected guests but wanting to stay close to help if needed.

"I've received a message from the Cutler farm on the other side of the village. Mrs. Cutler is in labor. Her baby will come tonight," Gemma began. "I've promised to go and help. So I probably won't be back until at least morning."

"Well, I can't come with you, obviously." Kyle looked toward his patient.

"It will be fine. I won't be the only one there. She has her sister as well. We can handle things between us. But will you be alright here?"

"Should be. I can send for Jerry or Stanley again if necessary. We can't use medicine from the Council of Doctors. The Corsairs wanted this man dead, and we're aiding and abetting."

"You don't think they'll come here, do you?"

"Don't know why they should. They left him for dead."

"Even still, you will be careful, won't you?" Gemma's eyes showed true concern for husband, stilling his earlier fears about her feelings for Sam.

He smiled, touching her cheek. "If you want me to."

She leaned forward to kiss him quickly before going to pack up the things she would need.

* * * * *

Sam did not have to think about his way to the cabin where he'd lived for more than a year before being discovered by Zacharias. He meandered through the woods, allowing his thoughts to wander freely as well. He felt the weight of his pack on his back as a burden. Zacharias had loaded him down with what food he could spare from the cellar; the rest of his needs he would find in nature. But it wasn't the physical weight that tired him. Nothing seemed easy anymore. He felt his muscles and heart slowing as the rivers in winter, slowing and freezing until a thaw releases them.

The cabin was higher in elevation than Jesse's Hollow, and the air was biting against his cheeks. He passed the lake, which had already experienced its first hard frost of the season. It was pockmarked with ripples in stasis as if it had frozen suddenly while in the middle of a windstorm. But in the places where the water still lived, the ripples responded to the caress of the wind.

The cabin under the pines revealed itself slowly as Sam approached. He was surprised to find the roof intact, and not only in good repair, but with a plume of smoke escaping its chimney. Nothing, apparently, would be as he expected to find it anymore. The crows crowded around the refuse pile behind the cabin, enjoying their feast. After years of hunting and surviving in the woods, Sam knew how to walk silently. He did so as he neared the cabin, peering through the eye-level windows. The inside of the cabin was clean and well cared for. The cabinets seemed stocked. But the woodpile next to the fireplace was low. He saw no inhabitants inside but assumed they would soon return to tend the fire. This would not be his refuge, then, and he would have to find solace elsewhere. He thought it fortunate he'd decided to pack his warmest clothes, for his time would be spent mostly outdoors as the weather continued to cool the air and his ire.

* * * * *

In the twilight hours, Gemma approached the Cutler farm on the edge of the village. The darkness descended earlier and earlier as winter neared. She wondered why this always took her by surprise, the early nights of winter. She pulled her wool coat more tightly around her, catching her breath in the cold wind blowing in her face. Seeing the lights from the farmhouse shining across the field, she stopped, dropping her heavy pack full of blankets, food, and supplies beside her. She held her lantern up above her head, waving it back and forth. Then took one of the blankets to cover it intermittently to achieve the signal she desired: *"Gone to the cabin. Kyle will ask after me here. Will pass by again in the morning."* The curtains shut once and re-opened, signaling message received. Then Gemma picked up her pack and walked on toward the forest. She needed to make a stop at the cabin before making her way to the lighthouse for her meeting with Aishe.

Gemma listened at the door of the cabin to hear if anyone was inside. The curtains were drawn; no information would escape the windows, though they seemed cleaner than when she last visited. She heard a wooden chair scrape the floor in the kitchen deep within, so she slowly entered the door, not making a sound. As soon as she'd crossed the threshold, a knife

49

was at her throat. Gemma's breath stopped as she turned slowly but could see nothing. The angle of the knife told her what she needed to know.

"Hey, kid," she said through a smile.

The knife fell, and a giggle escaped a little girl's mouth. She threw her arms around Gemma's waist and waited for her lesson.

"That was a good trick with the chair, Daisy. How'd you do it?"

"I had some string and pulled on it from behind the door."

"Clever girl."

Daisy was happy to know her efforts had impressed Gemma. "How'd you know it was me with the knife?"

"It was angled down, so I knew you were a child. Next time you'd better stand on a chair. Keep them confused."

"I will." Daisy picked up Gemma's pack to help her bring the things inside.

"I've brought you warm blankets and more food for the next few days. Where are the other children?"

"They went hunting. Oh, I almost forgot, I have a message for you from the Watch."

"Who brought it?"

"Someone new. Never saw her before. She called herself Cypress."

"Did she give the right passcode?"

"Of course. I wouldn't have talked to her without it."

"Well, let's have the note then."

On the page of a book Gemma didn't recognize, she read the circled words sprinkled around the page: *fort, night, trains, port, mid, night, and base.* The bottom of the page bore the signature *Cypress.*

Taking a deep breath, Gemma considered the meaning of the message. The guns and horses would be transported to the Corsairs' base at midnight two weeks from today. They must move quickly. Aishe needed to mobilize her people to cut off the transport.

Gemma threw the note from Cypress into the fire, then reached into the cabinet to the right of the fireplace. In old days, this was used to keep food warm. She used it to hide the couple of books in her possession. She pulled out *Dandelion Wine.* Flipping through its pages, she found the appropriate one. She hesitated to pull the page out from the cover. It was one of her favorite parts of the book. But it could not be helped. She had to use it. She circled the words: *under the stars, defender, citadel, withstand, assault.* Then at the bottom of the page she wrote: *Aishe and Foxglove.*

"Daisy, you'll need to take this quickly, sweetie, back to Cypress. Do you know where you can meet her?"

Daisy nodded her head.

"It can wait until morning. I don't want you going out tonight. Look what else I brought for you."

Daisy rifled through the pack to find an old game she didn't recognize. She shook the long thin box and heard the pieces within. Her eyes lit up to realize she'd have something to pass the time and play with her band of friends.

"It's called Checkers." Gemma loved bringing surprises to Daisy to see the smile in her eyes. Nothing gave her more pleasure in her life than taking care of the child. Sometimes her friends in the Watch would bring her games or books found in the old houses in the area, knowing she was taking care of the children. "We have time to play one game and read one story before I have to go. Alright?"

"I wish you could stay here with me or I could go back with you."

"I know you do, darling. I wish it too. More than anything. One day. Hopefully one day soon. But with as much as we're being watched, I don't want anything connecting you and me in case I'm captured. I couldn't bear it if the Corsairs came after you. So, for now, this is how it has to be. But it's what we're fighting for. It's why the people in the Watch do what we do so that one day, we won't have to sneak around like this. You do understand, don't you, darling?"

Daisy held the tears back from her blue eyes with great effort and forced herself to look at Gemma with a smile. "I do."

"Alright, then. Which first? Game or story?"

"Game."

4

WATCHING THE SKY

With the sun's short journey from east to west now complete and another day swept up in the wind-troubled night, Sophie lay next to Bridget in the child's bed, trying to coax sleep to wrap her in its arms. Leaning her head back against the chipped white headboard, Sophie's eyes closed as she recited again the story of Goldilocks and the Three Bears. With her daughter curled up beside her in the crook of her arm, Sophie absently played with Bridget's own golden locks as her voice sleepily ran through the story like a stream through a forest. She was startled to feel two chubby hands on the sides of her face.

"Mommy. Wake up, Mommy."

"I'm awake, Peanut."

"What do bears look like?"

"I think they're big and tall when they stand on their hind feet. They're brown or black all over with thick fur."

"Are they scary? Will they eat me for dinner?"

"No, love. The story says they eat porridge, like oatmeal." Sophie didn't mind telling white lies to her daughter to assuage her fears. She wasn't even sure bears still existed. There hadn't been a sighting of one for as long as she could remember.

"Where is my papa bear?"

"What?"

"There was papa bear, mama bear, and baby bear. I the baby bear. You the mama bear. Where's papa bear?"

"He had to go away before you were born, Peanut." Sophie's eyes fluttered as she started to doze again.

Bridget gently patted her mother's cheeks. "Mommy, Mommy."

"I'm awake."

"Mommy, I want a song. No more story. Sing to me, Mommy."

"Sing to you? What song would you like?"

"The 'I see you' song," Bridget giggled and snuggled in more closely.

Sophie grinned. "'Somewhere in My Dreams'? You like that song?"

"Uh-huh."

Sophie hummed a few bars first, inviting the song to join them in their warmly lit cocoon before she sang the first refrain. *"No matter where I go, I see you. In the butterfly's wing, I see you. In the tiny little flower, in the passing of each hour, in the love that's in my heart, I see you. So when my thoughts begin to stray, I know you're not far away. I'll see you always near me, so it seems. For you will always be here somewhere in my dreams."*

Any time she sang, Sophie's mind was pulled back to her birth mother, Sara, a woman burned into her heart and memory, though she had only had her for ten years. In another life or time, Sophie, as her mother before her, would have been a musician. Sara Bryan tried to hold onto lessons about music her own mother had taught her and pass them onto her tiny red-headed daughter, whose clear voice could be heard in her crib singing and making up songs to herself as a baby. She would sit at the piano with Sophie, whose legs dangled from the bench, and play happy, dancing songs loud enough to drown out the sounds of distant gunfire and screams.

When Sophie found her own farmhouse, she was overwhelmed with gratitude to whoever had gone before for leaving an upright piano standing, or rather leaning, in the front room. It was out of tune and some of the keys were missing or no longer hammered the strings. But Sophie spent many hours tinkering around with the piano that quickly became her friend. Her fingers would caress the worn black and white keys with bits of brown peeking out from under missing paint. She would play from memory the songs which still rang in her mind from her mother. In the attic of the ancient farmhouse, she had found an old wind-up gramophone. Of course, she didn't know what a gramophone was, nor what it did. But after some experimentation, she found it gave her some of the most beautiful music she'd ever heard, full of instruments she couldn't identify, yet thrilled to the sound of. Listening to the records expanded her repertoire and gave her new songs to learn on the piano. Songs from Before, which were a kind of bridge to a life she'd never known and didn't understand.

Hearing the deep and measured breathing of her sleeping daughter, Sophie tried in vain to roll out of the bed noiselessly. The creaking of the bedsprings filled the silent room, but Bridget didn't stir. A good sign.

Downstairs in the kitchen, Mrs. O'Dell waited for her to come down. The kindly old woman sat roundly in her abundance at the table in the glow of a beeswax candle. A lantern in the attic window, a signal from Sophie, had brought her over from the neighboring farm.

"Thank you for coming, Mrs. O'Dell. Bridget is sound asleep and should stay that way. I'm not quite sure how long I'll be. Are you alright to stay for a while?"

"Of course, dear. You do what you need to do." Mrs. O'Dell had learned not to ask where Sophie went on nights like this. She knew it had something to do with the Watch, and that was enough for her to know she wanted to help in her small way.

Gathering up a lantern, her rain slicker, and an old hat, Sophie headed out the door toward the ocean.

"Be careful, dear," Mrs. O'Dell called.

* * * * *

From their porch home, the weary wind chimes whistled a call to no one in particular, but an owl from the forest replied as Sophie made her way across her back field to the coast. Every sound seemed to her a warning, but she trudged on, telling herself it was only the wind. She heard the small dinghy before she could see it bumping against what used to be a fence post where it was tied off but barely hanging on in the rough waves. The moon shone bright enough that she didn't need her lantern. So she blew out the flame but brought it along anyway. She waded out in the frigid water to get to the boat she would row to the lighthouse. Strangled by the dance of wind and waves, she fought hard against the froth and surge. As she rowed out to the lighthouse, she felt the oars rubbing her hands raw, even within the gloves, and dreamt of a time when rendezvous like these would not be necessary.

As she looked back toward the shore, moving farther out, she could see the fires of the guard stations along the coast. There were only two left these days, one at the Southern Border and one at the Northern. After most of the boats were destroyed and the Border secured, they had nothing to fear from ghost ships of days gone by. Looking over her shoulder, she could see the top of the timeworn lighthouse looming in front of the moon, throwing a great shadow over her little rowboat. The roar in her ears made any vocal call to her captain impossible. Gemma stood on the catwalk, following Sophie's approach. As Sophie climbed up over the rail and tied off the boat near Foxglove's, she tried to maintain her footing on the slick metal surface.

"Though my soul may set in darkness . . ." Gemma called over the waves, shielding her face from the choppy water with her own raincoat.

"It will rise in perfect light," Sophie responded to the passcode. "Foxglove." She smiled and put out her hand.

Gemma gave her a firm handshake. "Thank you for coming out, Aishe. Let's go inside the light so we can talk a little easier."

Within the glass lighthouse, it was still damp with a couple of panes broken, but at least they didn't have the waves crashing on them and could hear each other speaking at normal levels without the need to shout.

Sophie took her hat off, shaking the water out of her hair. "I'm sorry for being late. I couldn't leave until my daughter was asleep, and that didn't happen as quickly as I would have liked."

A concerned look played behind Gemma's eyes. "I didn't realize you had a daughter."

"Why would you? We keep our private lives out of this work, don't we?"

"Is she going to be a problem?" Gemma had a chill in her voice that even she did not fully understand. Was it just concern for the mission, or did the thought of another woman having a child prick the inner longings of her heart?

"In what way?"

"I just mean it's harder to complete difficult missions when you have someone depending on you that you've left behind."

Sophie tried to see into her captain's eyes. She knew Foxglove was only doing her job and trying to protect the mission and the other people in the Watch. She came to the strange realization that you can know someone for years, yet never really know them, their thoughts, fears, strengths. What holds them back and what pushes them forward. She wished circumstances were different and they could have been friends just chatting about their lives on her front porch sipping tea. "Do you have a family?" she asked finally.

"A husband, yes."

"And does that affect your work?"

"Those I care about are always in my thoughts, but I find that propels me into the hard tasks rather than holding me back."

Sophie nodded. "Exactly. I don't think any of us are fighting just for ourselves. We all have someone we're loyal or devoted to. That's the only thing that makes all this bearable—those we fight for. Besides, is there any alternative to me completing this mission?"

"Not really, no."

"Well alright, then. I'll do what needs to be done as I always have, Captain."

"You're right. I have no reason to doubt you, Aishe. I apologize." Gemma relaxed slightly and reached out to put her hand on her compatriot's shoulder.

"So let's get down to business. Your message seemed urgent. We haven't met in person in a while."

"Yes, you're right. I'm sure you've noticed the increase in troop numbers."

"And in the number of messages from the Triumvirate. Just today, I saw them drag people out of a public assembly for not answering the motto."

"The barbarism continues. I predict it will only be a matter of time before the public beatings and executions begin again. But the urgency comes because we've also learned there will be two wagons of guns and a fresh herd of horses coming to the Corsairs' base from the northern road," Gemma responded. "They mustn't get through. We will divert the guns and divide them among our people. The horses will be hidden on farms along the coast."

"How many guards assigned to the transport?"

"Only four, we've been told."

"Well, that should be easy enough to take them by surprise. Pretty arrogant of them, if you ask me. We'll use the cave for the guns and

56

disperse them a little at a time among the Watch. If you can ensure the barns are ready, my troop can split up the horses to the farms that night. Has there been any news from the Wash District?"

"Only that the members of the Triumvirate seem nervous about something. More vigilant, added guards in the villages."

"I'm just trying to figure out what they could possibly need so many guns for. There are only seven or eight villages left within the Border. Could they be preparing for an outside attacker or another war?"

"We don't know yet, but we can't take any chances. Someone close to the Triumvirate has been leaking us information. They haven't been specific as far as their purpose, but only let us know of new shipments and troop movements. It seems as if he's trying to give us a picture with all of these puzzle pieces, but it's hard to know where they all fit if you haven't first seen the picture."

"When will the shipment take place?"

"At midnight two weeks from tonight. Remember, we don't want any casualties if we can help it. The Corsairs will be riled enough after the raid without adding murder to their charges against us."

"Very well. I should probably start back if there's nothing else you can tell me."

"Just out of curiosity, how old is your daughter?"

Sophie weighed the danger of giving out more information about her personal life but decided to trust Foxglove. "She's four years old."

"Your husband doesn't know about your Watch activities?"

"I have no husband."

"What made you want to join the Watch?"

"My daughter. The minute I first held her, I wanted to change the world for her, try to make it better. I knew she deserved everything I could possibly give her and more. I couldn't bear the thought of her growing up in fear the way we did."

"Then here's hoping we may ever be successful."

* * * * *

Sam's nightmares returned on the early winter nights as he lay huddled near his fire on the frozen ground. His body shivered from more than just the cold, while his mind stalked the twisted paths of memories from the wars he'd lived through. Smoke, gunshots, fire, and the dead all around him in mangled heaps. His dreams sent him staggering through razed and barren fields. When he woke, the sweat that had fallen down his face would be freezing in his beard. By the time winter had truly arrived, Sam felt like he had never known a warm day in his life. He was born cold, and he'd be colder still in the grave. He would vaguely recall stories about a thing called summer where everything is warm under a burning sun. But he wasn't sure he believed these stories in the dead of winter. They seemed mythological to him as he shivered under his blanket with the fire waning in the fog of early dawn.

He was used to nights sleeping alone. That had been his life for seven years. But this aloneness was different. It was loneliness without hope for the future, and that left a hole in him he could not fill. Through weeks of wandering forest and hills and border-crossing hunting trips, Sam sought meaning and purpose in the ruined lives of the people of Before. What could their stories teach him? Had they too lost loves, been thrown into the deep abyss, floundering for air? He knew the stories—those perpetuated by the Triumvirate and the more believable stories from Zacharias. The leaders painted them as fools and traitors, destined to be destroyed, no lives worth preserving. Zacharias told Sam the human stories of fear, desperation, and sacrifice for loved ones. Families huddled together in the last hours before only one or two were left from each decimated family. He told him of the type of lives they'd lived before the Disaster, stories of prosperity, creativity, and ease, a kind of life Sam could never fully understand.

And yet they *had* been destroyed. Their worlds had crumbled beneath their feet as Sam now found his crumbling. Would some traveler in the future find his bones among them and think him merely one of the mass wiped from the planet by their own indifference and arrogance?

What of his own parents? The first farmers and fighters, leaders in the First Revolution. After losing the war, living on the run with Sam in woods, caves, anywhere they could hide, until they were finally betrayed by someone among their own troops. They had loved, hoped, and trusted, and where had it gotten them? Exile and execution. Where had Sam's love and trust gotten him? Somehow both journeys ended in the same place, with Sam shivering in the unforgiving forest of loss and regret.

One morning, Sam woke to a thick layer of snow over him. Shaking it off, he quickly got up and stoked his fire to a size that could actually warm him. The barren trees looked like black cracks in the brilliant blue of the sky. He went to the tree where he'd hung up his pack to keep it out of reach of those creatures which would scavenge his food. But it wasn't in the tree. It lay on the ground as covered with snow as he had been, and its insides pillaged and stripped bare. All that remained were the inedible items, including the pistol Zacharias had pressed into his hand before he left—just for an emergency. It could have been an animal or a child that had relieved him of his sustenance, but it didn't matter now. What mattered was how and what he was going to eat.

He boiled a pot of snow, drinking it down to warm and hydrate himself. He could only hope to find something to eat from the land which the animals, children, or both hadn't already retrieved. Wandering among the trees and fallen branches, he felt himself like one of the little snowbirds, pecking the ground for any tidbit of food. He found a few berries left frozen on a bush and ate them quickly. Surveying his surroundings, he realized he was close to Teardrop Point, which looked out over the valley. Something in him beyond his control led him to the top. He ran as fast as could up the point, faster and higher than he'd ever been. Perhaps if he ran fast enough, he could shed the scales of the past holding him in a dying grip, like a snake sheds its skin. The thick wind chafed like a rope against his neck and face. Looking out from the point, he did what he'd always done, what he couldn't stop himself from doing, no matter his situation— he searched the landscape for Gemma's fire. But the clouds had settled below him near the base of the mountain, obscuring his view. They danced and skirted the ground, waiting to sprinkle another helping of snow. But Sam knew that wasn't the only reason he couldn't find Gemma. She was truly no longer his, no longer to be found in his searching eyes.

For days, Sam tried to make it back to Zacharias, back to the village where he could find respite and nourishment. But he had traveled far, and after several days without food, he found his strength failing him. He began sleeping in the day as well as the night. The specter of death haunted him, playing hide and seek like a child among the blackened tree branches. Sam wasn't sure he wanted to escape from its grip. Lying cold, dirty, and completely defeated in a snowdrift against a mammoth aspen, he contemplated the barren land before him. Devoid of color, sound muffled by the snow, he felt the void calling to him, beckoning him to let go. What use the fight? What purpose the struggle? It would be so much easier to just sleep. The emptiness of his stomach and heart felt like a great ocean he could simply fall into and continue falling, floating weightlessly in its folds.

Through the haze and delirium, Sam thought he saw movement in the snow, but all was white before him. He strained his eyes to see more clearly. Again, a short, jerky movement, but all white. Something brushed an overhanging branch, causing a shower of white dust to cascade down in a heap. That's when he saw it, the snow piled around its thin and muscular legs, a great white buck, which would have been completely invisible if not for its massive antlers growing like a tree from its head. The deer looked directly at Sam, standing perfectly still. In a corner of Sam's mind a memory prickled of the pistol he carried in his pack. But he had no wish to shoot this majestic creature, as pure as the snow it rivaled.

Sam hadn't fired a gun in years. The very thought of it propelled him into a state of almost panic. Days of need and desperation far greater than his current state. He closed his eyes tight, trying to wipe the visions from his eyes. Visions of Gemma, Kyle, and himself doing anything necessary to survive.

"Sam! Sam, we have to do this. We don't have a choice. We either attack now while we can take them by surprise, or we'll be dead by morning. You know they'll do anything to find us." Gemma stands with her hands on Sam's shoulders, trying to shake him into submission.

"I think we can get away, Gemma," Sam tries to convince her and himself.

"Why do you have to be such a coward?" Kyle chides. "Don't you want them to pay? They killed your parents, and now they're after us. Come on, there are only four Corsairs down there. We can take them if we go now."

Sam shuffles his feet in the bank of snow, creating a hole.

Kyle takes charge as always. He's older and assumes the responsibility to protect the group. "I'll take the two on the left. Sam, you take the one sitting down. Gemma, the one on the right. Once they're out of the way, we can raid the camp. Come on now, there will be food for a week down there. Move out!"

Sam grips the rifle to his chest. It's as tall as he is. He tries not to trip in the snow that's dragging his feet as they run down the hill. They each practically fall into the trunks of the trees they hide behind. Within a split second of stopping, Kyle spins from behind the tree, aims, and fires off two rounds in succession. His aim is flawless. Two soldiers hit the ground. Gemma fires before the second soldier has fallen. Her soldier on the right lands directly on top of his comrade. Sam's soldier, sitting on a fallen tree trunk, has risen and is reaching for his gun. The picture freezes along with Sam's shaking hands. He holds the rifle, aimed and ready to shoot, but he can't quite fire. The three soldiers on the ground lie in strange, unnatural angles. Their blood runs together in a pool beneath them, staining the snow and mud. The cabin they had sheltered in has been painted with a new coat of blood. Slowly, the soldier gets closer and closer to his gun. Now it's in his hand. Now pulled against his shoulder. Sam looks in his eyes and sees the tears about to run down his cheek. The soldier in Corsair uniform is as young as he is, maybe younger.

"Fire, damn it, fire!" Kyle cries in panic.

Sam closes his eyes and squeezes the trigger. It's done. They've won the skirmish. They will live to eat, sleep, and fight another day. Sam drops the gun at his feet, the muzzle sizzling in the snow.

"We had to do it, Sam. It'll be alright. They would have killed us. We had to do it." Gemma's words fail to comfort him, but she keeps repeating them for her own sake. "We had to do it."

Sam opened his eyes, half-expecting Gemma to be standing there. But the only creature looking at him was the buck, its chest puffed out in pride and majesty. He had not moved nor broken his gaze in several minutes. Sam knew what he had to do. He tried to convince himself this situation was different. He was starving. He wasn't killing a human being. But the innocence of the animal assailed him, rebuked him. The pistol shook in his hand, pointed at the ground.

"Go on," he shouted. "Get out of here!"

The deer gracefully took a step forward, and another. He was walking toward Sam, not away. And then a realization began to wash over Sam like the sunrise coming up over the mountains. He knew he'd been given a chance at redemption. The innocence the animal offered him was his own, and he was giving it freely to Sam, who would walk out of the woods a different man than he was when he entered. With great effort, he raised the pistol and fired a single shot, accepting and honoring the gift.

* * * * *

The gentle strains of Schubert's piano "Serenade" filled the yard from the gramophone on the back porch before being broken by the crack of an axe splitting wood. Music was sometimes the only thing that could soothe Sophie's frayed nerves. Music coupled with physical labor. She took out all her fears, frustrations, and anger on the chopping block before her, cutting them to pieces along with wood for the fire.

Although it was the middle of the day, Sophie had kept a large fire going in the fireplace to heat the fresh chicken soup she'd made for Bridget, who lay ill in her bed. She had taken sick the night of the Watch's raid on the Corsair's shipment of horses and guns. The raid had been a success but had taken all night. Even now, several of the horses resided in a barn obscured by a thick overgrowth of trees on the northern edge of Sophie's farm. But when she returned in the early morning hours after the raid, Mrs. O'Dell was ministering to her sick child, trying to control the fever. The fear welled in Sophie's heart along with the tears in her eyes. Bridget had always been such a healthy child; she'd never had to worry over a situation like this before. That was four days before, and the fever had yet to break.

Crack! Another piece of firewood broke and bowed to Sophie's will. She had tried all of the home remedies she knew to fight infection and bring the child's fever down. Teas, tinctures, oils, constant liquids. But still Bridget languished rather than rallied. The next day was Market Day when the Council of Doctors would be in town. Sophie knew she'd have to approach them for medicine for her daughter, but she dreaded it. Dreaded the risk of revealing her undocumented daughter, born illegally. She slammed the axe down, giving the soft white pine another blow with all the force of her fears.

"Still doing everything for yourself, I see."

The man's voice sent a chill down her spine colder than the air around her. Without turning around to face her intruder, she put another piece of firewood on the chopping block. "You shouldn't be here, Griffyth. We agreed, remember?" The axe came down again.

"We said a lot of things back then. I come to Market Day every week, but I never see you there anymore. I hate to admit it, even to myself, but I've missed you. I just wanted to see you for a minute."

"Well, you've seen me. Now you can go."

"Sophie, look at me, will you?"

She continued her task.

"I don't want to compel you, but you know I could."

Slamming her axe into the chopping block, Sophie wiped the sweat from her brow and turned around. Her red hair fell out of her braid in wisps around her face. She stared directly into Griffyth's cold eyes, although they held some heat for her.

"Where's the child?" he asked, looking toward the house.

"Do you really think I'd let you see her?"

"A father has a right to see his own child."

"The law doesn't recognize her, so it doesn't recognize your right. Besides, you have never been her father."

"I was curious about her, I suppose."

"Curious? Is that all we are to you, a curiosity?"

"Come now, Sophie, you and I never had any illusions about us. It was business from the start. You're the one who brought a child into the mix."

"I can't do this with you, Griffyth. Now, we made a deal. I wouldn't turn you into the Corsairs, and you'd leave us alone. I've kept my end of the bargain."

Griffyth stepped forward, running his rough hand across Sophie's flushed cheek. "Yes, you were always very good at keeping up your end of things. Can't we at least . . ."

With one swift motion, Sophie held the axe again in her hand and placed the blade almost gently against Griffyth's throat. "Can't we what?"

"Nothing," he hissed.

"Alright, then. Go on."

Sophie waited until he had left the yard to drop her axe, leaning over, her head between her knees. She breathed heavily, trying to work down the fear in her throat. She knew she'd pushed him too far. Griffyth was not one to forget slights or offenses. But she depended on the fact that Bridget held the proof of his guilt in her very veins.

In an effort to preserve valuable and scarce resources, the Triumvirate insisted on controlling all aspects of procreation. Extramarital attachments and relations were strictly forbidden. No one knew what the exact punishment was except that offenders were removed from the village and never returned. Sophie had no intention of being one of those people. When Griffyth had first approached her years before, she didn't feel she could refuse him. He was a government official, after all, holding power and influence within his grasp. He had set his sights on her and not relented. Sophie felt sick again at the thought of allowing him into her bed. But her saving grace in more ways than one had been the birth of Bridget.

"What do you mean you're pregnant? How is that even possible?" Griffyth paces in the kitchen, slamming dishes in the sink.

"I haven't taken the medications for years." Sophie tries not to smile about the serious situation but can't help feeling the joy of being a mother despite the fear it also evoked.

"For God's sake, why?" He takes a deep breath. He will not lose his composure. He is in control. "It doesn't matter why. You can't have this child without a permit, that's all there is to it. The blood tests for an identification card will trace it back to me. And I will not let that happen." He picks up his hat, turning his back on her as he walks toward the door. "Get rid of it."

There is nothing that will induce Sophie to get rid of her child. She's going to be a mother. She's going to love her child no matter what. And she's going to do it without Griffyth in her life. She is in control. She speaks with a measured cadence, "I'm going to have this baby, Griffyth. And you are never going to come back here again. I will not reveal you as the father. I will not register the birth. But you have to agree to leave us alone. For good. Do you understand?"

Griffyth says nothing and walks out the front door.

Sitting down on the back porch steps, Sophie heard the needle skipping on the gramophone record. The song had come to an end. Her legs were still shaking as she considered the consequences of what she had to do tomorrow. But she didn't have a choice. She wondered if she should have handled things differently with Griffyth just now. But did she ever have a choice in how she handled him?

* * * * *

The footprints were unmistakable and fresh, not yet filled in with snow, and the smell of smoke was near. Ethan knew he'd probably find Sam over the next hill. As he crested the hill, he was happy to see his quarry in the valley below. The journey had been tough, but not unexpected. He was glad they'd share a fire that night.

Sam heard the boy approach. "Sneaking up on me again, boy?"

"How'd you know it was me? Could've been an animal."

"Not likely. I heard you first. Then when I looked, there you were in the wide open with your black hair standing out against the snow like ink on a blank page. You've got to skirt the trees when you walk, son. Takes longer, but it's safer."

"Been looking for you for a couple of days, Sam."

"So I figured. Now you've found me." Sam chuckled to himself. "I guess that means I was the Lost Boy this time."

Ethan joined his laughter. "I guess so."

"Well, come and warm yourself by the fire, son. You must be near frozen solid."

"Just about." Ethan's senses perked up at the smells surrounding him of sweet burning pine and roasting venison.

Sam saw Ethan's mouth watering and the ravenous look in his eyes. "I suppose you're hungry too."

"Cold bread and greens can only do so much to help that."

"Well, you're right there. Go on and dish up, then."

The two ate in silence for a while. Ethan wasn't sure what to say to this man who had somehow become his father, yet whom he hardly knew. Neither seemed bent on conversation, and yet there were questions hanging in the air.

Ethan finally broke the silence as he fixed himself another plateful of venison. "You've been out here a long time, Sam. Weeks. Are you planning on coming back home?"

"Does Zacharias know you're out here, son?"

"Yeah, I told him I was going before he left to go to the Senate. He was going to try to find someone for me to stay with. I told him I'd rather come after you."

"And he let you?"

"He couldn't have stopped me. I'm not a little kid, Sam."

"Oh, you're not? You could have fooled me." Sam tried to control his grin.

"I was on my own before I met you. I can take care of myself."

"I'm sure you can." Sam knew how resilient children could be, how resourceful when survival was on the line.

"Tell me about the Senate, Sam."

"Well, long ago when the country stretched from one ocean to another, the people of Before had a president and a Senate of people they elected

65

to vote on laws for their country. After the Disaster, everything changed. People were dying in all of the storms and earthquakes, and starving, fighting over food and water. The government enforced martial law, where the army was in charge. When everything settled down, and new villages had been formed, the few leaders that were left created the Triumvirate of a president, vice president, and general of the army who were appointed instead of elected. They made new laws and kept a form of martial law with the Corsairs. But they allowed the people to elect one senator to represent each remaining village. They meet twice a year to discuss issues and make or change some laws for the villages."

"And Zacharias is a senator?"

"He is. Because he is one of the Old Ones from Before, people respect and look up to him. He has a lot he can teach us."

"Do you think he would teach me to read?"

"He taught me, so I don't see why not."

Ethan wanted to learn all the things Zacharias and Sam had to teach him. He knew there was an entire world of things he didn't understand, and more than anything he wanted to understand. After a few moments he asked his question again of Sam. "So, are you? Coming back, I mean."

"I am."

"You about done with what you had to figure out?"

"Did Z tell you to ask me that?"

"Nah, I just sort of knew."

That night as they lay on their pallets near the fire, Ethan again worried about Sam's stability. He'd learned to read the signs of distress in other people. He'd had to. Living in the wild and coming across all kinds of people, he had to be able to determine very quickly if someone was friend or foe, sane or insane, well or unwell. Whether they would be a help to him or someone he needed to help. He had learned to read a variety of signs to answer these questions. And everything he saw in Sam showed what the past weeks had taken out of him. "You gonna be okay back home?"

"What do you mean, son?"

"Without Gemma." Ethan always went straight to the point. He saw no value in wasting time or words in diplomacy or tact, and wouldn't have known how to use those tools if he had found them valuable. He had the straightforwardness of a much younger child with the insight sometimes of an adult.

Sam looked directly up at the clear night sky as he answered. "Have you noticed how the moon is in a different part of the sky every night?"

"I suppose so."

"Why do you think that is?"

Ethan shrugged. "Don't know."

Sam sat up before he continued. From under a nearby pine tree, he retrieved two small pinecones, one smaller than the other. With them, he demonstrated. "The moon circles the earth, and the earth also spins like this." He spun the pinecone on the ground, then picked it up again to circle around the other pinecone. "I think people are like that sometimes. We keep circling around each other, meeting people over and over as we circle through their lives, but always in different parts of their sky. I guess that's what happened with me and Gemma. She's just in a different part of my sky now. It takes time for things to change—it doesn't happen overnight. Like a caterpillar in a cocoon or the earth making its yearly revolutions, causing season changes. It all takes time."

"But will you be okay?"

"In time."

"It's hard, though, isn't it?" Ethan now looked up toward the full moon resting not completely still on the blanket of darkness. "Hard when someone you love isn't there anymore."

Sam reached over and tousled the boy's dark locks. He maneuvered between being awed by his wisdom and surprised by his innocence.

"It can be, but *though my soul may set in darkness, it will rise in perfect light; I have loved the stars too fondly to be fearful of the night*. That's a bit of poetry, written ages ago that Zacharias used to quote to us. It means no matter what, no matter how dark it may seem sometimes, there's always even a little bit of light to help you find your way." He pulled the boy in close for a hug before they both lay down again, looking in different parts of the sky for their own personal stars.

5

SURVIVING

As she rubs her eyes against the morning sun, Gemma instinctively throws her arm out, reaching for the bag she knows will be there. She pulls it open to find several days' worth of food and water. Every morning as sure as the sun rises, her bag is always packed this way, but not by her. She never asks the boys. They'd deny it anyway. But she thinks it must be Kyle placing the food there, always thinking ahead in case they get separated. It's what she likes about him, his reliability in an unreliable world. She knows Sam is protective of her, thinks Kyle is hard, and doesn't completely trust him. But the needs of survival sometimes have to cut the wait times on trust. Lying on the hard and frozen earth, she holds the bag close and is comforted by the predictable offering.

There had been a time in Gemma's life when she had liked the wintertime. She had found it fun to see the first snow, and to try to figure out all the animals that had passed by based on their tracks. Her heart had thrilled with the biting sensation of the cold air in her lungs and all around her. But as she trudged up the hill to Zacharias' house and over fields pregnant with snowdrifts, under a sky hovering like a gray ghost over her head, she felt trapped by the cold rather than exhilarated. And yet she smiled in spite of herself at the three-line triangle tracks of a tiny robin that had passed this way before her.

Walking in without knocking, Gemma thought she would find Zacharias in the front room, reading in front of the fire. But the fire was low and he was nowhere to be seen. She started cleaning up here and there the way she used to, feeling the guilt of neglecting her duties in the past months for the more pressing matters of the Watch and Daisy. So many people seemed to be depending on her, and she worried she was not up to the tasks ahead. She needed Sam and hated the need within her. But seven years had not made it less. She still needed his calm and stability, his comfort and care. She hadn't joined the Watch until after he left, but she was sure he would have joined with her. She had held a small hope of finding him here with Zacharias so she could at least see him again, maybe help him understand.

"What are you doing back in my kitchen?" Gemma heard Z's mockingly gruff voice behind her.

"Just picking up where I left off. Sorry I haven't been around lately."

"You think I can't take care of myself?"

"I'm sure of it," she laughed, holding up a hammer she'd found in the sink.

"Did you walk over here in the snow? It's too cold for that."

"I'm fine," she replied, still working over a week's worth of dishes. "But it feels like it's been winter forever. I wish it would go faster."

Zacharias gave her a small caress before settling himself at the kitchen table to shell the black-eyed peas for his dinner.

"Going faster isn't always better. You know," he began with a sigh, "we were all moving so fast Before, it was impossible for the world to keep up. Faster and faster in transportation, in information. Nothing was ever fast enough. We didn't have the chance to really see things like we do now that it's slowed down. The earth will keep its rhythm, its seasons. We cannot force it to spin faster on its axis. And soon it will demand of us that we slow down, find again our natural pace. Take time to ponder, be forced to wait. Plant when planting is called for, harvest only after the plants have found their full measure of potential. If only we were so patient with other people." He looked slowly over his shoulder at Gemma, who had stopped her cleaning to listen to him.

"That's very poetic." She paused and was quiet a few moments before continuing. "Where's Sam?" She finally cut to the subject of both their hearts.

"He's out trying to forget you. As you should try to forget him, or at least the place he held in your heart."

"We can't really forget people. I'm worried about him, Z. I never meant to hurt him that way, and I just want to make sure . . ."

"You can't be the one to help him anymore, Gemma. He has to learn to help himself."

"Z, I still . . ."

"I know. I know you do. You always took care of him, so you think that's still what you are supposed to do. But hard as it is, you have to realize your love can't do anything but hurt him now because your heart is no longer solely yours to give. Is it?"

Gemma looked down at the floor, pulling the dish towel between her hands.

"Just leave him be. Let him find his own way. He's stronger than I think you really gave him credit for."

"You don't know what it is to love someone and then let them go only to have them return."

"You act as if I wasn't the one who was here with you those seven years, as if I'm not the one who told you to move on and let him go just like I had to let my Jesse go."

"And what would you have done if she'd come back?"

"What wouldn't I have done to have that happen? You know what she was to me, maybe even more than Sam knows. I loved her more than my life. And if she came back to find me married to someone else, I'd be devastated, just like you are. But that doesn't change the situation you're in. You still have to let him go again."

"I know."

Gemma turned back to the dishes, trying to force her mind into other avenues not populated with images of Sam. Her hands moved slowly at her task as if she were carrying added weight. After a minute or so, she realized she'd been holding her breath. She exhaled slowly, trying to release the unwanted feelings within her. But she knew they would not leave until they were finished with her. So instead, she covered them as she would cover herself with a heavy winter coat. "Let's change the subject, huh? Tell me about the Senate. You just got back, right?"

"Oh, the Senate. What is there to really tell? We met. We tried to pass new laws, tried to lessen the grip of the Triumvirate. But the Reader of the Law was there, of course, ready to smack down any initiative we had."

"It's so insulting that the government insists on having a Reader of the

Law, rather than just giving us a copy of the laws. It's probably just so they can change the laws at will." She huffed in frustration. "How are they justifying the added troops?"

"As a response to 'subversive revolutionary activities' as usual."

"What were the issues on the table?"

"First, we were trying to eliminate the need to present identification when entering the town square and only when going to a different town. Second, we wanted to eliminate the blood test required at adoptions. We were hoping that they were just policies and not actual laws. But there's no way of knowing until we try to pass our resolutions."

"But the Reader said . . ."

"*Citizens wishing to adopt children must first submit to a blood test for both parent and child to determine if the parents are living registered citizens.* Straight out of the Book of Laws. So then we tried to pass a resolution to be able to submit requests for changes in the Book of Laws to the Triumvirate, allowing for only one request per session of the Senate. But the Reader said this was also prohibited."

"It's like running into a brick wall, over and over. Why even go back?"

"You know, I had a similar conversation with one of the other senators after the session. He wanted to fall down with gratitude that the government had even given the Senate back to us, such as it is. But I told him it's like the old placebo effect. People think they've given us back democracy because that's what they're calling it to lull us into a sense of control. But it isn't real, it's not the cure for this dying land. All they've really allowed us is the right to decorate the bars of our own cage. Then, of course, the senator told me I was taking a risk by speaking that way. But what do I really risk? My liberty? Because that doesn't exist anymore."

"No, Z, but we have to keep up appearances. We have to let them believe we're working within the system they've created for us. They can't suspect we're involved with the Watch. Besides, what would we do without you if you were arrested?"

"I think at this point they'd be more suspicious if I stopped speaking out. They're used to my bluster. I think that's more of a smoke screen than anything."

"Maybe so."

"And why should we work within the system they've created? Our ancestors didn't. If they disagreed with the system, they changed it or created a new one."

"Sure, but we've been through two revolutions, Z, and we lost both times. We don't have the resources to wage all-out war again. Much as our ideals may flinch at that thought, it's the hard truth we have to face."

"You know the thing that disgusts me the most? The fear. I could feel it in that room of senators like a film over everything. We got into this mess in the first place because of fear. Back when democracy still existed, people started letting fear guide their choices. Anytime fear is the sole motivator, it begins to strangle out all other good and noble purposes. Then I had to see the country begin to fashion its own noose out of the strands fear. And now we have to live with the consequences."

"Take it easy, Z. We're doing what we can."

"What we can. What they'll allow us. What doesn't cause too much suspicion. I wanted to make a difference with my life. I wanted to do something important. That's all Jesse and I used to talk about. She'd listen to her old Helen Reddy tapes and get all fired up, and we'd talk about all the things we wanted to do. All the things we wanted to become. And now . . . well, now, it's all become so much less."

Gemma had stopped what she was doing again. She walked toward this man, her adopted father, the one person she respected the most in the world. She noticed for maybe the first time the slope in his shoulders, the weariness he wore like a garment. She felt the urge to protect him as he had always protected her. Kneeling beside him, she told him what she thought he wanted to hear, but also what she truly believed. "You do make a difference, Z. More than you know. People look up to you. They follow you." She saw for the first time what his strength and care for other people all these years had cost him. She knew it was because she was experiencing something similar with losing Sam again. She would have to put her own feelings and needs aside to help her people and the cause.

Zacharias spoke slowly after a moment of silence between them. "I read something once about leaving a legacy. I suppose it doesn't matter what you do if you've changed the world in some way and left a little part of yourself behind."

Gemma took his hands in her own. "You've done that. We live in Jesse's Hollow, a town you practically rebuilt with your two hands."

"Would she be proud, do you think? No, don't answer that."

* * * * *

Gemma returned to her own home to find Kyle's coat and boots, wet with snow, dropped on the floor by the door where he'd left them after shoveling the walk. The snow was melted in a puddle beneath them, so she knew he'd been done for a while. The bloodstained pallet where their neighbor Jordan had lain for weeks was empty in front of the waning fire. She didn't relish the idea of having to clean up the effects of yet another run-in with Corsairs.

As she looked around the house, she noticed again how Kyle brought a ruffled, hurried look to any room he'd been in, the stain of his intensity left behind. He was different from the way he used to be, but then she was too. Since his return from the Corsairs, she hadn't been able to feel quite settled around him, though she tried harder than she ever thought she could.

In their bedroom, Kyle lay facedown, sprawled out on top of the covers. She could tell he was still awake by his shallow, quick breathing.

"Thanks for shoveling," Gemma said to his back.

"Hmm?" Kyle grunted.

"I noticed you shoveled the walk."

"Yeah, it needed to be done."

"Did Jordan and Ruth make it to the Border alright?"

Kyle took in a deep breath as he rolled over to face his wife. "Sure they did. Why wouldn't they?"

"I was just asking. It's the first time we've ever tried an escape like that. I just wanted to make sure everything went okay. It's not like we're professionals or like we have any experience with things like that."

"Not like the Watch, you mean."

"Sure. I still wonder if maybe we should have contacted someone in the Watch to take care of it, just so it couldn't be traced back to us."

"Have many friends in the Watch, do you?"

"No, but I assume there are ways to get in touch with them." Gemma hated lying to her husband but tried to hold his gaze so he wouldn't suspect the dishonesty. It was forbidden to tell spouses about membership in the Watch unless they were also members. This was to protect all concerned. She knew that in her mind, but it didn't make the lying sit any easier with her.

"Well, we were able to take care of it without them."

"What will they find out there, do you think? Have you ever thought about what it looks like beyond the Border now? If there are others like Ruth and Jordan, trying to make a new start?"

Beyond the Border. How could he explain to her the things he'd seen as a Corsair, the raids he'd been on beyond the Border? How could he tell her anything about his life in between when he'd been taken into the army and his return? "Not really. What's the use of wondering those things? How was Zacharias today?"

Gemma breathed heavily. "He's fine. I think he's feeling a little tired, though. Started talking about Jesse again. He always talks about her when he's down. I was thinking on the walk home of something he said to me."

"What was that?"

"It was something about leaving your mark on this world. It got me thinking of the mark I want to leave, my legacy. What in this world will say I was here after I'm gone?"

Gemma reached over to run her fingers along Kyle's forearm. He looked down and picked at the skin around his nails.

"Kind of heavy thoughts. Why all this speculation suddenly?" he asked.

"Don't you think we should try to do something, if we can, to make things better?"

"Better than what? What are you talking about?"

"I mean if we ever have kids. Wouldn't you want to improve the world we're living in?"

Kyle sat up straight, no longer relaxed. "Now you're blending subjects. Are we talking about joining the Watch or having kids?"

"Kids, I suppose. I was just thinking it might be time to talk about applying to have a child." Gemma turned and lay back on her pillow. She was tired and hoped this wouldn't turn into another argument. She wished they could find a way to get on the same page.

"Oh, come on, Gemma, this again? We've talked about it already. Talked and talked." Kyle tried to get up to walk out of the room, but Gemma pulled him on the bed, taking his hand to hold him there.

"What makes now the right time?" Kyle continued. "Does this have anything to do with you helping with that childbirth a few weeks ago? You've seemed kind of tense since that night."

Since she hadn't actually witnessed the childbirth, Gemma truly didn't know what it was all about. Maybe it was pure instinct, nothing more than chemicals and hormones. Maybe it was her interaction with Daisy. Maybe it was the jealousy that had gripped her when she realized Aishe had a child. But if she was being honest with herself, if she'd taken the time to stop and think about when her wish for a child had returned, she would have realized it was Sam. She and Sam had always talked about the children they would have together. And seeing him again had brought it all back. Every part of her she thought had died with him suddenly resurrected.

"No, it wasn't that really. It's just that I'm not getting any younger, Kyle. You know how much I've always wanted a child. And we're running out of time. Besides, it just feels right. Who knows how long it will take for the application to go through? Why are you still against it?"

"Aren't our lives, the childhoods we had to endure, proof enough that nothing in this world is certain? I was conscripted into the army without choice. Sam was sent off to the lumber camp for seven years. How much of our lives do we actually control? Then what happened with Ruth and Jordan doesn't make me feel better about the situation we'd be bringing a child into. Doesn't it seem selfish in a way?"

"Selfish to want to bring life into the world, to try to instill goodness, fair play, and maybe a little bit of beauty by raising a child? It seems like we'd be adding something to the world, not taking something away."

"Abstract ideals that don't hold up under the weight of destructive reality."

She sat up next to him and placed her chin lightly on his shoulder. "You and I have seen plenty of destruction in our time, more than we ever should have. That's true. But don't you feel the need to create something?"

"I don't know, Gemma. God! I'm just trying to survive."

"I'm tired of just surviving."

"What's the alternative?"

She put her face to his cheek and whispered the word like a secret. "Living."

* * * * *

Sam heard the sound before he saw its source. A rustling murmur not unlike a distant wave. Mother Nature's breath as she arose in the early morning. Then looking into the sky as blue as a cornflower, he saw them.

Starlings in flight, in what appeared as a choreographed dance, they moved like one entity with one mind, diving and swooping in unison. The tiny birds, when on their own, were vulnerable to predators, but as a group they became a new creature, an impregnable force. He marveled at the connection, the instant communication between them. Harper Lee's mockingbird was alone, David against Goliath. But these starlings had strength in numbers. Sam wondered if humans could manage to find that kind of connection with other human beings. Could they be brought into that kind of unity, and what would affect the kind of change that would bring them together?

As Sam cooked breakfast over the fire, he realized he was whistling a tune he hadn't heard in years. A song from Before that Zacharias used to sing to him and Gemma when they were children. He excavated his mind for the words, words he'd learned to read by. The smells of breakfast cooking, the fire, the accompaniment of the early morning bird chorus blending with the running tune, all beckoned his memories to come back to him. Mornings with Zacharias and Gemma in the early years, now bittersweet against his stark reality. The insistent lyrics floated to the surface like a diver coming up for air. *"Keep smiling through the day. Keep smiling through the night. The shadows fly away when they can see your light. If I can keep you with me in day and nighttime too, I know the dark won't find me because my light is you."*

Hearing Sam singing to himself woke Ethan from a light sleep. He stretched against the stiffness. He had been used to sleeping outdoors until arriving at Zacharias' house. Now his limbs and back protested against sleeping on the ground. He was glad they would be heading back home today.

"Ready for some breakfast, boy?" Sam called cheerily, trying to put into practice the words of the song to keep smiling. Ethan was relieved to hear the lightness in his voice.

"Sure, let me just get my plate."

"What's that in your pack there?" Sam noticed the strap he recognized.

"It's your old camera. Zacharias said you might want it."

"Let's have a look. I haven't laid eyes on this thing in years. Probably don't even know how to use it anymore." Sam winked at Ethan.

Over the years, during the exodus that led the citizens to Jesse's Hollow, Boswell, and other coastal towns, Zacharias had picked up supplies here and there. Things he thought might come in handy later. Sometimes just on a whim, with no logical reason in his mind, a discarded object would grab his fancy, and he'd pack it away like a squirrel. After he'd first found the camera in an old farmhouse robbed of its roof and inhabitants, he started hunting for film, paper, developing chemicals. He'd managed to get his hands on quite a few supplies in the abandoned cities before the Border went up. They resided now in his developing shed, a means of creating things which could then be traded on Market Days. He'd taught Sam his craft of photography early on. Their times together in the shed with the sharp scent of developing fluid in the air were some of Sam's fondest memories.

Sam felt the weight of the camera in his hands, turning it over, examining its intricacies, what had once been an extension of his own body. He looked into the top of the Rollieflex, a boxy, two lens-camera. He loved the idea that just a tiny box could hold and preserve people's memories.

"How does it work?" Ethan asked. He'd seen the photographs that Zacharias had on his walls and had brought some with him for them to trade at Market Day but couldn't imagine how they came from this little box.

"Well, it's not easy to explain. A picture is basically drawn on film with light, and then we transfer it to paper with chemicals. I'll have to let you watch one day when I'm developing the film. I guess I like to think of it as stopping time for a moment, or at least slowing it down."

"That's not really possible, though, is it, Sam?"

"Always the literal one." Sam tousled the boy's hair. "No, taking a picture doesn't actually slow time, but it holds onto a moment so you can always look back at it."

"What for?"

"After the Disaster, when the dust settled and people had learned how to survive again, they started to realize all the things they'd lost besides people, homes, electricity, transportation. They'd lost their memories. For years they hadn't had physical pictures like the ones I take with this camera. Z told me they somehow kept all their books, writings, letters, pictures, everything on their machines. Computers, they were called. I don't really understand it. But when the machines stopped working, they lost all those things. So when I bring my pictures to Market Day or take pictures of people, in a way it feels like I'm giving them their memories back."

"But that's what I mean. Why look back at all? Why does it matter if it all eventually goes away?"

Sam paused and thought about that for a minute. He knew the life Ethan came from and knew how much he wanted to forget. It was a strange dance in the mind between a longing for and a repulsion from something. He approached the sensitive area carefully, not wanting to throw off Ethan's balance. "Aren't there things or people you would like to have a picture of to help you remember?"

"There are memories of some things that never go away, even if you want them to."

* * * * *

Rising early, Sophie fixed her morning coffee quickly. She wanted to get to the town square for Market Day as soon as possible before the crowd grew. Maybe if she got to the Council of Doctors before everyone else, they would be more sympathetic. She didn't take time to put her hair up but left it down around her shoulders. She reluctantly lifted Bridget out of her sick bed, wrapping her tightly in blankets to ward off the cold in the air outside, and set out toward town.

The morning sun broke into a million fractured pieces of light over the snow-covered fields. Sophie should have felt the cold as she walked the two miles from her farm into town. But her daughter's fevered head lay on her shoulder as she carried her across the miles. Sophie was covered with the heat of her daughter, the heat of her own exertion from carrying a four-year-old, and the heat of fear radiating in her heart. Every few minutes, Bridget would jump or squirm to get out of Sophie's arms, making the walk a struggle to comfort and hold onto her daughter for a few more minutes.

"Hush, love. It's alright. Mommy's here. You're going to be alright." She tried to speak soothing words to her, sing lullabies in her ear, but the fever brought the fight out in Bridget.

Sophie knew the fight that lay ahead and knew she'd have to draw on her reserves of strength, determination, and persuasion to fulfill the task. Bridget was in desperate need of medicine, and though Sophie would have rathered do just about anything besides revealing her child as undocumented, she knew she didn't have a choice. She could only hope to play on the sympathy of the Government Office workers in order to get the medicine she needed.

Sophie counted on getting past the guards at the edge of town as she'd always done without showing Bridget's identification. The guards knew her and her daughter and had never questioned her, but they had always been friendly as she passed into town. On this day, the day she needed all powers of luck, chance, or providence to work in her favor, she was frightened to see five new guards she didn't recognize standing in the road on the edge of the town square. Their uniforms were the same color as the clear morning sky, crisp and new, not the faded blue of the guards they had replaced.

These were freshly minted recruits, not to be persuaded or reasoned with, their poised rifles a testament to their roles as bastions against all who would try to pass. Sophie knew she wouldn't be able to get Bridget through without proper identification. Strike one against her luck. She smoothed her daughter's hair down, wet with sweat. "Mommy needs you to be really quiet, angel. Okay?" Bridget's eyes were closed, and Sophie prayed she was asleep so she wouldn't hear the lies she was about to tell.

The leader, a sergeant, stepped forward, holding his rifle across his chest. "Present your identification papers for you and the child, citizen."

Sophie shuffled Bridget to her left hip, pulling her own identification card out of her pocket. Another soldier stepped forward to take and examine her card.

"Good morning, Sergeant. Where are the other Corsairs who used to be here?"

"Reassigned. It is not a citizen's place to ask questions. Where is the child's card?" the sergeant pressed, looking down at Sophie with empty eyes.

Holding onto Bridget a little more tightly, Sophie replied, "I found this child sick in the forest. I'm bringing her into town to register her for adoption."

The sergeant looked with more scrutiny at Sophie, sizing her up, trying to determine her level of honesty. His eyes were ice blue, almost white, and hidden under dark, unforgiving brows. Sophie didn't break her gaze, and even managed to smile at the soldier. "It's a shame there are so many undocumented children running around these days. We citizens must try to help them as we can."

"That is not my concern. You must obtain an identification card immediately."

"Yes, Sergeant. That's exactly why I'm here."

He looked at the two of them one more time. "Very well. See that you do."

* * * * *

An ancient railroad track, long devoid of wooden ties, ran from Jesse's Hollow to Boswell and from Boswell to the mountain range, making its way through trees, hills, and canyons. Walking between the long iron bands strangled in years of rust and corrosion, Sam and Ethan made their way out of the mountains, heading toward Boswell, not having the time to make it to Jesse's Hollow before Market Day was over. Sam took the heavier pack from Ethan, carrying the camera, pictures, and other trade items, including some smoked venison. The gravel crunched under their feet, and Sam thought he heard a faraway whistle. But of course, no trains ran anymore. He wondered how many people had traveled along these tracks, speeding toward unknown destinations. He had read of trains and tried to imagine their powerful speed, flitting from one town to the next like a dragonfly zipping across the water. The abandoned and rusted-out train engine stuck on the track ahead, an orphan from another time, didn't seem like it was capable of any movement at all. Some had thought trains and planes and other means of transportation had brought people closer together from all parts of the country and even the world. But for some, they had only driven them farther away from family and loved ones, all means of running and escape more easily accessible, the trains always one step ahead of those who would follow. He always felt sorry for the people he read about left on the train platforms, waving as the trains pulled away. That was before the machines of the world had come to a grinding halt with the Disaster. So now the people plodded on, one foot in front of another toward their destinations only within walking distance.

Boswell's market was smaller than in Jesse's Hollow. Everyone seemed to know each other. As Sam looked around for a place to set up his shop, he noticed too how they kept to themselves, no one smiling or talking to him, their trust of strangers long since abandoned. Every few minutes a child would run into the square, quickly grabbing an apple or a loaf of bread, then disappear among booths and patrons. Sam thought of Ethan having to live that way, and absently reached his arm around the boy's shoulders as they made their way through the crowd. Looking around the square, a flash of color against the gray clothing and white snow caught Sam's eye. He stopped, trying to find the source. A woman stood near him in the line for the Council of Doctors, trying to hold a sleeping child, who she shifted from one hip to the other. Every so often, she would look over her shoulder as if she expected to see someone. Sam was struck by her appearance. She seemed to embody all the colors of the sunset at once— her hair the fire of the setting sun, her eyes the color of the sky left behind.

"Sam!" Ethan's voice broke into Sam's consciousness. "Did you hear me? There's an empty booth over there a lady said we could use. Do you want to start setting up?"

"Sure. Why don't you bring the things over, and I'll join you in a minute."

Sam was only half paying attention to Ethan and what he was doing. He heard the woman talking to the young man at the window of the Council of Doctors. No citizens were allowed in the building until the government worker at the window determined if they would be able to see a doctor. Initial requests were filed at the window where the citizens were forced to wait in long lines despite the weather. Here this woman stood with a child wrapped in a blanket in the biting cold. She seemed agitated and worried.

Sophie tried to talk softly, not wanting to wake Bridget. "Joshua, you know me. Can't you spare at least a few doses of medicine to help my child?"

"Sophie, you know I would if I could. An extra ration of food here or there is one thing, but you know the medicines are more closely regulated. I couldn't possibly give them to you without being discovered."

Sophie felt the tears collecting in a painful lump in her throat. Her composure began to crack like the frozen lake in a spring thaw. Possible scenarios started to play in the back of her mind, including ways to steal the necessary medicine.

"What's going on here, Johnson? Why are you taking so long with this one citizen?" The voice grated against Sophie's ears as she saw Griffyth approaching. She hadn't known that he had been transferred to work for the Council of Doctors.

"The child is clearly ill, Mr. Credell. But her identification card has been lost," Joshua tried to cover for Sophie, hoping there would be some way to get her the medicine.

"Lost?" Griffyth questioned. "How very irresponsible. Well, then, there should be a corresponding card in the records office, shouldn't there?" Sophie thought she perceived a slight grin on his face.

"No, sir. Mr. Johnson misspoke. The child has no identification card. Her father disappeared before all of the appropriate blood tests could be taken."

She tried to keep the disdain out of her voice as she said the word "father."

"I'm appealing to your mercy to give her much-needed medication. After all, her parents' mistakes should not require her to suffer." Sophie's eyes, swimming in unshed tears, silently pleaded with this man she had known, yet not known to do one fatherly thing.

"And yet, that is the way the world works. We all suffer for the sins of our fathers and mothers. Your daughter is undocumented, so in the eyes of the leaders of the state, she does not exist. Besides, she could be a plant by a member of the Watch sent to entrap us, for all we know."

"She's four years old! Let the doctors check her and you'll see she's truly ill."

"We cannot spare the resources. In the end, it doesn't matter anyway. Undocumented, illegal conception outside the law. She does not exist within this state. Now, leave the premises before she infects everyone and I have you arrested."

Sophie thought she knew Griffyth, thought she knew what he would and would not do. She never thought he would knowingly put his own child in this kind of danger, especially after trying to see her only yesterday. She wondered at his cruelty and hoped he was just putting on an act for the benefit of anyone within earshot. Maybe, since he knew she was sick, he would try to sneak medicine to Bridget later. Sophie could only hope. She sat down slowly on the edge of the fountain which had long been dry, visibly trying to hold herself up against what seemed like impossible odds, the flow of her own strength slowing to a stop until she felt as dry as the fountain and thought she would crumble along with it. The panic in her heart moved up and began to constrict her throat. Her breathing was labored. She couldn't do this now. She couldn't fall apart. She had to come up with a plan to help her daughter. If only she could get a handle on her thoughts. She tried to cobble together pieces of a plan, but several sleepless nights paired with her worry created a poor space for thinking clearly.

Seeing the blanket fall around the woman's feet, he rushed to pick it up for her. Confused, Sophie looked at him as if she were looking at an extinct creature. She was unprepared to have a conversation with another person, much less a kind one. The rushing in her ears silenced, and she began to hear and see the world around her again. She quickly wiped the tears from her face. "Do I know you?" she asked, not unkindly. She wondered if she were truly capable of processing the world around her where strangers were suddenly being helpful, a most uncommon occurrence.

"No, I just arrived in your town. I overheard what happened about the medicine. Is there nothing they can do?"

"Nothing they *will* do. My daughter is undocumented, illegal. I imagine they will be sending the soldiers to take me away before long."

"Is her father gone?"

Sophie peered toward the Government Office. "Yes."

Sam felt as though this woman needed a friend, but he knew he'd asked too many personal questions already. "I didn't mean to intrude. I'm sorry. I'll just go back to my booth now."

"What is your trade?" Sophie asked as she got up and started walking with Sam toward his booth.

"I take photographs."

"Truly? May I see?"

"Here, these are just a few I brought with me. I have more in my own village."

"It is a wonder to see life frozen like this, as if it could never change from that moment. Like it will exist forever in just that way."

"Exactly."

Bridget began to stir and wake up. Sophie sat down on a nearby tree stump to examine her daughter's condition, kissing her forehead.

"Would you like a photograph of your little girl?"

"I have nothing to trade you for it."

"I think a smile would be just about the right price." Sam picked up his camera, capturing mother and daughter in his sights. Sophie held Bridget on her lap, waiting for Sam to let her know when to smile. She closed her eyes and pressed her face against her daughter's flushed cheek. Sam's camera quietly caught just the moment of pure love encircling mother and daughter. No one could ever tell them that it didn't exist.

"I'll bring you a copy when I come back this way in a couple of weeks," Sam said quietly, hating to interrupt such a tender moment.

"Was that it? Are we done?"

"That's it."

"Thank you. I don't even know your name."

"Sam."

"Sam, I'm Sophie. I'll meet you here in a couple of weeks." She touched his arm gently before turning to walk out of town, her head held a little higher.

* * * * *

"We did good work today, didn't we, Sam?" Ethan asked as he and Sam walked the path out of Boswell. The trail was paved by many footprints, melting the snow where so many people had walked. Ethan enjoyed helping Sam trade at the booth. He enjoyed learning how to use the camera, and Sam had even let him take a few of the photographs himself.

"We did, son."

"I want to help you and Zacharias develop the film. Will you teach me?"

"Sure I will. I don't think we'll be making it back to Jesse's Hollow tonight, though. It's already starting to get dark." Sam knew they were too far from the woods to find a good camping spot but saw something up ahead that warmed his heart in the chill evening. "Looks like there's a farmhouse up ahead. Maybe they'll let us sleep in their barn. We'll have to go up to the house and ask." Sam didn't relish the thought of spending another cold night out in the open.

"That's different than how my group would have done things," Ethan mused. "They would have just waited 'til the lights were out, then snuck in the barn."

"Not the safest or the most honorable plan, is it? Didn't your group live by the code?"

"I didn't know anything about the code until there was one boy, Toby, who taught it to me. He tried to get the rest of the group to do things that way, but they were kind of wild. They liked to just do what they wanted and preferred as little contact with citizens as possible. They didn't help people like the code says. They only stuck together because they were all strong or smart about different things, so they thought the others could help them. But any chance to take advantage, they took. I wasn't with them for very long. It's probably why they left me in the woods. I wasn't useful to them anymore."

That was the most Sam had heard Ethan talk about his time in the woods. He felt he was beginning to earn the boy's trust. He whistled to himself as they walked up the drive to the farmhouse, then knocked firmly on the door. Sam heard footsteps coming downstairs, then standing in the doorway in front of him, there she was. Sophie. Her shocked expression matched his own.

"Well, what are you doing here? You couldn't have my photograph already."

"No. I uh, I mean . . . Is this your house?" Sam stuttered.

"It is." Sophie smiled.

"I didn't know. I mean, we were walking back home and saw your lights on. We won't be able to make it back to Jesse's Hollow tonight, and I was going to ask the farmer if we could sleep in the barn overnight."

"Well, I'm the farmer, but I couldn't possibly let you sleep in the barn."

"I understand, we'll just be on our . . ."

"No, I mean it's too cold outside. You should come in and sleep by my fire downstairs."

"We couldn't intrude, especially with your daughter sick."

"I've tucked her in for the night upstairs. You wouldn't be intruding. Honestly, I would appreciate the company. Please, come in out of the cold."

Sam looked down at Ethan, who smiled up at him with a little pleading in his eyes.

"Alright, then. If it's not too much trouble."

Ethan and Sam knocked off the snow from their boots on the front porch and slowly entered the warm interior, warm from the fire in the front room but also warm from the beeswax candles throughout the house, the paintings that hung on the walls of sunset landscapes, and the smell of chicken soup that welcomed them.

"You can set your things down anywhere. Would you like some soup?"

"No, thank you," Sam refused. "We had some deer jerky on the road, we can't . . ."

Sophie stopped him with a look. She cocked her head to the side, and a smile entered her tired eyes. Sam knew she wanted to feed them, and it would be rude to refuse.

"Sure, that'd be great," he corrected.

"Perfect. You can wash up at the sink."

Throughout dinner, Sam continued to marvel at this strange creature who seemed capable of breaking down any barriers of shyness or lack of acquaintance not just with him, but with Ethan as well. The boy warmed to her immediately, as if he'd always known her. In between her trips upstairs to check on Bridget, Sam listened as she effortlessly coaxed stories out of the boy from his childhood on the road and even offered her own stories to show him how much she understood. Like many people around Sam and Sophie's age, she too had lived for a time out in the woods after her parents were taken. She hadn't had the benefit of a group, but she and her sister had foraged for themselves until being adopted by caring parents in the Romany village. Sam and Sophie discovered they'd often been within just a few miles of each other during their times in the forest. Sam was amazed by the fact that they'd never met before.

Seeing Ethan's head starting to droop over his bowl, Sophie reached over and ruffled his hair. "You look sleepy, honey. We should probably get you to bed," she said before even Sam had noticed his tiredness.

"Nah, I'm alright," he protested. "I can help clean up."

"Nonsense. A growing boy needs his rest. I've laid your bedroll in front of the fire, so you should be nice and cozy. Good night," she said as she walked him to his bed.

Ethan stopped suddenly, and with no warning turned and hugged Sophie around her waist. She hugged him back easily, as if it was an everyday occurrence for her to win the heart of a child.

Sam and Sophie stayed up for a little longer, cleaning up the kitchen and talking. Neither seemed to want to end the conversation.

"Ethan is a fine boy. You must be proud of him," she whispered, handing Sam a glass to dry.

"You know, I'm just getting to know him. I've only been back home from the lumber camp for about a month. I found him in the woods as I was traveling back. But I was happy to adopt him. He's what I would have imagined my own son to be like. What will you do about medicine for your daughter?"

"I've sent a message to some friends who may be able to help," Sophie replied, thinking that the Watch was her last chance to get help for her daughter. In the meantime, she would just continue to take care of her the best way she knew how.

"I hope they can. Oh, that reminds me. I have something for your daughter. I saw it in the market today and had figured on bringing it to you in a couple of weeks, but I guess now's as good a time."

Sam pulled a small rag doll with yellow yarn hair out of his pack and handed it to Sophie, who seemed to pause before taking it. "That's very kind of you," she replied. "What made you think of it?"

"I don't know. Sometimes kids just need something to carry around with them. It seems to ground them in a way, doesn't it?"

"Yes, it does. Adults too, sometimes." Sophie smiled, feeling suddenly shy. "I'll bring this up to her. Thanks again, Sam. Good night."

As she walked upstairs, Sam puzzled over this woman, so caring and giving but somehow reluctant to accept a gift. He felt intrigued and grateful for the chance to get to know her. As he lay down on his bedroll next to the sleeping Ethan, he heard a lullaby from upstairs. Sophie's voice wafted through the house, warm and sweet like the smell of baking cookies. He thought he recognized from far away the song she sang, *"So when my thoughts begin to stray, I know you're not far away. I'll see you always near me, or so it seems. For you will always be here somewhere in my dreams."* He tried to shake up his brain and travel back to remember where he'd heard it but couldn't quite place it. He fell asleep to her soothing voice and dreamed of a red-headed girl running through the trees.

6

GUILTY BY ASSOCIATION

On the far edge of Jesse's Hollow, several miles away from the town square, there stood a sagging gray house in the middle of a field. Its roof had caved in under the weight of snow from a hundred winters. Windows like black eyes squinted at anyone who came near. No path led to or from this forgotten residence. It rose up out of an over-growing field as if it too had been planted there and left to go to seed. When the citizens of Jesse's Hollow were settling in the town they found abandoned, this house was already too old and derelict to be inhabited. The fence had been torn down before anyone could remember. No trees sheltered this abode, every minor storm taking a shingle or a pane of glass until it looked like a carcass picked clean by scavengers.

Kyle often found himself sitting on the leaning porch steps when he needed to think. On this particular day, the snow had somewhat melted around the steps, exposing the dead grass beneath. He pulled at the flattened blades of grass. The dampness in his hands reminded him of the cold around him. He didn't know how long he'd sat there. Gemma would be worried, but he couldn't go home yet. Things had seemed simple enough before she started asking about children. Go to work, try to help people, be a good husband.

Although it was painful to leave his comrades in the Corsairs—especially Mark—when Kyle came back after being released, he thought he could have just taken up where he left off with his friends, with Gemma.

But too many years had passed. She had always been Sam's girl, but Sam was gone. It seemed only natural that she would turn to him to help her forget Sam. It all should have been so simple. But nothing was ever simple. They were both so changed from the people they had been. Other lives and loves had crossed into theirs, muddying the waters. Now she wanted children. A child would only complicate matters uselessly, but she wouldn't give up the subject and brought it up every few months. He was running out of things to say in response.

Things were too uncertain. The Corsairs were preparing for a war. He knew the signs. They would be sending more horses, troops, and guns. Kyle couldn't remember when he'd started referring to the Corsairs as *they* rather than *we*. They had been his brothers, his family. Mark and the others were the sole people he could depend on. Until his discharge. But all things change. Nothing was certain. There was always a job to do. Always a mission. For now his mission and his purpose was Gemma. Did that mean he had to give her everything she wanted? Children would only get in the way. He stared absently at the red berries on the bush in front of the shack. The only color on the frozen land, they looked inviting, though he knew they were poison.

Kyle looks down at his feet. The boots the leaders gave him look and feel too big for him. But they say he'll grow into them. He wishes the Corsairs had taken Sam with him, so he'd at least have someone he knew. Sam is lucky he got away. He couldn't handle the training. Kyle knows that. Better for him to stay with Gemma.

Kyle is shorter than some of the rest of the recruits standing next to him. They all stare straight ahead, the sun behind them, waiting for the leader to tell them what to do. Their shadows in the snow are jagged fence posts. He looks closely at his shadow, his arms, torso, and legs lengthened almost comically. His shadow seems to grow before him. Now it's wider than the rest. Now longer. It seems to fill all the empty space in the snow, a black shadow growing like a hole that will swallow him up. But it's not a hole, and it's not even his shadow. General Simeon Drape stands behind him. The man's great hands on Kyle's shoulders startle him.

A month passes. The tests and training are rigorous. Cruel. But Kyle is strong. He stands with his fists up, his nose bloodied. The boy in front of him is reeling from the last punch Kyle delivered. Spatters of blood pepper the snow like fallen holly berries. Kyle turns to Simeon, looking for permission to stop. He wipes the tears from his face. They will not have the satisfaction of seeing him cry.

"Don't test my patience, boy. You know your duty. Finish him. You could become one of the greatest officers in the Corsairs. But I warn you, do not cross me."

"Father."

"Do it. Make me proud I chose you as my son."

A crow caws from a branch, startling Kyle. He delivers a left cross, and the boy is on the ground. The fight was never fair. The other boy is much smaller than Kyle, but he hasn't kept up with his chores. The others have chosen him as a punching bag, and even the officers stage these fights once a week to toughen him up.

Kyle stands at attention, awaiting his next order. General Drape approaches slowly. Every step is measured. He delivers a swift slap to Kyle's cheek, but Kyle doesn't flinch.

"Never make me repeat an order."

The slap is followed by an embrace. Then the two stand at attention facing each other. Kyle's eyes focus on the medals on his father's blue uniform. He has to focus on anything to keep the tears back.

"This boy was just a child, not yet a man. Children are a commodity just like any other. Sometimes an asset to be treasured, sometimes a nuisance and a liability to be eliminated. Remember that."

Mark is the only one waiting for Kyle to walk back to the barracks.

A crow loudly cawed, looking down on him from the ridgepole of the roof. A brisk wind knocked loose a pane of glass barely hanging on. The shattering glass behind him startled Kyle. In his ears it sounded like the crack of the boy's nose under his knuckles the day General Drape made him a lieutenant over his fellow recruits. *Sometimes an asset, sometimes a nuisance.* Now all he had to do was get back to Gemma and hope he could distract her away from children for a little longer.

* * * * *

The room was dark except for a tiny candle swimming in a day's spent wax and the dying light of the fire that played on Bridget's face where she lay on her pallet on the floor of her bedroom. Sophie wanted to keep her as warm as possible on the cold night. Through the window, the moon hung in a murky puddle of gray, an eerie halo crowning the night. People look different by firelight. A softness descends with the evening, forgiving flaws, inviting closeness. Sophie sat in her rocking chair, just staring at Bridget. She tried to hold on to every piece of her, every blonde curl on her head, her soft cheeks, still like a baby's. Bridget no longer opened her eyes. She couldn't give her mother the pleading look that Sophie loved and dreaded. But her chest was still rising and falling with each labored breath. Sophie held a panicky hope that medicine would arrive from the Watch, that a miracle would come with the sunrise. Her ears ached, straining to hear someone walking up to the house or a knock on the door that didn't come. But she had never felt so alone or afraid. Even on the lonely nights in the woods as a child when the only voice she had heard for days was her own crying, she wasn't this afraid. It was as if she was watching her own life fall away before her.

The child trembled, and Sophie was immediately at her side. She lay down next to her and wrapped her daughter in her arms, stroking her hair, trying to comfort her. She spoke softly to her, "It's alright, my love. Mommy's here. I won't leave you."

Sophie gazed at the candle in the corner where it flickered and sputtered. She wrapped Bridget in the gentle lullaby that was a comfort to them both. *So when my thoughts begin to stray, I know you're not far away. I'll see you always near me, or so it seems. For you will always be here somewhere in my dreams.*

The melted wax formed a puddle in the candleholder. The tiny flame shuddered with a final glimmer, then slowly faded into darkness.

* * * * *

"They've started putting barbed wire fences along the Border. Miles of the stuff." Sam drew his finger along the map Zacharias had laid across the kitchen table. Ethan sat in the corner of the room, working on the alphabet Sam had given him to copy with chalk on a broken piece of slate.

In the week since returning from Boswell, Sam had tried to make a couple of trips across the Border but found his way barred with new guards unable to be bribed or circumvented and high barbed wire fences unable to be scaled.

"What could they be worried about keeping out?" Sam continued. "There haven't been border raids for years. Not even a hint of anyone trying to get in from the cities. And I've seen those cities. They are desolate graveyards."

"Or maybe what are they trying to keep in?" Zacharias mused to himself.

"You think this is to keep us in?"

"Maybe."

"What messages are coming from the Corsairs?"

"You'll be able to hear for yourself. There's to be a mandatory town meeting two days from now. Show me again where you saw the fences."

Sam looked down at the map full of pencil marks, shadings, crossed out sections. The map from Before bore the scars of a land changed through natural disaster and governmental borders. Z had painted the ocean in blue, miles inland from where it used to be, drawn mountains where there once were valleys, new rivers flowing through woods and fields. "They started here at the fork in the river, going southwest along the mountainside. But when I was in Boswell, I could see where they started at the oceanside and were building a fence along the Southern Border. And it looks as if they might even be starting one along the water's edge, as well."

"It doesn't make any sense. There have to be other villages and survivors outside those borders. Why would they want to separate us?"

"We can't be sure there are other villages. Maybe we're it." Sam didn't like to think of it, how many people would have died leaving only the few villages within the Border. But he'd seen and buried plenty of remains. Too many to count.

"You told me yourself you saw where there were new trees cut outside the Border when you were heading back from the lumber camp."

"They could have just been scavengers like me."

"Maybe. But maybe not."

"Tell me what you're thinking, Z."

"I don't know yet, I just . . ."

The front door crashed open, spilling Gemma into the room. Sam, Zacharias, and Ethan all turned to face her. She gulped air into her lungs, having run all the way from town. Gemma's eyes caught Sam's. They both registered fear from the other, seeking comfort in their silent exchange as they used to.

"Gemma, what on earth?" Z's question brought her back.

"There's been a public flogging. Today. In the square in Boswell."

"It can't be. They promised us." Sam sat down under the weight of the news. His thoughts turned to the woman he had met. Sophie had admitted to the Government Office that her child was illegal. Could they have flogged her for that?

"Then it's beginning already." Z's voice was as sharp as a razor, but calm.

"Who was it? Do you know?"

Zacharias noted the tightness in Sam's voice, full of anxiety.

"I don't have a name yet. But he was a member of the Watch, so I'm told," Gemma replied, but still looked at Zacharias, trying not to meet Sam's eyes again.

"He . . ."

"That's not all," Gemma continued.

"Here, drink some water and sit down and tell us calmly." Zacharias maneuvered her to the table while Ethan jumped in to provide the water.

"I don't have all the information. Just a short message from the Watch." Gemma paused to take the drink from Ethan. She gave him a smile that reassured him despite the fearful events she was talking about.

Sam walked over to her, giving her a look that asked her to wait to go on. "Ethan, could you take your writing upstairs?"

"There's no reason he shouldn't hear," Gemma protested. "After all, we may need to recruit him soon enough."

"Run along, son."

Ethan bristled at being treated like a child but didn't want to go against Sam. Once he was upstairs, Sam spoke sharply, "Gemma, I don't want him involved in Watch activities. I'll not have his childhood ruined. It's no place for a boy his age."

"You can't be so naive, Sam. Do you seriously think you can keep him out of all this?"

"I'm going to do my best to try."

"And what about you?"

"I'll help where I can, but I won't be involved in any killing."

"Well, that's what I came here to tell you and Zacharias. That's what started all of this. The message I received said a government official, Griffyth Credell, was found strangled last night in the G.O. in Boswell. Then this morning, one of our members was dragged into the square and flogged."

"Is he the one who killed the man, or do we even know it was a member of the Watch who did it?" Zacharias was skeptical that it wasn't all a trick played out by the Triumvirate and the Corsairs.

"The leaders of the Watch seem to think so. They've tasked me with finding the murderer or murderers and removing them from the Watch. I'm to send them beyond the Border."

"I'm still not sure it was someone . . ."

"We tried to be so careful to protect ourselves and the cause," Gemma talked over Zacharias, unable to stop her racing thoughts. "And now some over-excited, unthinking hot-head has brought suspicion and punishment down on us. Everything's at stake here. With the public floggings, it's only a matter of time before the executions will follow. All our care and planning has gone to hell!"

Zacharias tried to maintain an air of control. He knew how easy it was to let speculation run away with people, which always led to rash acts, maybe even what had led to this killing. "It may just be an isolated event. You said yourself we don't have all the information. Maybe they had no choice. I suppose they have the right to follow their own conscience . . ."

"Right? We have no rights! The Corsairs and the Triumvirate have all the rights, laws, and power. We are the ones left with nothing. Even still, we're losing what little ground we had gained. We can't resort to the methods of the Corsairs or we're no better than they are. This is not how we do things. There are rules for a reason. If everyone just goes out for revenge hunting, this will all turn into anarchy. I don't care what the motives were. This is not the way things are done. But now it doesn't even matter if one of ours did it or not. We're guilty by association. So now we're left with a choice. We can either publicly denounce the act and the perpetrator, or we can change our tactics, start fighting real battles."

"I'm not sure that's the right move," Sam spoke softly.

"Why am I not surprised?"

"Gemma, this is how it always starts. We're just reliving the same pattern over and over and over again. Aren't you tired of it yet?"

"You can't imagine I want violence. You know me better than that. I just don't see how we will have any other choice. Real battles fought out in the open may be our only recourse."

"One killing leads to another, then ten, then a hundred. And before you know it, a whole generation is wiped out. Honestly, we just don't have enough lives to give to the cause this time. It's already exacted too high a payment."

"The Corsairs dragged him out of his house in front of his wife and son," Gemma whispered, observing Sam's reaction as he visibly flinched at her words. His jaw tightened and he gripped the back of the chair. "They were on horses and dragged him between them into the square. Then they strung him up as if he were an animal to be skinned. They're not fighting fair. At least if we start real battles, they won't be murdering us one by one without any opposition. At least we'll have a fighting chance!"

"Will we?"

Gemma knew what he was thinking, who he was thinking of. She always knew. They shared a past, the same memories, nightmares, fears. She knew he had watched his own parents dragged out of their house after the First Revolution when their comrades had betrayed them to the Corsairs for their involvement in the war. Just as she had watched her own parents suffer the same fate. She knew she'd pushed him too far. But now was not the time for people to be burying their heads in the sand; that only ever led to burying more dead.

"I'll go up and see if Ethan needs any help," Zacharias offered, thinking he would leave them alone to work it out between them.

An eavesdropping Ethan scurried upstairs before anyone could find him crouched and listening.

"No, I'll go." Sam was up the stairs before anyone could protest.

Gemma looked pleadingly at Zacharias. "Z, bring him to the town meeting in a couple of days."

"We don't really have a choice now, do we?"

"You know what I mean. Maybe if he hears the propaganda and dictates the Corsairs are throwing around, he'll see they aren't giving us a choice."

"I suppose we're past the point of keeping up appearances."

"When you're on the chessboard, you can't just play your pawns or sit back and make no move at all. Eventually, you have to engage the enemy. We didn't make the rules, we just have to live by them."

"The rules seem to always be changing, don't they?"

* * * * *

That evening, Gemma went to the cabin to see Daisy before returning home. She felt an overwhelming need to check on her charge and the other children with her. She thought about what Sam had said about not letting

Ethan help with the Watch. Maybe she was wrong for letting Daisy be involved. Maybe she was putting her in danger. But then she thought of herself at Daisy's age, not even twelve years old. She knew she would have done anything to help fight the Corsairs with her parents if she'd been given the chance. She didn't force Daisy to do anything. The child wanted to help. Besides, she mostly just delivered messages, which seemed safe enough.

The cabin was dark and cold when she arrived. She lit a lantern and stirred the waning fire. Each of the children living there had created their own space in different corners of the large main room with bedrolls, knickknacks, and their own personal treasures stashed among what few things they possessed. Young Hughie had built a fort for himself and his twin sister made out of mismatched pillows, cushions, and boxes completely surrounding their blankets. Seth, one of the older boys, had collected bottles of all different shapes and sizes. Jake, as a semi-leader, had staked out the back room as his own. No one was allowed to trespass there, not even Gemma.

In Daisy's space, Gemma found several paintings she'd created on long pieces of bark, the paint derived from berries and plants found in the woods. The child was really quite talented. Gemma held a sunset in her hands that made her think of an entire world existing inside that piece of bark. She found herself wondering what other talents were hidden under the survival the citizens were forced to eke out. Sam used to talk to her about all the things he wanted to do, professions he'd read about in books. None of that was possible now. How many artists were toiling in the fields or working in government camps just for the privilege of survival? How had this type of life become normal?

Excited whooping outside the door broke into Gemma's thoughts. Five children came tromping into the cabin. They were each congratulating each other on their fine hunting skills. There would be a feast this night of two rabbits. The oldest two boys, Seth and Jake, walked into the kitchen to begin preparing their kill for the fire.

"Gemma!" Daisy ran to her friend, surprised by the unplanned visit. Gemma held the child's cold cheeks in her hands, noticing how chapped and red they were. This winter had been hard on her.

Gemma greeted all the children warmly. "I've brought you all some bread and apples to go with your feast. Daisy, will you do the honors?"

Daisy passed out pieces of bread and one apple to each of the other children. Little Hughie and Petal took their food and walked to their beds without a word. The twins would never speak when Gemma was around or allow her to touch them or come near. But they clutched the food gratefully in their hands and ate hungrily enough to let her know her gifts were appreciated. They both crunched into the cool apples, juice dripping down their tiny chins. Hughie reached his arm around his sister to help warm her after their sojourn in the cold night. Gemma often pondered about what horrors the little ones could have seen to make them so distrustful of adults.

"What made you come tonight?" Daisy asked, settling into the rocking chair with Gemma in front of the fire.

"I came to tell you that you must all be extra careful from now on. There's been an attack in another village. I don't know if the soldiers will be searching out children specifically, but they may be in these woods looking for members of the Watch. So try to avoid them if you can. None of the normal tricks or pranks, alright?"

Seth and Jake moaned at this, not wanting to give up one of their favorite pastimes.

"Have you seen the fences at the borders?" Gemma asked.

Daisy nodded.

"You'll want to steer clear of those as well."

"What's going on, Gemma? Why are things changing?"

Gemma ran her fingers through Daisy's hair as she talked to her. She wanted to make sure she warned her enough to keep the child safe. But how much fear was it necessary to instill in her? She wished again that she could bring them all back to her own house and keep them safe under her protection. "I'm not sure exactly what's going on, sweetheart. All I know is that it might get worse before it gets better. So it's best for you to all lay low."

"You mean no more messages, either?"

"Only when it's absolutely necessary."

Daisy put her head down on Gemma's shoulder. She tried to soak in the feeling of comfort and safety she felt in Gemma's presence, treasuring it like a special treat to be enjoyed later. Gemma always seemed to have an earthy scent about her mixed with the sweet smell of the tiny white fairy bell flowers, even in the winter. Daisy tried to remember what it was like when her own mother had held her this way, but Gemma had been the prevailing figure in her life for so long that her face had begun to blend into her mother's face, almost blurring into the same entity. She leaned her face into Gemma's neck. She didn't care if the boys saw her or called her a baby.

"I'll come to check on you as often as I can. I promise."

Daisy didn't respond.

Gemma held her more tightly. "And you can help me keep the little ones safe, right? I'm counting on you, honey."

Daisy nodded.

Gemma tried to glance unnoticed at the twins in their corner, wishing they too would let her in. And though they stared unashamedly at her and Daisy, they merely clutched each other tighter as Petal played with her own hair.

"Now, would you like a game or a story?"

Daisy followed Gemma's gaze toward the twins and gave the answer that would bring joy to them as well. "Story."

7

UNTIL THEY CAN STAND ON THEIR OWN

S mudged gray uniforms and soiled snow blended into a mass of gray in the square. Sam, Ethan, and Zacharias stood in a row with their fellow town members in front of the stage. The citizens of Jesse's Hollow were all clad in similar clothing, government issue of muted gray cotton tunics, pants, and tied leather belts. On Market Days one could expect to see tiny splashes of color, patterns, and various materials found in the old houses when the refugees had arrived. The people often traded swaths of fabrics on Market Day. It was the custom to try to find even a tiny sliver of individuality among the sea of gray. But on town meeting days when the citizens faced the Corsairs *en masse*, it was expected that they all look uniform. Sam searched the faces above the gray, trying to see a hint of the familiar.

He looked around to see if he could see Kyle with Gemma. He had not spoken to Kyle since his return. He hadn't found the strength or the necessity to do so. But Gemma stood without her husband in a row on the other side of the square. Sam wondered how Kyle had managed to get out of the required town meeting. He seemed to be always making up rules of his own.

"Attention! Silence!" a sergeant barked even though the crowd stood in silence already. "Give the captain your strict attention, citizens of Jesse's

Hollow!"

A barrel-chested man in bulging blue uniform approached the edge of the stage and looked over the crowd before speaking. Sam expected to hear him shouting as well, but an almost friendly voice emanated from the new soldier, as if he were reading a bedtime story to a child. "As a reminder, no citizen is allowed to enter the city limits of large cities or leave the borders marked by the guard stations. There are dangers lurking in the decimated streets of the large cities. Your government is aware of these dangers, which is why the Triumvirate has wisely taken this precaution for your benefit. We should all be grateful our wise leaders are helping us to stay the course."

"Stay the course," the crowd echoed in unison, like a chant.

"You will notice fences are being erected along the borders to further allow us to protect our villages from infiltration and attack. Anyone attempting to cross the fence will be shot without question." The words and his congenial tone did not match, grating against Sam's ears and nerves like the creak of a tree before being felled.

"Now onto our next order of unpleasant business. Sergeant, bring the man to the front of the stage."

A gasp went through the crowd, a concert of whispers and gulps of breath. Nothing could have inoculated the people from the shock of what they saw. Before them was a citizen, shivering in the cold with his tunic removed, back facing them. His flesh was torn in gaping red slashes. Though many had seen such injuries before, the time interim had dulled their memories of the spectacle. Mothers covered the eyes of their children, the Old Ones looked at the ground, the young clenched their fists. The desired dismay and fear meant to be engendered by the display fell short of the outrage and passion that still flowed in the veins of the citizens, however quietly it flowed.

The captain's dulcet tones continued, an insult to the scene before them. "A member of our esteemed government in Boswell has been murdered in cold blood. Citizens may be assured the culprit will be found and brought to swift justice. There will be one citizen from every village flogged once a week until that time. We are confident this will encourage your full cooperation with our investigation. If you have any information regarding this brutal murder, you will bring it to the sergeant in your village immediately. As always, stay the course."

"Stay the course." The citizens released the reply through clenched teeth or whispered it almost inaudibly. The air was thick with words not spoken and blows not struck.

As the crowd dispersed, Sam looked down to see tears in Ethan's eyes. Sam had tried to turn him away from the awful visual, but Ethan would not be swayed. He needed Sam to know he was no longer a child. And yet he could not stop the tears which wet his face and peppered his tunic in dark splotches. The boy wiped furiously at his nose, anger rather than fear shaking his young bones. He was angry at the Corsairs, angry he wasn't big enough to do something about it, angry at all the people who stood there just gaping and answering, blending into complicity and tolerance like a river of dirty water.

"Ethan, are you alright, son?" Sam tried to put his hand on the boy's shoulder but was shrugged away.

"How can you stand it? It's wrong for them to punish people who haven't even done anything. Why can't we stop them from doing things that are wrong?"

Sam tried to usher the boy out of the square in case they would be overheard. "Let's go for a walk. Z, we'll meet you back at the house."

They walked in silence toward the old bridge, one of Sam's favorite thinking places. Wooden pilings worn down with time, yet still not smooth. Sam grasped the railing, rough under his hands, and peered at the fish swimming under the frozen surface of the water in the creek. The ice was thinning. Branches, brown grass, and other vegetation awaiting spring renewal stood in dark contrast to the glaring white snow. Soon it would all be melted, the color returned to the land.

"I know how you feel, son. Truly I do," Sam began. "But there are times to fight, and times to keep yourself safe so you can fight another day. We all know what the Corsairs are doing is wrong. But until we can fight with some expectation of winning, it would be throwing our lives away for nothing. Wars can't be entered into lightly, and we can't always give in to our feelings, no matter how justified we feel in them. It's a hard truth, but it is the truth. And sometimes that's all we can hold onto. Do you understand?"

Ethan kicked at a small pile of snow up against the bridge piling. "You were in the war, though, weren't you?"

"Yes, I was."

"And you were just a kid."

"Not much older than you, but I didn't exactly have a choice. We were all called on to fight for our lives."

"Did you ever kill anyone?"

Sam paused, feeling the words like bile in the back of his throat. "I did. It's not something I would ever want you to experience."

"But like you said, sometimes we don't have a choice. How do you know when is the right time to fight?"

"Well, now. I'm not sure I know the answer to that question. Every situation is different. There's the question of knowing beyond a doubt you are in the right. There's protecting the innocent. There's common sense of knowing if you even have a chance of winning the fight. All of those things come into making the decision. It's why it's usually an adult's decision and not a child's."

Ethan stood as tall as he could, throwing his shoulders back and chest out, but still not even reaching the height of Sam's shoulders. "I'm not a child, Sam. I know things. I've seen things. And I've taken care of myself."

"I know all of that, boy. You've done very well on your own. And I don't want to take away from the things you've done and accomplished. But there are still many things you don't know. And until you do, it's probably best to trust my judgment for now, alright? When I think it's time to fight, I'll let you know, and I'll want you by my side. Can I trust you with that?"

"I guess so." Tiny crystals of snow covered the boy's rough boots as he kicked again at the pile.

"In the meantime, how'd you like to go back to Boswell with me tomorrow? We have some photographs to deliver."

Ethan nodded.

The fish continued to swim in their frozen stream. The warmer southern winds began to blow. And the child and the man set their decisions aside for another day.

* * * * *

A spring wind attempted to steal away Sam's hat. He pulled it down around his ears, looking down at the matted grass, wet from melting snow. A thaw was setting in. Just a few more weeks before the brutal winter would be over. Sam's body still bore the marks and the memory of his weeks on the mountain when he'd almost starved in the cold, but it felt like another lifetime. The boy at his side reminded him of the renewal he was feeling, the new energy that seemed to make him want to try harder, live more deliberately. He placed an affectionate hand on the boy's shoulder as they approached Sophie's house. Maybe it wasn't just the boy who was lightening Sam's step.

The sound of his quick rap on the farmhouse door rang in Sam's ears as he impatiently waited for it to be answered. He rifled through his pack, trying to find the photograph of mother and daughter, but was interrupted by the sound of the door opening before him. He looked up quickly to see an elderly woman standing before him, wiping her hands on her apron.

"I'm sorry, I was looking for Sophie Bryan. Do I have the wrong house?"

"No, this is her place."

"Is she around? I've come to deliver something to her."

"You may have to be satisfied leavin' whatever it is with me, my boy. She can't really be receivin' company just now."

"Has she become ill as well? How is her daughter?"

"Know her well, do ya?"

"We met a couple of weeks ago. I took a photograph of her and the child. Then she was kind enough to put us up for the night."

"Well, she is a kind one. Truth be." The woman seemed to be thinking something over and trying to make a decision. "A photograph, ya say? Well, now, that might be just the thing."

"What's happened?"

"Come in and I'll tell ya about it. Seein' as how she trusted you in her house, I suppose I can too. Yes, might be just the thing."

Sam and Ethan left their bags inside the front door and followed the elderly woman as she toddled toward the fire, stoking it, and motioning for them to sit before it. She made her way back to a large tub in the kitchen where she continued washing clothes as she spoke. Her hands were rarely, if ever, idle.

"I'm Mrs. O'Dell from the next farm over."

"My name is Sam, and this is Ethan."

"I'm happy this blessed winter seems to be ending. Truly was a hindrance on these bones of mine. No good for little 'uns and their sicknesses either. This little 'un isn't ill, is he?"

"No, he's fine."

Sam fidgeted with the picture, moving it from one hand to the other and turning it over and over. He wanted to know where Sophie was. Why was the house so quiet? Why was this strange woman receiving him? Was she a relative?

"That the photograph, is it?"

"What? Oh, yes. It is."

"May I see it? Been quite a spell since I've seen one of someone I know. Just the ones left in these old houses to look at. Not quite the same as seeing the likeness of a friend."

"Sure."

"Well, now, ain't that a wonder? Spitting image of her and the poor little mite." Mrs. O'Dell lifted the corner of her apron and wiped a tear from her eye. "One night over a week ago, I woke to hear this terrible sound. Never heard the like before. Sounded like an animal stuck in a trap, just a sharp cry, then a wail. I ran over because I knew the child had been sick. Found young Sophie holding the little 'un just so still in her arms."

Sam took a deep breath. Ethan regarded him carefully. He stepped closer to him and put his own hand on Sam's shoulder as Sam had done to him many times.

"Took me and Jim both to pull Sophie away so we could take care of things with the poor child. Sophie had stopped crying when we got here. She was just holding that poor baby. Rocking her like she was rocking her to sleep. Once we got her out of the bedroom, she just sort of went limp. So Jim carried her into her own bedroom. She stayed there for a few days, sleeping. Probably best, poor lamb. We buried Bridget in the back pasture under an oak tree, next to some other graves of the people who lived here before. And I've stayed here with Sophie since. At night, I'll hear her cry out once again like that first night. But she's not awake. I've found her a couple of times just wandering around, not awake. That first night, I'm almost sure she got out of the house and back in while I was sleeping right here in the front room. Uncanny, if you ask me. Yesterday, she got up, walked down the hall, in a daze like. Went to the child's bedroom, sat on the floor and started playing with her toys as if the child was there with her. I tell ya, I'm right scared for her. I've seen things like this crack a person's mind. No one knows the connection between a mother and a child. When it's broken, well, there's nothing fills that. The pain doesn't pass. Not ever. But if the mother's lucky, the pain will step aside from time to time. Losing a child is always hard, but this is something different."

"Every grief is different," Sam whispered.

"I suppose so."

"I'm not sure I should give her this picture now. Wouldn't it just upset her more?"

"No, it might be just the thing."

"I'm not sure it's my place, maybe you should . . ."

"Now, now. She'll not harm ya, my boy. You come on upstairs with me. She'll be in the child's bedroom again."

Sam looked at Ethan, who nodded he wanted to go with them. So the three walked up the creaking stairs to find Sophie sitting in the middle of the floor in Bridget's bedroom. The small bed was made, a coverlet of faded blue and pink flowers laying over the top. Sophie had a piece of what looked like an old yellow blanket hanging around her shoulders. Sam remembered seeing the child carrying it the day he'd met them in the square. The room was completely clean except for the few meager toys scattered on the floor around Sophie. One by one, she would pick up each toy, look at it, turn it over in her hands, hold it up to her nose, breathe in, then place it gently back on the floor. She had gone through this ritual several times before Mrs. O'Dell finally spoke.

"Sophie, dear, you have a friend who's come to see you. He's brought something for you."

Sophie didn't look up at the sound of the voice but went on with her ritual. A tiny elephant, squeezing it in her hands, then breathing it in. A doll with matted blonde hair and one shoe missing. A stuffed bear with only one eye.

"Go on, son." Mrs. O'Dell urged Sam into the room.

Before walking into the sanctuary where this mother was attempting to commune with her daughter, Sam removed his boots and left them outside the door next to Ethan. He approached her slowly, not wanting to startle her. He sat down on the floor across from her, the toys between them. Sam was shocked at the change in her appearance from just a couple of weeks before. She seemed much thinner, her cheeks were pale and sunken in, her red hair hanging in her face. There were dark circles under her red eyes, and Sam wondered when she had slept last. He still wasn't sure this was the right thing to be doing. He felt like an intruder into this woman's life, something he never wanted to be. And he marveled at the strange coincidences that had led him here.

"Hello, Sophie," he said quietly. "I'm Sam, remember? We met a couple of weeks ago."

Sophie finally looked at him. She seemed to be struggling to focus on him. Recognition crossed over her face, and she reached out for his hand, holding it for a minute before she spoke.

"You were the last person besides me to see her alive. I can't see her face anymore. It's hazy in my mind. She's like a song, but I can only remember a few notes or a phrase. I can see her fingers wrapped around mine. I can smell the top of her head. I can hear her laughing. But I can't remember her face. I thought maybe if I stayed here long enough, was around her things, I could see her again. But there's nothing."

Sam took a deep breath before delivering the photograph. He slowly turned it over in his hands as if he were handling a precious jewel, then placed it in Sophie's hand. She held it in the same way he had. She looked toward Mrs. O'Dell and Ethan, a questioning look in her eyes, not sure if what she was seeing was real. Then she turned back to Sam with the same questioning look. Sam slowly nodded, affirming it truly was her daughter in the photo before her. Seeing her daughter's face for the first time in over a week, seeing the child in her arms, her eyes finally released her unshed tears. Her face collapsed under the weight of her grief, and she fell limply into Sam's lap. She clutched the photograph to her breast and held it there as she would have held Bridget if she could. Sam held firm to her shaking shoulders, letting her cry as long as the tears continued to flow.

* * * * *

Later that night, Sam took himself to Bridget's grave to pay his respects. Moonlight shone in fractured pieces through the oak branches, lightly caressing her wooden grave marker and the older stones of those buried before. Sam struggled with the idea of death. He had seen too often the faces of the dying. One minute animated with life, the next stilled forever in death. Who was to know what happened to the souls of those who had passed through the shrouded portal?

Sam had left Sophie inside. She had finally spent all of her energy in crying and was sleeping peacefully in her own bedroom. He looked out at the Milky Way, smudged across the black sky with innumerable clusters of stars. Tonight, more than ever, he contemplated his place within that vast expanse of stars. They looked like tiny specks to him. But Zacharias said those specks were as big as or bigger than their own sun. How could something so large appear so small? Or maybe he and the earth were the specks, dwarfed by the expansive universe. You could never really determine the greatness or the smallness in another being, it seemed. Perspective changed it all and then back again. He breathed in the cool and cleansing air, filling his lungs to capacity, then breathing it all out again.

The cold air in his lungs and the sounds of Sophie's cries still ringing in his ears brought a forgotten memory flying forward into his consciousness.

Sam hears a muffled cry somewhere near but hidden in the trees. He pulls the knife from his boot and moves silently toward the cry. His ears strain to hear another sound. Scuffling to the right, up the hill. A girl's cry escapes, rolls down the hill to hit him in the chest. He has heard too many cries like that. Too many hearts ripped open with fear. His legs carry him like a deer over the snow. He surveys the situation quickly. A man holds the girl against a tree, his hands around her throat, her feet barely touch the ground, kicking as she struggles for breath. No one else around. Sam runs up behind the man, a foot taller than himself. He'll never be able to pull him off of the girl. He wraps one arm around the man's waist, and with the other, jabs his knife under his ribs. A grunt escapes the man's throat. He doesn't fall, but hits Sam with the back of his hand across his jaw. Sam is on the ground, so is the girl. They look at each other. She's gasping for breath, trying to stand. Her hand is in the man's blood on the ground. The man grabs her by the hair and pulls her head down hard upon the ground. Sam is up again, struggling to hold the man away from the girl. They're rolling in the snow, a fist on his jaw, a hand around his throat. Where is the knife? Hands cold on the ground in the snowbank, feeling for the knife. Sam's hand closes around the handle and plants the blade in the man's stomach. The man slumps forward, heavy on top of Sam. The fight is over. Where is the girl?

On his hands and knees in the mud and snow, Sam is coughing, spitting the blood out of his mouth. The cut on his lip stings. As the air fills his lungs, he hears it. Singing softly over his shoulder. A tiny voice, barely audible. The girl is under a tree, not far away. She lies on the ground, her hair like wet fire in the snow. Her arms around her knees, holding herself tight. She hums a tune to herself. Sam approaches carefully as he would approach a wounded animal. He stays level with her on the ground, holds his hands out where she can see, and talks in a soothing voice. "It's okay. I'm not going to hurt you. I'm just going to look at the cut on your head." He tries to touch her head, but she flinches, never stops singing the song. So he sits next to her, close but not touching. She falls asleep on his shoulder hours later. He sleeps too, holding the knife in his hand. He wakes to a layer of snow covering him and the tracks of the girl who ran away.

Ethan found Sam on his hands and knees in the snow, taking one deep breath after another. He ran to his side, not sure what was the matter.

"Sam! Are you okay?"

Sam looked up, startled, realizing what had happened. He could never get used to the flashbacks or how quickly they took over his brain and his body. He stood up and brushed the snow off of his clothes with shaking hands.

"Yes, yes. I'm fine, boy. Nothing to worry about. I just . . . um . . . dropped something on the ground. And I was looking for it. Nothing to worry about." Sam patted Ethan's shoulder and looked up again at the stars in the clear sky, continuing to take deep breaths to steady his nerves.

Ethan looked at him without full belief but allowed Sam to think he'd fooled him. "Will Sophie get better?" Ethan asked quietly.

"She will in time."

"I've never seen anyone cry like that."

"Tears can be healing. People need loyalty and devotion to something or someone beyond themselves to make life bearable. For Sophie, that was her little girl. Right now she's in pain because she's lost her. This is the hardest thing she's ever gone through, and she never wanted to survive it." Sam noticed himself talking about Sophie as if she were an old friend, someone he'd always known. But then, if she were really the girl he'd saved in the woods, maybe he had always known her. Sophie obviously didn't remember him or the incident. Maybe it hadn't happened at all. Maybe his mind had created a mixture of several events and people. God knows he had more than his fair share of violent encounters to pull from.

The boy shuffled his feet in the snow. "It's hard to watch."

"Yes, son, it is. Mourning is a terrible process, but she has to go through it and learn how to survive this. Mourning and the loss and pain we feel after a death, that's what reminds us we were able to love in the first place. It reminds us of that gift."

"So, what are we going to do?"

"Well, we have to remember the code, don't we? We share our fire, share our food, and stay with those who can't take care of themselves until they can stand on their own again. Right?"

"So you want to stay too?"

"Too?"

"I was already thinking I would ask you if I could stay with her."

Sam put his arm around Ethan, smiling to himself. "Good boy."

* * * * *

The smell of saltwater and damp vegetation swirled in the cold air filling the tiny cave. Gemma leaned against the cave wall despite its moisture, pulling her heavy coat tight around her as she waited for her contact in the Watch. She thought she could feel actual ice crystals stinging her face. This was one of many caves used by the Watch for temporary storage, meetings, and other purposes. The tide was starting to creep into the cave, making Gemma stand in wet sand, thankful for her winter boots. She worried if Tower didn't show himself soon, she'd have to leave without receiving the information he had to give her. But his spongy walk through the sand announced his presence minutes later.

"Though my soul may set in darkness . . ."

"It will rise in perfect light."

"Thank you for coming, Tower. We have to speak quickly before the tide comes in. Talk to me about Credell. What do we know about him?"

"He's worked for the government for years. Moved around between different offices. In the last year, he had been working with the Council of Doctors in Boswell. Administrative stuff. He wasn't a doctor."

"Why would someone want to kill him? What did he do?"

"Who knows? Especially considering . . ." Tower stopped and looked behind him, noting the tide creep up over his feet. He always seemed to hear things that would go unnoticed by others.

"Considering what? What other information do you have for me?"

"We think we know who did it, Foxglove. But are you sure you want to know?"

"I have to know. There's no choice involved. I have my orders. Tell me."

"It was Aishe," he finally blurted. "She's the one who killed Griffyth

Credell."

"What? It couldn't have been! This isn't like her at all. Are you sure?"

"The man who was flogged was a member of her group. He saw her leaving the G.O. late one night. He tried to talk to her, but he said she just walked past him like she hadn't heard. Almost as if she were sleepwalking. He went inside and found Griffyth dead. Strangled. Bruises on his neck. He tried to cover her tracks, make sure no one would trace the murder back to her. When the Corsairs investigated, they had no evidence except that someone had seen this man out that night past curfew. So they whipped him to make an example and maybe scare someone into giving evidence."

"What about Aishe? Has anyone seen her or talked to her?"

"Not since that night."

"Well, we have to find her." Gemma pushed her wet hair out of her face. She was struggling to put the pieces together, to try to make sense out of what she'd heard.

"You know I don't know where she lives. None of our operatives know where the others live for our own protection."

"You think I'm not aware of that? Have you tried to get a message to her?"

"Of course. She doesn't answer."

"Then I'll just have to get a messenger to disclose where she lives."

"That's breaking protocol. You'll be placing both of you in serious danger, and the messenger too."

"What choice do I have? The commander was very clear about my objective. We have to figure out what happened. Aishe is in danger already. We have to know why she did it. She could have information we don't." Gemma had to believe that Aishe, the Aishe she knew and trusted with her own life, had a good reason for what she'd done. Gemma couldn't leave her out there on her own to face the ruthless consequences of the Corsairs.

"Do what you have to do, I guess," Tower concluded. "We have to go now. And please don't ask me to spy on our people from the Watch anymore. It all just feels too confusing. I need a clear enemy, one I can see and know my reason for fighting."

"I understand. And as far as we know, we still have a clear enemy. We can't let the Corsairs continue to punish innocent people, though."

"Go safely, Foxglove."

"You too, Tower."

Gemma wanted to go see Zacharias that night but knew Kyle would be suspicious if she were gone too long. There had already been too many necessary meetings lately with Watch operatives. She needed to keep a low profile for her own safety and for his. The only way she knew to protect her husband from the questions of the Corsairs was to keep him in the dark about her activities. She would have to wait to see Zacharias, but she desperately needed his advice.

She knew better. Knew better than to have any sort of emotions about the people she worked with in the Watch. Hadn't she always preached at them not to get emotionally attached? It clouded the judgment, made people take stupid chances. It was part of the reason why they only used code names and didn't know anything about any of their personal lives. But when you fight on the same side for long enough, eventually the walls break down. You hear things, you become comfortable. You get to know another person's ways, characteristics. And when you've placed your life in someone else's hands and survived, well, it was just too hard to stay disconnected and objective. She supposed it was possible to never really know what people were capable of. Now, here she was with a friend who may have betrayed the entire Watch. She needed an outside perspective to help her know what to do.

* * * * *

Gemma forced herself to wait two days before going to see Zacharias. No one would be suspicious of her visiting him, but she didn't want it to follow too closely after her meeting with Tower. The minutes passed like hours as she thought of the situation with Aishe. It made her jumpy, anxious. She hated that she had to take all of these precautions, and she wished for a day when she didn't have to be looking over her shoulder.

"Z, it's me," Gemma called as she walked through Zacharias' front door without knocking. But she didn't find Z in his rocking chair where she expected him to be. Instead, Sam stood at the kitchen table packing his open bag.

"He's in the developing shed. Don't know how long he'll be." Sam didn't look up but kept on with what he was doing.

Something about seeing Sam packing again hit on Gemma's frayed nerves. "Going away?"

"Appears that way."

"Well, you've gotten pretty good at that."

Sam stopped his preparations. The past days with Sophie had been difficult, and though he was packing to return to her and was happy to be of some help to her, he had been grateful for some time to himself. He took a deep breath before turning to look at Gemma, really look at her. He knew something was bothering her. That was always when she lashed out at the nearest person. Also, her nails were jagged where she'd been biting them, tiny scabs and dabs of red were around the cuticles. She was nervous. He didn't want to know these things about her. He didn't want to wonder if there was something he could do to help her. He just wanted to go back to Sophie with as little fuss as possible.

"I do what needs to be done, Gemma."

Seeing the wounded expression in his eyes, Gemma knew she'd gone too far but somehow couldn't stop herself from continuing to poke at his wounds.

"Oh? And what needs to be done this time, Sam, that only you can do?"

"Are *you* really in a position to question me?"

"I'm just worried about Z."

"He's got you." Sam returned to his packing, walking through the kitchen and front room, gathering the few supplies he needed.

"It's always hard on him when you're gone. You don't know how much he misses you and depends on you when you're away from home."

"I'll be back from time to time to check in on him. This isn't a permanent thing."

"Sounds familiar."

Sam closed his pack, tightening the straps with more force than necessary. "God, Gemma. Do we have to do this?"

"Do what?"

"I thought we already said our goodbyes. Do we have to replay it over and over again? Can't we just say we took our own paths and be happy for each other? Don't you remember how it was when we were kids?"

"What do you mean?"

"I always gave you a way out, a means of escape."

"I don't know what you're talking about."

112

"Your bag."

"My bag?"

"Every night when you'd go to sleep, I used to make sure your bag was packed with food and water. Didn't you ever wonder why I did it?"

Gemma stared at Sam, trying to rewrite the story of her life she carried in her mind, changed now based on this new information. *Sam* had been the one to fill her bag every night, not Kyle.

"It was so you could know it was okay for you to leave any time you wanted, and you'd be taken care of for at least a couple of days. I wanted you to feel free."

"You did that?"

"Who did you think? Kyle?"

"I guess I thought . . . it doesn't matter. You're right. We should just go on our own ways. Good luck with whatever it is you have to do. I have to go."

"Don't you want to talk to Z?"

"I'll find him later." Gemma started toward the door. She felt torn between wanting to hug Sam and tell him all her troubles as she always used to and wanting to run away from him. With her hand on the door, she turned back. "Sam? Do you think I made a difference in your life?"

"*You are part of my existence, part of myself.* You made all the difference."

Gemma tried to get away from Zacharias' house as quickly as possible, but she heard him call her from the shed he used as a developing room for his and Sam's photography. She thought about walking on without stopping but knew she couldn't.

"Gemma, what is it, honey? What's going on?"

"I found out who killed the government man."

"And?"

"It's someone in the Watch. Someone I know well and have worked with often. Someone I trust."

"What are you going to do?"

"Daisy helped me get in contact with the messenger that delivers to her so I could find out where she lives."

"Gemma, that's crossing a dangerous line."

"I know that, Z. But I have to confront her. I've been ordered to get her out of the village, beyond the borders."

"Exile."

"It's necessary for everyone's safety."

"Is that really what you're going to do?"

"Those are my orders."

"That's not what I asked. You said she was your friend. You trust her. Are you really going to exile her without trial? Without giving her a chance at defense?"

"People aren't innocent until they're proven guilty anymore. Those days are over. In fact, it's probably more the opposite."

"That sounds like something the Triumvirate would say."

Gemma shivered. She told herself it was the cold.

"Isn't it the main mission of the Watch to counteract the Corsairs and the Triumvirate? How can we do that if we start to accept their ideology?"

"What do you think I should do, Z?"

"I think you already know what you should do."

8

A RESPITE

Zacharias sat in a pocket of sun on his porch. The morning had been cool, but a southern breeze and the sun on the rise was beginning to warm the day. *"Oh, wind, if winter comes, can spring be far behind?"* He softly spoke his favorite Shelley quote to himself. The damp and matted leaves now freed from the snow were beginning to dry out. A small purple flower was peeking its head from under the porch, stretching to absorb the life-giving rays.

The sound of distant thunder startled Zacharias from his reverie of renewal. Looking skyward, he saw only blue sky. He knew then it was the thunder of horses' hooves. His heartbeat hastened in his chest. Heat rose from his neck to his ears, while a chill ran over the rest of his body. He remembered his father had suffered from high blood pressure and used to take daily medication for it when such things were commonplace. Zacharias often wondered if he'd inherited the malady. As a rule, he tried to control it by staying calm as much as possible. Nothing could raise his blood pressure and heart rate faster than the sound of thundering hooves or thunder in the sky. They conjured unwanted memories and feelings best forgotten. The endless storms of years past. Battles and gunfire. Friends dragged behind mounted soldiers. Zacharias took deep breaths and tried to calm himself as a small squad of Corsairs rode up to his house.

As the sergeant dismounted, Zacharias began singing softly to himself. *"Keep smiling through the day, keep smiling through the night. The shadows fly away when I can see your light."* He stared past the sergeant into the empty fields still harboring patches of snow. The porch creaked as he rocked slowly back and forth, repeating the same couple of lines of the song over and over.

"State your name, citizen," the sergeant barked as he stood casting a cooling shadow over Zacharias, who didn't answer but continued to stare and sing.

"You are required to answer."

Zacharias rose slowly from his chair, turned, and walked into the house as if there was no one speaking. In the kitchen, he began pulling onions from a bin next to the sink, arranging them in an awkward, rolling bouquet on the table. "These are for my sweetheart. She loves wildflowers," he spoke in a childlike voice before beginning to whistle his repetitive tune.

The other five Corsairs had filed in through the front door and stood staring at him behind their sergeant.

"Old man, tell us what your involvement is in the Watch," he shouted as if he were speaking to someone hard of hearing.

"I like to watch the birds in the morning. If I throw seeds to them, they'll hop on the porch." Zacharias slouched his shoulders and shuffled around the kitchen as if he were looking for something he couldn't find.

"That's not what I mean, old man. We know you have connections to the Watch. Tell us who was responsible for killing Griffyth Credell. Stand still and answer me!" The sergeant jerked his head in the direction of his soldiers. Taking his signal, two of them walked to either side of Zacharias, holding him by the arms and forcing him to stand still and face the sergeant. But Zacharias continued to look past him, not focusing on his face.

With unexpected force, he felt a slap across his face that threw his head back. Then he did look at the sergeant. For a split second, Zacharias registered the coldness and hatred in the man's eyes before he forced himself to clear his mind and face of all thought, remaining a blank.

"You will tell me what I want to know, or I will personally . . ."

"Z, I'm about to leave for Boswell, but you've got enough wood out there . . ." Sam called as he entered the room with measured stride from the back door. "What's all this?" he asked, trying desperately to keep the edge out of his voice. He quickly assessed the situation tactically. He was outnumbered and had no easy access to a weapon. He would have to either

116

comply with whatever the soldiers wanted or find another way to subvert them.

The sergeant turned on his heel an exact ninety-degree angle to face Sam head-on. "Your name, citizen."

"Sam Erikson."

"What is your relationship to this man?"

"He is my adopted father. What is he accused of?"

"I will ask the questions. This man is obstructing an official government investigation."

Sam caught Z's eye, noticed the way he was looking around the room, not focusing on anything. He couldn't understand what Z was trying to do.

"Did you bring more flowers for my sweetheart, Sam?" Z asked in his childlike voice.

"No, no I didn't, Z," he said slowly. "You see, Sergeant, my father isn't exactly all there. His mind started to go awhile back. He thinks he's still courting his wife."

"Why are you going to Boswell?" The sergeant ignored Sam's explanation.

"Trade. As allowed by law."

"Don't quote the law to me, citizen! We have reason to believe this man has connections with the Watch and may have even instigated the murder of Griffyth Credell."

"With respect, Sergeant, that isn't possible. With these spells he's been having, he couldn't possibly be involved with anything like that. I assure you, he's harmless. I will take care of him." Sam started to walk toward Zacharias. The sergeant moved to intercept him and grabbed his arm so swiftly that Sam's other fist started to fly involuntarily before he stopped himself. The Corsair put his face uncomfortably close to his. Sam could smell the eggs and coffee the man had had for breakfast blended with the sweat of horses.

"We've found one accomplice already. And we know this man is involved with the Watch. I'm inclined to think you may be as well."

"I'm afraid you're mistaken, sir. He can barely get up and fix his breakfast in the morning, much less help any kind of group."

The sergeant gruffly released Sam's arm, reaching down to straighten his own uniform. "You are required to report any subversive activity at once."

"Yes, sir," Sam said through a plastered smile. "We'll be on the lookout for anything suspicious. Stay the course."

The sergeant cocked his head, unsure what to think of this man. His boots clomped loudly on the wooden floor as he and the other soldiers left as quickly as they had come.

Sam and Zacharias stayed almost frozen where they stood until they could no longer hear the sound of horses' hooves. When Sam looked at Zacharias, he was visibly shaking, holding onto the kitchen table for support.

"Z, sit down. You're pale."

"Glass of water, please, son."

"Absolutely." Filling a glass from the water bucket, Sam tried to calm his own nerves so he could help Zacharias. He busied his hands with wetting a washcloth for Zacharias as well. He didn't like being in such close proximity to Corsairs and especially having them in his home. He fought back the memories of his parents being taken away. Zacharias was the one who needed help now. He couldn't afford the distraction of a flashback now.

"Here, drink this slowly." Handing Z the glass, he then placed the washcloth on the back of his neck.

They both sat in silence for a few moments before Sam finally ventured a question. "What do you think they'll do with the accomplice?"

"I'm not sure I can even imagine."

"Do you think they're just going house to house, or targeting specific people?"

"I'm sure they're just beating the bushes, trying to see who will run out or give them a reason to strike."

"I don't want to leave you like this, Z."

"Nonsense, Gemma will be by later. You have to go help your friend. She needs you more than I do right now. Tell me you still have the pistol I gave you."

"I do."

"You know to keep it clean and ready even if you think you'll never use it?"

"Yes, of course. But I hope it won't come to that. Whatever made you think of acting senile?"

"I gave them what they would expect to find in an old man. Stereotypes can be useful sometimes if you know how to use them and then how to break them."

"I'm surprised they believed it. Surely they know you're in the Senate."

"They only know the minimal amount to carry out their assignment. When the Triumvirate is fully in control of the flow of information, don't think for a second that they're just passing around their intelligence, even to their own troops."

Sam took the washcloth Zacharias handed him, wringing it and twisting it in his hot hands. "There is no rest from it, is there? Will our whole lives be a struggle, a battle? The war is over, but it granted us no peace, and now this. Even when I was at the lumber camp, there was always the threat of some kind of punishment if we didn't fill our quota. I guess there can never really be a reprieve."

"Sometimes, once in a long while, life will grant a short reprieve. A few moments of respite. I remember one summer when I took my wife and kids to my grandparents' house down in Louisiana. They lived on a farm out in the country, much like here. I was happy to be out of the city. My grandfather took me and the kids out in a field of sugarcane, higher than our heads, and cut off a stalk of it, a piece for Max and a piece for Jill. They walked around chewing on them all day. There was an old hound dog that followed around at their heels. The air was warm and thick, sweet like honey. We spent hours just picking muscadines and honeysuckle. Weeks after we got back from that trip, the cloud seeders stirred up the storms. The tornadoes, earthquakes, and floods started. Then the drones started firing on neighborhoods all around us. Nothing was ever as peaceful as that summer again. But that was my respite I sip on slowly through the years like rationing water."

"What's mine?"

"Don't you know yet?"

* * * * *

Aishe's farm was much like Gemma would have imagined it, clean and organized. The fields had been lying fallow in the winter and would soon need to be planted. She wondered if Aishe had anyone who could take over the farm for her if she had to leave. The sun had already tucked below the horizon for the night, and the moon was rising, helping Gemma to find her way without the aid of a lantern. She didn't want to alert Aishe to her presence before she reached the door. During the walk from Jesse's Hollow, Gemma had been going over and over in her head what she would say but hadn't managed to settle on anything that met her satisfaction. She knew she wanted to ask questions and give Aishe the chance to explain. But how do you just waltz into someone's home and accuse them of murder, she wondered. Walking along the path checkered with moonlight through the trees, Gemma approached the back door quietly. A low fire was burning in the back yard, throwing dancing shadows around Gemma's feet. As she came nearer, she could hear the hum of voices inside through the back door which was slightly ajar. She wasn't sure who was speaking but thought she might learn more by listening to the conversation than from a direct confrontation. So she pulled herself as close as she dared and tried to stay out of the light.

"That boy said they met her at Market Day a couple of weeks ago. She'd actually taken the child into town to try to get medication, poor thing." An elderly woman was speaking, her voice moving closer and farther away as she walked around the kitchen. Aishe had never talked about her parents. Could this woman be her mother?

"That was a risk," a man replied.

"Well, sure. But when a mother is desperate to help her child, she'll do just about anything."

"Now don't get your back up, Martha. I'm not criticizing the girl."

"Well, I'd better not hear you try." Gemma heard a dish slam down on the table.

"I know how you dote on the girl, woman. I was just saying . . . Oh, it doesn't matter." The man's voice sounded kind, but a little frustrated.

"I just still can't believe the little mite is gone. How in the world is that girl supposed to go on with her life without her child?"

"We all face what life gives us, I suppose. Even death."

There was silence for a few minutes. Gemma assumed they were eating.

"When do you think you'll be coming back home so we can eat in our own kitchen again?"

"He should be back any time now to tend her. He's a kind one, he is."

"It's a good thing he came along, that's certain."

Gemma moved quietly back along the path toward the road. She tried to piece together what she had heard with what she knew about Griffyth Credell. Aishe's daughter must have gotten ill. Then she tried to get medicine for her. From the way the man in the kitchen was talking, it seemed as if the child must have been undocumented. So she was refused medication. Gemma's mind fought against the conclusion of that story, the death of a child for the mere infraction of being undocumented. Once she reached the road, she sat down near the mailbox and tried to catch her breath. She realized she had been running. Images of Daisy floated in her mind, and she wondered how she would react if something happened to her. If she lost the one person in the world she loved more than anything else. The person who depended on her completely. What wouldn't she be capable of if such a thing happened to her? No, she couldn't picture it. But she knew Aishe was not to blame for her actions, no matter how it affected the Watch. And beyond that, she knew she was in no position to pass judgment on this woman.

She reached into the small bag that hung from her belt and pulled out the book she'd begun carrying with her. Not long after Sam's return, Zacharias had given her the book, telling her Sam had brought it back from beyond the Border. *Little Women.* She'd read it straight through in one night, and as she did so, she knew why Sam had brought it for her. She could see herself in its pages. But she didn't want to admit this to herself or anyone else. She didn't want to know that Sam knew her better than she knew herself sometimes, that he could see her hopes, aspirations, and fears. She didn't want to feel the sting again of seeing him come back from the dead and knowing he could never again be hers because of her own choices. She resonated with the character of Jo, trying desperately to hold onto the happy parts of her youth but realizing it was impossible not to grow up and change into someone she didn't recognize. She thought of herself as the gull like Jo: *Strong and wild, fond of the storm and wind, flying far out to sea, and all alone.* Resonated like a guitar string being plucked. So instead, she just read the book again and again, whenever she walked, whenever she was at the cabin with Daisy. It became her touchstone and her anchor.

Gemma took the book in her hands now and turned to the page she wanted. She practically knew it by heart and so didn't mind using it to write a note to Aishe. She scanned the page, savoring the words again: . . . *that great patience which has power to sustain a cheerful, uncomplaining spirit in its prison-*

house of pain. She tore the page slowly and neatly from the book, and in the blank space beyond the last words of the chapter, she began to write.

My Dear Aishe,

Now is the time for courage. You've shown me "that courage wise and sweet." "And tho we are not now that strength which in old days moved earth and heaven, that which we are, we are; one equal temper of heroic hearts, made weak by time and fate, but strong in will to strive, to seek, to find, and not to yield." You have been a true patriot to the cause and reminded me what and who we're fighting for. Know that the Watch is with you. We will protect you. Return to us when you can. In the meantime remember that though I am your captain, I am the one who looks up to you.

With respect and condolences,

Foxglove

Gemma took the messages that had been left in the mailbox by the messengers and brought them back up to the house. She couldn't take the chance of someone finding them there. As silent as a cat, she went to the back door of the house and slid them through the crack, leaving them on the floor. Aishe would find them when the time was right, along with Gemma's newest letter.

As Gemma walked back to Jesse's Hollow, she started formulating in her mind what this new battle against the Corsairs would look like. She knew she'd have to be extremely convincing to get the generals to go along with her idea. But she also knew their choices were dwindling.

Sometimes, despite fear, it was necessary to begin anyway, *to strive, to seek, to find, and not to yield.*

* * * * *

Two men sat across a table from each other in a small concrete room lit only by a single bare lightbulb hanging directly above the table. The bulb was centered between them so it only partially lit each of their faces. The light buzzed and occasionally blinked with the limited electricity pumping from the generator outside. Neither windows nor light from under a doorway added to the illumination of the room. Simeon, the older of the two, sat silently reading through a file in front of him. He was in no hurry, but took his time, deliberately examining every page. The younger man,

Colonel Vance, noticed his shock of white hair as he bent over the file. Both men wore the blue uniform of the Corsairs. As Colonel Vance sat waiting for his superior to address him, he tugged at the neck of his uniform, which felt tighter than usual. He had never been in the same room with a member of the Triumvirate before, and his body hummed with an excitement not unlike the electricity of the light bulb.

"You will sit with both hands on the table, Colonel," Simeon said calmly, not bothering to look up.

"Yes, sir."

It felt like hours to Colonel Vance before Simeon finally looked up to address him.

"Did they arrest him?"

"The man was demented, sir. Talking nonsense. If you'll pardon me, I think we've got the wrong man. He can't possibly be in the Watch. His son was having to feed him and take care of him."

"You think? When did that become your role? You were not asked to think. Of course he feigned madness. He didn't want to be taken. Tell me about the son."

Colonel Vance cleared his throat several times before he was able to continue. "Well, as you can see in the file, sir, his name is Sam Erikson. His birth father was one of the ring leaders of the First Revolution."

"I thought we'd worn him down at the lumber camp. But now here he is, perpetuating a lie to deceive my Corsairs. Showing his true colors at last."

"Well, sir, he seems to be more of a pacifist by all accounts. No connection to the Watch. Doesn't fight as his father did. Would you like me to send out another detail, sir?"

"Never mind. I'll take care of it myself."

"What do you want me to do, sir?"

"What does anyone do who has outlived his usefulness?"

For the first time, Colonel Vance noticed the pistol sitting on the table next to the file folder. Simeon slowly moved it across the table toward him. It sat as a dormant volcano directly before him as a drop of sweat worked its way down his chin, dropping onto the barrel of the gun.

* * * * *

The next evening, Kyle walked slowly through the doorway, hearing Gemma moving around in the kitchen. She'd already lit the lamps, fighting off the encroaching darkness. "I'm home," he called.

"Take off your boots," she responded.

He knew to take off his boots. He didn't know why she felt she had to say it every day. Maybe he was just annoyed because he didn't want to have the conversation with her he knew he had to have.

"Hey, darlin', what's for dinner?"

"Tomato and lentil soup."

Gemma felt Kyle behind her, looking over her shoulder into the pot on the stove. The woodburning stove he had found for her in another village and brought all the way here so she wouldn't have to cook in the fireplace or outside over a fire like all of their neighbors. He kissed the back of her neck, then went to wash up at the sink. She wished he would have turned her around and covered her mouth with his. The way he used to when they were first married. She wished he'd take her upstairs, leaving the soup to burn on the stove while they made love. But the wishing did not fulfill her.

"I'm glad you're home," he said over his shoulder. "Is Zacharias any better since yesterday?"

"He's resting now. I'm going to bring him some soup later."

"I need to talk to you before you go over there."

"Well, it'll be ready in a few minutes. We can talk while we eat. Will you cut up some bread there?"

Kyle started slicing the bread absentmindedly, not waiting to jump into the difficult conversation ahead. He was never one to postpone unpleasant things. "An old friend of mine in the Corsairs came to see me today."

"Oh? What about? Do they have any more information about the murder?"

"No. It was about the Senate."

"The Corsairs don't have anything to do with the Senate."

Kyle placed the knife down deliberately and faced his wife for the first time since he'd been home. "Will you let me get through what I have to say?"

Gemma looked at him with questions in her hazel eyes but didn't say anything else.

"The Triumvirate is removing Zacharias from the Senate. They are going to replace him with someone else from our village. They believe he

124

has succumbed to dementia and can no longer serve. So at least his ruse worked in fooling the soldiers."

Gemma continued to look without speaking.

"It's really probably for the best," Kyle stumbled on. "He's tired so much lately. He needs to slow down. Honestly, I've been thinking ever since you told me what happened, it might not be a bad idea to try to get him across the Border. We know we have friends on the other side we've helped escape. He could find them, and they could help him. Just to keep him out of danger in case the soldiers come back. A slap across the face is the least they could do to him."

"May I speak now?" Gemma's voice had an edge Kyle wished he could avoid.

"Go ahead."

"Of course I know a slap is the least they can do! That's the very reason I want to keep him close. What if he's caught trying to cross the Border? There's barbed wire now. They could shoot him. And how do we know our friends on the other side could be any help to him? That's taking an awfully big chance. And who the hell does the Triumvirate think they are? The law does not allow them to choose the senators. *They* are going to replace him with someone else? Not even allowing a vote? This is out of control. This is just them tightening their grip more and more. And how do you even know you can trust this 'friend' in the Corsairs anyway? He's one of them, after all. We can't trust a Corsair."

"Alright, stop it. That's enough. You're the one who's out of control. You can't just say everything that pops into your head. Yes, he's a Corsair, but so was I. Not everything is black and white, Gemma. No one is either all good or all bad. It's just not that simple. Wouldn't it be nice if it were? He's my friend, and he's a Corsair. Now, as for the rest of it . . . who do they think they are? They're the Triumvirate! They made the law, so they can change it. Do I like it? No. But that's the way it is."

Gemma took a deep breath, turning back to the stove, and started serving the dinner. "Well, you know they'll pick someone they think they can control."

"Exactly. Someone they *think* they can control. Not necessarily someone they *do* control."

"Do you know who it is going to be?"

"Me. I can work in the Senate the same way Z did. I can carry on his work and let him rest finally as he deserves."

"Okay, okay. I was wrong about them controlling the person. Of course they won't control you. But I won't budge on sending Z over the Border. I'll bring him here to live with us."

"Now, that's not the best idea, given our situation with the Senate. We don't want them thinking he's controlling me either. Just think about the idea of sending him . . ."

"He's a grown man, Kyle. We can't send him anywhere he doesn't want to go. He's not a child. Besides, I can't send him away. He saved me and Sam. You have no idea what he sacrificed for us. No, I won't do it. No. No. No." She kept repeating the word. Denying all of the information that was overwhelming her.

Kyle walked over to his wife, placing his hand on her arm. He looked in her eyes, and for the first time in a long time, he considered the toll this life was taking on her. The tears were forming in her eyes, though she breathed deeply to hold them back.

"We're not going to do that," she continued. "We're not sending him away."

"I care about him too, Gemma. Will you just . . ."

"Nothing more to talk about. Your soup's getting cold."

* * * * *

The curfew never bothered Sam. He trusted his instincts and his ability to avoid detection. So he decided to go back to Sophie the night of the Corsair's visit to Zacharias after making sure Gemma would be with him. As the hill rose up to the left of the road, Sam saw the tall grasses bowing as if in prayer to the rising moon, having been brought low by the weight of winter snows. They had not yet regained their stature.

Sam considered the interrogations that had begun and how much they were like the pointless interrogations of his youth. The soldiers already had all the information they wanted before they ever started questioning anyone. He knew then as he knew now the only purpose behind the cross-examinations was to exhibit power and give the excuse for the soldiers to attack unarmed civilians when they were "uncooperative." It made Sam uneasy to see the patterns being repeated.

The blowing wind in his face, ruffling the grass free of its genuflection, reminded him of a sea breeze and the beach grasses. Even a few miles from the coast, he thought he could detect a hint of salt in the air. He imagined the waves at his feet, caressing him, calling him. The moonlit nights he and his friends had spent at the beach, avoiding patrols, digging for clams, finding fun even amidst the danger. There were times when the recess, the evacuation of the wave, would call to him to follow it out to sea. As it rolled back from the beach, his feet would grow cold, and he would begin to sink into the sand beneath him. He craved the caress and the intimacy of being one with the wave again. But did not follow it. He knew the dangers of chasing after something that would leave and then overtake him. That was not the way to happiness. The way to happiness was to learn to stand firm on the beach, sure of the strength in his own space. Happy to be with the sea when it returned, but knowing he'd be just as happy standing in his own footprints.

Sam's thoughts naturally turned to Sophie as he traveled back to her house. He was glad he had left Ethan with her for the boy's sake. He didn't need to see what had happened to Z at the hand of the Corsairs. Besides, the boy seemed to genuinely care about Sophie. The two had taken to each other immediately. In the past couple of weeks, as Sophie had fought her way through the horrific nights, dreaming of her daughter and her illness, sometimes screaming out as the pain ripped through her body, Ethan was always the first by her side to calm her, wipe her forehead with a wet cloth, and hold her hand as she fell back into an exhausted yet fitful slumber. Sam would stand in the doorway, aching to do something to help her, but feeling powerless to do more than be with her and be a witness to her suffering. As she would sit up in the bed, not knowing where she was, with Ethan wiping the sweat from her face, her eyes would look toward Sam. Her blue eyes, now gray more than blue, seemed to be lit from within, and they bored into Sam's chest with the heat of melted steel, questioning him, begging him for relief he was unable to give. *Why?* Her eyes seemed to call out to him. *Why are we only given people to love for a time? What's the point in us fighting for survival if, when all is said and done, we won't survive?* But he had no answers. No answers for Sophie, and no answers for himself.

As the night met the morning, the earth clothed herself in a robe of mist, clinging to the fields outside Boswell. Sam noticed a shadow moving over the horizon near the river, and he wondered who would feel as comfortable as he did in riding along the edge of the law. As the sun started to rise, he could see the fog in moving swirls around what he now realized were the legs of a horse. This was a rare sight, as all the horses Sam knew of were in the possession of the Corsairs and no soldier ever went out on his own. Something had to be wrong. They weren't traveling at a quickened pace but seemed to saunter along at the horse's will rather than the will of the rider. It made it easier for Sam to get closer while still avoiding being seen.

He ran across the field toward the rider, stopping at a live oak tree. An old rope swing hung among the tree's heavy and drooping branches, barely hanging on, with rope and seat long ago warped by age and rain. As the horse turned toward a barn almost hidden in the parent grove of trees, Sam realized where he was. This was the north field of Sophie's farm. And the rider of the horse, Sophie herself.

Sam's eyes had to adjust to the dark barn, but it took his other senses longer to adjust to the memories the smell of the barn evoked. Sweaty leather, sweet hay, and of course the smell of the horse itself. He thought of his father's barn, full of the farm implements, the care his parents took with animals before the slaughters began. Sam paused in the doorway, entering quietly.

Sophie stood just outside the stall. She and the horse seemed to be talking to each other without any words. He was a bay, his red coat shiny against the aged wood of the stall. Sophie ran her fingers through his black mane, touching her nose to his white one. Sam took a step forward, and the boards under his feet creaked.

The barrel of a pistol appeared at Sophie's waist without her moving from her position in the least. Still fully intent on the horse before her, she spoke quietly, "You'd better not move any closer. He tends to be kind of jumpy."

"Sophie, it's me, Sam. Remember? I didn't mean to startle you."

Sophie lowered the gun, placing it back in her belt.

"I guess that answers the question of whether or not you're alright to go riding alone." Sam moved hesitantly toward horse and rider. "I saw you riding out there. I just wanted to make sure there wasn't a Corsair sneaking around."

Sophie continued her private communication with the animal before her.

Sam pulled an apple from his pack, coming close enough that the horse smelled a treat, acknowledging Sam's presence for the first time. "May I?" he asked Sophie.

She nodded.

"What do you call him?" Sam asked as he introduced himself to the animal, announcing himself as a friend with the proffering of the gift.

"Pip."

"Good name. *Great Expectations* is my favorite book." Sam smiled at the added connection between them.

"I guess, in a way, I figured we were both orphans. That's why I named him that. Besides, he looks like a Pip."

Sam picked up a brush from a nearby shelf and began brushing down Pip's silky coat.

"You're good with him," Sophie observed.

"I had a horse once. Not for very long. It was during the First Revolution. Found him wandering in the woods after a battle. So I kept him. His name was Strider."

"What happened to him?"

"After the war, the Corsairs took him back."

"I guess you're wondering where Pip came from."

"I can guess. You don't have to tell me. It's just good to see you up and around."

"It's easy being with Pip. He doesn't need anything from me. I don't even have to speak if I don't want to."

"I'm sorry. I suppose I should leave you alone."

"No, that's not what I meant." Sophie's voice faltered for a moment before she continued. She ran her hands along Pip's long neck, taking her time to find her words. "I know you've been helping. You've been here for me, leaving your own life behind. I'm not sure I can repay . . . I don't know why . . ."

"Don't worry about that. It's the code, after all. You owe me nothing. But I don't want to overstay my welcome. If you feel like it's time . . ."

Sophie placed her hand lightly on his arm. He felt the heat coming from it, flowing into his cool skin.

"I'd like you to stay."

* * * * *

"I can't stay long, Tower. I'm expected back at home," Gemma explained. "But I needed your help."

"Did you find Aishe?"

The winter runoff from the mountains swelled the creek behind the cabin to almost overflowing. Its normal trickle was a rush that served to drown out their conversation in case any of the children should be about.

"Yes, I found her. But I'm not going to bring her over the Border. As far as anyone is concerned, she is still a member of the Watch and will take up her duties again as soon as possible. I will be telling my commander that she was set up."

"What really happened?" Tower pressed.

"That doesn't matter. And honestly, the less you know, the better. But I believe we can use this situation to fuel the rebellion, which will inevitably come."

"I'm not sure what you mean. Rebellion beyond what the Watch is currently doing?"

"I mean a real fight. Another revolution, and the last one if we can plan it right."

"You can't be serious. If past revolutions were crushed when they had more guns and resources, how can we possibly have a war out in the open?" Tower expressed Gemma's own fears as they both instinctively looked around them.

"We can use the Corsairs' own resources against them. We have operatives in all of the work camps, right? We can start siphoning the supplies from the camps and government farms. Then when the time is right, we will strike. Our last raid gave us guns and horses. All we really need is food and clothes to supply the Watch army."

"How will this situation with Aishe be a catalyst?"

"We can tell the commanders the Corsairs staged the whole murder to blame on a Watch member. The Corsairs are already retaliating. The floggings and interrogations have begun. When we don't deliver a scapegoat, they'll step up their punishments. They can't continue to rob people of their humanity piece by piece and expect us not to respond. The way I see it, we either resist or we're serving their interests."

"We, lie you mean."

Gemma sighed and realized convincing the Watch would not be easy. "It's not something they haven't done before. These punishments they're inflicting aren't justice. There's never been any justice. No trials. No laws that protected the people. Only executions, tighter borders. We would just be beating them at their own game. There's no bravery, courage, or even honor in a time like this, only doing what has to be done."

"You really think the commanders will get behind this?"

"That's where I need your help. You have to help me convince them. I need your military expertise. If we can approach them with solid plans and strategies, they'll be more likely to get on board."

"That's a tall order, Foxglove."

"But not impossible."

"No, I suppose not."

"When would you want the plans?"

"Next week. We need to strike as soon as possible."

Tower sighed, unsure if he could deliver what Foxglove was asking, but feeling the zeal and merit of her argument. "Next week."

"They've given us no choice. Now we've come to the place where we must live free or die."

"Live free or die. Sounds like you've already come up with the battle cry for the rebellion."

PART II

9
CONSTANCY OF CHANGE

Three Months Later
The Year of 43

Sophie stood at the creek's edge, letting the force of the water rinse the soap off the shirts in her hands. The sun warmed her back and face, but the water was cold against her already chapped hands. She dunked them again, rubbing the shirts against a large rock as her Daj used to do. The river was full to overflowing from the mountains weeping the melted tears of the winter. Sophie was reminded again of how painful renewal and rebirth could be, although necessary and even beautiful. She focused her mind on the repetitive movements of dunking and scrubbing the shirts. She had learned this technique of clearing her mind through repetition in the previous months, and it was often the only way she could stave off the echo of the hole left in her heart after her daughter's death. So many mornings she had awoken to the thought that there was nothing for her to get up for. She would force herself out of bed and make herself go through the daily motions of each task, no matter how meaningless it seemed. At least with Sam and Ethan around, she could tell herself she had to get up for them. They needed her to take care of the house chores. They needed her to make the meals. They needed her to be well. And so she pretended for them.

She heard a splash and a giggle a little way downstream and looked up to see Ethan playing with a turtle near the water's edge. He observed the turtle intently and helped him into the water before quickly jumping to his feet. He hopped on one foot over stones in the creek to reach the other side, and Sophie felt her heart leap with him. She worried he would fall in but resolved to let him have the freedom of play the spring day invited. It was good to see him playing like the child he was. So often in the past few months, she'd noticed how old he seemed for his age. He took on household responsibilities without being asked, helped wherever his small hands were needed, and often brought her the comfort of the wildflowers he'd picked for her during the day. Recently, however, she had begun taking him with her to the creek to wash the clothes. She would tell him she needed his help carrying the clothes in baskets to and from the house, but really she was only using that as an excuse to get him out of the house and into the outdoors for some leisure time, the kind of playtime children required and thrived on.

Ethan looked upstream, shielding his eyes against the bright spring sun. Seeing Sophie running her tired hands through her hair, he stuffed the rocks and worms he'd found in his pockets and ran toward her.

"Are the shirts done, Sophie? I can help you bring them back to the house to dry."

"Thank you, sweetheart. Yes, I suppose it's time to go back."

Ethan stood close to Sophie, putting his arm quickly around her waist before bending to the task of gathering the clothes.

"What would you like for lunch?" Sophie asked.

"Could I have an egg sandwich?"

"Sure you can. There's applesauce still as well. After we eat, you can bring Sam his lunch out in the field, okay?"

Ethan nodded, picking up his basket with one hand and taking Sophie's hand in the other.

Sophie was struck again by how tall he was getting. He was already taller than her shoulders even though he'd not even reached her shoulders when he first arrived. Everything changed so fast, season after season, the young saplings grew tall, expanding their leaf-laden branches. So it was with children, just as it always had been, the constancy of change.

* * * * *

Behind Kyle and Gemma's house, an old aspen tree held the place where life used to flourish. The tree had been struck by lightning and died years before. Now it was bereft of its outer shell, its fissured bark in pieces around its feet. The long white naked limbs stretched skyward, as it stood, the tallest tree in the forest, completely exposed. Kyle sat near the tree, using some of the branches for the task before him. Two large wooden poles lay on the ground, tied together with strips of fabric and rope. Kyle laced the strips together in a diagonal pattern between the two poles. He liked work like this where he didn't have to think but could simply let his hands take over and empty his mind of all thoughts.

Gemma called to Kyle from the back door before walking out to find him. She saw his jaw visibly tighten as she spoke. "What are you doing?"

"What does it look like? I'm making stretchers." Kyle kept his voice quiet, almost a whisper while he continued his work.

"But what for?" Gemma handed Kyle a strip of fabric.

"We both know something is about to get started between the Watch and the Corsairs."

"Why, what have you heard?"

"I just mean I can't imagine the Watch won't stand by for long with the Corsairs doing what they're doing with floggings and the Border fence."

"Has your friend told you anything about plans for the Corsairs?"

"He can't. He would be executed."

"You're right. I know you're right. I just thought if we had some way of knowing what they were planning . . ."

"Then what could we do? Get ourselves executed by consorting with the Watch?"

"Kyle, we've seen all of this before. Nothing is new. How can we sit back and do nothing?"

"I'm not doing nothing. I'm going to try to get some medicines and bandages from the G.O. We should try to be prepared for anything. I want to be able to help as many people as I can."

Gemma placed her hand lovingly on Kyle's shoulder. She found herself wishing again she could share her Watch activities with him, that they could work together and not always skirt around each other. "You really are a good man."

He stopped working and looked up into his wife's face with a slight grin. "Was that in question?"

* * * * *

The slicing of the digging fork blade as it cut through the soft earth made a singing sound in the damp afternoon air. Sam enjoyed the work of farming, its routine and order, the satisfaction of seeing the fruits of his labors. He basked in the repetitive actions of cutting holes in the earth and dropping seeds in. He'd plowed the field the week before to prepare for planting the peas, beans, and spinach. Sam was embarrassed when Sophie tried to thank him for his help around the farm. She and the O'Dells had always worked the two adjoining farms together. Sam didn't have to think about it, or even make the decision to help. He simply always did the next right thing that needed to be done. A field needed to be planted, so he planted it. Besides, physical labor helped Sam to work out his own inner demons.

Sam sensed the government's noose tightening around the villages. He drove his anger into the burgeoning ground with his digging fork. All around him buds and greenery were bursting from the confines of their winter shells. And yet the fences around the borders grew higher. The day before in the town square on Market Day, the smell of gunpowder hung in the air, burning the back of his throat. The Corsairs had shot a citizen of Boswell, supposedly for starting a fight with one of the soldiers, but Sam knew better. He'd seen the Corsairs pick fights with innocent people on too many occasions. And now their fights were turning deadly. It was fire and death that choked him. But here in the fields, his lungs filled with the green smell of new growth, sweet as freedom.

The sun was starting to set behind the rise beyond the field. A rising chorus of crickets and cicadas signaled the end of his long workday like the quitting bell at the lumber camp used to. He stood, resting his arms on the staff of the digging fork. He surveyed the field around him, taking it all in. Far in the distance, well beyond the borders, a large plume of smoke rose, muting the sun's rays. He knew there had to be a few people beyond the borders. He'd seen evidence of them in his travels, though he'd never seen them with fires as large as the one that was creating this much smoke. From his vantage point, he couldn't quite pinpoint where the smoke was coming from. But it troubled him. Could it be the Corsairs, or perhaps the people they were claiming to protect the citizens from?

Sam turned to see Sophie crossing the field toward him. He hadn't seen her in the fields for as long as he'd been in Boswell. She always stayed close to the house except when she went to the creek.

"How is the planting coming along?"

"Slow, but sure."

"You should let Ethan come out and help you."

Sam slowly kicked at the dirt under his feet. "I could, but he likes being with you. And he's asked if he can take the camera out to take some photographs to trade. He's really got quite a knack for it."

"That's definitely true. In fact, he asked if he could go back to the river this evening to take some. He's there now."

"Not too many, I hope. There's only so much film and developing fluid to be had, and when it's gone, it's gone. Still, I can't deny him the little pleasure. It's good to see him excited about things again."

"You're good with him."

"So are you."

"Sam, I wanted to tell you . . . I mean . . . this is hard to say . . .'"

"You don't have to say it, Sophie."

Sophie placed her hand in his. "I do. I do have to say it. You've been a great help. I don't remember a lot of what's happened over the past couple of months. But I know you've been here, and I have you to thank for my life. It's strange, almost as if I'm just waking up. I'm not exactly sure how to go forward or what to do with myself."

"Come with me," Sam said, leading her toward the edge of the woods. Along the straight line of the field he'd plowed, the trees and underbrush of the forest were barely held at bay. They seemed ready to push into the ordered lea and take over at any moment. Sam slowly approached one of the trees whose leaves shone bright green under the raindrops left by a morning rainstorm. "You see that drop of rain hanging from the bud of a new flower?"

Sophie nodded.

"Look closely at the raindrop. In the middle of winter, it can feel like there will never be another warm day or another sunrise. Nothing can ever escape the incessant brown and gray, I think sometimes. But then one day you wake up and there are little patches of green, tiny flowers opening up. There's life in a bud and a whole world in a raindrop. They don't think about those things. They don't try. They just embrace what's within them. People could be like that too, I think. What do you have inside of you?

139

What's inside of me?"

"It's a nice thought, I suppose. To think of the things we could do or be."

"When you were a little child, what did you want to be when you grew up?"

Sophie spoke softly, almost to herself. "Alive."

Sam paused for a moment, trying to push back his own harsh memories. "Of course, we all wanted that. But what profession?"

"It's not like we had a choice. But I guess I wanted . . . no, you'll laugh at me."

"Come on, try me."

"Well, it's not really a profession anymore, but I remember an old book my mother had about musicians. She could sing and taught me to play the piano. That's what I wanted, to just sing all day long. Not really possible anymore. What about you? You're a good farmer, and you worked at the lumber camp. Are those things you've always been good at? Did you ever want something else?"

"I wanted to be a writer of books. Like you say, not really possible anymore, but it's still fun to dream about sometimes."

"What's the use of dreaming in a world like ours? Survival is the thing."

"What's the use of anything, I suppose?"

"I've asked myself that question a lot lately. My purpose seems to be lacking. I need an occupation, something to help me feel useful again."

"Remember the raindrop." Sam was smiling down at Sophie. He started to lean toward her but stopped suddenly. "A raindrop," he whispered.

"Sam, what is it?"

"Look over there at that smoke. There shouldn't be able to be a fire that large outside after the kind of rainstorm we had earlier."

"What do you think it is? And where is it?"

"I don't know. But I don't like it." Sam sighed heavily, knowing there were no answers to be gained in this moment. "Come on, let's head back to the house."

"Right. That's what I came out here to tell you. Dinner's ready."

In the kitchen, Sam washed the dirt from his hands and lit the candles on the table as Sophie brought the pot of Brunswick stew over and laid out the three bowls. Sam thought of what she'd said about needing a purpose and knew it was time to give her the letters he'd found from the Watch. While Sophie had been her most ill, he had found them sitting by the door one day. He had suspected many times Sophie was involved in the Watch, but this was proof. He didn't know what messages they contained and didn't want to know. But he couldn't keep them from her any longer. He walked over to the cabinet where he'd stuck them, tied with twine, and brought the letters over to the table, laying them at Sophie's place.

"What are these?" she asked.

"I found them when you were ill. But I suppose it's time you had them."

Sophie read through the letters quickly. They were short messages mostly, asking where she was, why she hadn't responded to any contact. She realized what her absence had cost the Watch in resources and having to find someone to fulfill her missions. Then with the last letter from Foxglove, she was moved to know they had somehow found out about Bridget and cared about her well-being.

. . . *Know that the Watch is with you. We will protect you. Return to us when you can.*

Sophie ran her fingers over the words from Tennyson's *Ulysses*. How did Foxglove know this was a poem her parents had read to her over and over? How could she possibly know that? *Made weak by time and fate, but strong in will to strive, to seek, to find, and not to yield.* Sophie knew it was time to go back to the Watch.

"Do you know what these letters are?" she asked softly.

"Nope. Don't need to know. I figure they're your business. But it just might be that you already found the purpose you were looking for."

Sophie spoke slowly, "Sam, another war is coming."

"Now, how can you know that? The Watch may just continue their small missions, sabotage, minor subversions of the Corsairs."

"Is that all you think the Watch does?"

"I have no idea, really."

"Well, regardless, someone's going to make a move, either the Corsairs or the Watch. I mean the floggings and the borders are sign enough there's a change coming. What I can't figure out is why the floggings started again in the first place."

"A government official was killed here in Boswell. This is the Corsairs' retaliation, I guess. Some people think the Corsairs did it themselves to blame the Watch and give them an excuse to come down harder on the citizens. But I'm not sure. I'm not sure of anything, really."

Sophie looked over the letters and tried to piece what she read together with what Sam was saying. "Who was the government official?"

"Credell, I think?"

"Griffyth Credell?"

"Did you know him?"

Keeping her voice level, she replied, "A long time ago, I did." She fought against the images flashing through her mind: hands around someone's throat, blurred vision through tears. And behind it all she heard the words from Foxglove's letter: *The Watch will protect you.*

Sophie clenched her hands, forcing herself to stay in the present. "Well, regardless of what caused it, we can't continue in this purgatory, this limbo, indefinitely. Something's got to change. The question is, what will be required of us when the time comes, and will we be up to the challenge?"

"I've fought my wars."

Sophie focused in on Sam again. She realized she wasn't the only one with memories she'd rather forget. It shocked her sometimes to realize that others had suffered as she had. She reached out to touch his arm, but he moved quickly away from the table, pretending to go for the silverware to finish setting the places.

"Something tells me you're fighting them still," she said. "In my experience, we can take our time away to heal our wounds, but eventually, there are some fights that find us whether we want them or not. This clash with the Corsairs and the Triumvirate, it was only a matter of time before it caught up with us."

"I won't kill. Not again."

"What if we have no choice?"

"There's always a choice in how you react."

"But isn't that what the Watch is fighting for? To give us back our freedom and our choices?"

Sam turned to look into Sophie's eyes. The moment felt burdened with a truth he didn't want to carry. His heart didn't feel strong enough for the load. He was grateful when Ethan burst in so he didn't have to answer Sophie's probing glance.

"Wash your hands, boy, and sit. Our Sophie has made us quite the meal."

"I could smell the stew on the way up the drive. It's my favorite."

"How many pictures did you take today?" Sophie asked.

"Just three. I remembered what you said, Sam, about saving the film."

"I wish we didn't have to, boy."

"I know. But I think I was able to get a butterfly before it flew away. The sun was shining on its wings. I can't wait to develop it."

"I'd like to see that myself," Sam smiled at him.

They all sat around the table and began passing around the bowls of vegetables and fruit and the steaming bowls of stew.

"My sister used to love butterflies," Sophie mused, handing Ethan his napkin.

Sam stopped what he was doing and looked up at this remark. "I had forgotten you had a sister. It's strange. I mean, most families were only allowed the one . . ."

"I know. Laurie was born just after the First Revolution began, in the Year of 10. I'm not exactly sure how it happened. I was only five. But she became my responsibility. I loved taking care of her. And on the quiet days when the guns weren't firing, I would take her on short walks around our house. She'd always go searching for butterflies. This was her necklace." Sophie held up the thin gold chain she wore with a small green butterfly pendant. Ethan and Sam had both noticed it at times, since most jewelry from Before had been confiscated years ago by the Corsairs.

"Where is she now?" Sam wished he hadn't asked the question the minute the words were out of his mouth.

"After our parents were killed in the Year of 15—the year of the executions," she took a deep breath, "we lived in the woods for a time until we came across the Romany village and were adopted. We were happy with them. The happiest years of our lives, if truth be told. But when the Second Revolution came and everyone was being driven from the cities and towns, everything was chaos. I'm sure you remember. Our adopted parents were killed, and Laurie and I had to follow with the exodus alone. Then the Border went up, with a guard station every mile along their original jagged fence." She reached up and started twirling the lock of hair on the right side of her forehead, pausing before going on.

"Laurie and I were separated. I looked everywhere and couldn't find her. I went to the guard stations near where I'd lost her every day for months with no sign of her, no answers. Eventually they told me she'd been captured as a revolutionary. I knew she wasn't a rebel. I tried to tell them. But it was too late. Nothing could be done for her." Sophie looked for absolution in Sam's sympathetic eyes. She knew he understood, and she hoped his understanding would make her feel better about the past she couldn't change. But the guilt pressing on her heart still remained. "I lost her, Sam." Her last words came out as little more than a whisper.

Sam saw the story play out across Sophie's face. She always wore her emotions in her eyes, which seemed to tell more of the story than her words. His own experiences filled in the blanks. Years in the woods, fighting the Corsairs, and finally being adopted by Zacharias. With the history of their people written with the blood of their families, he knew he should have curbed his tongue before asking her too many questions. And yet something made him want to know every story she had to tell and to hear her telling only him. He finally looked down into his plate, unable to bear the pain in her eyes another second.

Ethan reached over and took Sophie's hand. She smiled at him through her tears.

"Maybe I could draw the butterfly for you so you can see it before we develop the picture."

"That would be lovely," she replied.

Sam cleared his throat and took a long drink of water, emptying his glass. "I'm going to have to leave in the morning to go to Jesse's Hollow for the mandatory town meeting. It won't do to raise suspicion about why I'm not there."

"Ethan can stay here if you like."

"Are you sure?"

"Of course. We'll have a grand time together, right, Ethan?"

The boy smiled at her. He wouldn't think of leaving Sophie alone while Sam was away.

* * * * *

Sam tried to remember what it used to be like when he'd go to the town square for Market Days and even for the town meetings when he was a young man, he and Gemma walking hand in hand behind Zacharias. Even with the Corsairs in charge in those days, the air seemed less heavy, less charged with hatred. He had had a sense then that Zacharias would always take care of them, somehow the strength of this man, his father, would fight back all the fear and unknowns. He had believed Zacharias would be able to one day rebuild the world as it had been Before. But nothing was rebuilt, and the only changes were the ones hitting Sam now, seeing more Corsairs patrolling, and now standing at the entrance to the town square, demanding ID cards be presented so they could ensure all citizens were at the meeting. They had never taken it this far before, but somehow Sam was not surprised.

On the few buildings he passed where Corsair advertisements and propaganda were painted, someone had thrown rotting fruit and smeared excrement across the fake smiles of the soldiers. It was a dangerous prank, one all the citizens would pay for, he was sure. And yet, he couldn't disagree with the sentiment behind the graffiti. He sometimes wished he was still a young man, full of the spontaneity and bravado that would have allowed him to do the same. He wished those things hadn't been squeezed out of him in the sweat of the lumber mill and the blood of the war.

He stopped at the blockade made of fifteen men in front of the square and walked slowly toward the captain.

"Show your papers, citizen."

Sam had his identification card ready and presented it.

"Where is the boy? It says here you have an adopted son, Ethan. Where is he?"

"He's sick at home." Sam's voice was low and smooth. He'd learned to lie before he'd learned to read. He couldn't let the Corsairs know he and Ethan had been living illegally in Boswell.

"Then you must bring him to the Council of Doctors. You will return home and retrieve the boy."

"It's not that serious. I'm not even sure he needs medicine. But he had a fever, and I thought it best that he stay home."

"You will return home and retrieve the boy," the captain repeated with measured venom. Then he took a step closer to Sam. "And I will send a detail of two men to accompany you to make sure you don't get lost along the way."

The two men were the same height. The captain looked probingly into Sam's eyes, the brim of his cap touching Sam's head. Sam met his gaze without flinching, but he could feel the sweat starting to form on his back and on his forehead.

145

"No detail will be necessary, sir. I can bring the boy back myself."

"I determine what is necessary! Harris! Wilson! Front and center!"

Two Corsairs jumped to stand on either side of Sam within a second.

"Wait, Captain, please, wait." He took a breath before continuing. He stepped back, rubbing the back of his neck and buying time. "I misspoke. Ethan isn't actually ill. I don't know where he is. I thought I would be able to find him before the meeting, but when I couldn't, I thought it was better for me to come alone. I intend to continue looking for him, within the borders, that is. I'm sure he was just out playing and didn't realize the time. I'll start looking again after . . ."

The back-handed slap across his face nearly knocked Sam to the ground. He bent over his knees, catching his breath and his temper before making another move. Caution ruled him and stayed his hand.

The captain leaned down and shouted in his ear. "You are guilty of deceiving an officer of the Triumvirate! I should take you to the base prison right now!"

Sam stood up, trying to reason with the Corsair. "Captain, please, I . . ."

A fist knocked the air out his lungs. Speech was impossible.

"You do not have permission to speak, citizen!" the captain spat at him. He raised his hand to strike again.

"Captain!" A commanding voice stopped the captain's movements. "General Masters says he is ready to begin the meeting. He asked me to find you."

The captain's face remained in a frozen snarl, giving him an almost comical look. He looked in the direction of the voice Sam heard from beyond his vision. Sam barely held himself up on his hands and knees, coughing and spitting blood from his cut lip. He tried to look up and squinted against the sun shining in his face from behind the new man's head. The captain said nothing, only turned and walked toward the stage. The other soldiers returned to their places as sentries, taking the ID cards of the other citizens who had lined up waiting behind Sam.

When the captain was gone, the man who had stopped him turned to help Sam up from the ground. "Stand up, and don't say anything until we're in the crowd," the man whispered in Sam's ear.

Sam struggled to walk with this man who he still wasn't sure he could trust, yet he had no choice but to follow him. Whatever his motives, the man had saved Sam from a beating, and possibly saved his life as well. For that, Sam was temporarily grateful.

Once they were in the back of the crowd forming in the square, Sam turned to look at the man for the first time.

"Kyle. I should have known." He shrugged Kyle's arm off his shoulder. "What the hell are you doing? Why did you interfere?"

"Is that all you have to say to me after almost twenty years?"

"What am I supposed to say?"

"It's not the first time I've saved your ass, as I recall," Kyle tried to chuckle, but the sound fell flat, hitting the wall that was Sam's face. "Not the first time you made a stupid mistake, either."

"Well, there it is. Just you rushing in to show me how stupid I am, as always. Things aren't the way they used to be. We're different people now."

"Are we?"

"Why did that Corsair listen to you, anyway? You aren't in the army anymore. He could have had you arrested."

"He knows me well enough not to try."

"Still chummy with the enemy, I see."

"Look, I just helped you, Sam. Shouldn't that make up for something, even if it doesn't make us even?"

"Sure, you saved me. But I still ask the question: why? You should have let him take me. Seems like maybe you wouldn't want to have me hanging around anymore. Might make things easier for you with Gemma."

"Do you think this is a game? Look around you, Sam!" Kyle's voice hissed as he tried to keep it low. "This whole place is a brush fire ready to burn out of control. People throwing shit on the signs, the Watch taking matters into their own hands, just stoking it higher and higher. All I'm trying to do is help people maintain a level of control and pick up the pieces when they can't."

"You really expect me to believe this good Samaritan act?"

"Believe what you want. Just try to be more careful. I won't always be around to pull your ass out of the fire."

Kyle turned and walked away to take his place by Gemma's side just as General Masters was beginning his speech. Sam wiped the blood from his face and looked around to try to find Zacharias, but he was nowhere. So he stayed where he was, trying not to think about the dull pain in his ribs. He hoped Z hadn't run into similar problems with the Corsairs.

Sam didn't want to owe Kyle anything. He hated him for stepping in just to show his control of the situation. He didn't believe for a minute that he'd done it out of any sense of friendship or wanting to help. Kyle always had at least three strategies going in his mind at once. At least that's how he used to be, and it wasn't likely the Corsairs had made him less strategically minded.

A hand on his shoulder made Sam jump just as the general was starting to speak.

"Easy, boy. It's only me," Zacharias whispered. "What happened to you?"

"Had a run-in with the guards. I'll tell you later. You're late."

Zacharias looked around to make sure no Corsairs were within earshot. "Meeting with the Old Ones."

"God, Z. Why do you take those kinds of risks?"

"Shhh," Zacharias warned. "And you're one to talk."

As the general droned on, neither of the men were listening to what he had to say beyond answering the call and response of "Stay the course" absently with the rest of the crowd.

On their way out of town, Sam and Zacharias stopped on the bridge to talk before Sam had to go back to Boswell.

"I don't know what's happening anymore, Z. There used to be a routine, a pattern to things, even if it was hard. I thought I could say what would and wouldn't happen. I thought I knew who I could trust and who I couldn't. I used to be able to trust my own instincts, at least. But now . . ." Sam's voice trailed off, following the way of the stream. He pulled at an overhanging branch, snapping a leaf off and tearing it to pieces before letting it float down the stream as well.

"What happened, son?"

"The Corsairs wanted to know where Ethan was and why he wasn't with me. I tried to make up a story, but they were going to take me back to your house, and they would have seen he wasn't there. I'm worried they'll be watching me more closely now, and Ethan too. Anyway, when they found out I was lying, they hit me. But Kyle came up and stopped them. Why would he do that? It doesn't make sense after . . . after everything that's happened."

"I'm going to say something you might not like, Sam." Zacharias paused, allowing Sam time to prepare. "I don't think Kyle meant to betray you."

"Come on, Z, how can you say that? Doesn't it concern you that he's still so friendly with the Corsairs?"

"Now hear me out. It wasn't his fault that he had to join the Corsairs. And as for Gemma, we all thought you were dead, and she had some choice in whether she married him. Don't you think it's been hard for him too? None of us knows what his life was like in the army or how hard it was on him."

Sam scoffed. He couldn't keep his hands still or meet Zacharias' gaze. "Z, has Kyle ever hurt Gemma?"

"No, he hasn't. And she's not yours to take care of anymore."

Sam looked as if he'd been struck again. Zacharias was sorry for that and placed his arm around his shoulders.

"Try to see things from his point of view, my boy. And hers. They didn't set out to hurt you. Just think about it, alright?"

Sam nodded. "So what was the meeting with the Old Ones about?"

"Oh, we talked about the Senate. The changes that are happening, and how the Watch plans to respond."

"What are they going to do?"

"I don't think you'd want to know."

"Is there going to be another revolution, Z?"

"*Those who make peaceful revolution impossible will make violent revolution inevitable.* A president of the former United States said those words a century ago. They're still true."

Zacharias looked toward the trees across the stream and the small hill of dandelions falling away into the underbrush. He wondered how many wishes he'd made in his life on dandelions. And how many other people had made wishes too? He asked himself why people continued to wish when all hope seemed to be gone.

"You know, when the First Revolution started off, it was a coordinated effort across the country. Our government had become untrustworthy. They'd thrown out the Constitution and were functioning purely as a military dictatorship. We used mail and couriers between the states, but eventually, communication broke down. We realized the electricity was not coming back. Nothing would be the way it was. We had no way of holding together as a solid force. The country was just too big. States began working independent of each other, and eventually cities and towns. They separated us. That's how the government won."

Sam knew Zacharias seldom talked openly about the previous revolutions. Those were painful times for him—for everyone.

"In the Second Revolution, cities were destroyed. They moved us around from place to place, plundering what was left behind."

"I remember."

"It was a pirate's kind of war. Did I ever tell you that's what the word *corsair* means? It's an old French word for pirate."

"Are we going to fight them again?"

"In order to move forward, we have to learn from past mistakes. We can't just keep beating our heads against a brick wall, expecting it to come down by the sheer force of our will. The wanting will not make it so. We have to fight smarter. We have to do things differently this time."

"So it is going to happen."

Zacharias did not respond. He didn't have to. Sam knew the answers to his questions before he asked them. His head felt light with the warmth of the day coaxing out the overwhelming perfumes of the cottonwoods and azaleas.

"Was the smoke I saw yesterday something the Watch was doing?"

"What smoke?"

"There was a huge plume of smoke from beyond the Border to the north."

"I don't know anything about that."

"Well, what could it be? It was too wet yesterday for the fire to have been out in the open."

"You're right. There was an old lumber mill in that area, but it was abandoned years before the Disaster, even. We just assumed it had been destroyed along with everything else. It was once a rebel stronghold. The mill had a large incinerator, though, that could have borne that much smoke."

"But who would be using it, and why? The Watch leaders would know it would draw attention."

"I truly have no idea. We'll have to keep a look out for it again."

"I could see it plainly from Sophie's north field. I'll try to see if I can get closer. Maybe I'll be able to find out more."

"So how long do you think you'll be staying with Sophie? You're breaking the law too, you know."

Sam looked down at the water flowing beneath them. On the raised bank, the roots of the trees clung to the edge, grasping at life. He wondered at his own hypocrisy of wanting Zacharias, Gemma, and even Kyle to keep the law to the letter for their own safety, and yet it never concerned him when he bent it a little. He rarely felt the full brunt of the danger beyond running back and forth between the towns to keep up appearances, and then today when he'd scuffled with the soldiers. Why didn't his own safety concern him? Why didn't he grasp at his own life as much as the roots of the trees did?

"I don't know, really. I think she still needs us. I at least want to get the spring planting done."

"Is that the only reason you're staying?"

"What do you mean?"

"I mean have you thought about making it a permanent arrangement?"

"Trying to get rid of me, Z?"

"Never. I'm just thinking about you. You obviously care about this woman. You've practically created a new family with her."

"It's not like that, Z. I would never . . . I mean, she's not really been all there until recently. It's been really hard for her to get past her daughter's death. I'm just trying to live the code."

"Ah yes, the code."

"Really."

"She's not Gemma, Sam. And from what you've told me about her, I don't think you have any reason to fear she'll hurt you."

"No, she's not Gemma." Sam smiled to himself.

10

ORDERS AND LIES

The concrete bunker felt close and damp. Colonel Mark Goodson could feel the moisture creeping from the wall to his back like an enemy sneaking up on him, chilling his body and his mind. He figured he'd have to change his uniform later in the day. He wanted to get back out into the open air.

"You will cut the rations for all towns within the borders, and I want the patrols doubled in the Forbidden Grounds beyond the borders." General Drape stood uncomfortably close to him. He could smell his tobacco with a hint of vanilla blending with the smell of his own sweat.

"Sir, the rations are already dangerously low. We risk having the people become desperate. Desperation breeds invention and, frankly, revolution."

"Do you think you are speaking to a stupid man, Colonel?"

That question would have frightened other men. They would have predicted their own deaths with that question ringing in their ears. But Colonel Goodson had known Simeon since he was a child. He was friends with his son, Kyle. They'd both been taken into the army the same year. Simeon's intimidation tactics were wasted on the colonel. He'd seen them too often and stood confident in the knowledge he was one of the few men Simeon liked.

"No, sir."

"Or a man who has not read and written history books?"

"No, sir."

"Do you imagine there is anything you can possibly tell me that I do not already know?"

"I don't know, sir."

"Ah, a little bit of arrogance behind that stoic face, Colonel. You do have some audacity. Possibly mixed with some stupidity, but nevertheless . . . audacity."

"May I ask why you would like the rations cut, sir?"

"We must weaken the enemy, Colonel. Weaken their bodies, their minds, and their resolve. Their desperation will lead them to seek help from supposed allies outside the borders. This will smoke out more enemies of the Triumvirate. Like rats. That's exactly what they are. Rats. And they must be treated as such."

"Has the leaker been caught, General?"

"The leaker has not done anything without our knowledge. They always think they are so smart. That they've thought of something that's never been thought of before. They don't realize how predictably history repeats itself, and how easily I can read them like a book."

"Maybe it's because they don't have books, sir."

"And you're funny, too?"

Colonel Goodson grinned despite his best efforts to keep a straight face.

"Scamp." General Drape gave him a rare smile in return. "One hundred more troops to the Forbidden Grounds and rations cut by one quarter. Today, Colonel."

"Yes, sir. Right away, sir."

"Oh, and, Colonel, has there been any word from my son?"

"Not yet, sir."

"You will let me know as soon as there is."

"Yes, sir."

* * * * *

Deep in the woods, too near the Border for comfort, there was hidden a cave, now at the highest elevation within the borders since the new fences went up. It sat between two boulders completely overrun with kudzu. A small stream split in two, running around the boulders and into a gentle waterfall flowing over a series of ancient stone terraces shrouded with green moss, giving the appearance of a carpeted stairway. Gemma climbed up a steep incline on her way to the cave to meet Commander Oak. Seeds and fluff from the cottonwood trees piled up on the sides of the path like snowdrifts. The air was purple with the weight of the unreleased storm and cover from the trees. There were other boulders scattered down the hill, marking the graves from the First Revolution. It was as if a great river had washed them down the mountain, leaving the stragglers behind. Gemma paused for a moment at one of the large stones, not knowing which ones marked the graves of her parents but knowing they were here somewhere. She kissed her hand and touched it to the stone as she always did when she passed this way.

Moving on, she endeavored to keep her footing along the slick stones. It wouldn't do to meet her commander in soaked clothes. Parting the kudzu like a curtain, Gemma spoke into the darkness where she knew someone was listening. "Foxglove reporting. *Though my soul may set in darkness . . .*"

"*. . . it will rise in perfect light,*" came the reply. "Welcome, Foxglove. We were just getting started with the meeting. We'll have to keep it short. There's a new patrol not far from here." Commander Oak stood with two other captains in the dim light of the cave, water dripping around them and flowing in tiny rivulets down the walls. "We obviously cannot mount an attack on the Corsairs without adequate supplies. And make no mistake, as soon as the first battle begins, the Triumvirate will shut down the Government Offices, leaving us to fend for ourselves. We all remember what it was like with people fighting over food after the First Revolution. We can't go back to that. So we must find a way to build up a store of supplies, and quickly."

"I have an idea about that, Commander," Gemma offered. "First, I must say that I received word through Cypress from one of our operatives within the work camps. It seems there is no clear reason why the government is cutting back on our rations. We're told there is plenty of food and supplies, and no indication of there not being enough in the future for the number of people within the borders, even if our numbers grew. So we can only assume the government has other motives for practically starving us."

"It's not hard to imagine what those would be," the commander replied.

"More control. More cruelty. That should be their motto rather than

'Stay the course,'" came the bitter response of a fellow captain.

"Second, we've managed to get our hands on some Corsair uniforms."

"How?"

"There was a squad bathing in a creek. My men literally picked the uniforms from the trees. It was a good harvest day." Gemma smiled to herself. "They shredded one and left it nearby, so hopefully they'll think an animal made off with them."

"Wonderful. Were they seen?"

"No, sir. And we've heard nothing in the speeches at the town meetings, so I assume the ruse worked."

"Now we must decide how to put these to work for us."

"That's where my idea comes in. If we send some of our people in Corsair uniforms to the work camps, we can both bring more people in to help us at the camps, and we can start moving supplies out of the government farms, ranches, and camps. They'll even be able to drive in wagons. If we send them on multiple missions like this and move them around between camps so their faces aren't known, we should be able to have enough supplies in a very short time."

"Excellent plan. What say you, captains?"

Gemma's fellow captains affirmed their support for her plan.

"And taking it a step further, once we've gotten all we need from the camps, we can either take over or destroy them. If we control the army's flow of supplies, we control the war," Oak continued.

"We may not even have that much fighting to do if we starve out the Corsair base," a young captain replied.

"I wouldn't count on that, Pine. We can't underestimate them." Oak marveled at how young his troops and captains were.

Pine continued in his zeal, "Well, I do think we should consider sending some of our people over the Border. There has to be something else out there. I don't believe for a second the government is trying to protect us. They must be trying to keep us away from something."

"Right now it's too risky. We'll have to wait on that for now. There are just too many soldiers along the borders."

"I agree with Pine on this one, sir," Gemma interjected. "We could have allies out there. What if we just sent one or two people in different directions with a message?"

"And what would this message say?"

"That would be up to you, sir. Something along the lines of asking who their leader is and letting them know we need help. They may not even know we're here."

"Very well, Foxglove. Choose two people from your team to take the message."

"I volunteer, sir."

"Denied. We need you here. And arrange to get the Corsair uniforms to Pine's troop. We'll make up a detail from his troop and Jade's to infiltrate the camps. Jade, you'll use the horse and wagon you have hidden on your farm for these missions. Let's begin one week from today."

"Yes, sir."

"You have your orders, captains. Now go in safety. Live free or die."

"Live free or die," they all chorused.

Gemma felt a thrill in her spine every time she heard the Watch's new motto. It reminded her again of the importance of the work she was doing and seemed to make up for the fear and danger she lived through every day.

Tower kept watch outside the cave while he waited for Foxglove.

"Tower, walk with me," Gemma whispered to her friend.

"Let's not talk yet. I just saw a patrol go by on the other side of the fence."

When they reached the main road, Gemma felt it safe to talk. "I haven't heard from Aishe in months, have you?"

"No. No one has."

"I assume she got the message I left. But I need to go to her. If things are worse with her, she may need me. And if not, we need her. I know she'll want to be involved in our current mission."

"You're taking another risk, Foxglove."

"I'm used to risk."

"Maybe so, but we need to start being more careful. I've just received a message from Cypress. She says the Triumvirate has sent spies into all of the towns within the borders, at least one in every village."

"Well, there's no great surprise there. Do we have any idea who they are?"

"No, but her contact says it will most likely be someone who's returned from the camps. The Triumvirate would try to make them blend in as much as possible and make their arrival seem normal."

156

Gemma's breath stopped. She felt the trees and even the air closing in around her. Sam couldn't possibly. Not after everything they'd gone through together. No, that was ridiculous. Just because he'd come back from the camps didn't mean he was a spy. She quickly banished the thought from her mind, wiping it away as she wiped the sweat from her brow.

"Do we have any other information to go on?"

"That's all so far. Just be careful, Foxglove."

* * * * *

Sophie floundered in her rare hour alone on the farm. Inside the house, she heard every creak and clatter of the walls and floors. Every tap of a bug on the window unsettled her. She finally took herself to the fields where at least she wouldn't feel the closeness of the walls of the house, suddenly grown more confining with the space that Sam and Ethan had left behind. Ethan had gone to take pictures, and when he hadn't returned after several hours, Sam had gone after him. She knew they would return in a short while but felt their absence lengthen the time before her. She wished Ethan was there to distract her from the thoughts and images assaulting her mind ever since Sam had said the name Griffyth Credell.

The midday sun lightened the sky to a translucent blue. A ripple of summer heat flowed over the reaching stalks of corn and beans. With no apparent map for their travels beyond basic instinct, bees and dragonflies jutted and darted through the neat rows of plants in haphazard fashion. Sophie walked slowly among them, feeling the soft dirt beneath her feet, sinking in, at one with the earth and yet a stranger. An eastern breeze swirled around her, through her cotton tunic, and brushed against her skin. She wondered if her presence would disturb the natural order of earth, plant, and insect, bringing chaos into a system that would possibly run more smoothly without her.

Someone had killed Griffyth Credell and now the Corsairs were lashing out at all citizens within the borders. A system, however flawed, had been disturbed, the scales tipped, and order marred. She didn't have to ask who had done it. Her nightmares told her all she needed to know. She had hoped it was only her mind's way of processing through her loss and anger, hoped she wouldn't be capable of the violence she saw under the mask of

157

darkness every night. She had planned to return to the village on Market Day and find Griffyth still scowling there to allay her fears of her own guilt. But now she knew no such relief would come. She could see her hands around his neck, see the fear in his eyes. The blood pulsed quickly in his veins, throbbing against the skin under her fingers. His muscles contracted, everything in his body fighting against her, and yet she had held on until he froze, then relaxed in death and all was still.

She wasn't sure how she'd gotten there or back into her house that night. She wasn't even sure of when it had happened. It had all seemed so far away, like all of her other dreams and nightmares, removed with the distance of time, blurring together with so many other memories from her past. She had never thought of herself as a cold-blooded killer, having only ever acted out of self-defense. But this . . . this was unforgivable. This was murder, and others were suffering for her crime. She had seen the scars left by the Corsair whips and wished she could feel the biting pull of the lash across her own back instead. Before she could stop them, the faces of the whipped citizens changed and distorted into the faces of Sam and Ethan. She knew she was putting them in danger too. Sophie felt sick and ran hard against the wind, away from the pictures in her mind, her hair whipping across her wet face.

At the edge of the field, she stopped, gulping the air to replenish her, holding her throat and willing her breakfast to stay down. The flower Sam had shown her was now in full bloom, its petals open and inviting, a velvet pillow of bright yellow, so bright in the noon sun it almost hurt her eyes to look at it. She reached out to touch it, feeling the warmth and delicacy beneath her fingers. Running her hand down, she approached the thorns of the wild rose, their jagged red spears piercing the air. She couldn't stop herself from touching them as well. One finger stopped, pressed down, felt the point of the thorn penetrate and draw blood, yet she held it there unflinching until it drew the tears from her eyes. She saw the blood form a bubble of red on her finger then drip down in a rivulet running along her finger, through wrinkles in her palm, and she let it bleed on. She marveled again at the frailty of the human body, so easily it bled, so quickly it stopped breathing. She knew then she had to do something. She couldn't continue to let others suffer for her. She needed absolution. She needed to turn herself in. She didn't want to leave Sam and Ethan, but she knew she couldn't continue to put them in danger, either.

A hand reached through the knitted branches of the forest, touching Sophie's and frightening her back into her own surroundings.

"Aishe."

"Foxglove! What the hell are you doing here?"

"We need to talk."

"Not out in the open. Come with me."

Sophie brought her captain to the barn where the only witness to their talk would be Pip. While they walked in silence, she thought of how to tell her the conclusion she'd just come to, how to explain her guilt and her determination to make things right, while damp warmth rose from the ground, encasing her in a circle of heat.

Adjusting their eyes to the dimness in the barn, the two women faced each other. Gemma thought Aishe looked worn and tired. She hadn't been sleeping, obviously. Gemma had hoped to find her better. She spoke first.

"It's good to see you, Aishe." She reached out and embraced her friend in an uncharacteristic gesture of affection. "We've been worried about you."

"I'm alright now, thank you, Foxglove."

"When I didn't hear from you, I feared the worst."

"I was going to send you a message. I only received yours yesterday. I assume you know I've been unwell."

"I know what happened."

"Everything?"

"I know about your daughter and about Credell."

"Does everyone else in the Watch know?"

"No. I didn't tell them. It's between us."

"But then, you know I have to turn myself in."

"I don't know any such thing."

"Foxglove, think about it. There are people being punished because of my actions. How can I just sit back and let that continue?"

"You won't. You'll rejoin our unit and take up your duties in the Watch to help defeat the Corsairs once and for all."

"I can't just live with this, knowing what I've done."

"You have to. How will your execution serve anyone? Your fighting will be much more valuable to the cause."

"But all those people. The floggings. I've seen it, up close. My parents . . ."

Gemma took a deep breath. A shiver ran through her as she thought of the man she'd seen just a few days before, his back ripped to shreds by the lash. She placed her hand on Aishe's arm. "Aishe, I know. It's hard to deal with. Horrible. And what they're doing is despicable, but it won't stop with you. This isn't the government meting out justice. Punishing other people for one person's mistakes is not justice, it's fear. They're using this to scare us. Fear is their greatest weapon against us."

"And what's our greatest weapon?"

"Hope, I guess. Listen to me, Aishe, if it wasn't this, it would be something else. Don't you think they'll come up with another excuse to punish us? We can't give in to them. Sacrificing your life in this way won't serve others."

"I see his face in my dreams. Griffyth."

"Tell me. Tell me how it happened."

"I only have a partial memory of it. It's all so blurred."

"Tell me what you know."

"He was Bridget's father. When she got sick, I went to the G.O. for medicine, but he wouldn't give it to me because she was undocumented. His own daughter. My daughter. I'll never know if I did the right thing bringing her there. Maybe I could have gotten medicine another way. Maybe she would still be here if I had been thinking clearly. I was just so tired and worried." Sophie's words came out in a flurry of confusion and pain, hard to follow, but easy to understand.

"*Suffering has been stronger than all other teaching and has taught us to understand what our hearts used to be. We have been bent and broken, but—I hope—into a better shape.* Someone I once knew used to read those lines to me."

"No one should ever know what those days were like, what it feels like to watch your own child slip away."

Sophie walked to the small window looking over the pasture. She took a deep breath but didn't feel revived. She breathed again, forcing herself to, willing the air into her lungs when her body just wanted to stop. She purposefully stopped her lip from shaking and wiped fiercely at her wet eyes before continuing.

"After she was gone, I was out of my mind with grief. It was like I was in a dream. One of my nightmares come to life. But I couldn't wake up from it. All I know is I left one night and found him at the G.O. late. I must have strangled him. I can see my hands around his throat. That's all

I know for sure." She stopped and looked at her hands, the veins forming blue lines through her pale skin. Her hands looked small. Too small to do what they had done.

"You said it yourself, you were out of your mind with grief. You aren't really to blame for what happened. You weren't in full control of yourself. It's like you were sleepwalking. You aren't to blame, Aishe."

As she turned swiftly to face her captain, the fire burning in Sophie's eyes roared, giving life to the anger, fear, and helplessness she was feeling. "Who else is to blame, then? Show me someone I can blame for who I've become. How could I have become this animal functioning on pure instinct? It's unforgivable, killing an unarmed man." She breathed heavily again, pushing down the lump in her throat.

Gemma thought for a moment before answering. How was she to know the answers to these questions she'd asked herself at times? "We've all done unforgivable things, I think. That's what makes mercy, forgiveness, the freedoms we're fighting for gifts. As long as we hold onto those, we hold onto our humanity."

"It all just seems so absurd. How can we go on living like this?"

"We can't. And we're not going to. The commander has given us new orders. We're sending several people across the borders to try to find help from the outside. We're also going to take over the work camps, build up our supplies, and mount an offensive attack on the Corsair base. We *will* bring an end to all of this, one way or another."

"I suppose it's time. We knew it would be soon."

"Are you ready for another mission?"

"Yes. I'll do whatever is necessary."

"Good. Then you are one of the ones I will send across the Border. Here is the message you need to take. Try to find whoever is in charge, a leader. Tell them how desperate our situation is, and try to negotiate for whatever help they can offer us."

"There's no way of knowing what to expect out there."

"I know. I want you to keep yourself safe. You'll bring a rifle with you. I wish you could ride your horse, but there's no way to get him past the Border fence without detection."

"There's something else. A man and his son have been staying here on the farm with me. You're lucky they weren't here, or they may have seen you. I'll have to come up with a story to explain my absence for the mission."

"Why are they here?"

"We met just before Bridget got sick. And then they stayed to help me. I think it's the code of the forest they're trying to live. They've been my salvation these past months. I don't know what I would have done without them. And I've come to care for them in a way I didn't think I was capable of after Bridget. I feel somewhat guilty leaving them. What I mean is, I've just been taking from them, and now I'm going to take off and leave. I hate having to lie to them."

"I know what you mean. But it's necessary. And believe me, I know how hard it is to love someone and have to keep yourself apart from them for their own safety and yours. I loved someone once, but never knew how to love him the way he needed to be loved. He was a lot like this man you're talking about. Believed in the code. He stayed with me, gave me space, protected me, worked for me. But in the end, I had to leave him. What did I ever give him? What have I given to anyone I really loved?"

"I'm sure we all ask ourselves that question at times."

"Well, all we can do, I guess, is our best, and try to help them and serve them how we can. We may all die in this fight before it's all over, but I'd rather die fighting than standing still."

"When do you need me to leave?"

"As soon as you're able."

"I'll go day after tomorrow."

"Very well. Go in safety, Aishe. We need you back here in one piece."

"I will. Thank you, my friend, for everything."

The two embraced again before Gemma snuck out of the barn to make her way back to Jesse's Hollow before Kyle missed her. Gemma was surprised to realize that when speaking of love and commitment, her mind had gone to Sam rather than Kyle.

Sophie started to wonder what this caring was she felt for Sam and Ethan. Had she felt it all along, or was she only now waking up to the fact, like waking up to the warmth of the early rays of sun on her face in the morning? The thought both warmed her and frightened her.

Neither woman knew how their connections to Sam joined them.

* * * * *

The sun beats down on their black caps. Simeon is dragging the drill out longer than usual. The boys stand in a line, each firing his rifle at the target in his turn. "Fire! Fire! Fire!" Simeon continues to shout. Kyle is hungry and sweaty. He smells his friends around him. But he glories in the fact that he's the best marksman among them. Even better than Mark. Mark's rifle reflects the sun into his eyes. Mark's own eyes sparkle with the hidden jokes he always keeps just below the surface. Kyle tries not to laugh. "Attention!" Simeon barks. The boys snap their rifles down, clicking their black heels together. "Squad, dismissed! Stay the course!"

"Stay the course!" they respond. Other boys run and scramble for the mess hall. Simeon marches away. Mark's voice is in Kyle's ear, "Stay the course, of course, to the steak!" He's snickering and jabbing at his friend in the ribs. "I could eat ten of those steaks, even if they do taste like mule." They throw their arms around each other's shoulders as they join the melee of cadets clamoring for food.

Kyle kicked up the dirt on the path to his house. He looked at his shoes. Hideous shoes. He missed the shine of his black Corsair boots, the tailored cut of his uniform jacket, and he hated living like a peasant. He didn't want to admit to himself that he missed Mark or his fellow soldiers. He had to keep his mind on his life now, that was the only thing to do. The town didn't feel like home yet, but it could. He still didn't feel comfortable with Gemma yet, but he could. It was just a matter of time. He just had to adjust. Stay the course.

"Going somewhere?" he asked from the door.

Gemma dropped the bag of clothes she was carrying. "God, Kyle, you scared me. What are you doing home?"

"Lunchtime."

"Oh, hell. I'm sorry, sweetie. I haven't fixed anything yet. I was just taking these old clothes over to a mother in the next town. Z told me about this lady who has an undocumented daughter, and she needed some clothes."

"Why do you insist in getting wrapped up in everyone else's problems?"

"I don't. But it's not so hard to bring these clothes over that were just going to waste."

"How did you get children's clothes?"

"I cut down a few of my old tunics. I won't be gone long." Gemma went to kiss Kyle on the cheek, but his words stopped her.

"Is that the truth?"

163

"What do you mean?"

"I mean where do you go when you take off for hours at a time?"

"Wow, just jumping right into the argument. We don't even get past the pleasantries anymore."

"Do you go to Sam? Are you two . . . together?"

"You can't be serious, Kyle. I just . . . I just can't believe we're actually going to go through this again."

"Just answer the question."

"I have answered it. Multiple times. I chose you. I still choose you. No, I'm not with Sam. I'm the one who tries desperately to cross the river of ice you keep between us, to get through to you somehow. But you won't let me in."

"How can I?"

"You mean when you don't trust me?"

"When I know you still love him."

"You don't know any such thing. Now, I'm bringing these clothes like I said. I'll be back in a while."

Gemma slammed the door behind her. Kyle felt himself relax in the silence.

* * * * *

Rippling and tripping water tumbling over rocks and through its worn bed, the stream pushed out the many other sounds Ethan's ears were tuned for in the forest. He stopped for a few minutes, closing his eyes and just listening to the rushing waters. He thought it would be nice to rest his hot feet in the stream since he'd been walking since early morning. Sam had allowed him to take the camera out for more pictures, and he'd wandered further than he originally intended, being pulled on from one natural beauty to another. A new green bud bathed in the sunrise. A squirrel hopping from branch to branch, following him only to chastise him with pinched, chirping exclamations. And before he knew it, he had found his way to the grove of pines at the base of the mountain. Pines neighboring with fur, oak, and cottonwood to perfume the air and cover the ground in their sweetness.

Ethan sat on the pine needles that lay like a carpet beneath him, took his shoes off, and just let the coolness of the stream overtake him. He wouldn't stay long. He knew Sam and Sophie would expect him back. He found himself wondering if he should have stayed to help Sophie. He felt a small stone of guilt enter his heart for leaving her alone with Sam in the fields. He liked helping her, liked just being around her. There was something so familiar about her that he couldn't quite grasp and chose not to examine too closely for fear the feeling would fly away like a butterfly. Nobody thought about or talked about home. It was a distant land best forgotten. But to Ethan, Sophie felt like home.

Before long, fish were swimming in and out between Ethan's feet, rubbing their scaly backs along his toes, tickling him. He reached for the camera and leaned over the stream as far as he dared, trying to get a picture of the fish swimming along the bottom. Though the water was running swiftly, the fish stayed in a shallow pool surrounded by stones rubbed smooth by years of rushing waters.

"What'cha doin' there?" a little blonde girl asked with a smirk.

Ethan jumped, just barely avoiding falling in the water, camera and all. The girl didn't even try to keep herself from laughing. The look on the boy's face was too funny.

"It wouldn't have been funny if I had dropped this camera."

"I'm sorry," she said, still giggling. Her laugh reminded Ethan of the stream. "My name's Daisy. What's yours?"

"Ethan."

"What's a camera?"

"It takes pictures so you can remember things later."

"What were you taking a picture of?"

"Fish."

"Why in the world would you want to remember fish? I'd rather eat them," she laughed again. Ethan noticed her holding a fishing pole. She wore a short gray tunic, almost too small for her, and gray shorts which had been torn off, having once been pants. No shoes covered her blackened feet, which took her to the stream where she deftly cast a line.

Ethan relaxed a little and smiled at this strange girl. "Can I sit with you?"

"Sure!"

After a few moments of staring at her, he finally said without obvious connection or reason, "You have blonde hair."

"And you have black hair."

"My mother had light hair too. Red more than blonde."

"Oh, really? I don't remember my mother. Not really. But I have a friend, Gemma, now."

"I've met Gemma!" Ethan was glad to have found a connection with this girl. He wanted a friend close to his own age and hadn't had one since Toby had left with the rest of his group before Sam found him. He had often wished over the past few months that he had someone to play with and talk to that wasn't an adult, even though he loved Sam and Sophie. "Is this Gemma's cabin?" he continued.

"No. She found it for us kids to stay here."

"Better than sleeping out in the open, I guess." Ethan tossed a pebble into the water, forgetting he would scare the fish away from Daisy's pole.

"Especially in the wintertime."

"How many of you are there?"

"Used to be more. But the older boys, Seth and Jake, took off. For a while I was watching out for the two little twins, Hughie and Petal, myself. But a new boy found us about a month ago. His name's Toby. I feel better having another older kid to help me. Sometimes I got scared on my own." Daisy looked at the water, wondering why she admitted this to a boy she'd just met.

"Toby? I wonder if it's the same Toby who used to be in my group. Me and him were friends."

"Come up to the cabin and see for yourself."

"Can I?"

"Sure! Hang on a sec. Let me just pull in the line. Oh! Oh! I've got something!"

"Well, reel it in!"

"I've got it, I've got it! There!" Daisy drew out a bass the length of her thin leg. She struggled pulling it out of the water, and Ethan ran to her assistance. They both laughed at the pronounced pout carved into the fish's mouth, an appropriate response to his being caught. "Fish for dinner!" Daisy cheered in triumph. "Come on, help me carry it back."

The two found the twins sharing the rocking chair in the middle of the room, looking at the pictures in a book. Toby stood in the kitchen, peeling potatoes left there on Gemma's last visit. Ethan noticed a smile cross his friend's face at the sight of him, but then he looked down again, seemingly bent to his task.

"Hi, Toby," Ethan offered.

"Hiya."

Daisy felt the awkwardness and jumped in. "Toby, you remember Ethan. He helped me catch this grandpa fish for dinner!" Her arm shook with the weight of the fish she hoisted one-armed above her head.

"Yep," Toby grunted. He ran the back of his forearm across an itching nose.

"Where have you been?" Ethan asked.

"Here and there. I left the group awhile back."

"Can I help you with those?"

"If you want."

"I um . . . I was adopted." Ethan turned a raw potato over in his hand.

"Well, that's great."

"I just mean I'm not mad you left and went with the other boys."

"Look, I should have stayed. I know that. I felt pretty bad about it. They got worse and worse until finally I left them, too."

"It's okay, Toby. I understand."

"So, you like your new family?"

"It's just Sam and now Sophie. But yeah. They're great."

"So what are you doin' here?"

"Just playin', I guess."

"Hm," Toby grunted. He never was much for conversation.

There was a cold storage bin cut into the floor of the kitchen where Daisy threw the fish before going to check on the twins. "Hey, kids! Game or story?" she called in a similar way to what she'd heard Gemma say to her countless times. In taking care of the twins, she mimicked Gemma's every move, her only point of reference for mothering.

"Story!" they called back.

"Which one you got there?"

"*Peter Pan.*"

"That's my favorite."

Ethan's ears perked up at the familiar name. "*Peter Pan?* Is that the one with the Lost Boys?"

"Yeah, how'd you know?" Daisy asked.

"Sam told me about it. Can I listen in?"

"Sure, come sit on the floor." Daisy took the chair while the twins and Ethan sat before her in the sunlight streaming through the window. She smiled when she looked at a picture of Wendy among the yellowed pages in the book in a very similar position. She could be Wendy, and they could be her Lost Boys.

Before the story was finished, a familiar voice called from the path through the pines. "Daisy, it's me!"

"Gemma!" Daisy dropped the book in the chair and ran to her friend. Gemma met her at the door, and the child hopped into her arms.

"Hey, kid. You're bigger every time I see you. I won't be able to carry you around like this much longer. Now just look at you. I guess it's a good thing I brought these extra clothes I made from my old ones. That tunic is just about done."

"Gemma, we have a new friend."

"Oh, yeah?"

"Hi, Gemma." Ethan stood to welcome her. The twins retreated to their fort in the opposite corner of the cabin.

"Ethan? What are you doing here? Where's Sam? Is he okay?" Gemma felt fear like bile rising in her throat.

"Oh yeah, he's fine. I was just out for a walk when I met Daisy."

"Does Sam know you're here?"

"Not exactly. But he won't mind."

"Alright, then." Gemma put Daisy down and gave her the clothes to try on. While Daisy was in her corner, changing behind a sheet she used for a curtain, Ethan took the chance to talk to Gemma.

"I've been wanting to ask you if I could help send messages for the Watch."

"How do you know about that?"

"I hear things. People think kids can't hear things, but we do."

"Ethan, buddy, I don't think that's a good idea. I know Sam wouldn't like it. And I have to respect that."

"Sam has to do what he thinks is right, and so do I. I'm old enough to make my own decisions."

"How old are you?"

"Eleven . . . I think."

"I think it's great you want to help, but still . . ."

"Sam doesn't have to know."

"Know what?" a masculine voice came from the doorway. Gemma and Ethan both looked to see Sam standing before them.

"How'd you find me?" Ethan asked.

"I'm an excellent tracker, and you leave excellent tracks, boy. I've told you."

"I didn't mean to be gone so long, Sam."

"Sophie was worried."

"Sorry."

"Alright. We'll talk about it later, son. Right now, I need to talk to Gemma. Outside?" He motioned her to follow him.

Sam didn't want to talk within earshot of the children, so they walked the short distance to the stream.

"Gemma, I don't know what your job is in the Watch, and I don't want to know. But I know you're involved. I've told you I don't want Ethan involved with them, and now I find him here at our old cabin with you. Are you turning him into a messenger?"

"Stop. Stop right there. I'm in no mood to be accused of one more thing today, Sam. I just met Ethan about five minutes ago. I came to bring Daisy some clothes and supplies, and he was here. They met by accident while he was out walking. That's it."

Sam's shoulders visibly relaxed. Gemma thought he looked tired under all his bluster. She wondered what his days were filled with, and what or who kept him away from Jesse's Hollow so often. She hoped it wasn't just to stay away from her.

"Okay. I'm sorry for accusing you," he sighed. "Who's Daisy anyway?"

"She's a kid I found that I help to take care of. In fact, I wrote you about her while you were away. Of course, you never got the letter. Anyway, now there are a few more children. I do what I can to help them."

"Why don't you adopt her? It's pretty dangerous for them out here alone."

"It's complicated," she bristled. "I'm trying to keep them safe in my own way. They can't be associated with me because of my connection to the Watch."

'There are no creatures that walk the earth . . . which will not show courage when required to defend themselves,' Sam mused, almost to himself. "God, the people of Before had a way of describing everything, even war. I sometimes think if we could just get back their words and learn to *talk* to people, maybe then we wouldn't have to fight."

"You can't be that naive. All their words didn't keep them from fighting then. Words alone can't save people. They have to mean something. Why do you think so much of them, the people of Before? Don't you think they got us into this mess?"

"I don't know."

"They prayed to gods who sent them liars and con men as leaders, breeding the liars and con men of our own time. We have them to thank for that."

"Gemma, do you really think the Watch is going to help make things better? Or are they just going to get worse?"

"Sometimes something just beginning can become an entirely new entity overnight. We can't know what's ahead."

"War changes people. We've both seen it. We've both fought for years to get past the horrors we saw in the last war. Killing changed us."

"You'd rather I sit back and do nothing as you do? Just try to pretend the world isn't falling down around our ears? You think you can stay removed, untouched by what's going on around us. But the very act of doing nothing changes a person. We can't look on injustice and do nothing without something changing within us. It forces us to build our own wall around our hearts. That is change. So yes, you're right. The fight, the war, will change us. We will have to deal with the aftereffects as we have our whole lives. But maybe, just maybe, the act of fighting against evil and injustice will change us for the better as well."

"Nothing I've seen in war changes people for the better. Look at what happened to our parents."

"The wars before were not our fights. They belonged to our parents. But this one is ours. It lies squarely on our shoulders, the responsibility to protect our children and their futures. What should we wait for? There's no one coming to save us. And the government won't change unless they're forced to by the will of the people. It's up to us."

A squirrel rustled in the underbrush, drawing Sam's attention absently for a moment.

"I don't want to see the children inherit a war like we did."

"If we handle it right, they won't. They'll inherit freedoms we never had."

"Freedom," he exhaled sharply. "Freedom I couldn't find in keeping the law or in going beyond the borders or going to a work camp." Gemma flinched at his mention of a painful memory for them both. "Can I ask you something, Gemma? I'm not hung up on it or anything, I just need to

170

know. Why didn't you send someone from the Watch to find me? In all those years you thought I was dead? Why didn't you make sure?"

"It was easier not to know, I guess. Besides, how did I know that you hadn't found someone else too?"

"You knew better than that."

"No, I didn't. You've always been so hell-bent on 'the code.' You could have picked up someone else to take care of just like you did with me and Kyle."

"And now it's you who takes care of Kyle instead."

"It's not like that with us."

"What is it like? Is he the same?"

"I don't know. You know, I wonder now if I've ever really known him. Or if I ever knew you, for that matter. How much can people ever really know each other?"

"I doubt anybody knows him. Hard to know someone who can change sides at the drop of hat."

Gemma felt her anger at Kyle still for his petty jealousies, but she knew he would never betray her. Not really. And somehow, she felt responsible for defending his honor to Sam. "What if he didn't change sides? What if he was always on our side?"

"The only side that Kyle knows is Kyle's side. He serves himself first and always."

"I wish you two could be friends again. I think it would be good for you both."

"Not likely. Look, I'm sorry, Gemma. I have to go. Good luck with the kids and everything."

Sam walked past the cabin, not going back in. "Ethan! Time to go, boy!" He walked quickly down the path, knowing Ethan would follow.

"Sorry, I lost track of time, Sam,"

"Want to join the Watch, do you?"

"Yes."

"Well, you know how I feel about it. But if you think you're old enough to make that decision on your own, I won't stop you. I do expect you to be upfront with me, though, and not go sneaking around behind my back, understood?"

"Understood."

"So, it looks like you made some new friends today."

171

"Toby was there, the boy I told you about who taught me the code. And I like that Daisy. We were reading *Peter Pan*, the story with the Lost Boys."

"Huh," Sam smiled. "That's a funny coincidence."

"Yeah."

"Well, I'm happy for you, boy. It's important to have friends your own age, I suppose." Sam tousled Ethan's hair, and the boy knew he was forgiven. "I haven't been much fun for you, have I?"

"You and Sophie are nice. She plays with me sometimes, and I like to listen to her play the piano."

"Even still, friends are more of a necessity than I realize sometimes."

Ethan took Sam's hand. He didn't want him to feel bad, especially since he'd found the only home he could remember with Sam and Sophie.

"Did you get any good pictures today?"

"I think so. Tried to get some fish, but they wouldn't stay still."

Sam laughed at the idea of trying to keep a wriggling fish still enough for a photograph.

Parting the branches in silence, Kyle leaned his rifle on one of the larger ones to steady it. He looked down the barrel, holding his prey in his sights. The gun felt cool against his hot cheek. His body held the midday summer heat after running. He'd had to move quickly to reach his spot after Sam left Gemma at the cabin. Listening to their conversation had given him much of the information he'd wanted to know, and he'd been rewarded for his efforts. He was a little surprised at how easy Gemma had made it for him to follow her, and he felt a stab of guilt realizing she must actually trust him. He held his breath and squeezed the trigger in confidence, knowing he'd hit his mark.

11

COMMUNION AND DIVISION

*S*am tromps with his friend deeper into the waist-high underbrush. "Come on, Kyle. I saw them here just the other day. I want to surprise Gemma with berries for dessert."

The ivy and moss-entombed branches allow for no brown in the rich landscape. It speaks of age and rains long past yet still nourishing.

"We're getting too close to the Corsair base, Sam. We should turn back."

"Just a bit farther. They're by the river just ahead."

Sam tries to break into a run but is slowed by clinging branches that trip him up. Kyle laughs at him sprawled on the ground before him. Sam enjoys the few times he's made Kyle laugh. He nearly falls into the blackberry bushes when they escape the tangle of the woods. Kyle stops. His face says he's listening intently for danger. He hears them before Sam does. Corsairs.

"Sam, listen to me. They're coming. They'll be here any second. They're going to want me, not you. I led the raid on the camp. Get in the river and stay underwater."

"No, I won't leave you. Let them just try to take us both."

"We don't have time for this. Do what I say."

"No, I can . . ."

Kyle pushes him into the river, stopping the argument. "Stay down!" he hisses before the Corsairs on horseback surround him.

Rippling water stirs the light through Kyle's ginger hair as Sam holds his breath beneath the surface. His brain is counting the seconds and the soldiers. One, two, three . . . seven, eight, nine. Too many to fight. The horses look like ancient monsters. The

Corsairs are pulling Kyle onto a horse. Why isn't he fighting? A minute feels like ten. Sam's lungs ache. He thinks they will explode if he's not allowed to release his breath and gasp for another. Two minutes. The horse monsters are turning. Kyle's colors are fading into the trees. Sam waits another thirty seconds before bursting through the surface of the river.

The shot cracked in Sam's ear just as a bird landed directly at his feet. "Holy shit!" He grasped Ethan by the arm, pulling the boy behind him from where he heard the shot originate. The bushes rustled before the shooter emerged, making Sam wish he was carrying the pistol Zacharias had given him.

"Kyle, what the hell?! You could have killed somebody."

"You know my skills better than that, don't you, Sam? I always hit what I'm aiming for."

"And just what were you aiming for?"

"This grouse, of course." He held it up in triumph. "I thought I'd surprise Gemma with a little something special for dinner."

"Oh, really? You, of all people, just casually carrying a gun and breaking the law?"

"Look, I've been worried about her since the rations were cut again. She's not getting enough to eat. I considered it a medical necessity, not just fun."

"Very well. Come on, Ethan."

"No, wait, Sam, I've been wanting to talk to you."

"Well, I don't want to talk to you."

"Can't we at least try to be friends again? I mean, what exactly do you hold against me?"

"How can you ask that? You joined the enemy. You became one of them."

"I didn't exactly have a choice. You were there, Sam. You saw them take me. We were surrounded."

"Maybe. Maybe it was just easier for you not to fight or not to run. Maybe you liked the idea of having a full belly for a change. I don't know what you were thinking."

"But you do know I tried to save you. You do remember that part, don't you?"

Sam grunted a reluctant affirmation.

174

"Is it that I left or that I came back that bothers you the most, Sam?"

"Does it matter?"

"It does to me. It does when I'm trying to build bridges and you're trying to light them on fire."

"The bridges were burned a long time ago."

"Then help me rebuild them." Kyle put his hand out, his eyes asking Sam to accept it.

"I wish I could believe you, Kyle."

"Try. Come to dinner tonight with me and Gemma. It'll be like old times."

"I can't. I have somewhere I have to be. Truly."

"Then maybe another time?"

"Maybe." Sam slowly reached out and gripped Kyle's hand. It felt strange to be this close in proximity to him after so many years, to hold the hand which used to be as familiar to him as his own, but to find only a foreign entity in the calloused palm. Nothing felt the same as it used to, and he was sure nothing ever could.

* * * * *

Sam and Ethan fit very well on the little farm by the sea. Sophie started to forget there was ever a time when they hadn't been there. They were so native to their surroundings that she imagined them springing up from the ground like one of the many flowering plants that had shot up in the spring. The partridge berry and wisteria were no more original to the land than Sam and Ethan. Sophie's stomach churned and tightened a little at the thought of leaving the two of them behind to go on her mission, but she knew well the necessity of her task. If things went as planned, she'd only be gone for a few days, a week at most. Her time with Sam on the farm had happened so naturally, there had been no need for a conversation addressing the future, but she wondered now if it was time to discuss long-term plans. She knew she had to ask him to stay while she was gone, although it was possible the O'Dells would help out on the farm if necessary. But she wished she and Sam could understand each other enough that such a conversation wouldn't be necessary. Maybe it wouldn't. Maybe he would just offer to stay. She wondered if he felt the same caring feelings toward her that she had for him, or if all these months he'd only stayed because of the code. When so much of her daily life focused on survival, it was hard to imagine or ask for more. Shouldn't she be grateful to be one of the ones left alive? Or was that enough?

* * * * *

Sam listened to the secrets told from the aspens to the willows. Secrets of sinking roots and liberating breezes. A blush seemed to darken the bark of a young willow whose branch had just been brushed by another tree. Or was it just a shadow? The air around him felt different, more charged with energy leading to these fancies whenever he stepped on Sophie's land. He wondered if this was always the case from the first day he arrived. Was it something particular to the spot or to the woman who inhabited it?

A craggy voice interrupted his reverie. "Sam! Sam, my boy, take a step over here and come sit a spell with me," Mrs. O'Dell called from her front porch.

"Run along, Ethan, and tell Sophie we're back. I'll be along directly."

Mrs. O'Dell settled herself into a rocking chair and motioned for Sam to take one as well. "Can I fetch you a glass of something? Cider, maybe? It's certainly a hot day."

Sam remained standing on the steps. "No thank you, Mrs. O'Dell."

"You've been here a fair piece, haven't you, my boy?"

"Yes, ma'am, I suppose I have."

"How long has it been?"

"A few months, I suppose."

"So it is, so it is. I reckon from keeping my ear to the ground that there'll be another war starting soon enough. I suppose you'll be joining up with many another young man."

"No, I don't have any intention . . ."

"I know. I know. So you say. They always say. But something always calls them to the fight, says I. Either way, you'll be leaving here by and by. And I just don't know if that sweet lamb could survive mourning somebody else."

"Do you mean . . ."

"Take it for what it's worth. But a woman can see the look in another woman's eyes. She's becoming attached. And I'm not altogether sure that's a good thing. Might be time for you to be thinking about moving on."

176

Sam considered his words before speaking. Mrs. O'Dell's insinuations and unsolicited advice had shaken him. He didn't know what he was more upset about . . . her assumptions about his relationship with Sophie or her telling him to go. He had no wish to offend the woman in her well-meaning offensive against his personal life. But he also wasn't one to be dictated to. He wondered if she was right. Had he been selfish in staying so long with Sophie? Had it only been the code? And what of Ethan? He had allowed him to get attached, to start setting down roots. Maybe it would be best for all concerned if he took the boy back to Jesse's Hollow. "I'll certainly think about what you've said, ma'am. I must be getting back now to see about the boy."

"Just so. Just so. I mean no offense, now, son. You know that?"

"I do. Goodbye, Mrs. O'Dell."

* * * * *

Just east of Sophie's farm, the sea crept ever closer, stealing perhaps an inch a year. Due to an almost imperceptible rise in elevation, there was a short strip of beach that remained exposed when the water was at low tide. It had not fallen beneath the encroaching waves that ate up the eastern shore like a starving man. On this beach Sophie walked in the late evening sunsets which hid behind the trees west of her farm, and on some days, she danced.

When Sam returned from Mrs. O'Dell's, he found Sophie there. She danced recklessly along the beach with the wild abandon of a child, but not a child from this world. Rather a child from Before, her arms flung wide as if she'd only ever caught good things in them. A child not hampered by fear, war, and the oppressive need for survival above all else. A child who had never had to worry about food or cold. A child who had never had to raise a stick over her head for protection, beating senseless an attacker. A child who had never slept alone in the woods listening to the not-so-distant sound of gunfire, wondering just how long it would take for the soldiers to find her. This kind of child, free from care and worry, would float along as light as a cloud through a summer sky, changing shape before your eyes.

But Sam knew Sophie had experienced all those things and worse and should have been barely mobile under the weight she'd had to carry her whole life. Yet here she was dancing across the beach, throwing off the worries of war and survival—a fairy, a nymph, wind in her hair caressing her in a way that made Sam jealous of the breeze. And in that moment, he saw her and knew her for all the things she was and could be. He saw her passing this freedom and lightness on to her future children. In that moment, he wanted to be a cloud-catcher and ride the sky with her, yet he felt privileged to have been in her presence even for just a moment.

She was one with all around her—the beach, the waves, the air, the taste of salt on his lips, and him. Deep in his bones he knew he'd never be free of her, never again have a moment when she wasn't in his thoughts and his motivations. She was part of him, but not like Gemma was part of him because of their shared past and memories. She was the air in his lungs, the blood in his veins, and the food that gave him strength. She was all the colors of the sunset as he had once thought, but more. She was the music of morning robins and evening swallows and the trip of the stream down its path, but more still. Sam knew even if he'd ever had the opportunity to be a writer in the time Before, the words would never have been enough to describe her, and his pen would have fallen down in deference to her grace.

He did not move or utter a sound, not wanting to disturb the beautiful reverie. But merely returned to the little gray house to hold his revelation close.

* * * * *

Kyle walked into his house, still cool among the trees. He was grateful Gemma had left the windows open, allowing the breeze to dispel any trapped heat in the house. He left the grouse on the porch, its mottled feathers stained with blood. He would clean it and dress it for dinner. He wished it was bigger or that he had been able to find more. But he couldn't take the chance of firing off more than one shot, which in itself was risk enough.

He'd picked some flowers for the table to add to the effect of the surprise dinner. He wanted to show Gemma that he could be thoughtful too.

Seeing Sam had affected him more than he thought it would. He tried to be sure he could leave the past behind him and do only what needed to be done now in the moment. But how was that possible when he had to draw on the past in order to get through to Sam? So much of their lives was always tied to the past. He wished he could be like the river, moving swiftly forward, always forward, never tripping back to the places it had been before. There was usually such a single-mindedness about Kyle that allowed him to focus on each new necessary task at hand. But something about Sam had unnerved him, jarred his thinking into a direction unplanned and unwanted.

He thought of Gemma and the argument he'd intentionally started earlier, and a feeling, rather than the necessity, weighed on him. Regret and sorrow for hurting her swam in his mind, forcing him to circle a drain that led to nowhere good or useful.

He looked around the empty house and realized he and Gemma didn't know each other at all. They'd grown up together, lived in the same house as man and wife, whatever that meant, but were strangers. In those moments alone he thought about how much he'd missed in not knowing her—her kindness, strength, and pure capacity for living. It all had seemed so easy when he first came back. It felt natural that he would marry her. With Sam gone, wouldn't it be expected? But he wasn't the same Kyle who had left, and she wasn't the Gemma he'd left behind.

He washed his hands and didn't recognize them. He washed his face and looked at a stranger in the mirror, lines around eyes that used to hold more kindness and love. He looked and felt tired. Nothing was the same or ever would be. Not now. Before he realized what he was doing, he was going through the marriage vows in his mind. "I do take this woman as my wife. I will keep her for better or worse, in sickness or in health. We pledge to work together to honor the Triumvirate and the laws laid out by them. We do this with solemnity and singularity of purpose. Stay the course."

Stay the course. Kyle went to the kitchen to start preparations for dinner but only stood pumping water over his hands, letting it run through his fingers and down the drain. He wondered if his choices, his life, were any more meaningful than that—water down a drain. He thought of his friends in the Corsairs and the oath of allegiance he'd made to them and the Triumvirate. When he first made it, it was meaningless to him. He'd been captured by the Corsairs and forced into service. Almost against his will, he began to enjoy their company, the camaraderie with his fellow soldiers. Then he'd met Mark. He didn't think anyone would ever take

Sam's place as his friend, but Mark was different. Mark had a similar sense of humor and fun as Sam had, but he and Kyle had more in common. It was easy to fall into a friendship with him. Easy to pledge loyalty and fight alongside him.

"Kyle, I'm home," Gemma called before she was even through the door. She saw him standing at the sink and hoped he'd worked through his anger from earlier.

He dried his hands and walked to her, taking her firmly in his arms and covering her mouth with his. There was an urgency, a need behind his kiss that surprised Gemma for its rarity. She let herself melt into it and tried not to think of anything but the feel of his lips on hers, the smell of his skin, his hands finding their way into her hair.

He stepped back and looked at her, seeing the tears in her eyes, and the pang of regret hit him again. "I'm sorry about earlier. I shouldn't have said those things about you and Sam. I was wrong."

Gemma tried to think if she'd ever heard Kyle say he was wrong before. "I just don't know where it came from, and I hope we're past it and that you believe me. There's nothing between us anymore."

"I do believe you. I do."

She kissed him again, slower this time, tenderly. He was so like a child sometimes. The clock in the hall struck six. They had to be thinking of dinner. "I saw you got a grouse. Where in the world did you find it?"

"Just in the woods past the stream. Thought it would be a nice surprise for you."

"It is. Thank you!" She put her hand on his shoulder before walking back into the kitchen to start dinner. She noticed the flowers on the table and was surprised again. A mix of yellow wildflowers, red clover, and pink dogwoods stood in a glass of water. "Flowers, too? This is quite the occasion."

"I wanted to tell you. I saw Sam."

"Oh? I figured you would at some point. How was it?"

"He's pretty angry still."

"About a lot of things."

"He holds too much in. Doesn't let things go."

"Did you have a fight?"

"No, I tried to be his friend again. In fact, I invited him for dinner sometime."

"That should be awkward."

"No, I think it will be good. Maybe like old times. I miss how we used to be."

"I don't know what to do with all this . . ." She started to say "softness" but stopped herself. Her mind quickly searched for another word. ". . . this tenderness, Kyle. Has something happened?"

"Yes. It was seeing Sam. It reminded me what it was like when we felt like a group, like a family. I've missed that. I know you and Sam went through a lot after I left. And that haunts me, not being there for you."

Gemma didn't say anything but let him continue. He walked out to the porch to begin pulling the feathers from the grouse. "Can you hear me out here?"

"Yeah."

"You know, sometimes I see men from the Corsairs I used to know. It's still jarring."

"In what way?"

"Well, because I was a part of them too, and now I'm not. It doesn't seem like I'm part of anything. You should see the way they look at me sometimes. I guess I'm still trying to figure out where I belong. I'm not counted one among them anymore."

"But that's a good thing, isn't it? Aren't you glad to be away from them and back with us?"

"Yes and no. I still miss it. I miss them. Do you know what it's like to be part of something greater than yourself, part of a purpose, and a group that looks after you? Then to just walk away and be nothing? Can a seed plucked from its parent tree not still long to become a tree itself?"

"Are you becoming a poet?"

Kyle was silent. She worried she had hurt him when she'd only meant to joke. She wiped her hands on her apron and walked out to join him on the porch. He was surrounded by discarded feathers dancing in the slow breeze, his hands covered in them, giving him a strange and almost comical predatory look so foreign to him as he labored over the bird he'd brought for her.

Gemma kissed the top of his head, the only clean spot left on him. He even had tiny feathers in his strawberry-blond beard.

"Sweetie, I know. I really do know what it's like. And you're not nothing. We're something, the two of us together, when we're not poking

181

and lashing out at each other. We can let our pieces fall in place here in this space between us, all the pieces from our pasts and from now. We don't have to be alone anymore. Alright?" She took his face in her hands and made his eyes meet hers.

"Alright."

"You know, you never told me why you were able to leave the Corsairs, anyway. I would think your adopted father would have wanted to keep you close, as general of the whole Corsair army."

"I was transferred out of his division. We hadn't seen each other in years. Then I got sick. Malaria. They let me have some time to recover in the hospital on base. But the doctors said I would never fully regain my strength, so they released me. Gave me the new assignment at the Council of Doctors."

"Well, heaven bless the mosquito that gave you malaria." Gemma smiled and went back inside.

* * * * *

With the day still not ready to let go of the light, Ethan asked if he could go out to the stream to play with his turtle after dinner. Sam and Sophie were both happy to let him enjoy the evening breeze and the sunset. They'd all been working hard on the farm lately and could use the rest. When dishes had been cleared and Sophie took in a sigh of contentment, she went where her heart often called her, to sit at the piano to try to pick out the tunes that ran in her head from her memories of her mother. She thought of the times she'd sat at a similar piano with her and played along with the tunes. Her mother could read the notes, but Sophie had been too young to learn.

Sam sat in the rocking chair, listening with eyes half closed as her fingers danced along the keys. Sunset light from the front window broke into rainbows along her thin arms and lit up her hair like fire, fire tied in a golden ribbon. He began tapping his feet to the lively tune she was playing.

Seeing the movement out of the corner of her eye, Sophie smiled. "Did you ever learn how to dance?"

"Who, me? Not at all. But something about music just makes you want to move, doesn't it?"

"It does. In fact . . ." Sophie stopped playing, spinning on the stool to face Sam. "I have a surprise. Stay here while I go get it."

He heard bumps and footsteps above the ceiling. She was in the attic. What could she possibly be bringing?

"Need help?" he called.

"No, I've got it. Stay there."

A few minutes later, she came down with a large wooden box in her two arms, holding a huge brass horn precariously in one hand.

"Here, give me that." Sam took the box and set it on the table as Sophie attached the horn to it. She put a round disc on the top of the box, then quickly turned the crank on the side. This seemed to make the disc turn. Then she moved an attached needle to run along the grooves in the disc and after a few seconds of scratching sounds, music began to emanate from the horn.

"They called it a gramophone," she said with a satisfied grin. "It's how they listened to music before all of their electrical machines."

"I've read about them, but I've never seen or heard one. It's amazing!"

"I know! I was so happy to find this in the attic when I came to this house. It was just pure luck."

"It is that. It's beautiful. What's the name of this song?"

"'The Cecile Waltz.' It's one of my favorites, and perfect for dancing."

"Oh, no, Sophie. Not me. I have no idea how to dance. I'll look silly."

"That's part of the fun. Now come on. We've both read enough about it in our few books. I know we're supposed to hold hands like this, and then you put your arm around me like this."

She gently placed his hands in the right places, and Sam felt his heart quicken and leap. She lay her palm gently in his, and its softness unsewed the heart from his chest leaving it hanging, helpless. It occurred to Sam he had never held Sophie's hand before, and the thought seemed strange to him. For as many times as he'd held her to still her nightmares, he'd never held her hand, never touched her skin, which rivaled every kind of light. And as he held it now, he was sure this was what it would feel like to try to touch the sun on a winter day, the heat and coolness running together through his fingers, solid and fluid at once. Her fingers were long and trailed around and through his like ivy on a tree. He noticed his own hand, brown and clumsy, and yet Sophie held on.

Sophie felt the slow 1-2-3 beat of the waltz and naturally moved her feet in time to the music as she and Sam turned round and round the room.

She felt light-headed with the spinning, the scent of pine that clung to Sam's tan skin, the feel of his lean arms holding her up and guiding her around the room.

"Did you ever dance with Gemma?"

Sam paused for a moment, taken aback by the question. Then his feet began to move again as he considered his answer. "How do you know about her?"

"Ethan told me what happened when you came back from the lumber camp and how he'd found you up in the mountains. You must have loved her very much."

"I thought I did."

"I've never felt that before. I'm not even sure I know what it is. I guess I've only ever known when someone wanted to possess or own me."

"I think you know more about love than you think. Your heart is deep. Like the sea. So deep you may not even know what's there, just like we don't know what's in the sea."

"That's fine, in the abstract. But you had Gemma. The great love of your life. You know what true love is. Even if it was never fully realized."

"I wouldn't call her the great love of my life. Maybe the great illusion of my life. All I ever really wanted was peace and maybe contentment if I was lucky. Gemma did seem like that for a while, that's true. But it couldn't last. Dreams never can. They're fake. Wishes. I tried to push and pull it, shape it into what I wanted it to be. But it wasn't what she wanted. In the end, I realized it was mostly an imaginary world I'd created in the image of all the romantic books I'd read. But not real. I want something real."

"What is real?"

"You are."

The music stopped and they heard the slow clicking of the needle on the record. The two of them stood looking at each other in the middle of the room. Sam noticed a bird calling from out among the trees. His heart was beating fast, perhaps from the dancing, or from Sophie's nearness to him. The scent of lavender was in her hair, wafting around him and through him.

Sophie began to feel nervous. She couldn't quite work out her feelings. Was it the sense of family she'd come to feel with Sam and Ethan both, or did she really care about Sam for himself? She thought about her upcoming mission and her muscles tensed. She realized she and Sam hadn't separated since the song ended. The needle continued to click against the record, and he held her still. Ethan would be walking in any moment, and she stood occupying the same breath as Sam. She would be leaving them both in a couple of days, but something held her there. She gripped Sam's hand tighter.

"Ethan will be coming back . . ." she started to say.

"Not 'til we call him."

"I have to tell you something, Sam."

"Not just yet," he whispered.

He freed his hand from hers and ran his fingers along her cheek, sending a ripple down her spine. As his trembling hand found its way behind her head, he untied the ribbon, releasing her hair in a wave. With the lightest pressure to the back of her neck, he pulled her to him and brushed her lips with his. Sophie closed her eyes, wanting to lean in, wanting to let him kiss her, but felt him pause.

"What is it?" she asked.

"I don't know if I can kiss you just once without wanting more. Maybe we shouldn't. I'm just worried . . ."

"I know. So am I. Close your eyes. Clear your mind." She spoke to herself as well as to him.

She cupped his face in her hands, feeling the heat of his cheeks beneath her skin, and kissed him, slowly at first, acquainting herself with his lips, his mouth. For a moment, just a moment, everything else fell away. All of her fears and hesitation melted. And in this kiss, she knew all she needed to know. Knew she could share her worries, fears, and dreams with him. Knew he would always be on her side and help her in any way he could. But then she knew too that one kiss would not be enough for her either, and if she didn't stop now, she never would.

She placed her hand on his chest and slowly pushed away from him.

"I'm sorry," he stumbled, "I didn't mean . . ."

"No, don't apologize. It's alright." She squeezed his hands and met his eyes with her own. She had never noticed his eyes were green before. Not a soft muted green, but a vibrant green, alive, like the forest.

"We really do have to talk, though, without Ethan here. Is that okay?"

Sam took a deep breath. "Yes, of course."

She walked to the gramophone, removing the record, letting the turntable spin out silently.

"I think you already know that I'm in the Watch."

"I do."

"Well, I have a new mission. I'm going to be gone a few days."

"Alright. Is it dangerous?"

"They're never exactly safe, Sam."

"Are you sure this is what you want to do, sure this is the way you want to handle things?"

"What do you mean?"

"Well, what's the Watch's end goal? They're fighting the government, but to what end? To replace it? An underground force only works if there's an above ground army fighting as well. So they're going to have to build an army, right?"

"What's your point?"

"Well, doing reconnaissance and sabotage missions are one thing, but have you ever fought in a war, Sophie? I'm not trying to antagonize you. I'm really asking. Have you?"

"Not exactly like you, no. But I have fought and I have killed when I had to." Griffyth's face flashed unbidden in her mind.

"Can I ask you another question? Do you know what you're fighting for?"

Sophie thought for a minute. She knew and yet she struggled to find the words. "I fight against anything that destroys individuality, the freedom to be ourselves, the one thing that separates us from the animals."

"Okay, that's a fine idea in the abstract, as you said earlier. But what are you fighting *for*?"

"Not what. Who. For Bridget." Her voice caught in her throat, holding back her tears. "For what she could have become if she'd been allowed to grow up. For the other children without parents. For the children we weren't allowed to be. For all the children and those yet to come. To restore the light in their eyes. To give them a chance to dream again. When you weigh it all in the balance, don't you think we've all been cheated out of our lives? That's all any of this is about for me. And that makes it very personal. *And tho' we are not now that strength which in old days moved earth and heaven, that which we are, we are; one equal temper of heroic hearts, made weak by time and fate, but strong in will to strive, to seek, to find, and not to yield.* My mother used to read me those lines. We are the only defenders left who will fight against the Corsairs, Sam, and we cannot yield. No matter what."

Sam looked down at the floor, the shadows of leaves playing with the last light of the evening. He stepped toward Sophie and again they stood facing each other in the middle of the room, and she felt as if they were floating in space, as disembodied as shadows. Sam didn't touch her but looked through the tears in her eyes and said, "Okay, then. I will help you."

* * * * *

Night draped herself over the valley with lengthened shadows and the sounds of the inhabitants of the woods calling their children home. In the fading light, Sophie found Ethan by the stream. She wanted to tell him herself that she would be leaving. They'd grown very close over the past months, and she didn't want to frighten him.

"You really like it out here, don't you?"

"Oh, Sophie. I'm sorry, I didn't realize how late it was. I'll come back."

"No, it's alright. I wanted to talk to you anyway."

"My mother used to take me on walks along a stream that ran beside our tent. I like to pretend this is the same one. I know it's not."

"You must miss her."

"Sometimes it's hard to remember her. I was just a little kid when they were captured."

"How did you get away?"

"My mother told me to run to the stream when she heard the soldiers coming. She said she'd seen a butterfly there, and I should go look for it. I actually found one, and I ran back to tell her, but the soldiers had them both and were dragging them away."

Sophie put her arm around the boy's shoulders. "Tell me about your mother, what you remember."

"It's just flashes of pictures really. And I know she used to sing to me, but I can't remember the songs. I try sometimes at night to hear her. It's just too far away. But you know that first night at your house? I'm kind of embarrassed . . . ."

"Why?"

"Well, I hugged you because you reminded me of her. She had red hair like you."

"You sweet boy." Sophie hugged him again, running her fingers through his hair. "Remind me to give you a haircut before I leave."

187

"You're leaving?"

"That's what I came to tell you. It's just for a few days."

"You're going on a mission for the Watch, aren't you?"

"Yes, I am."

"Take me with you, Sophie. I can help. I can do a lot of things."

"Oh, sweetie, I wish I could. But this one's super-secret. I'm not even bringing Pip. I need you to stay here and take care of him. Someone's got to bring him his apples. He'll be your responsibility while I'm gone. Sam can help you take him out for his ride at night. Okay?"

"I suppose so. I'd rather go with you."

"I know. And I'd rather have you with me. But we'll compare adventures when I get back. Now, let's head back up to the house before these mosquitoes have us for dinner!"

Sophie tried to laugh with him and make him think it was just a normal mission, but she knew the dangers of crossing the borders, and she had no idea what she'd find on the other side. Sam had given her a map he'd made of some of the areas in the Forbidden Grounds, so at least she wasn't going empty handed.

She thought about Ethan's mother, a woman who had brought this wonderful boy into the world. The woman fascinated her and seemed almost familiar from the way he had described her, but just as he had said—so far away.

* * * * *

The swing and chop of the axe felt good in Sam's hands. He'd always appreciated manual labor for its ability to still his mind and allow him to work out his frustrations physically. He had missed the lumber camp for that fact alone. Above the ringing of the metal through the wood, he heard Sophie's words and how they echoed Gemma's. In some ways, the two women were much alike and yet handled their similar thinking in different ways. Talking to Gemma earlier in the day had put his nerves on edge, angered him. But talking to Sophie about the same things only made him want to protect her. If he was being honest with himself, he wanted to protect them both. Even with the separation from Gemma, he hadn't lost his protective instinct with her, but had forced himself to ignore it.

Now both of these women were pushing them all forward toward a war, a war he wanted no part of. He knew he couldn't stop them from doing what they felt they had to do. Couldn't even stop Ethan. How could it be that all these people who had come through similar struggles and life experiences could come to face the world in such different ways? Gemma and Sophie's experiences spurred them on to fight harder, to fight until they won. His made him want to stay well away from violence of any kind.

Sweat dripped from his forehead, leaving dark spots on the circled stump before him. He stopped chopping for a few moments to take a breath.

Gemma and Sophie both wanted and expected him to fight with the Watch. But that wasn't where he felt the pull of his conscience, his only compass. The only thing he felt was his need to protect them both. Well, if they could spy and work reconnaissance, so could he. Standing out in the yard, he made his decision quickly. He would do his best to follow and protect them both. He'd stay out of the Watch so he could stay near them and keep them safe. Ethan's involvement would help him keep track of where they were, and they'd never have to know. At least this way, they'd all be doing what they thought was right and necessary. The code drove him, and the code he would honor.

* * * * *

The midsummer heat beat down on the heads of the citizens in the square of Jesse's Hollow. A thunderstorm was lurking, making the air heavy with unreleased moisture, dragging the latent human smells from the people around Sam and Ethan. Sam wished the Corsairs would get on with whatever they had to say. Why did the meetings have to be in the hottest part of the day, anyway?

Ethan was whispering something to him about Pip, but Sam was not paying attention. The heat distracted him as he looked listlessly around the square. It always struck him how few children there were in the towns. So many of them were living out on their own, parentless. He placed his hand on top of Ethan's sweating head. A boy stood in the front row, not much older than Ethan. He seemed to be struggling to stand still in the heat as well and looked longingly toward the shade of a tree.

Sam found himself almost feeling sorry for the soldiers in their thick uniforms. They stood on the platform in front of the crowd, a squad of red-faced, blue-clad boys, wanting the meeting to be over almost as much as he did.

"Sam, it's so hot. Can we go swimming after this?"

"Sure, son."

Finally, the leader took center stage. "Citizens of Jesse's Hollow, I am Colonel Mark Goodson. I bring you greetings from the Triumvirate. We know it is hot, so we will get right to business. It is well known that members of the rebel group known as the Watch have stolen a shipment of weapons and horses from a Corsair detail. A search for those stolen goods has already begun. And we will continue the search in homes, barns, and all buildings until they are found and the perpetrators brought to justice. Citizens would do well to cooperate with these searches and return the stolen items. Stay the course."

The crowd gave the expected echo.

"Item two, marauding rebels in the Forbidden Grounds outside the borders have made it necessary for the Triumvirate to take two added precautions. One is that there will be added patrols of Corsairs in the Forbidden Grounds to capture the rebels and protect our citizens from them. And two, rations must yet again be cut by one quarter as supplies and food have been stolen from the government camps."

A hushed murmur went through the crowd as they tried to think how they would survive on even less food than the meager portions they were already being given. But no one dared speak loudly enough to be pulled out of the crowd.

"Rest assured, citizens, that your leaders are aware of and have compassion for your struggles. To that end, to conserve the resources we have left, there will be no more permits given for couples wishing to have children until further notice. We must save our supplies for those citizens who are already living."

The crowd went silent at this, making it easier to hear the commotion which was beginning to erupt near the platform. A woman began to scream, holding onto a boy. The same boy Sam had noticed at the beginning of the meeting. A captain was dragging the boy up to the platform and seemed to be preparing him for a flogging. He removed the boy's tunic and tied him to the post at the edge of the platform.

When Sam registered what was happening, he and Ethan both made a move to get to the front of the crowd. Sam felt a strong hand take his arm in a vice grip from behind, stopping him mid-step.

"Don't," Kyle's voice whispered in his ear.

Sam spun around, trying unsuccessfully to wrench free of his grip. "Let go of me!" Sam hissed.

"Don't be an idiot, Sam," Kyle continued in a calm whisper. "Think about it! You won't be able to stop them, and you'll just get yourself killed in the process. You know I'm right, my friend."

Sam did pull away this time.

"Live to fight another day."

Sam looked down at Ethan, who was only waiting for his signal to jump into the fray. He knew and didn't want to know that Kyle was right. When he looked back up to the front of the crowd, there seemed to be a disagreement between Colonel Goodson and the captain who'd brought up the boy. He was close enough to the front now to hear the colonel reprimanding his subordinate.

"I thought I made myself clear, Captain, that there would be no floggings at my meetings, especially not of a child. How dare you disobey me?"

"But sir, General Drape has commanded . . ."

"You let me deal with General Drape. In the meantime, I am your immediate commanding officer, and you will follow *my* orders unquestioned. Now let this boy go and disperse the crowd."

The young captain hesitated.

"Immediately, Captain, or I will have you arrested."

"Yes, sir."

As the citizens of Jesse's Hollow began to go their way, Sam hesitated a moment, watching this strange colonel who appeared to have a drop of compassion running through his Corsair veins, and he was grateful.

"Anyone else want to question my orders?"

The other soldiers merely looked straight ahead, but one sergeant seemed to be holding in something he wanted to say.

"Sergeant, what about you?"

"I was just thinking that we gave them a heads-up that we'll be looking for the weapons. Won't they just hide them?"

"There is nowhere to hide. That is the point I want to get across to these people. Understood?"

"Understood, sir."

"Squad, dismissed. Mount up, gentlemen. I'll meet you back at the base."

"Mark!"

Colonel Goodson turned around to see Kyle standing before him. "It's good to see you, old friend. I was going to come find you before I left." He walked slowly toward Kyle and the two men held each other in a firm embrace.

"How's Simeon?" Kyle asked.

"The same as always. He asks about you. Wanted me to bring him news."

"Of course, of course."

"Look, is there somewhere we can go to talk? Not here. Some place we can be alone?"

"I know just the place."

12

RIPPLES

Soil, grass, and all the green things growing and taking over the gray house gave off an oppressive heat rising up to meet Kyle and Mark. They pushed through thick vegetation, breathing in the soggy air to reach the porch and hanging door. Kyle felt a wave of embarrassment rise up along his spine, over his shoulder, then his head as Mark waited patiently for him to scratch and pull and force the door open. Flecks of rust flew off the hinges to land on the creaking boards below, slats of mildewed dirt showing between them. Their presence seemed to draw groans of protest from the house with every move they made. Kyle had never brought anyone to this place, and it surprised him how much it changed everything and made him notice all of the many physical flaws of his favorite thinking place.

Musty air stirred by the hot breeze flowed in and around the walls inside the little house. It was almost overpowering to the point of distraction.

"Maybe we should just sit on the porch. Cooler there anyway," Kyle finally offered.

"Fine by me," Mark replied with a smile. He removed the black cap from his head, ruffling his dark-brown hair. Trying to find a measure of comfort, he took off his jacket as well as he settled down on the top step of the porch next to Kyle. He couldn't stop himself from looking at him. "I don't think I've been this hot since the day Simeon made us run a race on the hottest day of the year."

"And his idea of cheering us on was him screaming, 'The enemy doesn't care how hot it is!'"

"Then when we broke through the tape, we didn't stop running until we hit the creek."

They both laughed, breaking the awkward silence that had been hanging like the musty air of the aged house. Mark clapped Kyle on the back. Sighing with the waning laughter, Kyle hoped things hadn't really changed that much between them.

"It's been a long time," Kyle began.

"Too long. I'm sorry I couldn't get out here sooner. The Triumvirate was sending me all over creation making speeches and what-not. And before I knew it, six months had passed. But I've been transferred back to the Wash District. I'm close enough that I'll be able to get here more often."

"We all have our jobs to do, I suppose."

"Well, and I think the only reason Simeon let me come now is because he needed word from you and didn't trust anyone else."

"I can give you my report . . ."

"Not yet." Mark took Kyle's hand before he continued. He intertwined their fingers in the old familiar way. "God, I've missed you. I hate seeing you having to live like this. You should at least let me get you some decent food."

"I'm fine. Really. And it's not going to be forever." Kyle was struggling to communicate. All he could concentrate on was the way Mark's hand felt in his. He hadn't thought it would be this hard seeing Mark again. After months and years of keeping himself emotionally shut off from everyone around him, he found it hard to let his walls down, even with Mark. He hadn't seen him in six months, but they hadn't been together really in over a year. Why couldn't they just pick up where they left off?

"What's wrong?" Mark asked softly.

"What do you mean?"

"Don't give me that. You know I could always read you. Something's wrong."

"Sam came back. I knew he would eventually. I couldn't keep him at the lumber camp forever."

"Why did you arrange to send him away for so long?"

"For his own damn good, to keep him away from the Watch."

"Did it work?"

"Well, he's not a member, from what I've been able to gather, but he's making things more difficult than they need to be. When I saw him at first, I just wanted to run up and throw my arms around him after so long. But he hates me for having to join the Corsairs and now hates me for marrying Gemma."

"It's an impossible situation for all of you. He was like your brother. And Gemma was like your sister. You can't expect to be able to just go back to that easily."

"I don't expect us to go back at all. Any of us. It's been hard on Gemma especially, I think. I hate lying to her. I overheard them talking about me yesterday, and she was actually defending me. After what I've put her through. I wish there was another way sometimes."

"Listen, Kyle, I need to tell you something. I had hoped you'd guess it yourself. But I think we should start working together on something."

"Don't . . ."

"I'm the one who's been leaking information to the Watch."

"Don't. Don't tell me this, Mark. I can't hear this."

"Why not? It's perfect. No one suspects me. Not even Simeon. He tried to act like he knew who the leaker was, but he knows nothing. And with you here in one of their villages, we can do even more to help them."

Kyle was up on his feet in a second. His footsteps hitting the loose boards of the porch echoed around Mark. "Stop! Are you insane? Do you know what the Triumvirate will do to you if they find out?"

"I don't care. It's worth the risk."

"No, Mark. We just have to stay on mission. Trust the system and stay the course."

"Stay the course?! You sound just like Simeon. Like his little puppet. You were never that before. Listen, it does a ship no good to stay the course if it's heading for the rocks."

"The Corsairs are just trying to protect the people from the Watch. And that's all I'm trying to do."

"Do you really believe that?"

"Why wouldn't I?"

"You really have swallowed all of their rhetoric and propaganda. I thought you and I had the same idea—just play along until we could get out. It's not like we joined of our own free will. We were captured!" Mark now stood himself, taking the time to gather a deep breath with his thoughts. He couldn't believe the words he heard coming out of Kyle's mouth. Sweat dripped down his back and he shivered. He knew all too well the tactics the Triumvirate used to sway people to their way of thinking, and he couldn't bear thinking about Kyle having gone through their "reprogramming." It must have happened recently. He had been so sure that when Kyle agreed to the mission to go back to Gemma and the village that he'd done it to help his old friends. But now it seemed as if Simeon had finally broken him after all these years.

"Yes, we were captured at the time. It was necessary. But that doesn't mean the Corsairs are wrong or the Triumvirate is wrong."

"Doesn't it? It's not right, Kyle, and you know it. Would you stop pacing and look at me?"

Kyle stood before him like a soldier at ease, feet apart, hands behind his back.

"It's like when Simeon made you beat the shit out of that little guy. That's all we're still doing, just pounding the weak and helpless. Pounding and pounding away, and for what? To make us feel better about ourselves? I don't feel better about myself because I'm a Corsair. The floggings of innocent people, how is that helping them or protecting them? And it doesn't give us any more information out of them."

"We have to find the rebels. Some hard methods are sometimes necessary for the greater good."

Mark had him by the shoulders and was inches away from his face. "Listen to yourself, Kyle! Think back. I know you have sympathy for them. Or you did once. Hell, you were *one* of them before you were captured. And I'm not the one who let that woman escape from prison and earned himself a month of solitary confinement. Remind me who that was again? Oh yeah, that was you. I know you feel something for them."

"Not them, just her. She hadn't done anything. It wasn't her fault her husband was a rebel leader."

"None of them have done anything worthy of the punishments we're forced to inflict. They're just trying to hang on to a little bit of their humanity."

"No! It's their fault. If the rebels hadn't started these revolutions, we wouldn't have to live the way we do. They brought this on themselves. The Corsairs bring order. Everything else is chaos."

"What's wrong with a little chaos? The earth was created from chaos, wasn't it? And what do you think the Triumvirate, the rest of the Corsairs, and Simeon would think of us and what we're doing here? Order or chaos? Think about it, Kyle. Maybe if the rebels won, we wouldn't have to hide what we are anymore. Maybe we could live free too. Don't you want that? It's not the rebels that are keeping us apart. It's Simeon and the Triumvirate."

"Simeon is my father. He wouldn't do anything to hurt me."

"Adopted father. And I wouldn't bet on that. He'd turn against his family in a second if it served his purposes. He's already hurt you more than you know. You used to be able to see that. When did you change?"

"When I realized the rebels are responsible for everything, that they're the ones prolonging hostilities. The government wouldn't even need an army if it wasn't for the rebels."

"You mean when Simeon made you believe that." Mark took Kyle's hands in his own. He'd never felt so distant from him before, and it frightened him. He felt like he was caught in a current being pulled away from Kyle just as he was trying desperately to swim toward him.

"I know what Simeon did to you. I know how he singled you out for punishments over the years again and again. He was harder on you than he was on any of us. But try to remember. Remember the Corsairs and people like Simeon were responsible for your real parents' deaths. That's why you were fighting them in the first place."

"The rebel leaders were responsible. The Watch. They're the ones who took my parents away from me."

"Kyle, look at me. Eventually, there will be no one left to blame. Then what side will you be on? What do you believe in when there is no fight, no war?"

"How the hell should I know? I've never known a life without war, and neither have you." Kyle paused, measuring his next words. More than anyone, he needed Mark to be on his side, to see his true motives. "Try to understand what I'm trying to do here, Mark. I want to save others from being recruited by the Watch, from going through what my parents went through."

"I know you think you're doing what's right. You're a good man, Kyle. But how do you reconcile everything they've told you with how we feel about each other? They kill people like us! You know that. You've watched them drag men out of their beds and beat them to death. You've heard the speeches about purifying the human race. How does that fit in with what we have here? With us?"

"I don't know."

Mark hesitated before placing his hand on Kyle's cheek, red from the heat, sun, and anger. "You're more than just the product of the things that have happened to you. More than what the Corsairs tell you you can be. I see you. I see who you are. And that's who I love. But we have the chance to be a part of something bigger than the Corsairs, bigger than 'staying the course.' We have the chance to help these people change history, to *change* the course. You have to choose. I've chosen to help the rebels. Now, what are you going to do?"

* * * * *

In the fading sunset, dragonflies peppered the sky and lightning bugs lit the field, tiny candles among the twilight grass. The stars began to make themselves known, one by one. Gemma stood near the edge of the cornfield that bordered Zacharias's land. She watched each star wink its way into her sight, but while she was staring at one, the sky filled with millions more. She thought of how she and Sam used to try to count them before they fell asleep. How they tried to grasp something as vast as the sky and make it their own.

She looked down and noticed how loosely her tunic hung from her bone-thin frame. She would have to take it in again soon. She lifted it up a little, exposing her flat belly, almost concave, to the warm evening air. She was beginning to not recognize her own body. She placed her hand there, where a baby should be but would never be now. No more permits for child-bearing would be given, that's what the colonel had said. Going off the drugs and having an "accidental" pregnancy was too risky. She'd seen what had happened to undocumented children and their mothers. Wasn't Aishe's situation caution enough against breaking that particular law? But she understood the urge, the drive, the need to have a child of her own. She wondered again at a government that would expect its citizens to turn off their humanity. How was it even possible? The tears came unbidden to her eyes before she could think to hold them back. How she would have rushed to dry her child's tears.

There was still Daisy and the other children to be cared for, though they were still somewhat removed from her. She thought how unwise and impractical it was to love a child so much who was not her own. But the heart cannot always be dictated to, even hers.

The gravel crunched behind her as Zacharias approached. "I haven't seen you stargazing in a while."

"Not since Sam . . . We used to look up and try to imagine our place among them. But then I guess for a while it didn't seem like I had a place."

"And now?"

"Still not sure I do. Maybe that's what I'm looking for. You heard the message from the Triumvirate today. No more children. Kyle and I were waiting . . . I don't know what for. But now it's too late."

"What about those children you take care of?"

"How do you know about them?"

Z grinned to himself. "I know things."

"They don't have anyone to take care of them but me."

"So why not adopt them?"

"You know why."

"The Watch comes first."

"Well, I made my commitment to them first, I guess. I'm just trying to keep everyone as safe as possible."

"Gemma, I need to say something to you. Will you listen?"

"I guess."

"I've noticed you getting thinner and thinner these past months. Too thin."

"We're all on rations, Z. I'm fine."

"Don't give me that. Look at me, sweetheart."

Gemma found it hard to meet his penetrating gaze.

"Pretty soon I'll be able to see right through you. Have you been feeding those children out of your own rations? Tell me the truth, now."

"Maybe. Sometimes."

"Sometimes. All the time. Why, for Pete's sake, didn't you ask for help?"

"I feel like they're my own kids. My responsibility, my joy. Especially little Daisy."

"Well, it can't continue. You're killing yourself for them."

"But they're my kids. I can't abandon them. Did you and Jesse ever have children, Z?"

Zacharias paused before he spoke. He looked toward the waning pink in the sky as it gave way to blue, but not really seeing anything besides the faces of his children. "Jill and Max. I used to take them to the zoo. Not exactly the kindest thing we ever did to animals . . . putting them in cages to gawk at and appease our own curiosity. But Max and Jill loved the lions."

Gemma saw him enter the past, walking through a door of his mind he'd kept shut for some time.

"Did I ever tell you about the zoos?"

Gemma shook her head. He rarely talked about his past at all.

"Well, in big cities, they had these places with cages where they kept wild animals from all over the world for people to go and look at for entertainment. They would try to make these zoos look as much like the jungle as possible, to give the illusion that you were visiting these animals in their natural habitat. Then after the Disaster happened, it was clear the electricity was gone for good. We couldn't live in the same ways we were accustomed. The zookeepers had no means of taking care of the animals that were left—those which hadn't been killed by the storms or the bombings. So the keepers were ordered to put the animals down, to kill them as humanely as possible."

Gemma shuddered to think of the senseless killing.

"But I remember hearing stories of a few animals that escaped their cages before they could be euthanized. These lions, specifically. It's so interesting that animals born and raised in captivity never had any experience in the wild, but as soon as they were out of their cages, they reverted back to the ways of the wild—their instincts just took over. People thought they were tamed, that the cages would keep them as they wanted to see them. But nature goes deeper than that. Bars cannot change animal nature any more than government restrictions can change human nature. No bars or cages can make an animal less than what it is. The same is true for humans." Zacharias took a deep breath in and ran his hands over his face. His trip to the past had exhausted him.

"How much more can they take from us, Z?"

"I don't know. But in the meantime, I'm going to adopt those children myself and bring them here. And you're going to start eating again."

"I can't ask you to do that. It's too much for you."

"Oh, I'm going to expect your help. Besides, you're not asking. Now, the discussion's over. I assume you've been keeping them at the old cabin."

"Yes."

"Alright, I'll take care of it tomorrow."

"What if the Corsairs won't let you keep them for some reason?"

"We'll cross that bridge then. Now I'm going to have to leave you. An old man needs his rest if he's going to become a grandfather in the morning."

When Gemma looked back up at the sky on her way home, though she was surrounded in darkness, the stars lit her way.

* * * * *

On the moonless night, Sam stood in the ultra-black darkness under the oak tree that held the rope swing. The swing jumped and lurched in the wind. He caught the scent of herbs from Sophie's kitchen garden, and it made him hungry. Though he couldn't see the words on the page, he held *Great Expectations* in trembling hands and thought of the burial prayers he had scribbled in the front, the only remnants of past religions. After as many burials as he'd overseen, he had them memorized and stood mumbling them under his breath, almost afraid to raise his voice. *"The Lord is my shepherd; I shall not want. He maketh me to lie down in green pastures: He leadeth me beside the still waters . . . May all be free from sorrow and the causes of sorrow; may all never be separated from the sacred happiness which is sorrowless. From untruth lead us to Truth. From darkness lead us to Light."* These were the only prayers he knew, and he hoped and feared one of the gods might be listening. He never prayed for himself, but on this night, he prayed for Sophie.

Branches creaked and broke in the trees, shaken out of place by the forceful wind that spoke of storms to come. Startled by the sound, he instinctively reached for his gun, though he wasn't carrying it, and he probably wouldn't have fired it if he had been.

His prayers continued, and the wind continued to blow.

"What are you doing out here, Sam?"

He turned quickly to see Ethan standing behind him. "Well, you finally managed to sneak up on me. Well done, boy."

"Who were you talking to? I heard you whispering."

"Praying, really."

"Like to God? Like in the books?"

"Like that."

"Do you believe in God?"

"I'm not sure I know what 'God' is. I believe in the good that is in people, that feeling in your gut when you know what the right thing to do is. Maybe that's what God is, the demonstration of those things that are good and kind, those tender parts in us that make us vulnerable and human."

"But as a living thing, do you believe in God?"

"Listen, when I read this book in my hand, I become invested in those characters for a time. I'm emotionally wrapped up in them. I care about their hopes, dreams, desires. I want everything to turn out well for them. I believe it is the same as God watching our lives unfold. Maybe it's us who aren't real."

"But you were out here praying."

"It never hurts to take extra precautions."

"You're worried about Sophie's mission, aren't you? Why aren't we going with her?"

"If it's dangerous for one person to try to cross the Border, it's three times as dangerous for three people."

"So you're just going to let her go?"

"I'm pretty sure Sophie does what she wants and doesn't need me to let her do anything. But if you mean that I'm going to sit here and not do anything, that's not exactly true, either."

"What are we going to do to help?"

"I need you to saddle Pip and have him ready to ride before she goes. I'm going to try to make her mission just a little easier and a little safer, at least on this side of the Border."

Sophie's voice through the darkness gave Sam the same thrill it did every time he heard it. "Sam? Are you out here?"

"Yes, I'm here."

"What are y'all doing?"

"Just getting some fresh air. Run along now, son, and do like I said."

Ethan ran for the barn.

"Where's Ethan going?"

"He's just anxious to get started on his job of taking care of Pip for you."

"You know I'm only going to be gone a few days."

"I know. I'm not worried."

"Mm-hm." She took the book gently from his hand, knowing he wasn't reading in the book itself.

"Praying, Sam? Really?"

"Why not?"

"I used to pray for things too. A long time ago," she clarified. "Not things I would pray for now."

"Oh?"

"After I'd lost my parents, my adopted parents, and my sister, I prayed to die."

"Who did you pray to?"

"I don't know. Some idea of a god my parents left me. A father figure. A kind old man who wanted to please us, but not as much as he wanted to teach us a lesson. Anyway, I'd sit in the woods on cold nights, times when I couldn't find food, my stomach aching from the void, my ribs poking out from my translucent skin and clothes. I would just whisper the prayer over and over, 'I want to die. I want to die.' I didn't know where that would lead me, whether Heaven existed as a place to meet God or not. But I knew I wanted to be with my parents and Laurie, wherever they were. Even if I had to follow them to Hell. The funny thing is that by the time a crazy man came to deliver God's answer to my prayer, I had already changed my mind. I didn't want to die anymore, and the air he was strangling out of me was the one thing I wanted to hold onto more than anything else."

"Sometimes we don't know what we really want until there's the possibility of us not having it."

"Well, I definitely don't want to die anymore. I have things to live for now." Sophie paused. And when she spoke again, her voice was a whisper, almost inaudible among the heavy breeze. "It was you. You were there that night, weren't you? It was you in the woods who saved me."

She saw her answer in his downcast eyes.

"I'll always be there for you, Sophie."

"And I'll always come back to you." She took his hand in the darkness, and they were both glad there was no moonlight to reflect in their tears.

"You have the map I gave you?"

"I do, yes."

"I marked on there the guard station farthest away from the main roads.

They'll be the most relaxed. Might even be asleep." He tried to laugh. "It's better for you to take the long way to get there. Try to stay out of the lamplight."

"I know. I'll be alright, Sam. I can do this."

"I don't doubt it."

"See you in a few days, okay?"

"See ya."

The forced lightness in their voices hurt their throats.

As soon as Sophie was gone, Sam ran to the barn. Ethan had done his job well. Pip was saddled, and the saddlebag was packed with his pistol, water, and food. "Good job, boy. Just one more thing, and I'm off." Sam went to the back corner of the barn and pulled out two bottles of whiskey hidden under the hay.

"What's that?" Ethan asked.

"People used to drink this to make themselves feel good. I found them on the other side of the Border once upon a time. I'm going to use them with the guards."

"Be careful, Sam."

"I will, son. Now you run over to the O'Dell's until I get back."

"I can stay by myself."

"I'd rather not have to worry about you and Sophie at the same time. Alright?"

"Fine."

"Attaboy."

Taking the shortcut across fields, away from roads and the town, Sam knew Pip would easily get him to the guard station before Sophie. He didn't even have to push the horse to his fastest speed. The last leg of the ride did come to the road, and he threw stones at each lamp along it so he and Sophie could both approach the guard station in darkness.

He hadn't been wrong when he said the guards would be more relaxed here. Few people ever approached this guard station. Even still, bribery had long since been out of the question as a tactic. He slowed Pip to a walk a quarter of a mile away from the station and tied him in the thick trees that lined the path. He'd learned long ago how to approach someone undetected, and on this night the heavy wind was his friend. He looked through the trees. Two guards. One would leave every few minutes to patrol the perimeter, then back to the guardhouse. While one guard was out of the guardhouse, Sam silently locked his arm around the neck of the other guard, held just tight enough and long enough to knock him out. He positioned the guard in a sitting position against the wall, poured some whiskey down the front of him, and placed the half-empty bottle in his hand. He hid behind the guard shack and waited for the other guard to give him the same fate. They'd be reprimanded sharply by their superiors, maybe even transferred. But no one had to die tonight.

* * * * *

As the sun started to peek over the trees behind her, Sophie made her way into what had once been a city. She was still considering the luck that had gotten the two guards drunk on the very night of her mission. She had read about people being drunk in books but had never witnessed it. And seeing their incapacitated state, she wondered why people would have ever done that to themselves willingly.

She hadn't been outside the borders in over a decade, and even then had mostly stayed out of the destroyed cities. But Sam had marked the places on the map where there were most likely to be people, so that was where she went. Great mounds of concrete and metal rose up like megaliths grown from the earth. In some places it looked like stone had rained down over the city, and in others, as if a giant had merely blown down buildings like toys. The creak of metal scraping metal sent a shiver down her spine as she picked her way through the rubble. She'd been walking for hours and had not seen or heard another living soul. Even the wildlife had vacated this part of the world. But not the vegetation. Trees sprang up where once there were rooms. Automobiles were encased in kudzu. Cradled in mist, the morning air held a green smell mixed with sulfur.

Sophie lost her footing on some bricks and decided to stop and rest for a few minutes. This was as good a place for breakfast as any. She planted herself behind a wall with jagged edges along the top, pink bricks hiding behind the gray. Propping her rifle up to the wall, she pulled the boiled egg and bread from her bag. She began to wonder if this mission was a foolish idea.

Carried along the breeze, the first hesitant notes of a haunting song met

Sophie's ears. She couldn't quite make out any words at first, just a note here and a note there. Was it human, she wondered. She'd heard of places being haunted, and this was just that sort of place. The voice grew a bit louder. A woman singing something about smiling. Odd choice of words in this desolation.

"Hands above your head!" a boy's changing voice squeaked from behind her. She held her bread and half-eaten egg above her head. "Jimmy, get her gun!"

"Hang on, now. I'm not going to hurt anyone. Can I turn around?"

"Slowly!" Every word out of his mouth was a shouted command. He was overcompensating. When Sophie looked in his eyes, she saw how scared he was. The two boys were barefoot and wore clothes that looked like a patchwork quilt. Their hair was short but messy; smudges of dirt went from head to toe.

"Steady on, Ted. I've got her gun. Calm down." Jimmy was smaller than Ted. Sophie thought they might be brothers.

"Do you have any other weapons?" Ted shouted again.

"No, just the gun. Can I put my hands down now?"

"Alright, but slow. And keep your hands where I can see them."

"Very well."

"We've got to bring her to Gran."

"I know that, Jimmy. I'm not an idiot. Come on, you. Come with us."

"Can I bring my bag?"

"Give it to Ted."

The two boys led her across several mounds of rubble to the one building left standing fairly intact. The sign over the door was partially broken, but she could make out the word "school."

"Gran!" the boy Ted called. "We found a trespasser."

They led Sophie down a long hallway with pockets of light coming in from the rooms along the hall. At the end, they entered an office. An elderly woman, long white hair around her shoulders, sat in a chair with exploding cotton stuffing. Through a gaping hole in the roof, one bright ray of light lit up her white hair and piercing blue eyes. She was older and thinner than Mrs. O'Dell, Sophie's only point of reference for an elderly woman.

"Come in, come in, boys. What have you got there?"

"We found her down the block hiding in the old diner," Jimmy offered.

"I found her," Ted insisted. "She's got a Corsair rifle. One of the new ones with the silencer."

"Interesting. Alright, come get your breakfast."

The boys pounced on two open cans on the desk before her.

"Steady on, now, mates. That's got to last you 'til tonight. Don't bolt it. I think we've got a fair day's work ahead of us."

The woman walked around the desk to face Sophie. She too wore clothes of mix-matched fabrics sewn together in no particular pattern. Sophie noticed she had a strange accent she'd never heard before and wondered where this woman came from. She didn't look particularly menacing, but Sophie wasn't sure she felt quite safe here, either.

"So the boys caught you trespassing, eh? Who are you, then? You don't look like a Corsair."

"I'm not."

"Where'd you get the gun?"

"I stole it. In a manner of speaking."

"What does that mean?" The old woman was looking Sophie up and down. She walked carefully around her in shoes held together with bits of twine and fabric.

"I'm not sure I should tell you. I don't even know who you are. How do I know you're not a spy for the Corsairs?"

"Fair point. Fair point. You'd recognize a prison brand, wouldn't you?"

Sophie nodded her head as the woman raised her sleeve, exposing her inner left wrist where there was a tattooed number on her crepe skin.

"Okay, so you're not a spy." Sophie saw where the boys had set down her gun. She could get to it in a second if she needed to. This wasn't exactly the securest facility. She decided to take a chance. "I'm here looking for help. There's a resistance force forming against the Corsairs, and we need more people. Are there others here? By the way, my name is . . ."

"No, no, love. Nobody has names in this part of the world. Identity is dangerous. It's how they find you. Some folks call me Gran, but even that I don't always answer to. You never know when a soldier is undercover, trying to trap you."

"Wouldn't they just figure out where you live?"

"Not if you're always moving. Sometimes a school, sometimes a hospital. But you've got to be careful."

"Of what?"

"The patrols. Nothing is what it seems. Everything could be a trap by Corsairs, especially near food and water sources."

Sophie's eyes softened as she thought of her own days of dodging patrols in the Forbidden Grounds in what seemed like a lifetime ago.

"They burned all the houses years ago," Gran continued. "Every time a patrol comes through, they burn something else. The Fire Brigade. The Torch Brothers. Match Boxers. Flame Throwers. They have different names, too. You were asking about others. There used to be more people hanging about. But I reckon there aren't many of us left anymore. These little fellas didn't have anyone to look after them, so I let them follow me around. So where do you come from, love? You don't look like you've been living out in the open long."

"I live on the other side of the Border."

"You mean you came from over the wall?!" The old woman seemed excited and frightened at the same time. Her entire body seemed to resonate with emotion as if someone had plucked a string on an instrument.

"Wall? No, the other side of the barbed wire fence. What wall are you talking about?"

"The bloody great concrete wall that runs the length of the country, I expect. No doors. Too high to scale. But somehow the soldiers come across it. Never been able to catch them at it, though. I stopped trying to get over it years ago."

"Where is it?"

"Twenty miles or so west of here."

"So you mean there's a second Border?"

"And we're smack in the middle like a refugee sandwich."

"My God, we had no idea. So you're saying there could be other people on the other side of the wall?"

"There must be. Someone built the wall. And the fence you're talking about, it completely surrounds you?"

"Only on three sides. Like the letter 'C.' The fourth side is the ocean."

Gran's eyes lit up again with excitement and then with unshed tears. "You've seen the ocean? It's still there?"

"Right behind my house."

The old woman turned slightly away from Sophie and seemed to be talking to herself. "It's been so long since I've seen the ocean, I'd begun to think I had dreamed it." She paused, taking a deep breath and wiping roughly at her eyes before turning back to Sophie. "So, what's within the fence? Why is it there?"

"Four or five towns, I think. I've never seen all of them. Only heard of them. And I don't know why the Border is there. The Corsairs told us it was for our protection, but we never really believed that."

"Towns. And people live in houses, not out in the open?"

"Yes. Once the borders went up, we all migrated to what houses we could find in the area. Houses left behind by who knows what people or why. How did you get here?"

"I used to be married to a soldier in the Watch. Not like these blue-coated soldiers now, the cowards that patrol, rounding up innocents and murdering them. I was captured in the First Revolution. When I escaped, I tried to head back to where I'd last seen my husband and our group. But the borders had already gone up, and I couldn't find him or our children anywhere."

"You must have been in prison for a long time."

"Years," Gran whispered.

"How did you get out?"

"They used to bring in young Corsair cadets to watch the prisoners. Thought it would harden them. Mostly, it did." She looked out the window toward the rising sun as she told her story. "But this one little fella with strawberry-blond hair, he used to stand outside my cell, back to the bars, standing at attention and just talk to me. He'd been captured and forced into the army like most of them. But he seemed kinder than the rest. One day when no one was looking, he just opened the door and let me out. Didn't say a word, but just stood there with the door open. Probably gotten himself shot by now."

Sophie stepped closer to the old woman and put her hand on her shoulder.

"Anyway, when I got out, everything I'd fought for was gone, and everything I'd fought against was roaming free. All I could do was hide. Hide and survive. But what is that . . . survival?"

"I know what it is to be a survivor, the one who escaped, the one left behind. I know how it feels to be eaten away with senseless guilt that you're the one still alive. It makes me want make up for those who should be here and aren't, to do what they would have done if they had been left behind."

Gran's freckled and wrinkled face shone with understanding and more. She seemed grateful to be talking to another woman.

"Look, why don't you come back with me?" Sophie offered. "At least it's somewhat safer where I live than it is for you here."

"No, not yet. Who knows what events that would set in motion?"

"What do you mean?"

"Come over here." The elder woman reached out the broken window to grasp a few pieces of rock and brick. She tossed one of them into a bucket of water that stood below the window. "See those ripples? The rock has no say in where those ripples end up or what they touch. Every move we make, every choice is a rock in the pond." She took several more rocks and threw them at once into the bucket, ripples intersecting everywhere in indiscernible places. "Something as major as jumping the Border fence? Well, that's a damn boulder in the pond. For now, for your safety and mine, I'll stay where I am."

"How can I find you again?"

Gran smiled with a hint of mischievousness. "Who says you will?"

Sophie stayed for a short time with the little band, eating their breakfast together and talking about their different worlds before she decided to head back. Her meeting with Gran had given her enough information to know she would only find a few stragglers here among the Forbidden Grounds. Who knew what was on the other side of the wall? Another society? More Corsair troops? She knew one thing for certain, one person would not be able to make it over the wall alone. This was a job for a larger group.

After Sophie left, Jimmy, Ted, and Gran discussed their most exciting discovery in months. "Did she look familiar to you, Ted?" Jimmy asked.

"Yeah, like that crazy girl we called Red."

"Whatever happened to her?" Gran asked the boys.

"Last time we saw her," Jimmy answered, "she was running for the fence. Probably a Corsair shot her." He spoke not unkindly, but with the same detachment he'd speak of a squirrel or a rabbit, creatures just as doomed by their inevitable fates.

13

LINE OF SYMMETRY

*E*mbers of the charred house still smoke days after the fire has gone out. Kyle sits under a tree blackened by the blaze, his ash-colored face and clothes blending with his surroundings. His knees are drawn up, his hands numb from gripping the rifle so tightly. How long has it been since he moved from this spot? He hears movement near him, pulls the rifle closer to his chest, and stares at the embers. He sees feet, then legs, a face before him. He's aiming the gun, cocking it, ready to fire.

"Whoa! Hold on there. I'm not going to hurt you, buddy. Look, I'm putting my gun on the ground. Can you do the same? Go on now, put the gun down. I swear I'm not going to hurt you."

Kyle doesn't speak but lowers his gun.

"What's your name? I'm Sam."

Silence.

"Is this your house? Where are your parents?"

Kyle's eyes move back to the embers.

"Okay, well, why don't you come with me? You can't stay here. The soldiers will be back soon. I heard a squad of them not a mile away from here."

Kyle can't move.

"Come on, now. I'll help you, buddy. Let's do it together." Sam pulls gently but with unexpected strength to get Kyle to his feet. They walk through the forest with Sam holding Kyle's arm around his shoulders, guiding him to his camp. For at least a week Kyle is nameless to Sam, but Sam stays with him, teaching him slowly the things he'll need to survive in the woods. Sam becomes the constant in Kyle's life, filling the hole

where something called parents used to be, only blank faces now.

* * * * *

"I'm leaving for the Senate, Gemma. I'll be back in a few days."

Gemma reached around her husband's neck, planting a long kiss on his lips that took his breath away. "I wish you didn't have to go. Besides, there doesn't seem much point anymore."

He quickly picked up his bag. He wanted to get on the road before the heat took over the day. "We just keep doing what we can do. Stay the course, as they say."

"Please don't say those words to me."

He tired of her never-ending fight against the Corsairs. "Alright, alright. See ya in a few days."

"Be careful."

"Yeah, I will."

Kyle kicked at the rocks along the road. It would take him all day to reach the Wash District, and he dreaded the emptiness of it. Near the far Northern Border there was an old courthouse next to the Corsair base. That courthouse was home to the new Senate, being the only official government building nearest the old nation's capital. On the road just north of the courthouse, half of an ancient road sign swung and creaked in strong breezes. The sign used to point the way to Washington, D.C. in the time of Before. Washington, D.C., had long been underwater, and the letters that were left on the sign only read *Wash District*. So the area where the Senate met and where the Corsairs had their base was christened the Wash District.

As the humid heat came in waves over him, pushing up from the ground and down from the sun, Kyle felt trapped by it—trapped by everything. His commitment to the Corsairs and the mission that had brought him back within the borders. His loyalty to Gemma and Sam, wanting to protect them from the Watch. His love and history with Mark. How could all of these things that were a part of him be so conflicting? Order. Routine. Consistency. These were the things he needed and craved more than anything. He liked to imagine life as a woven tapestry, when in reality it was more like the tangled, unruly, and unrelenting vines of kudzu that took over everything. He needed to talk to someone, needed the old friendship with Sam the way it used to be, but hated the need at the same time. Kyle's drive for order and control pushed him to be the best, but that had always meant being better than Sam or it meant nothing at all. And where Sam had developed into a survivor, Kyle had become a soldier even before the Corsairs had found him.

Time was when he could talk his problems over with Mark, as well, when Mark was the only person who understood him. For years, Kyle had felt like he was the only man in the world who was attracted to other men. Thought there was something wrong with himself, even. But then he met Mark. Mark, who showed him he was not alone and there were others like him. Of course they'd had to lie and hide because of the laws against extramarital relations and Corsair rules against fraternization. But those were only logistical problems to Mark. He had convinced Kyle that all they had to do was be careful and bide their time until they could get out of the army and find a place where they could be together without hiding. Some place on the other side of the wall where survival and beating the enemy weren't the only goals. A house, a family, a life beyond the army, beyond the fighting. It had seemed perfect, a dream to look forward to. It had only been a matter of time.

But time was their enemy. Time kept them away from each other when they were assigned missions in separate places. Time made things awkward after long absences, worked on Kyle's memory, and gave root to guilt instilled by Simeon. Simeon often wrote to his adopted son when he was away on missions and reminded him of all that was expected of a general's son. The letters reminded him he was held to a higher standard of obedience, purity, and loyalty. Time was a river, with Mark on one side and Kyle on the other, and the longer and farther it flowed, the wider the river became. When Kyle allowed himself to think about it, he realized he'd wasted half his life waiting for it to begin.

Mark had looked wonderful in his uniform, and Kyle had been overcome with nostalgia and memories when he'd seen him again. But now Mark wanted something else from him. It wasn't enough anymore that they bide their time. It wasn't enough that they eke out chances to be together. Now Mark wanted Kyle to give up his other loyalties to join a fight he didn't believe in. How could Mark expect him to turn against the man who had saved him from starvation and death in the woods? Why couldn't Mark see that he was helping the wrong side?

But was it the wrong side? Kyle cared about Gemma and respected so many things about her. Yet she agreed with the Watch, too. And even though Sam was no longer a fighter, he'd always been against the Corsairs. What if they were all right and he was wrong? Was he willing to stake his happiness and dream of the future with Mark against it?

Kyle breathed heavily as he walked the path. He was grateful for the trees as shade against the oppressive sun. His fair and freckled skin burned easily. If it didn't, he would have removed his shirt, already soaked with sweat. Another half hour and he'd be in the Wash District. He'd been walking all day and felt it. A rider approaching on horseback from up the road annoyed him simply because he was riding while Kyle was forced to walk. He didn't ride quickly, just trotted at a leisurely pace.

Simeon's gaunt face looked strangely cool in the summer heat, tanned above his uniform. "Thought I'd ride out to meet you, son. How'd you like a ride into the District?"

Kyle squinted against the glaring light as he looked up. "I'd like it fine, Father, but I'm not sure it would help the mission if I were seen riding in with you."

"I wasn't being serious. But climb up. We need to talk before you go to the Senate."

* * * * *

Zacharias and Gemma made their way to the cabin early in the day. Even still, the sun beat down through his white hair, burning his head. He should have worn a hat.

"You know, I haven't seen this place since I found you and Sam here all those years ago." But it had been longer since he'd seen it before that. Not since he'd brought Jesse here to escape the city and the drones.

The birds called to each other from their nests, and a squirrel was fussing at them for passing too close to his tree. He remembered Jesse never liked the cabin but made do. She always made things work. Zacharias started to wonder if this was a mistake. Maybe he should have let Gemma bring the children to him. Why had he asked to come with her to the cabin?

"The kids have really done a great job with it. They've made it their own," Gemma replied.

214

Large dandelions populated the grass along the path leading to the cabin. Aged and browned with time since sprouting in the spring, the wishes still remained. As they made their way closer to the cabin, Gemma asked, "Did you ever feel an overwhelming sense of responsibility for me and Sam, and now with these kids?"

"In what way?"

"You know, it's more than just making sure they have food, clothes, shelter . . . it's up to us to teach them things. And how do I know I'm teaching them the right things?"

"I'm not sure you can ever really know. You try to teach them what you've learned, what's been important to you, or what you wish you'd known. But you can't know what kind of job you've done until they're grown."

The two walked into the cabin, their eyes adjusting as they left the glaring sunlight. The glass doors at the back had broken years ago and been replaced with uneven boards. The back of the cabin where the bedrooms used to be had collapsed when a bomb went off too close, leaving the building as just one great room and one falling-down bedroom.

The children were all sitting in their individual corners they'd made into their sleeping quarters.

"Who's this?" Daisy asked with friendly curiosity.

Gemma responded, "Come here, sweetie."

Daisy climbed in her lap in the rocking chair. The twins stayed huddled in their corner. Toby watched suspiciously. They didn't like new people.

"This is Zacharias. We call him Z, and he's my adopted father."

"Hello, Z." Daisy peered over Gemma's shoulder.

"Hi there, young lady."

"How would you kids like to come live in a real house near town and closer to me?" Gemma asked.

Daisy responded with a smile and a hug. The other children continued to stare. "Can we live in your house, Gemma?" Daisy asked.

"No, sweetheart. Not yet. But I'll be really close, and we can see each other every day. Z is going to adopt you so you can get ID cards. That way, we'll be able to get you all the clothes and food you need. Does that sound like a plan?"

"Sure!" Daisy spoke for everyone. "When can we go?"

"How about right now? Let's get everything packed up."

As they began to gather the children's things, Z tried to stay in the moment, tried not to let his mind wander to the past. But everywhere he looked, he was reminded of Jesse. He went to the rocking chair so he could close his eyes for a few minutes.

"Z, are you alright?" Gemma asked.

"I'm fine, honey. Just a little tired."

"We'll be finished in just a few minutes. Then we can get you back to the house. Are you sure you're okay with all this?"

"Yes, of course."

"Gemma, we can't forget the books," Daisy reminded.

Gemma walked to the side of the fireplace where she had placed all of the books she'd brought for Daisy for safe hiding.

"Here, I'll take those," Zacharias offered. "What's this?" He picked up the book from the top of the pile. *Peter Pan.*

"That's my favorite book," Daisy answered cheerfully. "I found it here."

He ran his fingers gently over the brownish cover. Peter Pan's face was fading, and the second star to the right no longer twinkled. This had been his children's book. They'd brought it with them the night they fled the city. Even now, he could hear Jesse's voice reading to their children. A tear found its way to his tired eyes.

* * * * *

Sophie had been gone two days. Sam knew he should have been working out in the field, but he sat in the house instead. Sitting by the window, he watched the dust float through rays of light in the air before him. He wondered if he had done enough to help Sophie on her mission. He should have insisted he go with her, even though he knew it wasn't possible.

He picked up one of the toys he was carving for Ethan, turned it over in his hands, contemplated finishing the job, then put it back down. He thought about going fishing, but what if Sophie returned while he was gone? It was killing him to just wait.

The back door fell open, startling him out of his chair.

"Sophie!"

His eyes quickly took in the situation. She was breathing heavily. She'd been running. Her tunic was torn, and her left arm was bleeding. He rushed to close the door behind her, checking to see if she had been followed. Then he sat her down gently at the table before going to the cupboard for bandages and alcohol.

"You've been shot," he finally said, tearing the bandages in long strips. Despite her injury, a wave of gratitude came over him seeing her sitting and breathing before him.

"Just a graze. I don't think they were really aiming to kill me. Just shooting around me."

"What happened?"

"Can I get a glass of water first?"

Sam busied his hands, getting her the water, washing her face with a cold cloth. He sat in a chair facing her, looking at her as if he were seeing her for the first time.

She took several minutes to still her breathing, adjusting to being in her own home.

"You're safe now," Sam said finally.

"I had to double back a few times, but I think I lost them. I got past the Border fine the first day. Coming back was a different story. I didn't dare go for a guard station. So I cut the fence with the wire cutters I'd brought. But the Corsairs heard, and a couple of them came after me. I guess I was just faster." She tried to laugh it off, choosing not to think of what could have happened if she hadn't gotten away.

Sam rolled up her sleeve, gently wiping the blood away with another wet cloth. He took the bottle of alcohol, pouring some over the wound, letting it trickle into the cloth in his hand. Sophie inhaled sharply.

"Sorry," he whispered.

"It's fine," she said through clenched teeth.

As he tied the bandage into a tight knot over the wound, he hesitated to speak again. He didn't know why he felt as if he'd lost the bottom of his stomach. "This might leave a scar."

"Probably."

"It doesn't look like it's your first one." His fingers gently traveled on their own to touch another scar on the side of her throat.

"I'm sure we both have our scars." She leaned forward, her breath cool on his neck. They sat holding each other for a few minutes, her head resting easily against his shoulder.

"I can bring up some water so you can take a cool bath if you want."

"That would be heaven. Thanks."

When her bath was done, Sophie lit the candles in her bedroom and stood in her robe for a few minutes, looking out the window. The sun was setting over the fields below. The cornstalks reached and stretched, brushing against the leaves of an overhanging mulberry tree. Everything seemed to slow down here. She was able to wash away the hurry and danger of the days she'd just lived through. A blue jay landed in the maple tree just outside her window, calling imploringly for its mate. The leaves on the branch threw shadows and patterns against her.

"Sophie, I thought you might need your bag. Oh, sorry." Sam stopped in the doorway, embarrassment showing in red patches on his face. "I'll just leave it here." He turned immediately to go.

"No, wait, Sam. Can you come here?"

Turning back around, he saw her red hair still wet and pinned up. Her robe was closed, but loose. Her freckled skin shone in the flickering candlelight with the damp of having just been washed. And he thought he'd never seen anything so beautiful before.

"Where's Ethan?" she asked.

"Z adopted those kids from the cabin. So I let him go and spend the night with his friends. In fact, I thought about maybe going over there myself. I just wanted to make sure to be here when you got back. But, you know, there's probably a lot that Z needs help with over there." He spoke rapidly, not allowing for a second of silence between words or sentences.

"Or you could stay here." There was something so innocent about the invitation. Sophie stood before him as they breathed the same air.

Sam's mind felt hot and muddled. How did she always smell like lavender?

"Sophie, you know I want to as much as you do. But it's against the law. It's dangerous. What if someone found out?"

"No law that I recognize. Besides, who would find out? Can't we try to forget ridiculous laws for now? I mean, where is the line? If a law is evil, what moral obligation do we have to follow it? The law to turn in our neighbors suspected of rebellious behavior could turn into a law that says we have to shoot our neighbors in the back. The law against intimate relationships without marriage or against having a child without a government permit—what right do they have to tell people how or when to love, anyway?"

She took his hands in her own. "You're trembling," she whispered against his ear.

"We just have so much to lose," he whispered, so quietly Sophie wasn't sure she had heard him.

"I know everyone you've loved and lost has taken a piece out of you. Won't you let me try to give something back? I want us to have this moment and know that no matter what, we can always come back to it, wherever we are."

"Is a moment enough for you?"

"Maybe not. Maybe I want more than a moment with you." Sophie no longer sought control over her circumstances, but connection. Not just any connection, but connection with Sam. And just being close to him was not enough. She kissed him slowly, fully, hungrily, as if his lips here the bridge to his soul, and the kiss her transportation. She led him to the bed and removed his shirt. He too had scars she noticed from fights long past. Tracing the line of symmetry that ran the length of Sam's whole body, she ran her thumb softly down his furrowed brow, his nose, the almost imperceptible cleft in his chin, his Adam's apple, the hollowed line down the center of his chest and stomach. When she reached the waistband of his pants, she stopped and looked at him once again, his living green eyes, pools of wonder looking back at her.

Sophie thought of the last time a man's hands had been on her body, and it was not a pleasant memory. She tried to clear her mind because she knew Sam would be different. She knew him to be kind and gentle. And she knew that when her eyes met his, she could at least try to not be afraid. She felt him on her and around her, felt his hot breath in her mouth. And though she tried to stay in the moment, tried to tell herself she was safe with him, she felt her mind move down and away from her into a dark cave where she had no control, where all she could do was lie still and wait for it to be over. The room was spinning, down was up. She looked at the ceiling and stayed there, counting the planks of wood, noting the lines and crevices, well removed, while what was happening in the bed continued without her.

All of Sam's senses were mixed up and screaming. In the wide vibrating air, the world entered the room with them. The ocean roared in his ears as their bodies intertwined. He tasted purple, smelled blue, and felt as though he were falling. He tried to slow down and experience every tiny piece of her, every gesture, every freckle. But when he looked at her face, there were tears in her eyes, and she was looking at the ceiling. He knew she had been hurt by others before, and now he knew how she'd been hurt. He held himself very still, looking into her face and waiting for her to return to him in her own time. "Sophie, come back to me. You're safe now." He saw her eyes, but she seemed to be looking through him, not at him. "I would never hurt you. But we don't have to do anything tonight if you don't want to. If you're not ready."

He lay down next to her, slowly putting his head on her chest. He felt the blood moving in her and through her. This thumping against his ear was the mechanism giving life to them both. Without the thump, thump, thump of the heart beneath his head, his heart would stop as well.

A few minutes passed, and Sophie came back to herself. She was somewhat embarrassed to have had one of her episodes with Sam. She still wanted to be with him, and knew she had to take this chance to put the past behind her and create new memories. She needed to try again. Turning over, she lay on top of him. "I'm alright now."

"Are you sure? Where'd you go?"

"Let's not talk about it. Just be patient with me, alright?" She kissed him, caressing his top lip with hers. For the rest of the night, they each loved as they had never loved before. In memory and tears as she felt the most lost, she knew lying here next to Sam she had been found. The warmth of his love melted her defenses. The candlelight and their love forgave them of all imperfections.

* * * * *

In a meadow beyond the Wash District, a stream ran into a large pond. As it tripped and made its way into the pond, its current ran and rippled toward its final destination where the larger body engulfed the smaller, all signs of current or resistance lost in the greater waters. Simeon brought Kyle to this familiar spot, the place where they'd first been acquainted after Kyle was drafted into the Corsairs. Simeon felt Kyle behind him on the horse, shivering despite the heat.

"Get down," he commanded.

Kyle made his way to the stream, automatically standing at attention when he reached the edge. His eyes looked straight ahead, focusing on nothing. Simeon approached behind him and commanded him to look down at his feet. There, a large anthill came up out of the grass, and all around it, tiny ants scurried to their collective jobs.

"Look at them," he began. "Every ant crawling on the ground is convinced he will be the one ant who will live forever, so he works like his future immortality depends on it. But every ant is wrong." He lifted the toe of his boot, bringing it down on several ants, twisting and working their miniscule bodies into the ground. "Humans are no different. We can't conceive of anything past our own consciousness, so we assume we will go on in some way or another. This knowledge makes most people's actions very predictable."

Kyle saw the whip out of the corner of his eye, then felt it tap him lightly on the shoulder.

"Stay the course," Simeon said.

"Stay the course," Kyle echoed.

Simeon watched Kyle's muscles ripple and stiffen the longer they stood next to the stream. He held the whip just within Kyle's line of sight. As with a broken horse, all Kyle had to do was see the whip for it to have the desired effect. As Simeon continued to speak to his adopted son, he would tap him occasionally on the shoulder with the whip.

"You remember the Box, don't you?"

Tap.

"Yes, sir."

"A most effective teaching tool, don't you agree?"

Tap.

"Yes, sir."

"How long were you in there?"

Tap.

"A month, sir." Kyle's eyes were straight ahead again, no longer seeing the ants, the stream, or the trees in the distance. All he could see were the darkened, scratched cement walls of his month-long solitary confinement. All he could feel was his body baking in the oven they called the Box.

"And what did you learn?"

Tap.

"The Corsairs bring order, everything else is chaos."

"The Corsairs bring order, everything else is chaos," Simeon repeated. "Correct. And who gives you your orders?"

Tap.

"You, sir. For the Triumvirate."

"For the Triumvirate."

Tap.

Just as easy as breaking a horse, Simeon thought. So predictable.

* * * * *

The next morning, Sam rose early. He was glad to be awake first—it gave him the chance to bring Sophie breakfast in bed. She was awake when he returned to the bedroom with eggs, toast, and hot coffee on a tray. A red camelia from the bush outside the front door lay next to the plate.

"Good morning," Sophie grinned. For the first time in as long as she could remember, she didn't dread waking up, but was happy to see the sunrise.

"Good morning."

"I'm starving," she said. "We didn't exactly have dinner last night."

"Not exactly." He sat on the bed next to her. "You want to talk about what happened?"

"Not really."

"Sophie, you can trust me. I understand, really."

Sophie picked at the food on the tray, not meeting Sam's eyes.

"Were you . . . did someone hurt you?"

"Sam, what do you think happened to girls and women out there in the woods when we encountered strangers? What do you think that man was after the day you saved me? Do you think everyone followed the code like you did?"

"You can tell me."

Sophie took his hand and spoke quietly, "What's the point? It's over and done. Now I'm with you, and all of that fades into the background like a bad dream."

Sam thought of his own nightmares that plagued him and knew she was right.

"Now, we need to talk about my mission," she continued, barely skipping a beat.

"What did you find out there?"

"A few people living in the Forbidden Grounds, but more importantly, they told me about a second Border wall twenty miles west. Did you ever see it?"

"No, I stayed pretty close to our Border, except when I went south to the work camps."

"There was this old woman. Never told me her name. She's the one who told me about the wall. I don't think she was born in this country."

"Why do you think so?"

"She spoke English, but she had a strange accent. She was a little strange herself, honestly. But I can only imagine what living out there would do to a person."

"What kind of accent?"

"I don't know. I never heard it before. And she was singing this song about smiling."

Sam sat up straighter, intrigued now. "Do you remember how it went?"

"I don't know. She was kind of far away when I heard her singing it. I don't really remember."

"Did it go like this: *Keep smiling through the day, keep smiling through the night. The shadows fly away when they can see your light* . . . ?"

"Yes, I think that was it! How could you possibly know that song?"

"Z used to sing it to me and Gemma. Weird that this woman would be singing that, of all songs. Z always said it was an old song when he was a boy. Not really a popular song that everyone would know. Strange. So where is she now?"

"She wouldn't come back with me. I hated to leave her out there, but she refused to come with me. What could I do?"

"Well, it's not like you could have forced her."

"Oh, Sam, as hard as we've had it here, it's so much worse out there. You've seen what it's like. Can you imagine living out there for more than a few days, constantly looking over your shoulder?"

"It's how we grew up."

"But to do that for decades after being in prison and losing everything. And it seems to have gotten worse than it was when we were younger."

"So, what's the next step? Where do we go from here?"

"I'll have to go make my report to my captain. Then we'll decide what's to be done. I think we need to send a squad to try to get past the wall.

There has to be a way through or over it, even though this woman said she's never seen it."

"It could be anywhere."

Sophie sat back, sipping her coffee, thinking of the woman out there on her own, having lost her family and everyone she cared about. A tightness came into her stomach as she thought about it.

"Sam, I need you to promise me something."

"Anything."

"Are you on my side? Are we in this together?"

"Of course."

"I need you with me. I need you on my side."

"I'll always be on your side."

The sun peeked in through the curtains, sending a shaft of light onto the bed. And their day was slow to begin.

* * * * *

Down in the creek on his stomach, Zacharias swims upstream. The cold water stings the bullet wound in his arm, but at least he's out of sight of the soldiers. He'll be at the cabin in a few minutes where Jesse is waiting. Slithering among the rocks of the creek, he wonders again what he's gotten his family into. Maybe things could have been different. Maybe they didn't have to be the ones to fight. But if not them, who?

Jesse throws down the clothes she's been mending and helps him through the back door to sit at the table where she can see to his wounds. One bullet, several grazes, a bump on the head. It's a miracle he got through at all.

"I don't know if we can stay here," he's panting. "It's only a matter of time before they find us here. We're going to have to go somewhere else. There are other members of the Watch farther upstream. We can join up with them."

"Now's not the time to decide that, love. Let's get you fixed up first, eh? God, look what they've done to you."

"Makes me wish I was invincible. For you and the kids."

She scoffs, concentrating on her task of bandaging him up. "No one's invincible. That's the whole point, isn't it?"

"What do you mean?"

"Aren't we fighting for the little fellas, the ones that can't fight for themselves? Maybe no one is invincible. Maybe we were never meant to be. That's what being human is, accepting our weaknesses and the weaknesses of others, trying to be a little stronger

tomorrow than we were today. Isn't that all any of us can ask of ourselves? Doesn't mean we're broken or beaten. Just means we're human."

Zacharias flinches as she starts cutting the bullet out. The pain radiates from his arm down the entire left side of his body. But at least he knows he's human.

Peering in the door of the shed, Sam noticed the dark curtain pulled shut, so he closed the door quickly behind him. "Z, it's me, Sam. Can I come in?" He didn't want to interrupt Z's process of film developing.

"Just a sec," Z called. "These prints are almost ready. Ethan has been taking some good shots. He got some pictures of the new children. Gemma wanted one of Daisy."

"I'm glad Ethan's found some friends."

"Alright, come in."

Sam looked at the photos Zacharias showed him of a little blonde girl peeking through flowers and wild oats. "These are good."

"Did you come to take the boy back?"

"Yes, but I wanted to talk to you first."

"About Sophie's mission."

"Yes, how did you know?"

Zacharias looked at him with a slight smile accentuating his wrinkled skin. "How long have I known you?"

"You're right."

"What did she find?"

"There are people living outside the borders. But Z, there's another Border. A wall."

"Interesting." Zacharias walked outside to sit on the bench under the oak tree that shaded his developing room.

"There were destroyed cities, of course, that Sophie went through, same as I've seen, but worse now. It's hard to imagine that level of destruction. Makes me wonder if everything is destructible."

"Not everything, boy. Love lasts." Zacharias patted the seat beside him for Sam to join him.

"Z, how can you say that when your Jesse is gone?"

"The love remains." Zacharias breathed in heavily and rubbed the spot on his arm that still ached sometimes.

"I wanted to ask you something. Remember that song you used to sing to me and Gemma?"

"Which one?"

"'Keep Smiling.'"

"Yes, I remember."

"Where did you hear it or learn it from?"

"That's an odd question."

"Just bear with me."

"As a matter of fact, it's one that Jesse used to sing to our kids."

"Jesse sang this song? Could you have heard it anywhere else?"

"I'm sure I did. It was an old song but was still popular for nostalgic reasons when we were young. Why this sudden interest?"

Sam hesitated before continuing. He didn't want to shock Zacharias or get his hopes up for nothing. He looked up to a moving branch as a squirrel jumped and flitted along to find a less crowded spot.

"What is it you're not telling me? Out with it, Sam."

"Alright, it could be nothing, but Sophie said this old woman she met was singing that song."

Sam saw Z's tanned skin turn suddenly pale, and he reached out to him, worried that he'd faint right before his eyes.

"I'm okay, son. Just took me by surprise, is all. Do you know what I miss sometimes almost more than anything? Jesse's homemade lemonade. You never tasted a lemon before. But it has the cleanest, freshest taste. Like sunshine. Jesse would squeeze the lemons herself and mix them with honey and ginger. She'd smile and sing with the breeze blowing through the kitchen window. And when I looked at her, it was like I was looking at the sun. Then she'd start singing that song or some other one. She was always singing to herself."

"But other people could have known that song. That woman in the Forbidden Grounds could be anyone."

"True. She wouldn't come back with Sophie?"

Sam shook his head.

"You never told me what happened to her, Z. Or your kids."

"No, I didn't. It was easier somehow not to think about it. But you know, the dead are never really dead, the past is never really gone. They live in the nooks and crannies of our lives. They pop up unexpectedly sometimes and remind us they still exist. We can't wipe them out or erase them as if they didn't exist because the *feeling* of them remains. Always. And all you can do is take them with you."

"Do you remember what happened?"

"Do I remember? How could I forget? She wasn't from this country. She came from the other side of the world. Australia. And there was something so indescribably Australian about her. I couldn't put my finger on it then, and I still can't. It was something wild and exotic. You could see it in her eyes. It was like trying to tame a lion. You could never really do it."

Sam let Zacharias talk on without interruption or question, let him float into the stream of reminiscing that took him along with its current.

"There was a wisdom in her, some called it a second sight. An ability to see into the future. She believed in the inevitability of what was coming. She didn't want it, she thought it was wrong, but it was already in motion. And see, I . . . I was arrogant enough to think I could stop it or change it. She loved me enough to fight with me. But by the time the real fighting began, it was already too late."

14

JESSE

2020

Zacharias heard the strains of Helen Reddy with Jesse's voice overlaid in sweeter tones coming from the kitchen. Barbra Streisand was her favorite, but she was cooking. She always listened to Helen Reddy when she was cooking. And somehow, no matter what artist she was singing along with, she always made them sound better than they sounded alone. She'd missed her calling.

He watched her for a few minutes, singing and dancing around the kitchen. Her white shirtsleeves were rolled up, and she wore her blue flowered apron, a gift from her mother. Her bare feet skidded along the floor as if she were on a stage. As she did a spin, she saw Zack watching her, stopping her in her tracks with a laugh. She was past being embarrassed. He'd caught her dancing before. In fact, it was how they had met.

At a psychology conference in Melbourne, Australia, there was an impromptu dance in the bar of the hotel. It never took much to get Jesse moving when music was playing. And as she'd twirled through the bar, she bumped into him, spilling his drink all over both of them. They had both been grateful for dancing and mishaps ever since.

"Hello, love. What do you have there?" she greeted him as she opened the oven to check the chicken.

"The new iPhone! I've only been waiting three months for it."

"Oh, no. Tell me that isn't why I've been holding dinner for an hour. Not because you've been waiting in a bloody line for that thing. Zack, the kids are starving."

He knew he should have called her; knew she'd be angry. And she was. Her Australian always showed more when she was riled up.

"I know, I know, honey. And I'm sorry. But look at it."

"I don't want to look at it. Jeez." She threw the towel she was holding into the sink, taking a deep breath. It was hard to be angry with a man when he lit up like a Christmas tree over something so silly.

"Where are the kids?"

"Playing in the yard. I told them no screens today. Ironic, don't you think?"

Zack laughed, walking up behind his wife to put his arms around her. He buried his face in her neck, kissing and breathing in her scent, more enticing than whatever she was cooking.

"Zack, they'll be in here any second."

"And they'll see their daddy kissing their mommy. It's healthy for them."

"So says the professional. You bloody idiot," she laughed, swatting him on the arm as she pulled away to set the table. "What am I going to do with you?"

Sunlight streamed through the glass doors, illuminating her auburn hair, their children's screams and laughter tumbled in around them. In that moment, Zack thought he had never been so happy.

"Just love me, I guess. I am who I am. I can't change." He gave her another kiss before walking over to turn the television on. He settled heavily into the couch to relax after his long day.

"Well, then, I'm so confused about what we both do for a living. Therapists helping people change their lives?" She chuckled to herself. Her laugh could fill the room. "Oh, come on, now, love. No screens today, eh?"

"I just want to catch the news. I heard there was another bombing at a church."

"Do we have to listen to it at dinner?"

"Just a minute, okay? Siri, stop music."

With her music silenced, Jesse listened to the newscaster droning in the background. "The fifth bombing in as many weeks has police stumped. Although suspicions have turned to the possibility of terrorist ties, no group has claimed responsibility for the bombings of the five different religious facilities: a Catholic church, a Jewish synagogue, a Baptist church, a Mormon chapel, and a non-denominational church. Protesters have gathered, calling for the dismissal of the chief of police if he is not able to bring the perpetrators to justice."

Jesse didn't want to hear about bombings and crimes. She would rather focus on her own family. "Are you still wanting to take the kids to the movies this weekend?"

"Huh, what'd you say, Jess?"

"Movies. This weekend. Me, you, Max, and Jill. You think we'll be able to go this time?"

"Don't know. This has been the first day without a storm in two weeks. Maybe it's letting up."

Jill and Max ran in from the back yard straight toward their father.

"Shoes off, kids. You're full of mud," Jesse called, but it was too late. She'd be mopping it up again tonight.

"Dad, what'd you bring us?"

"Nothing today, guys. Now come on, your mom's right. Let's get cleaned up for dinner."

Max ran to the table, grabbing a roll with muddy hands.

"Come on, mate. You know you've gotta wash your hands. Go on with your dad to the sink." Jesse smiled in spite of herself, seeing so much of her husband in her son's upturned face.

The newscast continued in the background as activity stirred through the house. "In international news, a magnitude 8.2 earthquake has struck Melbourne, Australia, causing massive damage to most areas of the city. This is the strongest onshore earthquake ever recorded in Australia. Very little has remained unscathed. This comes after a week of extensive flooding in Sydney and Canberra. Officials are calling for citizens to go north and seek higher ground, with mandatory evacuations along the southern coast as entire cities are now underwater. It is unknown when rescue workers will be able to return to the Melbourne area to look for survivors, as flood waters are rapidly moving west from Canberra."

Jesse stopped what she was doing, gripping the couch and looking in disbelief at the television screen. She struggled to recognize the places she knew from the horrific pictures on the screen of cars floating by buildings, roads being covered in mudslides, and streets completely disintegrating into the ground. She listened to the water running and her children laughing from the bathroom. She smelled the chicken in the oven being cooked past the point of edibility. A ringing came into her ears, and her hot tears stung her eyes before they fell.

"Oh, my God," she whispered, almost as a prayer.

"Mum, what's wrong?" Jill lisped, placing her still wet four-year-old hand into her mother's.

Zack followed his daughter into the living room and caught the end of the news story. Jesse looked at him with questions and fear in her eyes. He tried to put his arm around her, but she quickly moved into action.

"I have to call my mum," she said, wiping the tears from her eyes and looking frantically for her cell phone.

"Honey, the lines may not be working. I doubt you'll be able to get through just yet."

"I have to try."

"Dad, I'm hungry!" Max called from the table. "Can we eat?"

Zack set about making plates of food for his children while Jesse tried to reach her mother.

* * * * *

"The president has ordered a ban on all international civilian travel until further notice, citing the escalating threats of earthquakes and severe storms across the globe. In his press conference today, he assured the citizens of the United States that he is committed to finding a solution to these climate issues. In this same press conference, which covered a variety of concerns, he further promised to create a special military task force whose sole purpose will be to find the perpetrators of church bombings which have continued across the country. He is quoted as saying, 'The safety of America is our first concern.'"

Jesse wondered how news anchors could deliver strange and terrible news with straight faces and emotionless voices. She knew that was something she would never be able to do. Every emotion she felt made itself known in her face and her voice. There was very little she could hide. Zack always said that was a good thing; it meant she was genuine. But sometimes it just made her feel completely exposed.

Sitting up in bed, she pressed the power button on the remote. She couldn't take any more news today. She threw the covers off of her. Although autumn was beginning to caress the air with a chill, she was hot, lying in the dark bedroom in only a t-shirt.

The lamp turned on from the other side of the bed, and she saw Zack jump back. "Jeez, Jess, you scared the crap out of me. Why are you just lying here in the dark?"

"I just turned off the news."

"Yeah, I was listening in the car." Zack plopped himself on the side of the bed, beginning to remove his shoes and pants. "The library closed today. Did you hear that? I still can't get used to it, having all the books uploaded to the cloud. I'd still rather hold a book in my hand."

Jesse didn't respond. It was hard to concentrate on what her husband was saying with all of the thoughts and concerns swirling in her head like bilge water. Her mind jumped to thoughts of the sea. Melbourne. Home.

"Did you hear me, honey?"

"What? No, I'm sorry, love. I was just thinking. I'm not going to be able to fly to Australia next week with this ban on international travel so brilliantly thought up by our fearless leaders."

Zack could feel her fear and worry under her biting words. "Maybe it won't last long."

"I haven't heard from my mum in weeks, Zack, not since the earthquake. My home is most likely gone, fallen into the sea. The only way I've been able to combat my anxiety over that was knowing I was going over there, and I'd be able to look for her myself."

"I know, babe. I know. We'll get there as soon as we can."

"Where've you been? It's late. How'd you get past the police after curfew?"

"I had my work pass. Told them I had clients."

"You never have clients this late."

"Nah, I actually went to a meeting."

"What kind of meeting?"

"I found this group on Facebook. They call themselves the Watch. Basically, we just talked about what we can do to try to do the best things for the country and maybe hang on to some of our civil rights."

"Wacko militia types, huh?"

"Not really. They were making some pretty good sense." Zack climbed in the bed next to his wife, placing his head on her chest while she stroked his hair. "What are you thinking right now?" he asked.

"I don't know. It's hard to put into words. When you were a kid, did you ever go into a scary place, and you just knew that something was going to jump out at you, but you went in anyway? You would have no way of knowing it was going to happen, but beyond all logic or reason, you just knew. Like in a horror film. And every sense was heightened, every muscle strained so you could hear it, sense what it was before it happened. Did that ever happen to you?"

Zack nodded. "Sure. Every kid went through something like that, I'd imagine."

"Well, that's what I feel like right now. All the time lately. Something's coming. Something is getting ready to jump out at us."

"We've been through other tough times in the past few years."

"Sure, we've dealt with some frightening things that happened politically in the last few years. But this isn't that. This is beyond politics. The bombings, the task force, and now we can't leave the country. Any time leaders take away freedoms in the name of protection and safety, we're on a slippery slope."

"They shot down an alleged terrorist with a drone this week. Here in America."

"Is that what we've come to? I mean, so much for innocent until proven guilty. He didn't even get a trial. I just don't know what to believe anymore."

The thunder bellowed through the night sky and the lights flickered. As they lay in silence, Zack and Jesse were startled to hear a series of raps and taps on the window. First one or two, then several together, until a wave of plinking percussion overtook the night.

"Hail!" Zack sat up. "It's the wrong time of year for hail."

"It sounds small enough."

"It's gonna scratch the damn cars."

"Least of our worries, love."

A large clap of thunder made them jump, sounding as if a tree cracked in two. Suddenly, they were in darkness.

"Well, there goes the electricity," Zack complained, fumbling for a flashlight in the nightstand.

"We need to sleep anyway. I've always liked sleeping during a thunderstorm." Jesse was tired of her own complaining and worried thoughts, so tried to find a positive.

"I give it five minutes before the kids are in bed with us. What do you wanna bet?"

"I'll bet you a massage that it's less than two minutes." Jesse grinned unseen in the darkness, but Zack could hear the smile in her voice.

"You're on." He leaned over to where he thought her face was. Lightning illuminated the room for a split second, lighting his way to her mouth.

"Mummy! Daddy!" Both children were screeching from their bedroom.

"Ha! I win!" Jesse laughed. "Let's go get them. And I'll take my massage first thing in the morning, thank you, sir."

* * * * *

Autumn gave way to winter. And winter surrendered to spring. Snuggled down under the covers of the king-sized bed, Jesse wrapped her arms around her two children, one on each side, holding a book between them. She had soft music playing and read as loud as she could to distract them from the thunderous sounds rattling the windows and jingling the breakables on her dresser. Every few minutes, she would feel one or both of them jump in her arms, but she read on. She wished for maybe the hundredth time in a week that her own mother was there to wrap her in her arms, or even that she knew where her mother was.

As Jesse read of Peter Pan, the little boy without a mother, being thrilled and waiting anxiously for his friend, Tink, she clung more tightly to her babies.

A deafening boom from outside sounded as if it were at most a block away. Jesse held her children tighter.

"Jess! Jesse!" Zack called through the house over the sound of the slamming door.

"We're up here," she called.

Zack ran quickly into the room and started going through the closet. "It's time to go, babe. It's started. Where are the bags we packed?"

"In the kids' closet." Jesse felt the adrenaline coursing through her body, the excitement mixing with fear in an uncomfortable cocktail shaken in her heart. Jill and Max clung tighter to her, watching their dad rush into the other room.

Jesse had seen the smoke stains on his face and wondered what he'd gone through to tear his shirt as it was. She knew that whatever he'd managed to get through, she'd soon be facing it as well, and facing it with her children under her wings. Her stomach felt sick.

"Mummy, I want to bring the book with us. Can we?" Jill pleaded.

"And Billy Bunny. Where's Billy Bunny?" Max added.

"Yeah, sweeties. I'll bring the book to Daddy to put in the bag. Max, your bunny is already in there. I've got to help Daddy get the things in the car, alright? We're going on a trip, like we talked about."

Jill started jumping on the bed. "Can we go to Disneyworld, Mummy?"

"Nah, love. It's not that kind of a trip. It'll be more like camping. You guys stay here while I go help Daddy."

The light from the kids' lamp filtered through the animals on the lampshade, making it look like they lived in a zoo, with animals climbing the walls.

"Where's the car, Jess? Why isn't it in the driveway?"

Jesse put *Peter Pan* in Jill's red backpack. "The car's gone. Someone stole it. I heard them drive off with it about an hour ago."

"Are you kidding?! Shit! It wasn't supposed to be like this. Jesus, everything is going insane." Zack took a deep breath. He sat down on the bottom bunk, running his hands through his hair. "Okay, let me think. The Jeep is at the office. I can help you and the kids get past the perimeter. We'll have to walk there."

"How did you get here, then?"

"Charlie dropped me off. I'll call him to meet us there."

"Why?"

"He was going to pick me up here. I've got to help him take care of some things before we go."

"Jeez, Zack. I need you to help me get the kids out of here."

"I'm gonna meet you at the cabin. Come on, now. We've got to get going. They're already starting to set up roadblocks all around the city. The traffic is crazy."

They only had two blocks to walk to Zack's office, but with dodging the drones and trying to avoid the looters who were already mobbing the stores, it took more than half an hour to get there. They would start down the sidewalk and Zack would pull his family quickly into an alley just as people with guns ran past. With every explosion or vibration of the ground beneath them, the streetlamps blinked, giving the darkness around them a strobe light feeling. Jesse wondered why she thought of being in a dance club at a time like this. The same pulsing lights, booming vibrations. Her ears and all of her senses feeling assaulted.

"Mummy, I don't like this trip. I want to go home." Jill began to cry.

"We can't stop yet, love. Come on, sweet girl. Come on, love. Just a little farther." Jesse handed the two bags she was carrying to Zack and picked up her daughter.

Zack was relieved to find their Jeep still in the parking garage attached to his office building. And though the green paint was scratched in places, it still maintained all of its tires, and, God willing, still had gas in the tank. He threw the bags in the back of the car and handed Jesse the keys once the kids were buckled in. Jesse closed the car door so they couldn't hear her conversation with Zack.

Before she could speak, Zack reached behind him and pulled a pistol out of his belt. "Take this with you."

"I've never fired one of these in my life!"

"Take the safety off, point, and squeeze the trigger. You don't even have to cock it. Here's an extra magazine."

"I can't do this."

"Yes, you can. You probably won't even have to use it, but I want you to have it just in case."

He placed the pistol into her trembling hand.

"One other thing, no matter what, don't get out of the car. You have a full tank of gas, I just checked. That's more than enough to get you to the cabin, even if you're sitting in traffic for a while. Whatever you do, don't get out of the car."

Jesse saw a look in her husband's face she'd never seen before. He looked like he'd witnessed things he had never thought he'd see. He had an appearance of resolution mixed with fear. But there was something else. A purpose? A goal? She couldn't put her finger on it. But somehow, it unnerved her and made her think the insanity of the world falling down around her ears wasn't temporary as she hoped it would be.

"Zack, this is insane. Just come with us."

"People are counting on me."

"We're counting on you!"

"I'll be right behind you, I promise. We can do this. Now, here are the keys. The cabin is fully stocked with everything we'll need. Charlie and I have been packing stuff up there for months. Don't forget about the tank with water in it on the back patio just in case we lose running water. I'll be there before morning. Give me a hug, then y'all better get going."

Jesse threw her arms around him, burying her face in his neck. His skin was hot and smelled like the smoke in the air. Her tears blended with his sweat. She pushed away thoughts that told her this could be the last time she would see him. The one thought that remained and revolved around her brain like a record was that it hadn't been enough. She had never gotten enough of him, and she never would. Not enough lazy Saturdays before the kids were born when they would stay in bed all day, but not sleeping. Not enough pizza Fridays watching silly movies with their friends. Not enough laughing at his ridiculous jokes. Not enough of his scent in the morning covering her like a blanket while she was still half asleep. She needed more of him, not just now but for the rest of her life. She hoped and prayed her will and faith were enough to keep them all together.

"Please come with us," she begged one more time.

"Go on now, baby. I'll see you in a few hours, okay?"

Zack finally pushed her from him and helped her into the car.

"I want to stay with Daddy," Max cried as soon as the door was open.

"I need you to be a big boy and help Mummy, okay buddy? Can you do that for Daddy?"

"I'm five years old. I'm a big boy."

"That's right. I'll see y'all in the morning, okay?"

Max stuck his chin out, his way of trying to look more manly.

Zack stood under the blinking fluorescent lights of the garage, watching as Jesse drove away. He waited until they were out of sight to shed his own tears.

Jesse wanted to put the pedal to the floor so she could get out of the city as quickly as possible. But she was forced to take it slow to avoid the people dodging in and out of the street. None of the traffic lights were working. They all were blinking red, but no one seemed to be paying much attention anyway. She was shocked to see every church she passed either engulfed in flames or the remnants smoldering on the ground.

There were some cars parked in the middle of the road, abandoned with doors left open. Alarms and sirens were going off from all directions. Jesse watched a man pushing a grocery cart overflowing with televisions and other electronic equipment. Others had dropped their loot as they ran, forcing her to drive the road like an obstacle course.

"Mum, you're driving on the wrong side of the road!" Max called from the back seat.

"I know, mate. It might be best for you to close your eyes for a bit. Alright?"

She quickly stomped on the brake, just barely missing a teenager darting into the street. He slammed his hands down on the hood of her car, shouting incoherently.

"How about we sing a song, guys?" Jesse spoke reassuringly to her children. Jill hadn't uttered a sound since they'd gotten in the car, but Jesse knew she wasn't asleep. *"Keep smiling through the day, keep smiling through the night,"* she began singing. "What are the next words, Jilly? Something about shadows?"

"The shadows fly away . . ." Jill almost whispered the words.

". . . When they can see your light," they all joined in, *"if I can keep you with me in day and nighttime too, I know the dark won't find me because my light is you."*

Jesse looked at the Apple store on the corner. Its windows were broken, and she could see the shelves inside were empty. A block further up the street, a car bomb went off in front of the bank, and she felt the earth groan in protest as a crater opened up where the car had been. A bumper landed just in front of their car. "Shit!" she cried.

"Shit's a bad word, Mum," Max offered from the back.

"Not when you're really scared, it isn't, love."

She steered the Jeep down a side street, heading into a neighborhood. It was a longer way, but maybe she'd avoid the bombs and the looters.

"Shit, shit, shit, shit, shit . . ." Max began repeating.

"Alright, mate. Let's not wear it out. Let's sing our song again." She hoped they couldn't hear the lump in her throat she was trying to speak through or the shakiness of the tears entering her voice. She glanced down at the pistol in the front seat. It looked so foreign, unreal, almost movie-like sitting there. She wondered what her life had become.

Turning down side street after side street, trying to avoid the main thoroughfares, Jesse had no exact route set. She knew only she was heading in the general direction of the interstate, which would bring her east to their cabin. As she came to a stop sign, she saw a woman and her baby huddled against someone's yard fence in the shadows thrown from the winking streetlamp. The woman tried to stand and move further into the shadows when she saw Jesse's vehicle approaching, but she appeared to be injured and slumped down again.

Jesse sat at the intersection for a few moments, watching the woman and her baby, looking around to see if anyone else was out on the street. She looked into the inky sky for drones. They seemed to be alone on the abandoned street. As she edged her car closer to the woman, Jesse pulled toward the curb. Again she sat, waiting, thinking. She heard Zack's voice in her head: "Whatever you do, don't get out of the car. Don't get out of the car. Don't get out of the car." She looked in the rearview mirror and saw her babies had fallen asleep in the back seat. She rolled the passenger-side window down and called out to the woman. "Are you alright? Can I take you somewhere?"

"Please. We're fine. You should go. You're putting yourself in danger." The woman's voice sounded hoarse from screaming, or maybe from the heavy smoke in the air. Upon closer inspection, Jesse could see blood running down her forehead and matting her hair on the side of her face. The baby was crying in her arms.

"No, really, it's okay. Come get in the car. I'll give you a ride."

"Please, just leave us."

Jesse sighed heavily. She looked around again. No one. Her blood pumped harder and hotter in her veins. She remembered feeling this same sick excitement just before Max was born. She threw the car into park and got out, leaving her door open. As she ran toward the woman, she stopped short when she saw a child's shoe and some toys sitting on the ground near the curb. There was a thin layer of ash beginning to gather on them. And somehow this sight bothered her more than all the other shocking things she'd seen that day. They had to get out of here quickly. Running toward the woman, she called, "Come with me." She leaned down to help her up, this woman who could barely stand on her own feet. "Come on, love. I've got you." She gently pulled the woman's arm around her shoulders and helped her toward the car.

"Don't. Please, you'll put yourself and your children in danger."

"Don't be ridiculous. I'm not leaving you here. Now, get in."

Jesse took the gun off the front seat and stuck it in her belt. For a moment the woman in her arms looked frightened.

"It's okay. It's just for protection. My husband insisted. You sit here in the front seat. You'll have to hold the baby, but I'll drive as safely as I can." She got them situated in the car, then ran around to the driver's side. Closing the door, she looked in her side mirror and saw him, a man running at the car from the bushes.

"Oh, hell no!" she whispered under her breath. She reached for the door lock button, but he was already pulling her car door open. She pulled and struggled in the opposite direction. She was strong and had the urgency of helping her children pumping adrenaline into her veins. But he was stronger. She instantly reached for the gun, swiping the safety release in one movement. There was no hesitation as she held the pistol in her steady hand. As she placed the gun against the man's chest, he took several steps back, arms raised. She heard the woman in the seat next to her breathing heavily and wondered if this man had anything to do with her.

"Just walk away, and I won't shoot you." Jesse's voice sounded calmer than she felt.

She looked at the man's face. A twisted, gnarled crust of skin covered him. She couldn't tell his age. The tattoos on his upheld arms were wrinkled, distorting the pictures beyond recognition. She wondered why his face didn't register fear. Amusement, defiance, challenge—all played through his bloodshot eyes, but not fear. For a second, she saw those eyes dart toward the back seat, taking in the fact that she had children back there. She couldn't imagine what his intentions were but knew they couldn't be anything good.

"Don't do it," she said.

But it was as if she had said the opposite. The man made a leap for the back door but never reached his destination. One shot cracked the violent air, piercing through the myriad sounds in the night. The bullet stopped his chest, the rest of his body folding in around it as he fell in a twisted heap in the middle of the street, leaking an oozing dark river of blood beneath him. Jesse didn't wait to see if he was dead. She quickly shut her door and drove away as fast as the Jeep would go, dropping the gun on the floor beneath her feet. The woman in the seat next to her simply looked at her in awe.

"You did the right thing."

"Who knows what's right anymore? There's only what's necessary. Let's just get the hell out of here."

Her hands shook on the wheel as the adrenaline made its frantic trip through her veins, and she felt a film of sweat forming along her back and forehead.

Fifteen minutes later, as they drove toward the edge of town, Jesse finally spoke again. "So, what's your name?"

"Aabirah."

"I'm Jesse. What happened to you?"

"The drones shot up my neighborhood, so we had to run. I was separated from the rest of my family—parents, husband. I kept hearing shots behind me as I ran."

"Because you're Muslim?"

The woman looked at Jesse with suspicion.

"I don't mean anything . . . I mean, it doesn't matter to me. Really."

"I suppose it was something like that. I took the hijab from my head so I could try to blend in."

"If you reach in the glove box there should be some bandages for your head. You should try to stop that bleeding."

Aabirah tried as best she could to cover the cut on her head with a bandage in one hand, holding her baby in her other arm.

"Now, what's this?" Jesse's voice sounded tense as she slowed the car, reaching for her gun to place it in her lap. There was a roadblock ahead. They wouldn't be able to get to the highway this way. Pulling to a stop, she looked at the people in her car who were counting on her. There was no way she was going to try to get past the soldiers on the road ahead.

"Okay, Aabirah, here's where you make your choice. We're heading out of town, and I don't know when we'll be able to get back. Do you want me to drop you off somewhere, or do you want to come with us? It's up to you. You're welcome to come with us."

"There's nowhere else for me to go. I can try to contact my family later, once we're safe."

"Right, then you're with us. And it looks like we're going off-roading, kids. So hang on."

Jesse thought about where the next interstate on-ramp was. There was a patch of woods along the frontage road between where they were and where they needed to be. She just hoped the underbrush and the trees weren't too thick for them to get through, but they had to try.

It was well past one o'clock in the morning before the little group finally arrived at the cabin. Once they'd managed to reach the interstate, traffic was at a slow crawl. Most of the gas was spent barely moving down the highway, so they had to abandon the Jeep about a quarter of a mile from the cabin when the gas tank was empty. Jesse and Aabirah carried the children and their bags the rest of the way to the cabin. Jesse noticed moving flashlights every now and then from deeper in the woods. But she chose to believe it was other people like them just escaping to their cabins, trying to avoid the violence in the cities.

Flipping on the lights, Jesse was shocked to see how much her husband and his best friend Charlie had managed to bring up here without her knowledge. The cabinets, refrigerator, and freezer were all fully stocked, and the hall closet contained more food in addition to sanitary and hygienic supplies. There was a large wooden box near the back door that contained about ten different kinds of guns, from pistols to rifles. Looking through the glass doors to the back of the cabin, she turned on the light on the back patio and saw, to her astonishment, a garden in full bloom with vegetables, beans, corn, melons, and more.

She wondered what had prompted them to start preparing like this so many months ago. What did they talk about in their meetings with "the Watch" and what did they know that she didn't know? The preparation disheartened rather than comforted her.

Aabirah's baby started to cry. The children had all slept through the long car ride. Jesse had placed Max and Jill in their bed in the back bedroom. Aabirah sat down with the baby, trying to comfort him. "I think I might have left his bottle back at the car."

"I'll go get it," Jesse offered.

"It's too far. I can't let you walk all that way alone."

"Maybe you're right. I'll lock the door here since the kids are just sleeping. And you and I can walk back together. Let me just grab the pistol and a flashlight."

The two women hadn't talked much in their few hours together. They each knew the other was worried about her own family. What else could be said that would be useful? Empty speculation about what would happen in the coming days? A useless occupation that wouldn't make their current situation any better. So they walked on in silence, sharing the moment and their thoughts without the exchange of words.

The light from Jesse's flashlight bounced along the ground as they walked down the long drive toward the Jeep, making the darkness of the woods feel like it was trying to crowd them out. Jesse listened in wonder to all of the distant night sounds—crickets, birds, animals. She had never felt fully comfortable among American wildlife. There was something that seemed foreign and exotic to her. And now there was an added danger of not knowing if there were people intent on harming her and her children hiding among the shadows.

She didn't remember the car being this far away from the cabin. It should be coming up soon. Jesse held her flashlight up and swung around in a wide arc, looking all around them. She saw a reflection off something shiny in the distance. "That must be it," she said out loud, her voice sounding empty in the thick night. But the reflection moved and came closer. Aabirah was just ahead of her on the path, holding her baby close to her, the movement of walking having put him back to sleep.

"Aabirah, I don't know what that is, but I don't think it's the car. Does it look like it's moving to you?"

"Yes, it does."

"Let's head back to the house. I'm sure we can find something for the baby in there."

"Alright."

Jesse sent Aabirah on ahead of her toward the cabin and kept her eye on the shiny movement behind them. Suddenly, she heard it, a soft whirring. The shiny thing was coming closer.

"A drone! Aabirah, run! Get to the cabin!" Jesse didn't care who heard her anymore.

They ran as swiftly as possible over the gravel drive, thankful they weren't among the trees and underbrush. But stepping wrong on a rock, Jesse's ankle turned, and she'd fallen to the ground before the gunshot pierced her ears. One. Two. Three shots.

"My God, the baby," she whispered to the rocks in her face on the ground. She got up quickly, wincing at the pain shooting up from cuts on her leg, and ran to Aabirah. She had dropped her flashlight somewhere but could see a little in the gray light of predawn.

"Aabirah! Aabirah, where are you?"

She nearly tripped again, this time over the drone in pieces on the ground. Someone had shot it down. But Jesse heard no one else about.

"Aabirah!" She strained to listen for any movement or sound. A groan came from a few feet away.

Aabirah was on the ground, still clutching the baby to her.

"Aabirah, are you alright? Were you hit?" Jesse gently lifted the mother and child into her arms. She felt the hot, sticky blood on Aabirah's back. "What have they done to you?" The tears ached in the back of her throat. She looked at the baby and listened for breath but could only hear her own and Aabirah's ragged breathing. There was a dark hole in the blanket around the child that wasn't there before. Jesse knew what she didn't want to know, that the baby was dead, and the mother would soon join him.

"Is he . . . is he alright? The baby. You must take . . . my baby." Aabirah struggled to get the words out.

"Shhh . . . of course. He's alright. I'm going to get you both up to the house. You're going to be fine," Jesse lied. "Don't you worry."

"Thank you . . . so kind . . ."

"Don't talk. It's going to be okay. I've got you."

One. Two. Three breaths. Aabirah was gone.

Jesse sat there holding the mother and child until her legs ached beneath her, her sobs muffled against their still forms, tears and blood mingling in a hot paste on her face.

Zack walked heavily into the cabin. The day had robbed him of his home and his best friend. He was relieved to see Jesse at the kitchen table. Her head was down, and all the lights were on. He had seen the Jeep at the end of the drive and was happy to know she and the kids would be sleeping in the cabin, waiting for him. But Jesse wasn't sleeping. Her shoulders were shaking. She was crying.

"Jess, honey. Are you alright?"

Jesse jumped when she heard his voice. She stood up fast enough to knock her chair over, pulling the pistol from her lap and aiming it at him.

"Whoa, Jess, sweetie, it's me, Zack."

She seemed to look straight through him, not recognizing him. She was covered in blood on her clothes and face. Her hands shook violently as she tried to hold up the gun.

"Jess. Jesse, baby, it's me. It's okay. It's just me. I'm not going to hurt you." He spoke slowly and quietly as he started to inch his way toward her. He reached his hand out as he moved one step closer after another. When he stood close enough to his wife to smell the smoke, woods, and blood on her, he reached one arm around her shoulders and took the gun from her with his other hand. Jesse collapsed in sobs in his arms. They stood for several minutes, frozen in fear and anguish.

"It's okay, baby. Tell me what happened. Where are the kids? Are the kids okay?"

In those moments, Zack had played out every awful scenario he could think of for an explanation of the blood on his wife's clothes. He hated himself for letting her come out here on her own. He should have listened to her and come with them. For all his talking of fighting the enemy and standing up for what was right, he hadn't protected them.

As Jesse started to catch her breath again, she sat down and looked up at Zack, seeing him for the first time.

"Yes, the kids are fine. They're asleep," she whispered.

"What happened, sweetie?"

"There was a woman and a baby when I was driving out of the city. The woman was hurt, so I brought them with me."

"Where are they?"

"We went back out to the car to get the bottle for her baby, and a drone . . . a drone . . . shot them. I didn't even know her baby's name. Zack, how the hell have we come to this place when machines are shooting unarmed people and children?"

"Oh, my poor darling."

"What's going on, Zack? Why are the drones after us? Tell me . . . just please tell me you're not a terrorist, you and the Watch."

"God, no! Jess, you know me better than that."

"I thought I did. But I don't know anything anymore. Nothing makes sense. And then I come here, and you've got all these guns."

He sat down next to her and looked her directly in the eyes, puffy and red from hours of crying. "Know this . . . I love you. I haven't blown up any churches, and I haven't killed anyone."

Jesse looked down and whispered almost inaudibly, "I have."

"What?"

"I killed someone!" Her tears ran hot again. Her mouth was dry. She was dehydrated.

"Tell me everything that happened."

"This man came at the car when I stopped to pick up the woman and her child. He was going to hurt the kids. I tried to just warn him with the gun, but he . . . I don't know . . . he had this crazed look in his eye. I didn't have a bloody choice. So I shot him. Now *you* tell me everything. Why are the drones after us?"

"I'm not sure I can tell you."

Zack saw a look on his wife's face he'd never seen before. Somewhere, it registered in him that it was because she was feeling things she'd never felt before. Neither of them knew how to navigate this new territory they had been thrust into.

She spoke firmly, but slowly. "I just ran out into the night with my children like some kind of fugitive. I've been attacked, shot at, killed a man, and had a woman die in my arms. So I'd say I bloody well deserve to know what's going on. Tell me."

"I think they must know I'm in the Watch. We've been planning and carrying out a series of focused and necessary attacks against the military. And before you say anything, no, we're not terrorists. We never target civilians. But the minute they declared martial law, they declared war on the American people."

"You're talking about treason, Zack! About another goddamned civil war. Do you know how crazy this sounds?"

"Shhh . . . you'll wake the kids."

"Did you think about the kids when you made this decision without me? Since when do we do things without discussing them with each other?"

"I know. But I couldn't. And I don't believe it's right to just do nothing while they take away one freedom after another. This country was built on the principles of freedom and justice . . ."

"Now is not the time to preach at me about freedom and justice."

"I mean it. We can't abandon those. But it wasn't supposed to be an all-out war. That's not what we wanted. But I have to tell you, Jess, the church bombings weren't terrorists. They were staged by the government to look like terrorists so they could have cause to declare martial law."

"You're sounding crazy like a conspiracy theorist, Zack."

"You were shot at by drones tonight. That's not a theory. That's fact. They're coming for us."

Jesse paused, trying to take in everything he was saying. She went to the sink in the kitchen and washed her face and hands without speaking.

"What are you thinking right now, Jess?" Zack finally asked.

"I don't see how we can win if they've been planning this for as long as they would have had to in order to stage everything. I mean, they have bombs, drones, and soldiers. Hell, with the storms being what they are, it may not even be an option. It may all just be inevitable."

"So you think we shouldn't fight? Just hunker down and wait for it to be over?"

"No, that's not what I'm saying. Sometimes even when things are inevitable, you have to fight so you can still call yourself human."

Jesse heard her children from the back of the cabin quietly singing their song to themselves. She looked to the window. The curtain edges glowed with the light of dawn in a frame around it. The sun would continue to rise and set again. The foreign-sounding American birds would announce the different times of day. The cabin would become more familiar, become home. And in the end, what else could be done except what had to be done? When there was only one path before you, you either took your first steps or stood still, and she had never been one for standing still.

15

SET APART

"The short version of the story is that we fought together through some of the First Revolution. She was at my side as often as she could be."

Zacharias paused in his story. He was looking at the cracks in the wooden slats of the shed. Then he noticed the cracks in his wrinkled skin. Old skin. Older than he ever thought he'd be. He'd survived half a lifetime without her, and it was killing him. The air started to feel cramped and suffocating, heavy with a coming thunderstorm. He could see lightning far in the distance over the mountains.

Sam was at his shoulder. They'd come this far in the story; Zacharias knew he had to finish it. But he'd never said these words before. Never told the horrors of what had happened in those early days of the war, and he felt as if he were tearing the flesh from around his heart.

"Z? You okay?"

"That's a strange word . . . okay. It can cover a multitude of feelings and states of being. Am I alive? Yes. Am I functioning? Mostly. Am I in pain? Absolutely."

"You don't have to finish. I shouldn't have asked . . ."

"No, I do. I have to say it out loud. It's what I used to tell my patients in that other life. You can't keep things bottled up inside you. They always find a way out. But it always hurts—the letting out."

"You can say anything to me."

Zacharias smiled. "I know I can, son." One deep breath and maybe he could get the words out. "On the day we had planned to leave the cabin to join some other members of the Watch, I came home to get Jesse and the kids. But they were gone. I waited for a little while, thinking they'd be back. Jesse knew how to take care of herself. I wasn't scared at first. But hours went by. I went out back to start looking for them down by the river. The river . . ." More deep breaths. He was gulping in air now, thick air. Humid air. Liquid air. He felt like he was drowning.

"Slow. Slow breaths, Z."

In a daze, he finished his story, seeing it play out before his eyes in the swirling, building clouds that loomed over the mountains.

"The river ran red that day with the blood of American citizens gunned down by the government soldiers. I never found their bodies—my Jesse and our kids. Just their clothes covered in blood. I buried those."

"My God."

"Yes, we call on God in times like that. But we seldom find him in the violent world of our own making."

"Violence. Killing. So much bloodshed, Z. We've both seen it and been a part of it. It's why I'm staying out of it now."

"That's not always the answer either."

"What do you mean?"

"If Jesse and I had stayed out of it, that wouldn't guarantee she or my children would still be alive. Then I'd have the added burden of knowing we didn't take a stand for what we believed in. Knowing that we had helped the other side a little by our acquiescence."

"Just because I don't believe in the war doesn't mean I sympathize with the Corsairs or the Triumvirate."

"Oh, I know that, son. I know you've tried to stay out of it. You thought you could protect the people you love by not fighting, not killing. But sometimes the fight finds you, whether you want it or not. That's what happened in the Second Revolution with your parents, and it's what's happening now. This was always meant to be your fight."

The two men stood in silence even as the first raindrops started to fall and darken their clothes. After a few minutes, Zacharias spoke again. "You know what haunts me the most to this day? Why she was at the river in the first place. It looked like she'd gone down there with a gallon jug for water. But there was water in the tank by the cabin. So why did she go to the river?"

"Z, what if this woman Sophie found . . ."

"No, no son. I can't allow myself to hope or even think about it."

"But what if . . ."

"No! I mean it, Sam. I don't want to talk about this again. I can't."

Zacharias walked slowly back up to the house. He looked older than he had when he'd started speaking. The sheets of rain enveloped him in their gray release. Sam couldn't imagine what their conversation had taken out of him.

The rain through the trees soaked Sam's hair and ran down the back of his neck, cooling him. He didn't attempt to cover himself but stood looking after Zacharias long after he had entered the house. An accent, a song, a feeling. Sam hadn't told Zacharias about some of these things, especially the nagging feeling in his gut that wouldn't let him let go of the belief that this woman was Jesse. There would be time for that later. He would honor Z's request and wouldn't speak of it again. But that wouldn't stop him from trying to find her.

* * * * *

Lush and rejuvenated by the rain, the flowers, wild oats, and grass by the river dipped and swayed under the weight of nourishment. In this primeval temple with walls and ceiling of mottled green and filtered light, Sophie stood by, watching the river run full to bring more life to other parts of the land. She hadn't been prepared for the storm, and her hanging clothes on the line had fallen heavy with water to the ground below. She would have to wash them again. The wet grass stuck to the basket and her legs. Everything stuck and mashed together in what the rain had left behind.

She saw Ethan running toward her, Sam struggling to keep up. The swish and squish of the grass and mud beneath them made her smile.

"Welcome back!" she called.

Ethan wrapped his arms around her waist, then picked up the basket to begin helping her with the laundry. While the boy's back was turned, Sam stole a kiss. He didn't know why he felt the need to sneak.

"There's going to be a town meeting in a couple of days. Ethan and I will have to go back to Jesse's Hollow. But we'll only be gone the day."

"Do we know what it's about?"

"No idea. As usual."

"How are the other children with Zacharias?"

"They're settling in. Pretty quiet for little ones. It may take them some time to adjust to not being on their own. I kept pretty much to myself for a while after Z adopted us. But it's best for them."

"Of course." Sophie looked at Ethan, wishing again he could be truly hers.

"What are you thinking about, my Sophie?" Sam tucked a curl of hair behind her ear.

"It's hard to explain," she spoke softly. "Walk with me for a minute."

She called to Ethan, telling him she'd return soon to help him.

"Sam, Ethan is your son now. By law, he can't be taken from you."

"And when did you start caring about the law?" Sam tried to smile at her.

"I'm serious."

"I know. What is it that worries you?"

"I hesitate to say. This is all so new, and with everything that is happening around us, how could I hope for . . . or ask for . . ."

"Sophie, just say it."

"I love Ethan. And I love you. But what binds us? What is to say that I couldn't lose you both? If the Corsairs found out you were living here instead of in Jesse's Hollow as they believe, they could take you away from me."

"I see. Well, I could say the law is not always a protection, especially when it changes as often as it does. But I know that wouldn't comfort you."

"Did you hear what I said?"

"What?"

"I can't believe you're going to make me say it again," she laughed with embarrassment. "I love you, you silly man. I've never said that to a man before."

Sam took her face in his hands. "And I love you. I should have said it. But I guess I thought some things go without saying. Yes, Sophie, I love you."

"So what's the answer, Sam?"

He looked down at his mother's golden wedding band on his little finger, dwarfed by the size of his hand. How could something so small carry so much meaning? A ring. A word. A law. What bound them, she wanted to know.

"You and I both know nothing is certain. There's not a lot we can count on in this world. The only thing I'm sure of is how I feel about you. The answer is that the government can say what they want. But if you want me, I am with you and for you from now until the end of my life. To me, that means we're married. And if you promise the same, what other promise or loyalty could mean more than that to me?" He took the ring off his finger and placed it on hers. Sam looked at the ring he had worn for so long it had become a part of him, and he marveled at how easy it was to give that part of himself to Sophie.

"Just like that?"

"Just like that."

Sophie looked at the ring. She looked at the dragonflies skipping over the river. She looked anywhere but at Sam.

"Listen, I know the risks of not applying to the government for a marriage license," he continued. "But after what happened the last time, the risk of filling out the application actually frightens me more. They sent me away for seven years, Sophie. I don't think I could go through that again. Not with you."

Hot tears stung her eyes and the back of her throat. She knew he was right, and she had known what he would say before he said it.

"So, will you?" he smiled.

"Will I . . . will I what?"

"Promise me."

"Of course I will." She hadn't looked up at him yet. Her tears dripped onto her hand and made the ring shine brighter. "What if this—us here—what if it doesn't last? What if this is the only time we have?" She placed her hand on his chest, feeling his heart beating as quickly and intensely as her own.

"All we ever have is the light we're living in here in the moment. We can't bask in yesterday's sunrise, though we may remember it. And we can't be guaranteed the sun will rise tomorrow. So we enjoy and are grateful for the light we have today."

"That's fine, but isn't it our responsibility to try to ensure light for tomorrow, not just for ourselves, but for those who come after us?"

252

"Sophie, look at me." He gently lifted her chin. "It's about Ethan, isn't it?"

She didn't need to answer. He could see the fear in her eyes, see the remembrance of Bridget. She had let Ethan into her home and her heart, and now she was terrified of losing another child.

"Ethan is yours just as much as I am. He's our son. And as long as I'm breathing, I won't let anyone or anything separate us. I know that won't be enough forever. But who knows how things are going to change in the future? What new laws or restrictions they're going to come up with? I don't want to do anything to draw their attention to us. Isn't it better to keep our family here between us and not let the government get their hands on it?"

"Of course it is." Sophie folded herself into Sam's arms, fitting her head just under his chin, listening to his heart beating. She held on as tightly as she could, and she felt his arms tighten as well. She wished their arms were strong enough to keep them together always.

Then just as quickly, she stepped away. "Go on, now, you. The garden has to be seen to. I think the wind from the storm may have knocked over some of the tomato plants. And I need to help Ethan take care of the laundry."

"Wow, that sounds like quite the honeymoon—tomatoes and laundry!" Sam laughed.

"I'll show you a honeymoon later on," she grinned. "But for now, there's work to be done."

"Yes, ma'am!"

Sam walked away whistling the tune Sophie had heard the old woman sing, and it both comforted and frightened her.

Reaching into the pocket of her tunic, Sophie pulled out the message she'd written to Foxglove earlier in the day. She hadn't been sure she'd be able to get the message to her through the storm but was grateful for the break in the weather.

She had used quotes from Sam's own book *Great Expectations* to relay the message but hadn't wanted to pull the page from the book, and so copied it in her own hand.

Foxglove,

We came to Miss Havisham's house, which was of old brick, and dismal, and had a great many iron bars to it. Some of the windows had been walled up; of those that remained, all the lower were rustily barred. There was a courtyard in front, and that was barred . . . always creep in-shore like some uncomfortable amphibious creature, even when the tide would have sent him fast upon his way; and . . . coming after us in the dark or by the back-water, when our own two boats were breaking the sunset . . .
Aishe

She hoped Foxglove would be able to discern her meaning but wouldn't know unless she showed up on her beach at sunset.

"What'cha got there?" Ethan asked curiously.

"A message for my captain."

"Let me take it, Sophie."

She heard an excitement in his voice. He wanted to be part of things, but it was too dangerous. Her arms ached to hold onto him. "I don't know, Ethan."

"I can do it. I know how."

"What does Sam say about you working with the Watch?"

"He doesn't like it, but he said I'm old enough to make my own decisions about it."

She ran her hand through his hair. He wanted to be an adult, but there was still so much of the child left in him. His idealism, wanting to join in, wanting to feel important—didn't they all point to his youth? How could she send him off to a job that would endanger him?

"He might be right, sweetie."

Ethan sat down on a large rock near the river. "You know, sometimes I think there's no point to anything. There just seems to be so much darkness, and all I have is a little match to light it up. There's no way that my little match could make a difference. You know what I mean?"

"Like on a cloudy night when you can't see the stars, and everything looks blacker than normal. But that doesn't mean the stars aren't still there. The stars are always there, always sending their light to us, no matter what. No matter what we're able to see of them, no matter if we even acknowledge their existence."

"So you mean that we should continue to do good, even in our little ways, even in the dark?"

"It's what we do. It's who we are, even on a cloudy night."

"Can I tell you something, Sophie?"

"Anything."

Ethan pulled a string out of his pocket, playing with it, twisting it around his fingers as he spoke. "Awhile back, Sam and I saw a flogging in the town square. Everyone just stood by and didn't do anything. I knew the citizens outnumbered the soldiers, but we didn't do anything because we didn't have any weapons."

"Well, that's just the point, honey, you don't . . ."

"I'm not finished."

"Sorry."

"That wasn't the first flogging I ever saw, though. When I was little. Just before my parents were taken, the soldiers beat them like that. But on that day too, I didn't do anything. I was too little."

"Oh, sweetie . . ."

"But I promised myself that when I was older and bigger, I would do something to stop them. And I think that's what you mean too—about shining on a cloudy night. This is something I can do, Sophie. It's something you can let me do."

"You're right, Ethan. I know you are. How can I ask you to sit by and do nothing when . . ."

She knelt in the wet grass by the water, running her fingers through its quickening current. *This is what holding onto a child is like—trying to hold water in your hands.*

"Alright. You can take the message."

He jumped up from the rock, ready to go.

"But I want you to use the chain of messengers. Don't go right to Foxglove, even if you know where she is. That's for everyone's safety. Understood?"

"Understood." He saluted.

"And you and the other little messengers. I want y'all to be careful. Stay near the river and don't go anywhere the Corsairs would question. Then come right back here when you've delivered the message, alright?"

"Absolutely. Thank you, Sophie. I won't let you down." He ran off faster than she'd seen him go in a while.

Using children to fight against tyranny. Well, maybe their innocence was the perfect weapon. But children—

* * * * *

"Run! Hide! He'll catch you!" the little girl Daisy shrieked. "There's a place over there! Run!"

Anyone listening would have thought it was a children's game. Daisy loved to play games and loved teaching the games she knew to her friends.

But this wasn't a game. A Corsair on horseback had surprised her and Ethan in the woods and had seen them pass the note between them. Running through thickly crowded trees, they'd managed to slow him down. He had to get off his horse to be able to fit between the trees as they went deeper and deeper into the forest. Near the Border, a tree had been blown over in a storm months, maybe years, before. Who could say? The felled tree was home to a colony of gray lichen on its rotting trunk. Hiding in the dank depths of what had once been its life-giving roots, the children crouched in the crater underneath, which was just big enough to hold them.

Ethan was breathing heavily. Maybe Sophie and Sam had been right. His first message delivery, and he was almost caught. His embarrassment stung more than his fear.

"Shhh," Daisy whispered. "You're breathing too loud."

The Corsair's boots crunched on the dead branches that littered the ground. Even after the rain, their brittle sounds helped to let Daisy and Ethan know how close their foe was.

"Come on out, kids." His words sounded more like an entreaty than a command. "You won't be in trouble. I just need to see the note."

Daisy shook her head at Ethan, letting him know a Corsair's word was not to be trusted.

"You know, I used to be the best at hide and seek. I'm going to find you eventually."

She shook her head again.

The way they heard the Corsair walking was not in a straight path, but meandering, roaming all over the woods. He hadn't seen where they'd gone.

Ethan took a deep breath. It was wet and stank inside the old tree trunk. It smelled like mildew and wet earth, and he was pretty sure he felt something crawling over his hand. His nose twitched. He had to sneeze. Daisy saw the look in his eyes and knew she had to think fast. She covered his mouth with her hand and tossed a large stick as far away as she could to cover the sound. If there was one thing Gemma had taught her, it was misdirection.

It worked. The Corsair heard the stick and started running away from them. He was far enough away now that they could risk running in the opposite direction.

"Come on, let's go," she whispered, and took off with Ethan close behind her. "Give me the note," she called to him. "We have to split up. I'll deliver it. You run home. Take the long way!"

Ethan handed her the note mid-stride, and they left each other with no more farewell. He made his way to the rusted-over railroad tracks he and Sam had walked along before. With each step toward home, he felt as if he himself were carrying the weight of one of those ancient locomotives, the movers of people and freight. He had taken on the responsibility and put himself in the danger of an adult, but he felt like a child as he ran away.

* * * * *

The warm wind in his face told Kyle the storm that had passed would come again. He needed to make it home before the rain. But more than that, he needed some time to himself before going back into the fray. The gray and green, vine-covered shack beckoned and welcomed him, creaking hello as he walked onto the porch. He wasn't sure what always drew him back to this place. Perhaps it was only the seclusion. Or maybe it reminded him of a life half-lived in his childhood. But regardless, it was his. And maybe that was all he needed to draw him back.

"Simeon said you wanted to see me."

Kyle whirled around to see Mark standing in the thick weeds by the porch.

"Geez! Mark! You scared me."

"Sorry."

"How did you know I was . . . I didn't tell Simeon . . . I mean, never mind."

Mark had removed his blue jacket and cap. His white shirt flowed openly in the breeze under his suspenders. Kyle noticed his heavy brows shrouding his crystal blue eyes as if they were protecting precious jewels. Mark joined him in the shade of the sagging roof, sitting on the steps.

"So what's it all about?"

"Mark, nothing is simple. Even choices you would think are easy black-and-white choices aren't. I'm not the man I used to be. And frankly, neither are you. We've all been changed by our experiences, the things we've seen and done."

"Are you alright? You seem . . ." Mark grasped Kyle's hand like he was trying to reach a drowning man being swept away in the current.

"Don't!" Kyle didn't mean to shout. "Please," he whispered. "I can't say what I need to say if you're touching me."

"So that's the way it's going to be. You've made your decision."

"I have."

Mark stood to face Kyle again, dragging his coat behind him. It took more energy than he thought he had to raise himself and move away from him. "All in love is fair, I suppose. But this isn't love. It's cowardice. I never saw you as a coward before."

"I'm not a coward! But you said I had to choose. And the Watch has to be stopped. They can't be allowed to spread their lies and treason anymore."

Mark listened to the bees and hornets buzzing around the encroaching bushes and weeds. Robins made their way from branches to sky in fluid movements, shadows against the gathering clouds.

"You know, Kyle, I believe that you believe that. But if you silence everyone who disagrees with you, eventually, all you'll have left is silence. Even those who support your own ideas will be silenced too. I hope you're prepared for that."

Mark couldn't look at him anymore. He didn't recognize the man who sat before him. There was something familiar in the way he ran his hand through his hair and to the back of his neck. Something in his earnestness. But the warmth and gentleness were gone. Feeling his feet move beneath him, Mark let them take him away from Kyle.

"So, that's it?" Kyle called after him. "You're just going to walk away? No goodbye or anything?"

"I'm not the one who walked away."

* * * * *

Back to Gemma. Back on mission. Kyle had to stay focused. He couldn't let what happened with Mark deter him. It was a distraction. That was all. The Corsairs brought order. Everything else was chaos. And all he had to do was stay the course.

"How was the Senate?"

"Pointless, as usual. Not sure I'll go back. Not sure there will even be another session."

"You sound like Z."

"I doubt that."

Gemma tilted her head. She didn't want to fight with him. Not today. She needed connection. She needed to lean on him as she used to. With her hand at the back of his neck, she pulled him in for a kiss. Taut and hot against her hand, his neck stiffened.

"You hungry?"

"Yes, thank you. I could eat something."

"You wanna help me fix dinner?"

"Sure. We could do that."

He seemed formal and rigid to her. She almost felt as if she were entertaining a guest in their home.

"How are the kids that are now with Zacharias?" he asked with a note of sincerity laid across the surface of his voice.

"They seem to be doing okay."

"Tell me again how he found them? Just stumbled upon them in the woods?"

"Not exactly. They were staying at his old cabin where he took his wife after the Disaster. I suppose he went out there to reminisce or something."

"That's not really like him, is it?"

"What is this? An interrogation?"

"Did you know these children already, Gemma? Did you lead him out there to them?" he persisted.

"Let's change the subject, huh? What do you say?"

"Sure, okay."

Kyle felt as though he were reciting memorized lines written by someone else. Nothing about him felt genuine anymore. Looking around the room, he was a prop, just another piece of furniture fulfilling the function it was built for. He walked over to where Gemma stood at the sink, taking her in his arms. He buried his face in her neck, slowly kissing the hollow behind her ear.

Gemma held him in her arms but still felt the tightness in his muscles. Nothing about him felt relaxed or natural. It was as if he were forcing himself to be near her.

"Kyle, I can't keep up with you. One minute it seems like you're picking a fight. The next minute you're kissing me. How do you expect me to act?"

Kyle dropped his arms. His face was a blank. "I don't know, Gemma. I'm just sorry, okay?"

"Sorry for what?"

"For everything."

"You'll need to be more specific."

"I'm sorry for leaving and coming back the way I did. Maybe I'm even sorry for marrying you and putting you through all this. I just wish I could take it all back."

"You wish you didn't marry me, is that what you're saying?"

"It doesn't matter, does it? We can't undo the past. We have one chance to make the decisions that will shape our lives."

"I wish I understood you. I want us to be together, to be a couple. But how can we when you're constantly shutting me out, Kyle? We can't keep doing this. Either let me in or let me go."

He walked to the door, opening it to the shower that covered the outside world, a light steam entering with a breeze.

"Where are you going? I thought we were going to make dinner."

"I should go to the Council of Doctors, see if I'm needed there. At least I'd know what was expected of me."

Gemma couldn't understand her husband's erratic behavior. Sorry for leaving and coming back the way he did, he had said. Unwillingly, her mind jumped back to what Tower had told her—the Triumvirate spies would most likely be people returning from the camps. But it would make sense as well for it to be someone who had returned after serving with the Corsairs.

She tried to fight back her feelings of suspicion. But nothing made sense anymore, least of all Kyle.

* * * * *

At the bridge where she and Sam used to play, Gemma stopped to peer into the river, which was pregnant with rain. It flowed and moved, ever-changing. Her reflection was twisted and lined with the water's movements, and yet she found more truth and beauty in that reflection than in reality. There was something soothing about the way the reflections shifted. Something less soothing when it happened on this side of the reflection.

Her encounter with Kyle had left her uneasy, so she walked to return to Z's house, the only place where she felt safe or secure these days. As the evening passed away, her anger did not pass with it, but grew. She breathed in shallow bursts and felt as if her anger could set fire to a barren earth. She had never really thought about how certain kinds of love could weigh you down like chains or carrying an uneven load. Maybe it was because she'd never felt anything different.

A pigeon flew across the path, dropping a feather on its journey that spun, floated, and flitted to the earth so slowly it looked suspended in air. Gemma knew she had to be on her way as well before the next round of showers hit. The thunder was already announcing their arrival. Stepping across the bridge, she turned to look back once more. Lightning struck the ground mere yards away, shooting into the river, creating a series of explosive splashes along the surface of the water. Gemma had never seen anything like it. Nothing could have prepared her for the spectacle.

"You're back soon." Z sat in his rocking chair on the porch, watching the storms roll in over the valley. "So many comings and goings today."

"Kyle and I had another fight. I didn't want to stay in the house. Where are the kids?" Gemma was hoping to get to spend some time with Daisy.

"Out playing somewhere in between storms. They were feeling a little stir crazy. It seems like you and Kyle are fighting more than usual lately."

Gemma leaned against the railing of the porch. She felt the breeze against her neck, ruffling her hair. "I know. I can't understand him, Z. I try, I swear. But it's like he's living in another world removed from me now, and I can't get through. Ever since Sam came back."

"Now, now. It's not Sam's fault."

"No, that's not what I mean. But it's like it changed something in him. Turned on his suspicions or something. Hell, our whole life together seems to be nothing but suspicion."

"What do you mean?"

"I know you didn't know Kyle before like Sam and I did. You've only known him since he came back from the Corsairs, so you can't compare how he is now with how he used to be. But if nothing else, before he left, he was always so sure of what we were fighting for. Sure of his allegiance. And now, it feels like he doesn't know which side he's on. Like he's fighting against himself."

"Well, maybe we're all . . ."

"No, listen. I have to say this before I talk myself out of it. Z, I'm worried Kyle might be a spy for the Corsairs. Tower and Cypress told me there are at least one or two spies in every village, people coming back from work camps or from being away, infiltrating back into the groups that once trusted them."

"Well, by that logic, Sam could be a spy too."

"I know. Don't think I haven't thought of that."

"Gemma, what other evidence do you have that Kyle is a spy?"

"None. It's just a feeling. Just a suspicion. Like I said. But how can I go on living with a man I no longer trust? I just wish I had someone who could see the whole picture telling me what to do."

"Well, we all wish that. It never gets any easier as you grow older."

"Isn't that what your gods used to be? Someone to tell you which way to go?"

"Do we need to be told what's right or wrong? Or do we just need to be still and quiet enough to listen to what our hearts and consciences are telling us? Maybe a god is made up only of our belief in him. But still we have to ask ourselves—what are we fighting for? And who are we standing with?"

Zacharias observed the crows flying above trees in shadow against the ever-darkening sky. Led by instinct, something beyond their consciousness telling them to seek shelter.

"I know why I fight." Gemma blurted out the words as if she'd been trying to hold them back.

"Why do you?"

"Absolution, to somehow make up for my mistakes."

"I don't understand."

"I never told you exactly what happened when my parents were taken. It was too soon. I couldn't talk about it. Never even told Sam."

"What did happen?"

"There was nothing I could do, Z. I couldn't even watch. I ran away and left them there. I left them."

"You were a child."

"That's not all. I remember when I was running from the village, there was a little boy hiding behind a building that was on fire. He was frozen with fear. Couldn't move. His tears made white lines down his dirty face. Everyone was running. Chaos everywhere. But I just looked at him. Our eyes met through the smoke and debris. I tried to get to him, to pull him away, and get him to run too. But suddenly, the building collapsed. And he was just gone. I couldn't save him . . ." When the words could no longer be wrung from her throat, her tears fell, washing her in the feelings she'd kept at bay so long. She threw her hands up to her face, an unconscious shield.

Zacharias went to her side, stooping a little to look her in the face, gently taking her hands in his, forcing her to face him. "Gemma, that wasn't your fault. None of this is your fault. You take too much on yourself."

"We humans have figured out so many ways to do horrific things to each other. But we're adults," she spoke hoarsely. "What about the kids? They are always the ones to suffer the most, and they are the innocents. What have our actions done to our children?"

"I'm finally starting to understand you. Listen to me, the things we've experienced leave scars, not just on our bodies, but in our very souls. Constantly poking at those scars won't change anything, believe me, I know. You and I have a tendency to look in the wrong direction. We won't find the meaning or the purpose we seek in the past, but in the future."

"Maybe so. But my future and my purpose seems to be to keep the Corsairs from continuing this campaign of taking more and more from us."

"I'm not sure they could have taken anything that our original apathy didn't give them."

"And I'm not sure it's as simple as all that."

The children tromping back from their adventures interrupted them before Zacharias could finish explaining his meaning. Toby and the twins ran and giggled among themselves. But Daisy held back, shuffling behind them quietly.

"Alright, kids. There's apple juice inside. We'll start on dinner shortly. Come on in and clean up." Zacharias led them into the kitchen. But Gemma stopped Daisy before they entered the house.

"Hey, kid. You alright?"

"I'm okay."

"You're not looking at me."

Daisy impulsively threw her arms around Gemma, burying her face.

"Hey, now. What's all this?"

Daisy looked up and could tell Gemma had been crying. "Were you worried about me?" she asked.

"I always worry about you. You want to tell me what happened?"

"I have a message for you from Aishe."

"Well, that's nothing new. What's the matter, sweetie? What aren't you telling me?"

"When I was getting the message from one of the other kids, we were almost caught by a Corsair. That's never happened before. It just surprised me, I guess."

"Scared you, too, I'd say."

"I'm not scared."

"Daisy, being scared is nothing to be ashamed of. I'm scared all the time. Did you know that?"

The child shook her head.

"It's what we do with our fear that matters. If it keeps us from doing what needs to be done, that's not good. But if it makes us more cautious so we can live to fight another day, then that's a good thing. You had every right to be scared of the Corsair in that situation. So how'd you get away?"

"We hid in an old tree trunk, then I distracted him so we could run."

"You did everything right, then. Well done."

Daisy hugged her again.

"Is that what you were worried about? That I'd be disappointed?"

"Maybe a little," she mumbled.

"Never. I'm always proud of you. You remember that." Gemma held onto her a little tighter, hoping that her own fears weren't seeping through. "Now, let's see that message."

Horses hooves splashed in puddles and clomped along the road. A squad of Corsairs was coming close. Gemma and Daisy looked up, still clinging to each other. Daisy was sure they were coming after her, and

Gemma wondered the same. She whispered entreaties to no one in particular that the squad would continue riding past the house. "Please ride on. Please ride on." But they turned in at the drive, the sergeant staring directly at her. Daisy and Gemma stood facing them. Where the child had sought comfort by her closeness before, she now offered support and solidarity. If she had been taller, the two would have been standing shoulder to shoulder as they faced down the soldiers together.

16

BURNED AS COALS

Sounds and smells of men on horseback assaulted Gemma's senses. Jangling stirrups and reins, neighing and whinnying beasts pushing in and pushing out. Orders were shouted across the yard. Flowers and plants trampled. All that existed to these Corsairs was their group and the mission. Everything else was out of their scope of vision. Gemma felt the note from Aishe growing limp in her sweating palm. She had to find a way to hide it. She dropped to her knees on the porch and pretended to tie her boot laces, sticking the paper within the folds of her leather boots.

She whispered to Daisy, "Run inside, sweetie. Tell Z to make sure everything's hidden. Quickly. Then you and the other children head for the cellar."

Daisy hesitated. She didn't want to leave Gemma to face the soldiers alone.

"Go now, kid."

Daisy ran inside just as the sergeant clomped his heavy boot on the porch.

"What can I do for you, Sergeant?"

"Do you live here, citizen?"

"No, I'm just visiting my father while my husband is working at the Council of Doctors. You may know him. Kyle Drape. He used to be a Corsair as well."

"That's enough, citizen. We are here to search the premises for illegal weapons. We will proceed with no further interference from you. Stand aside."

"Just as you say, Sergeant. May I offer your men and horses some water? There's a pump just out back."

"Don't patronize me. Stand aside!"

Gemma took one step to the left as the sergeant passed roughly by her.

"You men search the shed in the back. The rest of us will go inside."

Zacharias sat in his rocking chair with the children surrounding him, rather than in the cellar as Gemma had instructed. He hummed a tune quietly to them. The twins, Hughie and Petal, were crying silently. Toby faced the soldiers with squared shoulders and defiance in his eyes. Daisy sat on Z's lap, following Gemma with her eyes wherever she went.

"Good day, men. Come in, come in. I know you have a job to do." Z's voice was calm, though a little breathless. His face was red, with sweat glistening on his brow.

"You will rise in the presence of a Corsair, citizen."

"Just so. Just so," he groaned as he tried to raise himself from the chair. "You're free to search the place, but the only thing I fight these days is getting out of this blasted chair." He chuckled.

"If you tell us where the weapons are, it will go easier on you."

"There are no weapons, Sergeant. I've told you. I fight nothing and no one."

"We will see about that."

At a nod from the sergeant, four Corsairs spread out through the house to begin the search. The group in the living room watched helplessly and listened as they knocked over every piece of furniture, ripped pictures from the walls, threw food out of the cupboards. There was no order or pattern to their search. They behaved more like tantrum-throwing children rather than adult men. Zacharias held himself back as the soldiers ransacked his house with everything of necessity and comfort flying through the air before it crashed to the ground.

"Sergeant, I found something!"

Gemma felt her stomach rising into her throat as she held Daisy and the twins close.

A young soldier, too young to even shave, came tromping down the stairs holding several books high above his head. "Books, Sergeant. He had them in a secret cabinet."

The sergeant turned to face Zacharias. "So, old man. You're hiding books. I'm sure that's just the beginning. I'll ask you again. Where are the weapons? We know you people have stolen them from a squad of Corsairs. You will tell us where they are!"

"I've already told you, I haven't got any . . ."

The back of the sergeant's hand flew across Z's cheek, sending him reeling back into the chair. With that, the children could be kept in check no longer. Toby led the charge with a leap onto the sergeant's shoulders, hitting him in the face as he clung to his neck. The twins hit the floor and attached themselves to the legs of running soldiers, bringing them down in a heap. Daisy ran straight into the sergeant's gut, ramming him into the wall.

As Gemma tried to collect her senses in the scuffle, her veins were running with pride mixed with fear. She loved that the children were trying to defend Zacharias and their new home, but she knew this would all end badly. She couldn't let them be taken away.

"Children! Children, please stop. Come here. Come to me now!"

Her words went unheeded as the melee continued. She saw with horror that one soldier was reaching for his whip as the sergeant was also fumbling for his gun. In a second, Gemma had wrenched the whip out of the young soldier's hand and stood before the sergeant, who had aimed his gun at Toby, now lying sprawled on the floor.

"No, Sergeant, please. He's just a boy. They were frightened and didn't know what they were doing. Please, Sergeant. I beg you for mercy, sir. You've searched and not found the weapons you came for. Please have mercy on these children and old man."

"Drop the whip and stand aside, woman!"

"I can't do that. I can't let you shoot that boy."

"You can't let me? You can't let me," he laughed. "You do know you're looking down the barrel of a gun, don't you?"

"I do. And you know the power over life or death today lies in your hands. But my question is, what will you do with that power? Did you enter the army to fight children and old men? Or did you join to try to bring a sense of order into a world of chaos? We're told to stay the course with the Corsairs. Very well. We submitted to the search. And now I'm asking for mercy to be shown to these frightened children. Can you do that, Sergeant?"

Gemma looked in his eyes and saw his determination waiver. She knew he didn't want to shoot a child. He rubbed his cheek where Toby had hit him, lowering his gun back into the holster.

"Very well." The words released the tension in the room as quickly as a bubble bursting. Gemma dropped the whip, and the children corralled themselves around her and Zacharias, still sitting in the chair where he'd fallen.

"But I'll be taking that boy with us."

Gemma's fists and shoulders tightened. "No, Sergeant, please. He's just a child. He won't survive prison."

"Oh, I'm not taking him to prison. He's going to be conscripted into the Corsairs. There will be no more discussion. Come here, boy." Toby stepped forward. "What's your name?"

Silence.

"The first thing you must learn is obedience. You will tell me your name, or I will force you to tell me."

"His name is Toby," Gemma offered.

The sergeant threw an angry look in her direction.

"Private, take this Toby and put him on a horse. We're moving out. Now!"

The soldiers jumped at his command, leading Toby roughly out into the encroaching storm. No farewells, no ceremony. Gemma didn't know if she'd ever see the boy again. She knew how upset Ethan would be at the loss of his friend as well. Standing in the doorway with the children, she looked through the sheets of rain to see him sitting with matted hair and dripping clothes in a saddle that dwarfed him. He looked like a man in miniature upon the large animal's back as the soldiers rode away.

"Z, are you alright?" She finally turned back into the house. Zacharias sat in the chair, rubbing his aching head.

"I will be."

"Oh, Z, what are we going to do?" She looked at the mess the soldiers had left behind, both in the room and on the faces of the children. "They bring destruction wherever they go."

"We're going to go about our lives and do what we can do." Z got up, walking to the closet with the hidden door. The first door was off its hinges, the contents of the closet strewn about. But the inner door stood in place. They hadn't seen the guns which stood behind it.

269

"And what's that, exactly?" Gemma asked with anger in her voice as she tried to see to the children's minor cuts and wounds.

"First, we'll clean this up. Then we'll make dinner. You'll return home. And tomorrow, we'll start all over again."

"There has to be a reckoning, Z. They can't continue to get away with things like this!"

"We have to keep our heads down for a while. Try not to draw their attention. They'll be watching us after today's events, expecting us to run for help. So for now, we lie low."

"If we all just run and scurry to the corners to hide, how are we any better than the rats?"

"You know better than that question, Gemma. This is just your anger talking. But we can't allow ourselves to be led by the flights of our feelings."

"I am angry! That soldier had no right to hit you or take Toby. I could . . ."

"Now, that's enough." He held Gemma by the shoulders, letting his eyes wander to the children who stood watching her, ready to take her lead. "How can anyone ever really know who's to blame for anything? He hit me because someone hit him. So and so did this because of that. And this person did that because of this. You can trace it back and back to Cain, who first killed his brother. Further than that to Eve, who ate the apple, introducing human failings. And further still to God, who placed the apple and told Eve not to eat. But to what end? Why blame someone else for an event or series of events when at the end of the day, each person is faced with the choice of how to react or how to let go? How do we move forward from here? And in that, every human being is exactly the same."

"You're right, Z. I know you're right. It's just so frustrating." Gemma looked to the window where the shadows of branches mimicked sentries on patrol. She pulled Daisy and the twins to her, feeling their trembling bodies in her own shaking hands.

"I don't like the storm," Petal said. The first words she'd ever spoken to Gemma.

"Neither do I, sweetheart. But storms become flowers, and flowers become wishes, baby girl. You just remember that."

Later that night after Gemma had gone, Daisy couldn't sleep. She took a walk through the house, peeking in to check on the twins in their new room. They slept bundled together in the center of the bed. As she padded down the hall, she heard muffled crying coming from somewhere. Walking down the stairs, she moved slowly to avoid creaking the wood underfoot. Z's room was on the main floor off the kitchen. Looking under his door, there was not even a sliver of light. The house was in complete darkness. But as she got closer to his room, she knew the old man was the one crying, his choking sobs muffled in the pillows. She wondered if she should go in and check on him but thought he wouldn't like it. The sounds of a man crying scared her more than seeing Gemma so upset earlier, more than Toby being taken away. If the soldiers could make Zacharias cry, what would they do to her, she wondered.

* * * * *

The muggy summer afternoon stifled the square in Jesse's Hollow, and yet Ethan stood uncomfortably close to Sam.

"What is it, boy?" he asked as they waited for the colonel to begin the meeting. "You've been quiet for days, and now you're practically shaking in your boots. What's the matter?"

"Nothing, Sam."

"Are you not feeling well?"

"Yeah, that must be it."

"We'll go to the Council of Doctors after this, then. See what we can do about that."

"I don't think I need to. Really. I'll be alright."

"No arguments. I'm not taking chances."

Ethan shoved his hands in his pockets, hiding his fear behind an angered brow and whispered defiance. "I'm alright."

At the front of the crowd, the Corsairs began to file onto the platform. Sam was concerned to see them leading and pushing a group of people from Jesse's Hollow, both men and women. It was obvious they had been beaten recently, and savagely, too. Several of them cradled broken arms. Others limped across the platform. All had cuts and bruises on their faces.

A colonel unknown to Sam stood to address the town. Sam wondered if the somewhat kinder Colonel Goodson would make an appearance today, and he found himself hoping for it.

271

"Citizens of Jesse's Hollow! The Corsairs are here to protect you. We have found traitors among you, those you see here before you. Your leaders cannot allow their actions to go unpunished. The trash here on the stage with me were found impersonating Corsairs and stealing from the government's farms and work camps. Stealing the very food out of your mouths!" He paused and waited for a reaction which was not to come. The townspeople stood silent and frozen on the summer day.

"We would remind you," he continued undaunted, "it is required by law for any and all citizens to report knowledge of treacherous activities of this nature. If we all stand together in this difficult time, we will stay the course."

"Stay the course," came the mumbled response.

"Now, for your safety and for your remembrance, we have brought these traitors to face their punishment publicly."

Sam looked frantically around the crowd for Gemma. She and Kyle stood near the front of the townspeople, and Sam saw that Kyle had a tight grip on Gemma's arm, as she seemed to be struggling to pull away from him. In those actions, the story revealed itself to Sam. The people on the platform were members of the Watch, maybe even members of Gemma's own squad. And he hoped Kyle would keep his grip on her.

Ethan looked at Sam, who would not meet his gaze but fixed his eyes rigidly on the ten citizens standing among the Corsairs on the platform. With a shouted command from the colonel, a squad of ten Corsairs shuffled quickly down the stairs to face the citizens on the platform. A captain stood to the right of them, shouting the orders. "Ready!"

Sam clenched his fists

"Aim!"

He took a step forward.

"Fire!"

A thud of bodies hit the wooden platform.

In the thick, moist shade of moss hanging from oaks, ten haggard, unarmed people were cut down with a volley of merciless bullets. Screams rang out like tolling bells through the town, pulled from throats trained to silence.

Something beyond consciousness sent Sam forward toward the platform as the colonel continued his speech. "Let this be a reminder to you all of who the real enemy is and where your loyalties should lie. Stay the course!"

Not one person responded, but the crowd dispersed with tearful faces turned to the ground. Sam felt a tight grip on his arm and thought it might be Kyle trying again to hold him back.

"Sam, isn't it?" a brittle voice crinkled in Sam's ears. He turned to see a general with his hand on his arm. On the shoulder of the man's blue uniform, a silver snake swam in the confines of a triangle too small to hold it. It was the snake and star insignia of the Triumvirate. Sam had heard enough about the leader of the Corsairs to recognize Simeon Drape when he saw him. But he was unprepared for the strength he felt in him.

"I wouldn't do that if I were you, son."

"Do what?"

"What you were about to do."

"You have no idea what I was about to do."

"So predictable. Look around you, boy. No one would have come to your aid. They would have watched you die just like they watched these other people die. And it would have been for nothing." Sam stared at this strange man, not sure how to respond or if to respond at all.

"My son has told me a lot about you," Simeon continued almost genially. "Walk with me for a minute, won't you?" He kept his grip on Sam's arm and held a whip in his other hand.

Sam considered for a moment before reluctantly following Simeon.

"Kyle tells me you're a pacifist, that you don't want to join the Watch. I hope this is true. I hope what you've seen here today reminds you of why this is the wisest course of action, to do nothing to interfere. It's best to take care of number one, eh?"

Sam continued to stare in silence.

"Don't have much to say, do you? You know what I think? I think my son is wrong, and that you're not a pacifist after all. I've seen the look you have on your face right now too many times to mistake it. You see, we're not that different, you and I."

"I am nothing like you."

"Oh no? Then ask yourself what your plan was to stop what was happening here today. Did it involve any kind of attack? Any violence?"

"I don't enjoy violence as you obviously do."

"No, the difference is that you think violence for your cause is justified, and you think violence for mine is not."

"Those people today were killed in cold blood. They didn't have to die. Where was the justice in that?"

"Of course they had to die! Someone always has to die in order for the rest of us to appreciate life. We live life in opposites, don't we?"

"That's bullshit. Fucking bullshit. You don't appreciate life. You appreciate nothing," Sam's voice gurgled with simmering rage.

"Such language! What have you been reading, boy? No one from your village has used those words in more than twenty years. Find yourself some old books, did you?"

Sam's silence spoke his surprise.

"Oh, yes, I know you can read. And I know what you read. Perhaps *Catcher in the Rye* or *Salem's Lot*? But you didn't really like those because you didn't take them with you . . . Did you really think we would leave something as important as the flow of information up to chance? You're smarter than that, aren't you? Now, I want you to remember today. Remember our little chat before you make any decisions in the future. Understood?"

Simeon walked away without waiting for an answer. From across the square, Sam heard him call out, "Goodson! You're with me." So the Colonel Goodson had been there after all and hadn't stopped a thing. Maybe Simeon was right about one thing: No one was coming to help.

The perfumed sunset was assaulted by rifle smoke still hanging in the square.

As Sam and Ethan walked home in silence to Boswell and Sophie, they both tried not to think of the carnage they'd just witnessed. In the dimness of the waning moon above the sunset, the fire of the day meeting the night burned as coals.

"Why did you hide your face from that Corsair as we were leaving Jesse's Hollow?" Sam finally asked.

"You saw that?"

"Obviously. What's it about?"

"I didn't want him to recognize me."

"Recognize you from what?"

"Don't get upset, okay?"

"Just tell me."

"When I was carrying a message for the Watch a few days ago, he saw me in the woods. Chased me and this other kid for a few minutes. But we got away."

Sam felt his lungs tighten and breathed out a long sigh to try to relax. "This is the type of thing I was worried would happen."

"It won't happen again, Sam. I'll be more careful. Besides, I saw you today. You wanted to fight them too. I know you did."

Sam stopped walking, kneeling down to look at Ethan face to face, and saw how much of a little boy he still was. He still had hope and sparkle in his eyes, even if they were clouded with a film of fear. "Of course I did. But that doesn't mean it was the safest thing to do—for me, you, or Sophie. We have more to think about than just ourselves, son. Sophie loves you and is terrified of losing you. We have a responsibility to her, don't we?"

"Yes, Sam. But she's in the Watch, too. She understands."

"I know."

"I'll be careful."

"I know you will."

Sam remembered his own childhood, and how it was ripped away from him, remembered having to make grown-up decisions far too early. He had hoped to save Ethan from that. Hoped he and Sophie could have given him a semblance of a childhood. The farm by the sea had seemed like a haven, an escape for a little while. But there they all were, having to face it all again, just like before.

"Sam, what's going to happen to us?"

"I don't know, son."

"Are the Corsairs going to kill us like they killed those people today? Like our parents? And if they are, why don't they just get it over with? What are they waiting for?"

"I don't know that either, Ethan."

"I wish you did."

"So do I. But hear me when I tell you I will protect you and Sophie. No matter what. Do you understand?"

"I do."

"Alright, then, let's just go home."

* * * * *

After dinner, Ethan went up to his room. No one had really spoken throughout dinner. Wilting asparagus hugged the edges of their plates. Nettle soup no longer steamed but sat in cold silence in the bowls. The deaths of the members of the Watch weighed heavily on them, bringing fear as an unwelcome guest to the table. When Ethan had gone upstairs, Sam and Sophie sat staring at their flickering plates in the lamplight in protracted silence.

"I wish they wouldn't make the children go to those damn meetings. It's beyond cruel." Sophie's voice sounded hollow in the room.

"They're growing fear. That's the whole point of all of it."

"To what end? We're already frightened. You reach a level where you can't be frightened anymore."

"Maybe they're trying to establish where that level is."

"What, like a kind of experiment?"

"Maybe."

"It makes no sense. None of it does."

"I saw the smoke again today on my way home from Jesse's Hollow. I wish I knew what it meant."

"I wish I knew what any of it meant." She got up and started clearing the dishes away while Sam pumped water into the sink for washing. "I'm going to take Pip out for a ride now that it's dark."

"Do you have to today?"

"He's been cooped up in the barn for days because of the rain. He's getting restless. I've got to let him out."

"Just stay away from the roads and the lanterns, then, alright?"

"I will. Don't worry, sweetheart. I won't be long." She kissed him on the forehead.

"I do worry."

Feeling the cool saddle under her and the moist air through her hair, Sophie felt as though the earth had just been washed clean only to be soiled again by the terror the Corsairs were bringing down. She had met with Foxglove a couple of days before and given her report of the mission. But she'd received no word yet on how the Watch wanted to proceed. Now with the executions having begun again, she had no idea what to expect, but waited anxiously for word from her captain. They could be thrust into the middle of another war within days. And what of the others, the people beyond the borders? How would another war affect their lives?

Ever since returning from her mission, she couldn't stop thinking of the woman who called herself Gran. She kept wishing she had brought her back over the fence with her. At night, she would wake up from firelit dreams of the old woman running from Corsairs, darting out of burning buildings. Sometimes she would see her sister Laurie with Gran, grown older than her now, withered with time and suffering. Their faces would be covered with ash as the trailing smoke and flames leapt behind them.

Sophie pushed Pip to ride faster, letting the wind whip her face as Pip chose the direction through fields and trees, always on the lookout for a Corsair patrol. Before long, she found they'd reached the Border and pulled him up just short of the barbed wire fence. The wires crisscrossed along the length of fence so there was no way to lift or maneuver them to get through. The only way across the Border was at the guard stations or to cut the fence. Razor-edged barbs punctuated the crosses, and they sometimes held onto fur or flesh from animals attempting to sneak through.

Sliding silently from the saddle, Sophie tried to quiet Pip from his exhilarating ride. She knew a Corsair guard from the guard station would be passing within minutes, but she stood looking through the crossed wires. Where would Gran be sleeping tonight, she wondered. Had she been able to find shelter from the storms?

A barb pricked her finger, jolting her out of her musing. She needed to move quickly to get herself and Pip out of earshot of the Corsairs. But when she turned to go, she felt a tug on her tunic. It was caught on the fence. The moon was too low in the sky by now to assist her with even a hint of light. Pulling and tearing wasn't working. She was held fast. Her nimble fingers fiddled, turned, and tore along the barbs, dripping blood onto the offending tunic. Still it would not come loose.

From the right, she heard the Corsair whistling. He was coming closer on his ten-minute patrol. Pip was snorting and pulling at the reins she held tied around her wrist as he tried to escape without her.

Seconds felt like hours. She was sure she'd be caught when she finally ripped the bottom of her tunic free.

She forced herself to walk somewhat slowly as she led Pip in the opposite direction from the Corsair. She couldn't risk the noise they'd make riding away. As they got deeper into the woods away from the Border fence, she finally allowed herself to mount and ride Pip to the safety of her farm.

After she'd fed and watered Pip, Sophie walked the length of the field back up to the house. It stood black against the gray dawn rising. She silently berated herself for falling into such pointless danger. There was no reason for her to be at the Border in the middle of the night. It was a childish mistake to have made, and one she couldn't afford to make again.

Her neck and shoulders ached from the tense ride. She ran her hands down the back of her neck, pushing into the knots in her shoulders. Then she felt it. Her butterfly necklace was missing. She patted her neck and her clothing, hoping to find it clinging there. But it was well and truly gone. It could be anywhere between where she stood and the Border. The chances of anyone finding it were slim, but her heart ached with the thought that she'd lost Laurie's necklace, her one connection with their shared past. And all for what? For a reckless midnight ride. She walked into the house and up the stairs, defeated.

A bird called through an open upstairs window, standing out against the usual morning wildlife sounds. It didn't sound like a normal call, but distress, chirping and crying in ever increasing volume. Sophie wished she could cry out that way to express her fears.

As she entered the darkened bedroom, Sam rolled and tossed in the bed, mumbling in his sleep as he often did. She'd grown accustomed to his night sounds. She removed her clothes, replacing them with a nightgown before climbing into bed beside him. He didn't settle as she hoped he would but kept turning and kicking at the covers. His mumbling grew louder and more pronounced.

"No, don't take them!" he cried. "No, come back!"

Sophie ran her hand along his sweating forehead, trying to calm him, whispering in his ear. Moving away when she was almost hit by his flailing arms, she knew she had to wake him.

"Sam. Sam, wake up, my darling, it's just a dream."

Still sleeping, he jumped out of bed and started for the window.

"Sam!" She barely reached him in time. As she pulled him away, he cried out, his voice jagged as the blade of a knife. He stood looking at her in the rising light, not knowing her right away.

"Sam, it's me, baby. It's Sophie. You were having a dream. It's okay. You're safe now. Come back to bed."

He didn't utter a sound but allowed her to lead him back to bed. She covered him up, cradling his head against her chest. "Shhh, it's alright now. You're safe. I guess we all have our demons, don't we?" She stroked his wet hair. "It's okay. Go back to sleep." She began singing her song quietly to him. *"In every bird's refrain, I hear you. In the brook that speaks your name, I hear you. In a child's unbridled laughter, in the peace that follows after, in the beating of my heart, I hear you."*

Sam lay there, still. He breathed deeply. And though the air filled his lungs in the bed, she imagined he could still smell the burning of the forest and hear the screams of his dreams. Sleep was lost to him.

PART III

17

SHEDDING LIGHT

Sam stood at the gate leading to Gemma's house, waiting. He couldn't bring himself to go up to the door and knock, so he just waited for her to come out. The days were starting to look and feel differently. Summer was coming to an end. Autumn wrapped the fading green summer day in her vibrant red robes, taking up the burden of brilliance. Summer was shedding her colors, fading, and stepping back from the brightness. He remembered summers he'd spent with Gemma and thought of how slowly and subtly their lives had changed, the colors draining from their days until now when he hardly even recognized her. He questioned again if he should be interfering now and bringing her the information he had. Surely Sophie knew what to do with the knowledge she'd gained on her mission across the Border. He knew she must have already met with her commanders. So why then was he here getting Gemma involved?

If he were honest with himself, it wasn't about getting the information to the Watch but to Gemma herself that was important to him. It was about following the code. He needed her to know and be prepared for what he sensed was coming.

"Sam?"

The voice coming from behind him startled him. He had expected to see Gemma coming down the drive from her house.

"Oh, there you are."

"Were you waiting for me?"

"I have something to tell you."

"What is it?"

"Have you heard anything in the Watch about a second Border? A high concrete wall past the Border fence?"

"Yes, I know about it. But how. . ."

"So what's going to be done?"

"What do you mean?"

"Are they going to send people to try to get over the wall?"

"We don't know yet."

"Well, I think it's time to get in touch with your contact from the government, the one who's leaking information."

"Now, hang on, Sam. First of all, we can't just get in touch with them. They've always contacted us, and only through several layers of messengers. So we have no idea who it is or how to contact them. But secondly, the bigger question for me is how *you* know all this."

"That's not important. Something has to be done. That's the important thing."

"Something is being done. The Watch is going to handle it. But I mean it, how did you come across all this information?"

"Maybe I shouldn't tell you."

"You need to tell me, Sam."

"I got married. My wife went on a mission for the Watch. We talk about things." He let the words fall out quickly. Sam thought he saw fear seep into Gemma's eyes. "But believe me, Gemma, the information is safe with me. I'm not going to tell anyone else. I may not be a member of the Watch, but I will keep your secrets."

"Stop. Please stop talking. I've heard enough."

"She doesn't know that I know you. I recognize there are code names for safety. Honestly, I don't even know hers."

"Please stop, Sam. Let me just take this in, okay?" She gripped the gate, steadying herself. Her knees and her voice were shaking. Nothing about this was in her control. She clutched the gate tighter.

"What's the matter?"

"What's the matter? Can you really ask me that?"

"I don't understand."

"This isn't about the Watch. How did you think I would react to hearing you're married?"

"I don't know. I didn't think you'd have much of a reaction at all. I mean, you married Kyle. Did you think I'd just stay alone for the rest of my life?"

"Do you love her?"

"Of course I do."

"And will you take care of her?"

"Always."

"Then that's all that matters, isn't it?"

"I'm still not sure I understand you."

"You never did. Change of subject. Since this conversation is just an exchange of information, you should tell Ethan his friend Toby was taken by the Corsairs. Conscripted."

"What?! How did this happen?"

"A search at Z's house. The kids went after the soldiers, and they decided to take Toby as retribution."

"I swear, it's like Ethan is just reliving my life."

"The pattern continues until we stop it."

"I don't see that there's much we can do."

"Don't you? Look, I have to go. Goodbye, Sam." Gemma walked through the gate, closing it between them.

Her head was spinning. How could one five-minute conversation completely overturn her world? Sam was married. And to Aishe, her only friend. So this is what he had felt that day when he came back to her and she'd told him she'd married Kyle. The same feeling. Even almost the same place.

Maybe he was telling the truth. But maybe he wasn't. What if he was the spy and just making up a wife to attribute the information to? Maybe this was all a trick to force a move by the Watch. Could this man she'd known her whole life really betray her and everything she stood for? Married to Aishe or a spy for the Corsairs. Were those the only two options? Gemma wasn't sure which prospect scared her more.

* * * * *

"I can't tell Ethan about Toby. I just can't."

Sophie turned on her piano stool to face Sam, still standing in the open doorway. The last chords she'd struck on the piano as he walked in were still hanging in the air. The last phrase of music playing in a loop through her mind. The song hung unfinished. Sophie hated to hear about children being taken and struggled to control her own emotions about it. "You understand what he's going through more than anyone else, honey."

"It's because I understand that I know nothing I could say will help. I want the boy to be able to have his own feelings about it and not be influenced by mine. Could you please just tell him?" Sam was already starting to shift, moving toward going back outside. He looked like a little boy ready to run away.

"If that's the way you want it."

"I do. I'm going out to the field. We've got to get started on the harvest."

"Sam, are you okay?"

"I don't know. I just don't know."

The force of the closing door struck discordant strings on the waiting piano.

Sophie found Ethan in his room, where he often stayed lately. He didn't venture outside as much as he used to, and she had worried about that. It wasn't good for him to be inside and alone as much as he was. And now she was coming to deliver another blow. She wished she could have protected him from it, kept the information to herself. But he would find out as soon as he went to Z's house anyway. There was no protection from it, no insulation from pain. Wasn't that what life had always taught her?

Standing in silence a few moments in the doorway, Sophie waited to enter Ethan's room. He was near the window, closely observing a spider building its web. As the spider swung nimbly from one end of the window to the other, Ethan followed him with his eyes. In his face, the crisscrossing paths of thought were like the web before him, trying to make a pattern out of chaos. In his lap, he gripped a book tightly but did not open its pages.

"What do you have there?" Sophie finally asked.

Ethan turned, surprised to see her standing behind him. "It's a book Z let me have."

"Can I see it?"

He offered the book to her.

"*Peter Pan.* I like this story."

"You know it?"

"I sure do."

"It's why Sam sometimes calls me the Lost Boy."

"But you aren't really lost anymore, are you?"

"No, I guess not."

Sophie's smile could not hide the sadness Ethan saw in her face.

"Sophie, did something happen to Daisy?"

"Who's Daisy?"

"One of my new friends. She lives with Z now."

"No, I'm sure Daisy is fine."

"But something else is wrong."

"How do you know that?"

"Your eyes say just about everything."

"Sometimes I wish they didn't."

"You can tell me. I can handle it."

Sophie was in awe again at the strength in this little Lost Boy. She wished she could whisk him off to Neverland where he would never have to grow up. Never lose his friends or see the terrible things he'd seen. But there was no Neverland, no place of fairies and magic. She wondered if there was even a place where humans could find their humanity again.

* * * * *

From the top of the piano, Sophie pulled down the picture of her holding Bridget. She wondered if she would be acting differently now if Bridget were still with her. She probably wouldn't have gone to the Border at all that day if her daughter had still been alive. She looked at her daughter's blonde head laying on her shoulder, the kiss she'd planted on her forehead. She saw again the fever in her cheeks, the useless suffering. And she knew she had to hold on to every piece of her family. Every reminder of love found and love lost. If humanity was going to survive, it would be in the mementos treasured, the kisses shared, and the family remembered.

Sam stood knee deep in the deep green sea of beans, bending, snapping, and plunking them into the bucket he carried with him. Sophie knew his back would be sore later. She'd have to remember to bring the bottle of liniment to rub on him that night. As she walked toward him, she felt the warm, damp soil caress her toes. She loved being barefoot; it was her preferred state.

"Sam, I brought you some water."

Wiping the sweat from his forehead with the back of his arm, he stopped what he was doing. He gratefully took the glass from her. Drinking it in one large gulp. "How'd he take the news?"

"Better than I would have expected. Like the little man he is."

"He's a strong kid. He'll be alright."

"Will he? He's had a lot of shocks lately. I'm not sure how much more he can take."

"He can take it, Sophie. Trust me. It's not what any of us wanted, but he'll survive. Like we did."

"Maybe so. Listen, I've got to go look for my necklace I lost."

"You really think you're going to find it?"

"Maybe not, but I've got to try."

"Where are your shoes?"

"Not going to wear them. Better for sneaking." Sophie tried to laugh unsuccessfully.

"Let me go with you."

"No, it's dangerous enough with only one person. I'll try to be quick."

"Why do you have to do this? No one's going to find it, and even if they do, they have no way of connecting it to you."

"That's not why I'm going. It was Laurie's necklace. It's all I have left of my family."

"So you're risking your own life and what you have with this family?"

"That's not fair, Sam."

"Maybe not, but it's the truth. Laurie isn't here anymore. But Ethan and I still are. We can only protect and fight for the ones that are still alive. We can't recapture what is gone."

Sophie took the glass back from him and turned to leave. There were no words she could say in response.

"Sophie, wait."

"I'll be back later," she called over her shoulder.

* * * * *

There were two guards at each station who walked the Border fence from one station to the middle point between stations. Sophie knew from watching them many times that a guard passed the middle point every ten minutes, and the stations were never left unattended.

She approached the fence silently, every position of her feet a slow, silent settling in the earth beneath. Hiding in the hanging vines of an aged tree, she waited for the guards to pass so she could time herself at the fence from the time of their arrival to the time of their return. Her ears tuned into every sound around her, cataloguing them as normal nature sounds or perking up to any unexpected noise. Every lift of the breeze seemed to portend an approaching threat. Finally, she saw them. One guard, then two. They nodded to each other, turned, and walked back along the paths they just marched. She had ten minutes to look near the fence for her necklace.

She moved quickly and silently. She knew the green of the necklace would blend in with the underbrush. Her hands moved swiftly through the leaves. Maybe Sam had been right that this was a useless undertaking. She still saw movement everywhere, and every sound startled her, but she continued looking, counting silently in her head. Seven more minutes.

But then something did move on the other side of the fence. Or maybe she just imagined it. Leaves rustled and something darted from behind a tree. Frantic panting and wheezing. It wasn't an animal, but a person. There was a woman running for the fence.

Sophie watched her approach, fighting the urge to grab at the fence, knowing it was useless to try to get the woman through without wire cutters. The woman's hair was long and would have been red if it had been clean, a shade lighter than Sophie's own hair. Her face was streaked with smoke, and for the first time, Sophie smelled the burning air.

"I knew it was you. I hoped you'd come back," the woman spoke between gasped breaths.

"Do I know you?" Sophie tried to see through the dirt and smoke to the woman's features underneath.

"It's me, Sophie. It's Laurie."

Sophie couldn't stifle her cry but covered her mouth in the attempt.

"I found my necklace the other night here by the fence and knew it must have been you that dropped it. And then I knew you'd come back for it, and you did."

Sophie's tears were blocking her words. She couldn't bring her thoughts into focus. "Laurie," was all she could whisper.

"We don't have a lot of time." Laurie looked around, listening and almost sniffing the air to sense if the Corsairs were near.

"What's happened to you, Laurie? Were you in a fire?"

"The Corsairs burn everything they come across, buildings, people. It doesn't matter to them. They just light it up. They found where I'd been living."

"I'm going to get you out. I thought you were dead. Laurie, they told me you were dead." Sophie couldn't stop her tears. She reached through the fence, grasping her sister's hand.

"There's no way out. They'll catch you."

"No, I've crossed the Border before. I can do it again. Listen, you stay close to here. I'll come back. I'll cut the fence. We'll get you out. I promise."

"Soldiers will be coming back. You have to go now."

"I don't want to leave you again."

"No choice."

"I'll be back. I swear, Laurie. I won't lose you again."

"Corsairs," Laurie hissed. She heard them approaching before Sophie did. "Run." Laurie pulled away from the fence, leaving the necklace in her sister's outstretched hand.

Sophie could hear nothing but the pounding of her heart in her ears. But she ran anyway. Ran away from the fence, away from her regret and the shame she felt over having left her sister. Ran toward the only comfort she knew. Sam.

* * * * *

Listening only absently to Simeon, Kyle stood at attention but noticed the leaves on the ground. Always before, Kyle gloried in the autumn, loved the smell in the air as it cooled, and the crunch of the brown and golden leaves beneath his feet. It had been his favorite time of year when he lived in the woods. Not to mention that it was easier to hear an enemy approaching. The leaves formed a sort of alarm system. A gift of nature. But these leaves were different; their green and supple bodies should have been clinging to life on the branch, but instead they sacrificed themselves before they'd even lost the green in their veins.

"Once I convince that weak-minded president this is the only way, we'll have to move quickly before the information is leaked to the Watch. Timing will be everything. I'm relying on you to now be the calming force. Are you listening to me?" Simeon struck the whip against the back of Kyle's legs.

"Yes, sir. Couldn't we just send them to work camps away from the influence of the Watch? Surely, there's a way to save some of them." Kyle fought the urge to rub the back of his sore legs, remaining at attention in the general's presence.

"Are you questioning me? So I still haven't convinced you I know what's best for these people."

"Sir, that's not what I mean. I didn't mean to question . . ."

"Silence. When will you understand? The land *must* be cleansed. We've tried the tactic before of separating the children from the influence of their rebel parents. And they still grew into another generation of rebels. It only takes one to spread the poison to the others. One spark alone can start a blazing fire. That's what I must make the president understand. As for you, you'll do as you're told. One tiny spark. That's all it takes, my boy. Remember that. Now, you have your orders. Take care of that little problem in the Watch we talked about. Beyond that, calm the others. Deny any possibility of a Corsair attack. Let them know everything we do is for their own good."

"That's the truth, isn't it?"

"Of course it is."

* * * * *

Tower was nervous. He'd asked Foxglove to meet him at the cave behind the waterfall, knowing he had sensitive information to give her. So the most serious precautions had to be taken. Very little sunlight filtered through the thick trees, which bristled in the wind, constantly making Tower look over his shoulder. Every movement, every broken twig could be a Corsair moving closer. But then he told himself he was just being paranoid. Just up over the step stones and he'd be in the cave. He hoped Foxglove wouldn't keep him waiting long.

Was that just a branch rustling in the wind behind him, or did it sound more like real movement? An animal, maybe. Tower threw a quick look over his shoulder before scrambling up over the slippery rocks. Just a few more yards.

That branch definitely broke behind him. It couldn't be the wind. He saw no animal. No movement. Wishing for more light in the woods, he took one last look around before entering the cave.

* * * * *

The smell of smoke pricked Kyle's nose. He could expect more of that in the coming weeks as the weather turned colder. Although it did seem early in the day for it. He walked the familiar road to his thinking place. How often in the past days had he passed by it, hoping to find Mark there? He knew it was a fruitless hope. He'd sent Mark away, and he knew him well enough to know he wouldn't return to the place where their last meeting had happened. Maybe he'd even ask for a transfer to get away from Kyle. But Kyle knew none of that really mattered now. Not with the job ahead of him, and not with what he'd just done on Simeon's orders.

Yet despite everything, he longed to see Mark and couldn't wipe the longing away with all of his rational or logical thought. He wished he could talk over his thoughts about his father with Mark. Simeon was gearing up for a major push against the Watch and using Kyle to help him. He wondered how much Mark knew. Even with Mark leaking information to the Watch, Kyle questioned how much of it was true and how much of it was made up to further his father's plans. How he wished he and Mark could be on the same side again.

Kyle pushed through the overgrown bushes and weeds, thankful he had on his Corsair boots, knee high and a protection from the thorns he was swimming in. He squinted against the fiery sun backlighting the shadowed trees ahead. But as the smell of smoke grew stronger, he realized the orange behind the trees was not the sunset, but fire. The house was on fire.

Running the rest of the way, he felt the heat burst upon him as he neared the house. It had gone up like kindling, completely engulfed. The roar and blaze overwhelmed him, making him turn his face away. And then he saw it. A horse with a Corsair saddle was tied up in the trees behind the house. The mount snorted and neighed, trying desperately to free himself and bolt from the fire. But where was his master? Where was the soldier who had left him there?

"Mark! Mark!" Kyle screamed, hoarse and coughing in the choking smoke. "Mark! Where are you?"

He ran to the back of the house, hoping to find a way in. He could be in there. Mark could be inside the inferno.

"Mark!" he called again, tears streaking down his blackened face.

He moved to start pulling at the flame-licked timbers, the dripping ash falling like red and orange raindrops around him.

"Kyle?! Kyle, stop! What are you doing?"

Kyle turned to see Mark standing in wet clothes behind him.

"I found it like this. I thought maybe . . . maybe you'd done it yourself. So I went for water, but it was no use. God, I'm glad to see you."

Kyle flung himself at Mark, clutching him in a fearful embrace. His soot-covered hands on the sides of his face, kissing his mouth, not thinking anything except how glad he was that Mark was still alive.

"I thought you were dead. I thought you were dead," the words escaped through his sobs.

"It's alright. I'm alright. Come on, let's get away from these flames."

Mark took the reins of his horse and walked with one hand in Kyle's and one hand trying to steady the animal. They went down to the river, neither of them speaking until the sound of the rushing stream drowned out the sound of the flames in their ears.

Both men threw water on their faces from the river, washing away the smoke and the tears.

"I thought they'd killed you," Kyle finally said when he could speak again.

"Who?"

"The Watch."

"This isn't something the Watch would do. It's not one of their tactics."

"They could change their tactics."

"Think about it, Kyle. Who do you know who uses fire as his weapon of choice?"

"No! The Watch could have done this to trick us."

"To what purpose?"

"How should I know? To turn me against my own comrades."

"And who knows about this place besides the two of us?"

"I didn't think anyone knew about it."

"And who has the resources to have you followed and the motive to frighten or punish you?"

"I know what you're saying, and you're wrong. My father wouldn't do this to me. Especially when I've been carrying out his orders."

"What do you mean? What have you done?"

"We can't talk about this, Mark. I'm glad you're okay. But our situation hasn't changed."

"Kyle, please try to reconsider. Just think about things logically. Remember your parents. He burned your house then. And he's done it again. He follows the same pattern. He's as predictable as he claims everyone else is. And far more cruel."

"I can't. I can't do this. It's too late."

"Kyle. Kyle!"

But Kyle was gone before he could hear Mark calling after him. As he walked away, Kyle closed his eyes, losing himself again in the smoke caught beneath leaves above his head. Leaves that would soon be on the ground, leaving empty and reaching branches behind.

* * * * *

A strip of orange leaves lit by the sun infiltrated into the gray-green forest like a visitor. The sun was setting, and Gemma would soon be surrounded by darkness. She had to move fast to get to the cave where Tower was waiting.

As she hurried, she thought of Kyle. They hadn't really talked in days. Something was off with him, but she didn't know how to get through to him. She thought of her life before Kyle. The hollow rooms and emptiness she felt with Sam gone. She had fallen into a void and a loneliness not even Zacharias could pull her out of. She never told anyone, but she had actually thought of taking her own life in those years without Sam. It had all seemed so pointless without him. She would sit in her room with the very revolver she carried now in her tunic, spinning the empty cylinder holding only one bullet. She never could bring herself to pull the trigger. Fear and a sense of responsibility for Daisy stayed her hand. However much she loved the child, though, she knew that relationship could never be enough.

Then Kyle came back, and everything changed. She'd felt really needed again. He hadn't shared with her what his life had been like in the Corsairs.

It wasn't hers to know. And she hadn't told him about her depression before his return. They both trafficked in secrets and hidden stories yet clung together in the midst of it all. And there they were in the swirling mass of lies and missed connections. She had no idea if they could truly ever make it work between them.

As she got nearer the cave, something in the air made her slow her pace. Something didn't smell or feel right, but she couldn't put her finger on what it was. She had learned to trust her instincts, so she stepped lightly. Tower was vague in his message to her requesting the meeting, but she sensed he had word on who the spy was. Gemma tried to figure out what felt different about the area of the woods around the cave. Then she realized the birds weren't making any noise. The forest was almost silent. Not a sound but the breeze stirred around her. She looked up through the boulders to the hanging vines of kudzu and broken branches in front of the cave. Just off to the left among the trees, the joints and curves of the branches looked almost like human limbs. She took another step up and looked again. They *were* human limbs. Tower was hanging from a rope in one of the trees. His eyes were open, almost staring at her. His face blue with strangulation. His whole body seemed twisted and unnatural. As her mind fought against the image she was seeing, an unbidden scream started to rise in her.

As the sound was tearing through her throat, a hand covered her mouth, and impossibly strong arms pulled her away to another part of the forest. Movement of her arms and upper body was completely futile, but she kicked her legs fiercely in the air. It was several minutes before they stopped and she was set upon the ground. Falling against a tree, she was finally able to look into the face of her captor.

Sam.

Through blurred eyes, she locked her gaze on him, not wanting to accept the thoughts that raced through her mind. In a second, she had her revolver in her hand, pointing the shaking barrel at him.

"Whoa. Hang on, Gemma. It's me. Put the gun down."

"I know it's you! Tell me I'm wrong. Tell me you didn't do this. I want to be wrong. Please just tell me I'm wrong!"

"You've got to get control of yourself and try to be quiet. The assassin could still be around. That's why I had to take you away like that."

"How do I know you're not the assassin?"

"Why would I have tried to keep you quiet if I was? Why would I have come out of hiding at all?"

"I don't know. Nothing makes any sense anymore. Just please, if you ever loved me, tell me you're not the spy. Tell me and make me believe you." Gemma talked through broken sobs. She didn't know if she could shoot Sam. But she didn't know if she could believe him, either.

"Of course I'm not the spy."

"But you knew about the mission. And now you're here."

"I told you how I knew about the mission. And I'm here because . . ." Sam didn't want to finish his sentence. He felt suddenly exposed.

"Why? Why are you here?"

"I came across that man in the tree by accident just a minute or two before you did."

"That doesn't explain why you're here."

"I was following you."

"Why?!"

"To try to protect you."

"Protect me? You're not making any sense. None of this makes any sense!"

"The code still makes sense. Helping people still makes sense."

"That damn code. *Share you fire, take care of them until they can stand on their own*, right? Well, I can stand on my own now, Sam. You don't have to take care of me anymore. You've got a wife now, anyway."

"Fine, I'll go, but you shouldn't stay here in case the murderer is still around."

"Wait."

"What?"

"I still don't know that you're not the murderer."

Sam looked into Gemma's tear-filled eyes. He hadn't seen her this frightened since they were children living in the wild together before they even met Kyle, when she would wake up screaming in the middle of the night. He walked a few steps forward, placing his chest against the barrel of the shaking gun. "Yes, you do."

Gemma dropped the gun and fell on her knees before him. "He was my friend," she cried. "This is my fault. I got him involved. Now he's dead. My squad members killed in the square. It's all my fault, Sam."

"No, it's not. It's this war. It's the Corsairs." He knelt and took her by the shoulders, resisting the urge to wrap his arms around her. "It's like Z says, we can only control how we react. We can't control their actions. Now come on, Gemma. You can't do this here. We've got to go. Come on. Walk with me. I'll go back to Jesse's Hollow with you."

"No, you go. You have to get back to . . . to your wife."

"I can't leave you here."

"Yes, you can." Gemma wiped her face, pulling in her tears with a deep breath. "It'll be good practice for you. I can take care of myself now, Sam. I have to."

"I'm sorry about all this, Gemma."

"So am I."

* * * * *

Just as Sam was walking up the drive home, Sophie came across the field to join him.

"Did you find the necklace?" he asked.

She held it out for him to see as they came into the shadow of the porch, moonlight falling around them. Sam saw a sparkle of tears in her eyes.

"Sophie, I'm sorry about earlier. I was wrong. I shouldn't have said what I did. I know it was important for you to find it . . ."

"That's not it," she interrupted.

"What is it?"

She tried to speak, but felt a tightness in her throat, a lurching in her stomach. "I think I'm going to be sick." The words tumbled out as she ran for the bushes.

Sam held her hair back until the episode had passed.

"Feel a little better now?"

Sophie nodded.

"What's wrong? Did something happen?"

"My sister. She's alive. She's been living in the Forbidden Grounds."

"What? That's incredible!"

"Oh, Sam, she's been out there for years! You know what it's like in the woods. If I had known . . . even thought there was a chance she was still alive, I would have gone after her. But they told me she was executed, even gave me her necklace as proof. Why did I believe them? Why didn't I keep looking for her?" Sophie was breathing quickly, still feeling sick to her stomach.

"Everything was crazy in those days. You probably would have just gotten yourself killed if you had tried. Sophie, we can't keep looking back. That's not where the answers are. All we can do is try to go forward now. We'll help her. We'll bring her back home. That's all we can do."

"Is it? Is that all we can do? I've got to try to make this up to her."

"Let's take one thing at a time. Let's bring her home safely first. Alright?"

18

THE COLOR OF BLOOD

The taste of smoke was bitter on Kyle's tongue. Smoke still seemed to be all around him, in his hair, his clothes. He could hear the roar of the flames as if they engulfed him along with the deserted house. He sat on the back porch of the home he shared with Gemma, waiting for her to return, wondering if the fire still burned. Although fire was a necessary part of his existence, Kyle had always hated it. The smell, the sounds, the blinding orange glow that stayed within your eyes even after you looked away. He hated it all. And as he stared into the twilight, he thought he saw the flames rising up over the horizon, moving nearer.

There was no fire except in his memory. No light on the horizon except those of the lightning bugs. No hissing or crackling, only the cicadas singing their nightly tune. But in his mind, it all blazed up, leaving him with nothing but smoke.

He heard Gemma's steps in the house, heard her calling for him. But he continued to sit in the smoke left behind.

Gemma's hand was on his shoulder. The minutes of her search for him had vanished; her quick appearance startled him. "What are you thinking about?" she asked with a hesitation in her voice.

Silence borne on the still air gave Gemma her answer.

"There's a strong smell of smoke in the air tonight," she forged on.

"Soon everything will be smoke." Kyle's voice was a whisper. Gemma wasn't even sure she'd heard him.

"What do you mean?"

"Everything, everyone I've loved, is eventually just kindling for the fire."

"Even me?" Her voice shook. She took a deep breath to calm the shiver that went deeper than her skin.

"How many lives do you think we've lived?" He ignored her question.

"I don't know. I feel like I've lived about four I guess: one with my parents, one in the woods with you and Sam, one with Z, and now one with you and me."

"Do you ever feel like we're just living the same life over and over again until we get it right?"

"Maybe." There seemed to be some hope in his question. She started to think maybe it wasn't too late for them after all.

"Remember that time I was sick and you made me soup out in the woods? You said it was the soup your mother had made for you when you were a little girl." Kyle continued to stare into the encroaching darkness. The only light was coming from the lantern in the kitchen behind them and spilling around their feet.

"I remember. It's one of my fondest memories with you. When you let me take care of you."

"And you sat there feeding it to me, wiping my head down with a cold cloth, dripping water from the river. No one had ever done anything like that for me before. And nothing was ever quite so simple again."

"Kyle, are you alright?"

"Did you do it?" he whispered.

"Do what?"

"Or was it just your friends in the Watch?"

"I have no idea what you're talking about."

He stood quickly, knocking over his chair, turning on Gemma like a wild animal, growling his answer. "Burn down my house. Someone did it. So just tell me, was it you?"

"Kyle, let's not do this again. You aren't making any sense. How can I possibly answer your questions if I don't even know what you're talking about?"

"What aren't you telling me? I know you keep secrets."

"Oh, really? And what aren't you telling me? Why did you have another house? What is all this about?"

"We'll never really trust each other, will we?"

"How can we if the only conversations we have are made up of accusations and suspicions?"

Gemma heard herself in his accusations. Heard the fear and suspicion she'd heaped onto Sam. And hearing it made her ill. Kyle was right. None of them trusted each other anymore. How could they?

She wondered how they'd gotten so far away from the tight-knit group they used to be. Wondered how anything or anyone could have come between them. And part of her longed for the simplicity of living out in the woods with Kyle and Sam, knowing who they could trust and knowing clearly who the enemy was. Nothing would ever be so clear again. But this was what happened when you lost people. The losing wasn't always all at once, but sometimes a little at a time. First you lost time with them. Then the trust would go. Eventually, there would be nothing left of the people or relationships that once were.

That night, sleeping alone in the bed while Kyle slept on a thin pallet downstairs, Gemma dreamt of the river. She and her boys and the river. All being pulled and torn by the lashing waters and relentless current. In her dream she reached for Sam. She couldn't see through the rapids where he was looking, but he swam away from her. Water constantly assaulted her mouth and nose as she tried to keep her head higher than the waves. She tasted the metallic taste of the water, felt the twigs and grass in her mouth. The water stung her nose and the back of her throat. Turning to see where Kyle had gone, she glimpsed him gasping for air as he went under, until all around her was only water and rocks as far as she could see.

* * * * *

Sophie closed the kitchen window, blocking out the chill and fog in the morning air. The sun shone through the gray mist, sparkling in the tiny crystals of dew. Autumn was coming. Sitting back down at the breakfast table with Sam and Ethan, she picked listlessly at her food. She yawned and wished she could just go back to bed. Ethan looked like he was sharing the same thoughts.

"You're not eating, sweetie. Can I fix you something else? There may still be some strawberries in the garden," she offered.

Ethan shook his head, staring down at his plate.

"You've hardly eaten anything in days. Can you tell me what's wrong?"

"You're not eating either," he said into the grits now cooling on his plate.

"I'm not feeling very well this morning." Sophie's voice was hoarse. She took a bite of her food, forcing herself to swallow, and knew almost immediately she'd made a mistake.

"Me either."

"Do you have a fever?" She felt his forehead with the back of her hand.

"No. Can I just go back up to my room now?"

"I suppose. What are you going to do today?"

Sam didn't want to watch Sophie beat her head against a brick wall anymore. The whole meal was becoming uncomfortable for him. He knew she was just trying to help. But she was pushing too hard. "Ethan, run on up to your room, boy. I'll call you when I'm heading out to the fields. You can help me start the harvest, eh?"

Ethan nodded and ran upstairs.

Picking up her plate and Ethan's, Sophie dumped their contents into the compost bucket. The splattering sound almost sent her running for sink, but she held down her food valiantly. "There's something wrong with him, Sam," she spoke through tense throat. "He's not himself."

"He's had a hard few days. He just needs time to adjust."

"Maybe we all do, I suppose. But have you noticed something about the children? Not just Ethan. They don't cry anymore. They just hold everything in as if they think it's pointless. I just wish he'd talk to me. He could always talk to me."

"He'll talk when he's ready, sweetheart. Why are you pushing so hard on this?"

"I don't know. I'm just worried about him. I want to take care of him. I want him to know I'm here for him, no matter what."

"He's not Laurie, Sophie. I know you think that you let her down. But you didn't. And you're not letting him down either."

Sophie gripped the side of the sink, fighting down the nausea and back the tears. She wished she could just close up her body like you close a door.

Stepping behind her, Sam rested his chin on her shoulder. "He'll talk to you in time. Now what's all this about you not feeling well? Do we need to take you to the Council of Doctors?"

"No, my stomach is just still upset and I feel a little dizzy, that's all. If you grab me some ginger from the garden, I'll make a tea that should help."

"I will. But even still, I'd feel better if a doctor saw you."

"Sam, it's nothing."

"Tea, and then we'll go to town." He was already heading for the back door.

"You're not going to let this go, are you?"

Sam only grinned.

* * * * *

They heard it before they saw it—the sound of skin on skin, bone on bone. Walking into Boswell, Sam and Sophie turned the corner toward the square. There, in front of anyone who would watch, two Corsair soldiers were beating a man on the ground on the side of the road. The man no longer moved but lay with his arms around his head and his knees up under his chin. But still the soldiers hit him, taking turns in a team effort like they were chopping down a tree. Blood turned the dirt under him into red mud.

Across the street from Sophie and Sam, two other men walked by close enough to be splattered by the man's blood. One stopped and looked as if he wanted to intervene. "Shouldn't we do something?" he whispered.

"Stay the course," the other man answered, pulling his friend past the unpleasant scene.

Sam thought how strange this dance was they were all locked in together. The Corsairs taking one aggressive step forward after another, and the citizens always taking a step back.

Sophie moved as if she were going to cross the street and try to do something about it. Sam put his arm around her shoulders and continued walking forward, blocking her way. "There's nothing we can do right now, Sophie," he whispered.

"I have to try."

"No. No you don't. Try to think about it rationally. The man is probably already dead."

"That's worse."

"What would you be killing yourself for?"

"For what's right."

"Would you dying here today change anything?"

"Maybe it would."

"No, it wouldn't. You can do more good if you stay alive, now come on. We have to get you to the doctor, alright? Come, on, Sophie. Please."

They walked the rest of the way in heavy silence.

A breeze blew the fog clear of the square, catching leaves along the way, marking the beginning of the year's long farewell. Sophie felt sick with all the words she'd never said, all the times she'd had to walk past and say nothing or do nothing about the atrocities the Corsairs visited upon them. She was filled up with them until she thought she'd burst. Just the thought of Laurie living all those years on the other side of the Border, alone in the broken-up world of the past, was enough to make her feel as if she'd throw up. She felt like a river filled up with all the rageful storms, flowing and racing out to the sea, but not fast enough. Already, she felt her banks and old levees of the past built to shore up against an overflowing river now cracking, collapsing, breaking with the weight of the water that could no longer be held back.

The square was filled with other people as silent as Sam and Sophie. They all went about their own business, speaking only when absolutely necessary. The birds went about their jobs of finding food, building nests. The squirrels silently did the same. Looking at the ground as he walked, Sam saw a line of ants crawling and slithering like a snake toward their goal. And they all moved together like gears in a clock, but separated, silent. The only sounds were the continued blows of the Corsairs on the man on the ground.

Into this busy silence of everyone knowing and keeping their place, an old man stumbled and reeled his way into the square, falling into line behind Sam and Sophie at the Government Office as they waited to see a doctor. He spoke quietly to himself as if he were having a normal conversation. A smell of sweat and urine emanated from his slouching form. Sophie and Sam turned slightly to see him shuffling in place behind them, from one foot to the other. His clothes were tattered and worn, transparent in places. They wondered how long he'd been living out in the woods and if he even had the identification papers necessary to get him food and new clothing. He seemed uncomfortable, but more than that, he seemed genuinely frightened. Crumbs from his last meal decorated his chest-long beard, white with hints of black and gold. He was a calico cat who had forgotten how to clean himself.

"Are you alright?" Sophie asked.

Sam tugged at her sleeve, trying to signal her to leave it alone.

"Never a thief that takes from none. Never a soldier that marches without killing. A winking, twinkling star is brighter than the moon."

"Can I do something for you? Maybe you'd like some water."

"No feast, no feast tonight," he continued, looking all around him, but not at anyone. "Have to wait until the battle's over. Hungry after a fight."

"Sam, I think he was a soldier."

"I wouldn't doubt it. Let's just leave him alone, alright."

"He needs help."

"Never!" The man's shout startled Sophie. She clutched her lurching stomach. "Never gonna catch us. Not us. We'll find a hiding place, eh Jarom?"

Hearing this, Sam leaned down to put his face just in front of the man's. "What did you say?"

"No better place to hide from the traitors than down by the—No! Won't tell. They'll never make me tell."

"Sam, what is it?" Sophie was starting to be genuinely concerned, not just for the old man but for all of them. She felt as if some outside force had thrown them all together, stirring them in a pot of pain, memory, and fear. In her mind it was as if she heard just a piece of an old forgotten tune, grasping and reaching at something she couldn't quite remember. Looking in the eyes of Sam and then the old man, she knew they both felt the same.

"Nothing. Just turn around."

"It was that damned redhead. Can't ever trust a redhead. She gave us all away. Gave us all away."

Sam and Sophie moved forward in the line. The old man grabbed Sophie by the shoulder and whirled her around.

"You! It was you. Gave us all away. Sent Jarom to the executioner."

"Sir, I'm sorry, I don't know you. I think you're mistaken."

Sam took a threatening step toward the old man, placing himself between him and Sophie. "What are you talking about? What happened to Jarom?"

"She-devil. She-devil did the deed. Do the deed, plant the seed." He laughed to himself. "Raining under the shadows of the bridge. Slipping into the general's camp. She-devil!" He pointed a crooked finger in Sophie's face.

"Let's get out of here, Sam. I obviously remind him of someone else. We can come back another time."

They started making their way out of the square, feeling the eyes of other citizens on them. The last thing they needed was to draw attention to themselves with the Corsairs close and bent on punishment. The old man fell out of line behind them, shuffling along the road in their wake, following them with a barrage of incoherent mumblings. The edge of the town square gave way to the woods, and they hoped to lose the man among the trees, but he stayed close. Too close.

"She-devil. Evil in the eyes. Always the redheads. Can't make me tell, though. Never did. Never did."

"Sam, what are we going to do?" Sophie whispered. "I feel like he needs help, but he's frightening me."

"Just keep walking for now."

"Too much rope to hang a man, just enough to tie him up."

Suddenly, the man took up a strange and wandering tune, blended pieces of songs and poems he'd heard in whatever life he used to live. *"Gone in the valley, the valley below. Always the children crying in snow. If I should die before I wake, I pray the Lord her neck to break."* He began to giggle uncontrollably as he ran around to block the path in front of Sophie and Sam.

"Sara! Sara gave us all away. Jarom gone. All gone now. Sara! Sara did it!" The man stood unexpectedly straight and tall with an accusing finger piercing the air between himself and Sophie.

She had turned pale, gripping Sam's arm and trying to hold herself up.

"I pray the Lord her neck to break!"

Before either of them could move, the man had his hands around Sophie's throat.

It took Sam a moment to register what was happening. When he came to himself, the man, crazed with memory and fear, had Sophie up against a tree, strangling her. Putting the old man in a headlock from behind, Sam was amazed at his strength, and was struggling to pull him away. Moments of scuffle and struggle felt longer as Sam fought to stay in the present. His arms were beginning to tire as he tried to use enough force to stop his foe, but not so much as to kill him.

Sophie's face over the man's shoulder was turning blue. Sam knew he had to act quickly. Other faces flashed before him. His father being dragged into the square to be executed, his mother right behind. The first man who tried to kill Sophie in the woods. It all came flooding back, swirling around him like fetid water. And suddenly he was falling into the water, into space, into a world made of silenced breaths.

He wrenched the man to the ground, heard Sophie coughing and sputtering behind him. He couldn't let the man up, not yet. Not while he struggled. He couldn't be sure he wouldn't attack again.

The noose tightening around his parents' throats as they stood on the gallows. Sophie gasping for air. Kyle pushing him into the river. So many Corsairs swirling in the waves of the river. Reaching out to grasp at something, or to hold it at bay. Sam battled to draw air into his lungs. He was coughing and choking on his own tears. A hand was on his shoulder. He shrugged it away. Sophie's voice seemed to float to him from far away as if he were just waking from a dream.

"Sam. Sam, let go. Sam! Let him go."

Looking down at hands he couldn't quite recognize as his own, Sam saw his grip on the man's neck as he lay on the ground beneath him. The old man no longer moved or breathed. A stillness fell around them more hostile than the fight. Sam fell back into damp leaves covering the ground, pushing and clawing himself away from the still form. His vision began to blur. The bark of the trees dripped and ran in rivulets to a ground moving beneath his stumbling feet.

"Is he dead?" he whispered.

Sophie crawled over, moving the man's beard to feel for a pulse on his bruised neck. After a few moments: "I think so."

"Are you alright?" Sam saw the bruises rising on Sophie's own neck.

"Yes, I will be," she said hoarsely. She joined Sam to sit beneath a tree as they stared at what they'd just done in disbelief.

"I killed him."

"You didn't have a choice."

"I was out of my mind."

"He didn't give you a choice."

"I've seen him before."

"Where?"

"I think he was my father's best friend."

"How can that be?"

"I don't know. I don't know." Sam buried his face in his hands, pushing hard against his eyes, trying to wipe the memory away. "We can't do this now. You have to go back to the house, and I have to bury him before the soldiers find him."

"Sam, let me help you."

"No! Please, just do as I ask and go home. Please."

Sophie felt the anger in him, and it wasn't only anger about what he'd done or even anger about the man attacking her. No, Sam was angry with *her* for the first time ever. And she didn't understand it.

"Fine. I'll see you at home, then. Be careful."

Sam didn't answer but retrieved a large branch and started digging in the moistened earth. As Sophie walked away, she heard his huffed breathing as he drove the stick harder and deeper into the earth, and his feelings deeper within himself.

Hours later, Sophie sat outside on her porch, leaning against a post with her head thrown back and her knees drawn up into her chest. Her neck ached under the bruises as she tried to sooth the swelling with a cold cloth. For once, she was grateful Ethan was holed up in his room. She needed time to think before she could even attempt to explain to him her injuries. She had no wish to frighten the boy more than he already was.

The chill evening air was warmed by the setting sun peeking in under the roof of the porch. From the great sighing earth, she drew breath, holding it in her lungs until her own body forced her to breathe it out again. Just as she was beginning to worry that Sam wasn't home yet, she saw him shuffling slowly up the drive without his usual jaunty step. He looked at the ground at his feet, never raising his eyes toward the house.

When he reached the porch, Sam slumped down next to Sophie on the other side of the post.

"Is it finished?" she asked gently.

"Finished."

"Sam, I wish things were different. I . . ."

"Tell me what you know about your parents," he interrupted.

Sophie took a minute to answer his abrupt question. "Very little."

"Your mother's name was Sara, wasn't it?"

"Yes."

"Did she turn against her people in the Watch?"

"I don't know. I was just a girl. How can we possibly know what really happened all those years ago? One day I had loving parents, the next day,

I didn't. It was the same with you."

"Not quite the same. My father's name was Jarom."

"And you think based on what that man said that my mother is responsible for your father's death."

"It would make sense."

"Nothing makes sense, Sam! That's the point. The Watch, Corsairs, the Triumvirate, patriots, traitors, spies. Look around us. It all defies understanding. We can make ourselves crazy trying to figure it out. In the end, though, the color of blood looks the same no matter which uniform it stains."

"What do you mean?"

"I mean if we're all going to die in this fight, which I have no doubt we are, all that really matters to me is what happens right here between us. This is our life now."

"How can we really know what there is between us if we don't know ourselves or where we came from?"

"You can't be serious." Sophie sat up and tried to reach for Sam's hand, but he pulled away.

"I just can't . . . I'm sorry, Sophie."

Sam walked quickly into the house, shutting the door behind him. Even with all his nightmares and the many things they'd lived through together, Sophie had never seen him like this. It frightened her. She knew if she allowed this gap between them to continue, it would grow into an unbreachable chasm. They had to work through whatever they were both feeling here together, or they would always be apart.

So, against her instinct to leave him alone and give him space, Sophie followed Sam inside. She found him sitting at the kitchen table, his hands folded before him, looking for all the world like he was praying, but to whom?

As he sat at the table, his eyes closed, he heard Sophie enter the room. And the wave of unexpected information washed over him again. Sophie's mother was responsible for his parents' deaths. How could he look at her again? He knew she was not to blame. The children could not be responsible for the sins of the parents. But then, could he just forget this strange connection that bound them? Or could he forget all the days and nights they'd shared together? He wished his mind was a slate, able to be wiped of all undesirable knowledge, holding only that which was good.

Pressing his hands together until the knuckles were white and his fingers went numb, he realized something he'd never known before. Realized you could want to know something, crave it with your whole being. Questioning, searching, seeking to find it, and never realize how heavy it would be to carry it once you did know.

He stood up, still unable to meet Sophie's gaze. He had wanted to get a glass of water but placed his hands on the table and bowed down again. His body bent and buckled under the weight of his own actions, not Sophie's parents or his parents. He had killed a man when he had sworn to himself and to Sophie that he'd never kill again. The guilt was almost too much to bear.

She watched him for a few moments, afraid of how he would react. He had told her so many times he would never kill again. Never again. And yet he'd done it—and for her. Because of her. Because of who she was and who her parents had been. She walked slowly behind him and folded herself over his back, covering his body with her own, wishing she could cover up what had happened, erase it from both their minds. Standing up slowly, Sam turned around to face her. She felt ashamed when he looked questioningly into her eyes. She couldn't hold his gaze and looked away.

"Some people live for the struggle and the fight," he said finally. "I've tried to live my life in a way that I would never have to fight or kill again. This will be the third war in my lifetime. These wars seem to follow me. I can't escape them."

"Sometimes we have to make hard decisions, do hard or painful things to protect ourselves or others. You didn't want to kill that man, I know that."

"It doesn't matter. We can't lie and kill and still call ourselves different or better than the Corsairs. The result is the same. A man is dead by my hand. More blood on my hands. I can't forgive myself for that."

Sophie wondered if she could tell Sam what she knew she had to. But the banks and the levees of her river finally collapsed, and she could be silent no longer. "Well, then, can you forgive me?"

"For what?"

"I'm the one who killed Griffyth Credell, the government worker in Boswell. I was out of my mind with grief, sure. But he would have gone on killing. He was an evil man who caused the deaths of others, not in self-defense, but just for the hell of it. There would have been no justice if I had not done it."

"It's not the same thing. You weren't in your right mind. It wasn't a conscious decision."

"I'd venture to say that neither was yours a conscious decision. But the result is the same regardless. The point is we've all done things we regret that we wish we could undo. That doesn't make us bad people. It makes us human. No one is perfect, Sam. But you've come closer than anyone else . . ."

"Don't!" Sam couldn't listen to her go on about how good he was. Not when he knew his Sophie was almost touching perfection. He knew he'd never be worthy of her. "I'm not perfect. I need redemption or absolution—something! Something to pull me back from the path I'm constantly being pushed toward. My whole life. All the wars, the killing. You don't know the things I've done. People have died because of me! So no, I can't do enough to make up for that. Everything I've done has been to purchase my absolution."

"Absolution can't be purchased. It's freely given." She reached out to touch his arm, but he jumped at her touch. When he saw the pain enter her eyes, saw the bruises again on her neck, he could no longer stand it, but rushed out of the house.

* * * * *

Simeon Drape sat on what used to be a park bench, surrounded by large chunks of broken concrete, tattered sidewalks, and fallen trees. There was a gray, chopped-up quality to the world around him, like a quarry. Here they had mined for a new world, driven the monstrous drills deep into a society hardened by greed and apathy. They had saved the people, saved them from themselves, from their historical myths that bound them to nonsense.

Simeon was rarely this relaxed. But he felt the threads he'd woven finally coming together into a cohesive whole. His feet rested on the severed head of a statue. He believed it was probably Thomas Jefferson. No matter; it made a fine footrest after the long ride from the wall. He shielded his eyes from the afternoon sun with his lowered hat, waiting somewhat impatiently for President Gabbro and Vice President Craven.

He heard movement behind him before the voice, "It's strange to see the remnants of what used to pass for civilization to these people. Good day, General."

"Good day, Vice President Craven." Simeon stood to salute him. "This is, after all, the only place on the planet where we can be sure we won't be overheard or spied on."

"Very true. The president should be here shortly."

"The president is here now." The voice came from behind a half-fallen wall a few feet away.

Though General Drape was a tall man, President Gabbro dwarfed him. His large, boulder-like head rising several inches above Simeon's. The president, as all members of the Triumvirate and administration, wore the bright-blue uniform of the Corsair army. He pulled a large handkerchief out of his pocket and held it up to his nose, looking around him in resigned disgust. Those who saw the three men of the Triumvirate together often thought the vice president looked to be a cadet in the army, so slight was his form. Only when they saw the snake and star insignia of the Triumvirate did they salute and give him deference.

"I can't abide this smell of old things, General," President Gabbro was saying. "Let's make this meeting quick. Why have you called us here?"

"Sir, I need more troops to be able to crush the rebel army."

President Gabbro scoffed. "Army, what army? You mean that rag-tag group they call the Watch? A nuisance at the worst. They are not a threat, General. They have no army."

"Do you think they aren't planning for an attack, gathering allies?"

"We've heard this same argument for years, but the evidence doesn't bear it out. Besides, it doesn't matter what they plan. They simply don't have the manpower to stand up to us. No, I believe the experiment is at an end."

"They can get more manpower."

"From the few stragglers we've seen here in the Forbidden Grounds?" Vice President Craven joined in, choosing to remain on the president's side of the argument.

"General, as always, you are exaggerating the threat." The president spoke as if he were soothing a frightened child.

"And I don't think you're taking it seriously enough. We must kill off the genetic line of rebellion. No DNA trace of resistance must be left."

"We've beaten the rebellion out of them. It's over. We can't continue to prolong this, waiting to find other rebels. We must move forward with Phase Two of the plan."

"It's my considered opinion that they're past the point of being useful citizens. The rebellious streak runs too strong in them. They will poison the pool. We must go forward with the executions for the sake of the greater good, Mr. President."

"We can't kill them all. We have to get the children out. They've done nothing."

"They've aided the rebel cause."

"They're only children."

"And as I'm sure you'll remember in the last revolution they used 'only children' to fight against us. Many of my comrades in the Corsairs were killed by children. Then these children will grow into rebels. No, they must be eradicated like a disease. We must kill all the diseased cells. If you don't win, you lose. If you don't kill something, it kills you. That's the way the world works. Dog eats dog."

"I've made my decision, General. We'll pull the children out and send them for reprogramming. Then we can move on with Phase Three, if we must. Do you agree, Craven?"

"Yes, President, I do."

"Very well, Mr. President."

"It's time to begin to put an end to this. It's been forty-three years since the Disaster. We can't continue to allow this land to go to waste. I want this ended within the year. Is that understood?"

"Yes, sir."

* * * * *

Picking among grasses under a ruined and leaning merry-go-round, Gran found the wild garlic and chamomile growing in a bent shaft of sunlight. She'd be cooking up a soup tonight with tea besides. She had found some carrots in an ancient garden, scrawny though they were. They'd go fine with the squirrel the young fellas had left her before they took off. She took it as a peace offering, an apology for leaving her. The young ones never stayed long. Skittish, they were.

The rusted swings on the old swing set creaked in the breeze, startling her. She almost hit her head on the upturned merry-go-round. Stretching her back, she mused on the new aches and pains that were coming over her lately. She could feel even the slightest chill just in the small of her back, reaching down into her knees, and twisting her so she'd have to stretch and consciously remind herself to stand straighter and taller. She thought of the playground like this one that used to be down the road from what had once been her house. The playground where she took her kids every Saturday. It had a slide with a lion's mouth, and another that looked like an elephant's trunk. The merry-go-round was horses and zebras. She could hear her kids squealing as she ran, pushing them faster and faster around. "Faster, Mummy, faster!" Even now, their voices were clearer and more real to her than the ground on which she stood.

"I can't abide the smell of old things, General . . ." the muffled growl of a man jolted Gran from her reminiscing. Darting behind a half brick wall that used to be part of the park clubhouse, she lay flat on the ground, holding her breath in silence.

". . . these children will grow into rebels . . ."

". . . pull them out for reprogramming . . ." the voices continued.

Corsairs, my oath!

"Very well, Mr. President."

The dawning realization that she was listening to the Triumvirate began to make her sick. The dank, stale air in the corner of the wall assaulted her senses as she choked back the rising bile from her stomach.

She lay there longer than she thought she needed to, making sure the men were gone before she stirred, all the while thinking through the plans she'd heard. The Triumvirate was going to round up all the children. But where? Over the fence, or over the wall? She couldn't understand some of what she'd heard. And in her immediate thoughts, she thanked whatever luck existed that they hadn't seen her and that their plans didn't include the Forbidden Grounds. She was bloody well out of it.

As she stood, brushing leaves and grass from her tattered clothes, she saw again the merry-go-round, the rusted swings, the fallen slide. Her children's faces among the ruins streaked with mud and her tears. She remembered her early days in prison, wondering what had happened to them, hoping they'd found safety and shelter, but never knowing. And she thought of the other mothers who unknowingly had the same loss racing toward them. Some other mother would miss her children and wonder what had happened to them. Some other mother's arms would ache with emptiness. That other mother would never sleep another night without dreaming of the horrors that had befallen her babies. No, she could not allow someone else to go through what she had, not if there was the slightest chance she had the power to stop it.

That evening, Gran prepared what would be her last meal in the Forbidden Grounds. She counted the moments out in breaths. Long ones and short ones. Gasped breaths and held breath. Hot breath and cold. She rested for her journey in the time it took her to take in the world around her in an inhale. The night draped a gentleness over the earth, a gentleness not felt in the glaringly oppressive day. In the company of unfettered stars, she knew there was freedom to be found somewhere, even if not on this earth.

* * * * *

Meeting at one of the guard stations along the Border, General Drape took Colonel Goodson for a walk as if they were just two friends having a chat. He always had the air of one who was in complete control and so was completely at ease, especially in a subordinate's presence. Even as they walked in the breeze that was picking its way through the trees, nothing of the general's hair or clothing rustled with the breeze as he defied even nature with his control.

"I've come to give you the orders from the Triumvirate, Colonel, as I trust you above all others to carry this out." Simeon patted Mark on the shoulder in the good-natured way that could sometimes make people mistake him for a kind man.

"Thank you, sir."

"You will round up the children and bring them to the old lumber mill outside the borders, is that understood?" He spoke as if he were asking him to bring him a glass of water.

Mark stopped walking. He almost forgot himself to grip a fence post for support. Though he held himself erect and at attention, he could not make his feet move before him. "But I thought Phase Two was reprogramming, sir. That is not the reprogramming facility."

"I am aware of that." Turning to face Mark, Simeon's face held his surprise at the response, while his eyes held his natural coldness.

"But, sir, you can't mean . . . they're children."

315

RACHEL ANNE COX

"Are you hard of hearing, Colonel? Do I need to have you removed from your post and sent to the lumber mill yourself?"

"No, sir."

"Then you will follow my orders."

"Yes, sir."

"And you understand what is to be done with them once they are at the mill?"

"Perfectly, sir," Mark choked out the words.

"Excellent. Now, be on your way. I expect immediate results."

* * * * *

From a hollowed-out hole in the trunk of a maple tree, Gran drew out the rust-laden tools she'd accumulated in the past few years. Wrapped in molding canvas, they clinked and clamored into her hands, heavier than she remembered. There was a hammer, a screwdriver, wrench, jack, and finally the wire cutters she was after. She could leave behind the others for some other poor soul to find. She'd not be needing them after this. Her knotted hands gripped the dark red handles and tried to work the cutters out of their frozen rust. Two good clips, the only job they had left to perform before being discarded. She dropped the other tools, bag and all, with a thud back into the hole and made her way to the Border.

She chose a spot farthest from the two nearby guard stations, watching and timing the arrival and departure of the Corsair guards from behind a fallen tree. Her joints ached as she crouched, making her wish the guards would hurry up. One, then two. They tipped their hats to each other, turned, and walked back to where they started. Gran slowly stood to make her way toward the fence, wire cutters in hand.

"Hello?" a timid voice came from behind her.

Gran swung around to a bright-red head of hair and two tear-filled eyes swimming in a dirty face. "Jesus, girl! Get down before the whole Corsair army sees you!" Gran whispered hoarsely.

Back behind the fallen tree, the two consulted.

"Are you going over the fence?"

"That obvious, am I?"

"Well, I thought I might . . . no, I don't know."

"You're welcome to come along, if that's what you were going to ask."

"No, I'd better stay here. She said she'd come back, and I won't know where to find her on the other side."

"Who?"

"Sister."

"So that must have been the other one I talked to who looked like you."

"You met her?"

"Had to have been."

"I promised to wait for her."

"Well, I'd venture to say you'd have a better chance of finding her on the other side."

"Do you think so?"

"I do. But we don't have any more time to talk about it. So either come with me or stay, but make your decision now. And if you come with me, we've got to cover up that hair. You can be seen from a mile away. Here, take this scarf."

Laurie tied the proffered scarf, gray with age, around her head.

"Come on, then," Gran whispered over her shoulder, crawling toward the fence. She figured they'd talked for about five minutes. That meant they had five left to cut the wires and get far enough away so they wouldn't be seen. Plenty of time, if they worked quickly.

Gran pulled out the wire cutters and began the task of carving out a hole without being whipped by the freed wire full of barbs. It would take more than two cuts to get them both through the intricate wire weaving. With every clip of the wire, the young woman behind her jumped and looked around in panic. Three more and that should do it. But the rust on the wire cutters had caused them to jam. Gran was struggling to open their jaws.

"Let me help," Laurie offered.

Gran gladly handed them over. "Yes, just there. That's it."

One more, and they'd be through.

"You there!" A shout zipped through the trees, striking Gran in the chest. "Stop!"

"Come on, we can make it," Gran insisted as she began squeezing through the hole in the fence, tearing new lashes into her already shredded clothes.

"No, you go on, I'll distract him."

The Corsair was running swiftly toward them, pulling his gun from his shoulder. Gran was through the fence, now on the same side as the soldier, who had his site homed in on her and was getting closer by the second. Laurie wriggled through the fence, wire cutters in hand. Just as the soldier got close, she swung them toward him, barely missing his head with the tip of rusted metal. In one second, he'd turned and fired on her. One shot, and she was down.

Gran wanted to call out to her but realized she didn't even know her name, this woman who had tried to save her. She stood in shaking silence, staring down the long barrel of the Corsair rifle.

"You will halt, woman!" the Corsair continued to shout, even though he was in close range.

Gran stood with empty hands exposed as another soldier ran up behind her.

"What are you waiting for?" the new soldier questioned, quickly ascertaining the situation. "She's an intruder who has breached the Border. Shoot her!"

Gran saw the youth of the Corsair before her. He couldn't have been more than sixteen. A child with a gun.

"I just . . . I just thought . . ."

"Thought what?" the older soldier pushed.

"I thought we might bring her in for questioning."

"No questions required. She crossed the Border illegally and the punishment is death."

"But what if she's working with someone else, shouldn't we get more information from her?"

Gran knew better than anyone what the problem was. This boy didn't care about information. The girl had been the first person he'd ever shot, and he was terrified. He could barely even hold his aim this close. He'd pop her in the leg if he got up the courage to fire.

"If you don't shoot her, I will."

"What's all this, men?" Colonel Goodson approached on horseback.

"I caught this woman crossing the Border, sir, with that one there on the ground . . . wait, where is she?" They all looked to where the young soldier was looking. There was blood among the leaves on the ground, sure enough. But Laurie had vanished.

"He lost a prisoner and now won't shoot this one, sir. He's scared. Fresh out of programming, I'd say."

"That's enough, Private. You'll stand at attention when addressing a superior officer."

"Yes, sir."

"You seem quick to sell out your comrade. I'm not sure you couldn't do with a dose of programming yourself."

"Please, sir."

"Enough. I will handle this situation from here. I will take charge of the prisoner, and you will both return to your posts."

Colonel Goodson dismounted, but was still able to look down at his fellow soldiers, towering a head above them. He pulled the pistol from his holster, taking Gran by the arm.

"Move!" he shouted as the soldiers each turned in opposite directions to return to their guard stations. Waiting until they were out of earshot, he put his gun back in the holster and surveyed the woman standing before him.

He always hated seeing those who lived in the Forbidden Grounds. They looked like walking rag dolls, most of them, dreadfully dirty and starved. But this one was different somehow. The woman looked as if all color had been scrubbed off of her with a hard brush. The years had not been kind to her body, but her face seemed strangely young under her white hair, hair that faded into white skin and almost white-blue eyes. He'd seen those eyes before. Taking a step closer, he knew where.

"You're the one, aren't you?"

"Who?"

"The one my friend helped escape from prison. I remember you."

"He was your friend?"

"Yeah. Was."

"They didn't kill him, did they?" she asked anxiously.

Mark was touched by her concern. "No, they didn't kill him."

"Then he's alright?"

He wished he could tell her Kyle was still the same kind boy from back then. Wished that he could tell her he wouldn't have shot her himself probably if he were now in Mark's place. But he couldn't say any of those things.

"He's alive, yes."

"Oh, thank God."

"Well, look, I guess I can't very well undo what he did, can I?

Everything has ripples, right?"

"You think so too, eh?"

"Jesse's Hollow is due east from here. You'll want to find a man named Zacharias or a woman named Gemma. They'll know how to help you."

Gran caught her breath, and Mark worried she would collapse.

"You're okay, aren't you?"

"Why are you letting me go?" she managed to get out.

"Who knows why any of us do anything anymore? Now go on before the others return."

"Thank you." Gran took the colonel's hands in hers, kissing them and covering them with her tears.

* * * * *

Making her way across the bridge and following the directions a young man had given her to the house of this Zacharias, Gran tried to tell herself this couldn't be the same Zacharias. He couldn't have been this close all this time. It seemed too wonderful and cruel. She was walking slowly through the bright fall day, squinting against the sea-blue sky. The light seemed different on this side of the Border; she couldn't understand it. Cleaner, somehow. Not filtered gray.

Zacharias stepped off the porch. The children were making the midday meal, but he needed a walk. The house had seemed confining lately. It wasn't the children. It was him. He couldn't stand the walls of his own home anymore. It didn't seem like home. He found himself wishing he'd never told Sam about Jesse. He had been right to keep the feelings at bay all these years. Easier not to think about or talk about her or the children. Now she seemed to be with him, haunting him all the time. He would turn a corner and think he saw her there. He imagined what she would look like now, how the years would have changed her or not changed her. Of course she would still be beautiful. Even now as he approached the bridge, he thought he saw her there. It had to stop.

But the illusion was not disintegrating as he got closer as they usually did. This mirage was gaining clarity and focus with each step he took toward it. There was someone on the bridge. A woman from the town, probably. But he'd never seen someone in town with such long, flowing white hair. And the clothes. The clothes didn't seem right for someone from the village. Zacharias drew closer, but somehow felt as if his stomach were dropping out of his body.

White hair surrounding a youthful face. Eyes of light. Impossibly high cheekbones. The old smile.

Jesse.

Her beauty hurt him. Different and yet so much the same. And before he knew it, she was standing directly before him on the bridge, her hands on his face, in his hair, looking searchingly in his eyes.

Her first words, "Did they hurt you?"

"Of course you'd ask that first. The one question I've been wanting to ask you for almost forty years." He tried to laugh but sobbed instead.

His arms still fit around her, like a hand in a glove. Her face was in his neck, their tears and bodies mingling.

When they could talk again, "No, they didn't hurt me," he answered. "Not physically. I fear your answer will be sadder than mine. The worst pain they inflicted on me was taking you away from me."

"And our children? Jill and Max? Did they escape with you?" She looked around as if she expected to see them running toward her.

"I never saw them again after that last day," Z whispered. He felt as if he'd struck his wife, and he hated himself for having to give her the news.

Jesse flinched, clutching his hands tighter. "Oh, Zack!"

"I thought you were all dead together. But secretly, I hoped. I hoped if you were alive that they were alive with you. I'm so sorry, Jesse. I'm so sorry."

They were in each other's arms again, holding each other up under the pain of years of fruitless hope finally being let down.

"We lost our babies, Zack," she sobbed into his shoulder. "It happened forty years ago. So how can it feel like it just happened today? We should have grown old . . . together . . . with our children and their children around us."

Moments, hours, it was impossible to know how long they stood, soaking each other in, reacquainting themselves. As the afternoon sun began to dip lower in the sky, Zack held his Jesse in a long-awaited kiss. And in that sunlit kiss, they tasted the bittersweet emptiness of the years between them and what their lives might have been if one of them had just crossed the Border.

19

LOST BOYS

In the moonlit autumn night, Jesse and Zacharias sat on the front porch in two creaking rocking chairs, holding hands and rocking slowly in unison. All the children except Daisy were in bed. Zacharias had sent her for Gemma so they could discuss the information Jesse had brought them. He knew Daisy, of all the children, could pick her way through the woods, taking shortcuts to Gemma's house, more safely in the dark than in broad daylight. And he and Jesse figured the Corsairs wouldn't be able to start rounding up the children for at least a day or so.

Jesse laced her fingers between Zack's. They felt the same as she remembered, and yet different. The moon reflected in his white hair and hers, creating a kind of halo around them. She thought of the way she used to describe herself back then, in the time Before. Daughter, wife, mother. They were more than roles or jobs to her. They had been her whole identity. Then, as each one was ripped from her, what had she become? A prisoner, a fugitive, caretaker of children, survivor, old woman. But here she sat with Zack as she'd always imagined them together. A wife again. A mother, still missing her children.

Zack squeezed her hand. "What are you thinking about?"

"So many things."

"Tell me."

"I didn't know the last time I held them or sang to them or read to them would be the last time. All the little last times I missed out on. If I had known, I would have held on longer and tighter."

"So would I. If I had thought it would be the last time, I'd never have left you in that cabin alone. I'd never have dragged you into all of it . . ."

"Now, now. What did we agree? None of that, love. I'll not have you cloaking yourself in all the blame for everything that's happened. It wasn't your fault. We both did what we thought was right. And life took us on its own journey. That's all."

"So many ripples, though, from every action we take."

"So many ripples."

"What was the last song you listened to before the electricity went out?" He tried to change the subject.

"Oh, wow. Let me think. Let me think. I think it must have been the soundtrack to *Hamilton*. I do miss our music from Before," Jesse sighed. "What about you?"

"I was listening to Radiohead on my phone. 'No Surprises' was the song. Ironic, huh?"

"Yeah, it is. What do you miss from Before?"

"You know, you'd think I'd say something about electricity, technology, or something like that, wouldn't you?"

"Maybe. Maybe not."

"But you know what I really miss? Hamburgers. Big, juicy hamburgers with everything on them. I try to be grateful that we just have food at all. I eat the never-ending cornbread, eggs, vegetables, and I try to imagine a soft hamburger bun instead. Sometimes, I swear, I dream about the food from Before."

"I knew it! I knew you were going to say hamburgers!"

"You did not!"

"I did. My oath, I did."

They both laughed. In the back of her mind, Jesse wondered how they could with all that was happening around them and all that was about to happen. But sometimes, she just couldn't help herself. After years of thinking, *I wish Zack were here so we could laugh about this together,* now he was actually there. And she promised herself she would enjoy every single laugh.

Jesse sighed at the end of her long, throaty laugh, squeezing Zack's hand tighter. "And what do you see when you close your eyes, my love?"

Zacharias caught his breath, then exhaled slowly. He'd forgotten what it felt like to be with someone who could see directly into his soul. "I see you and the kids in those last few days. I see the fear in your eyes and know I have to do something to take that fear away."

"That's what you've carried with you all these years?'

"What about you? What do you see?"

"I sometimes see my mother on Brighton Beach. I see my babies when they were born. I see the happy tears in your eyes when they each held your finger for the first time in their little fists. I see their first steps. The sun peeking through the clouds and lighting up the tops of their heads. I see every happy memory with all of us."

Zacharias found it hard to believe the joy she was still capable of. Joy she seemed to carry with her like a gift, despite all she'd been through.

"Z! Where are you? Zacharias?!" They heard Sam calling from inside the house. He had come in the back door without their noticing.

"Quiet, boy. The kids are asleep." Zacharias met Sam in the front room, noticing immediately how frightened he looked. "What is it?"

"Z, I've done something. Everything's changed. I don't know what to do."

"Calm down, son. Calm down. Come have a glass of water."

"I don't want a glass of water. And I don't want to calm down!"

"Then come outside with me so we don't wake up the kids."

Sam was pacing frantically through the room but followed Zacharias outside. He froze in the doorway, seeing Jesse rise from her chair. "Who's this?"

"Sam, this is my Jesse. Jesse, this is my adopted son, Sam."

"It's lovely to meet you, Sam. Zack has told me all about you and Gemma. You're more of a man than I imagined from his description. I half-expected to meet a teenaged boy." She held out her hands to Sam, but he hesitated.

"So I was right, then? Sophie did actually find her?"

"Yes, you were right."

"I'm sorry, Jesse. Yes, of course, it's nice to meet you. Please forgive me." Sam took her proffered hands. Then he slid onto the top step of the porch, letting his head fall into his hands.

"Why don't you tell us what's going on?" Zacharias laid a heavy hand on Sam's shoulder.

"You, know, Zack, I can go on up to bed if the two of you need to talk.

The boy's just met me, after all."

"No, you can stay," Sam spoke through his hands, muffling the sound. Jesse could hear tears in his voice. She and Zacharias sat back down in the chairs behind Sam and waited patiently for him to begin his story.

Sam was amazed at how comfortable he felt sitting there with these two people, the love he felt between the two of them wrapping themselves, the house, and him in a kind of cocoon of safety. He marveled at the events that had led them to this moment and found himself wondering if he would have felt as comfortable with his birth parents and if he could have sat here like this, sharing his most troubling thoughts and fears. But he would never know, never know the relationships or events that might have been if his parents had not been executed. He heard two crows shouting back and forth between each other in a nearby tree, somehow making the silence of the night even more pronounced.

"The moon is brighter than the fires tonight," Sam spoke finally.

"It's what the people of Before used to call a Harvest Moon, back when there were real harvests. Supposedly, the brightness of the moon was enough to let farmers continue their work of the harvest well into the night, lengthening their day." Zacharias always had an explanation for everything.

"I killed a man!" Sam blurted out. And without giving Zacharias or Jesse a chance to ask any questions, he spilled out the whole story of the crazed old man, what they'd learned from him about Sophie's parents being traitors, and how Sam had finally been forced to take the man down. He told his story in fitful spurts, hitting at loose boards on the porch. And when he could sit still no longer, he told it while pacing through the dew-soaked grass.

"After the last revolution, I swore I'd never kill again. But as soon as someone threatened Sophie, what did I do? I'll never be fit to be around decent people. Love shouldn't lead you to do such terrible things. A life is worth more than that. And I just snuffed it out with my bare hands. A human life is irreplaceable. You can't make up for that loss to the human race as a whole. Nothing we would win is worth what it would cost us."

When he finally paused for breath, Jesse asked, "Do you think all life is worth the same?"

"Jesse . . ." Z interrupted.

"No, let the man answer."

"I'd like to think so," Sam replied.

"I'd like to think a lot of things too. I'd like to think my children are coming back. But Simeon and the others like him made that impossible. And what do you think it would cost us in human life to leave someone like Simeon to carry out his horrific plans? He wants to round up the children, and he wants to execute us all. Those lives are irreplaceable as well."

"I still say I don't ever want to kill again. It changes you, robs you of a piece of your humanity—no matter who you're killing—until eventually there's nothing left."

"I know what you mean, my boy. Believe me, I do. And maybe that's part of the sacrifice we've been called upon to make. Have you noticed the leaves changing colors, son? In the middle of summer you would swear they'd be green forever. Nothing could change them. Then the temperature drops, the sun shifts in the sky, and suddenly the whole world looks different. We can't be so sure of our own beliefs that we don't notice the changes happening around us. If we don't rid this world of evil but allow it to flourish and take over . . . well, I sure don't want to be the one responsible for that."

"And how can I be responsible for making the choice of whether someone is good or bad?"

"None of us wants to kill. We try as hard as we can to win the fight without it. But we do what we have to do to protect the greater good. Sophie is part of your greater good, and you were protecting her."

"How can I ever go back to her when we don't even really know where we came from?"

"Pish tosh!"

"What?"

"I only met your Sophie once, and I know exactly what kind of person she is. I know you know her too and the real person she is. She didn't know her parents were traitors, and even if she did, she can't be held accountable for their actions. She loves you and your boy, Ethan. Nothing on this earth is worth more than that. Trust me. Now, I've said more than my piece."

Jesse sat back down, suddenly aware that she'd been lecturing this young man she'd just met. What in heaven's name would he think of her? Zacharias simply smiled at the woman he had missed like air when you're underwater.

"Maybe you're right," Sam finally said in a calmer voice. The truth of her words washed over him like a cool summer shower on his hot cheeks.

"Of course she is!" Z chimed in. "Look, son, just preventing death— that's not enough, is it? What are we doing to improve the quality of life? That's the thing. Haven't you felt that surviving, just staying alive, isn't enough? Sometimes we have to remove evil in order to improve the quality of life for the whole human race."

"I've tried so hard, Z, in my own way."

"I know you have, my boy. You've been trying so hard to be perfect, for Gemma, for Ethan, then for Sophie. But we can't be perfect. And this world we live in isn't perfect. All we can do is try our best to be good. To give good an equal chance in the world. And you're doing that."

"I just wish I could wish it all away."

"I know the feeling. I lived in that space for forty years. But what if we did wish it all away and were able to win our freedom by wishing? I wonder if we would even appreciate it."

Zacharias placed his hand on the back of Sam's neck and pulled him in for a rough embrace. "I'm going to send you home to Sophie now. Curfew or no curfew. You've been gone from home too long, and she and Ethan will be worried."

"Thanks, you two. I'm glad you're back, Jesse." Sam stooped to kiss the old woman's smooth cheek.

* * * * *

Daisy peeked her head around the corner of Gemma's house. All was quiet inside. She could see a lamp burning at the kitchen table, and Gemma sitting within its glow. She couldn't see Kyle anywhere, so ran quickly inside.

"Gemma! Z needs you to come to his house right now."

"Daisy, sweetie, what is it? Is anything wrong? Is he hurt?" Gemma was on her feet immediately, her arms around the trembling Daisy.

"Not hurt. But there's news. And Jesse came back."

"Jesse?!"

"His wife. It was the first time I saw him smile."

"Where did she come from?"

"The Forbidden Grounds. She overheard the Triumvirate's plans, so we need you to come."

"Slow down. Slow down."

"Can't slow down. We've got to go."

"Alright, just give me a minute . . ."

"What's all this?" Kyle was walking down the stairs. He had a strange look in his eye that frightened Daisy. Even though she'd never met him before, she disliked him immediately. "Going where?"

"Kyle, this is Daisy, one of the kids Zacharias adopted. She says he needs me."

"Is he sick? Perhaps I should come with you."

"I don't think that will be necessary. If it turns out I need you, I can always send Daisy back."

"Breaking curfew."

Daisy felt Gemma's body stiffen next to her. She felt something from her she'd never felt before. Gemma was afraid, something Daisy hadn't thought possible. And more than that, she was afraid of her own husband. Daisy stood closer to her friend, squared her own shoulders, and looked directly into Kyle's eyes. He would not see that she was also afraid, and if she could, she would try to cover Gemma's fear.

"I think it's a risk worth taking for Z," Gemma continued.

"He asked me to come get her. Said she was the only one he wanted."

"Well, if you really think it's necessary . . ." Kyle seemed to hesitate.

"I do. I do."

"Very well. When can I expect you back?"

"Tomorrow probably. It all depends."

Kyle stared at the child holding Gemma's hand, a child she had supposedly met only weeks before. "It's nice to see that you two have gotten so close so quickly. You be sure to stick close to Gemma, young lady."

"Yes, sir."

Kyle patted Daisy on the shoulder and kissed Gemma's cheek before allowing them to go on their way.

* * * * *

The journey back to Boswell brought Sam through the moonlit night and into the morning mist. He pulled his coat closer around him in the cool, damp air. All around him, the trees made their presence known with vibrant colors and the raining sound of the leaves. Yet Sam rushed on, not heeding their beauty. He knew Sophie would be worried.

From between two trees—a crooked but strong oak and a straight, white-limbed birch with yellow leaves brighter than the sunrise itself—a stranger stepped out to block Sam's path. Sam instinctively reached for a gun he didn't carry. Though the man wore the citizen-gray tunic, Sam recognized the imposing figure as Colonel Mark Goodson of the Corsairs.

"You're Sam, aren't you?" The colonel made a 360-degree survey around him, scanning for other soldiers.

"You know I am, Colonel Goodson."

"Then you know me?"

"I know who you are, yes." Sam's voice was tense and shook with the chill. He had once hoped this colonel would have been an ally when he saw him stop a flogging. But when he failed to stop the last round of public executions, Sam had categorized him with all of the other Corsairs.

"I'm a friend of Kyle's," Mark continued.

"That doesn't improve my opinion of you . . . sir."

"None of that 'sir' business, here, Sam. Today, I'm just a citizen like you."

"Not likely. What do you want?"

"I've come to warn you. On orders from the Triumvirate, soldiers will be coming to collect all of the children." Mark waited for a reaction, but Sam's face was inscrutable. "You've already heard about this, apparently. But what you don't know is that General Drape has given me specific orders to do away with them. All of them."

Sam started forward, fists clenched, and stood threateningly close to Colonel Goodson, close enough that he could smell the forest on him. He looked deep within his eyes, trying to find truth or a lie, but didn't know if he could trust what he saw there.

"If you can't get word to all the families with children in time—and I sincerely doubt you can—I can tell you where the children will be held so they may be rescued."

"Why should I believe you? This could be a trap."

"You're just going to have to trust me, Sam."

"There's no such thing anymore."

Mark decided to trade in the last chip he was holding. "Did the old woman find Zacharias?"

Sam looked genuinely surprised at this. "How do you know about her?"

"I let her through the Border. I've been trying to tell you, Sam. I'm on your side. Who do you think has been getting the information to the Watch all this time?"

Sam still didn't trust it. He could be trying to catch him admitting to some offense. "How can I trust you, or anyone for that matter, in the midst of this war?"

"War? Sam, there is no war!"

"What do you mean? Of course there is."

"There was never going to be another war. The Triumvirate wouldn't allow it. Haven't you figured out yet where you are?"

Sam looked confused. His head was spinning. He couldn't seem to process all of the new information that was being heaped upon him.

"You're in a prison camp, all of you that are left. Everything within the borders is a prison."

"All of the towns?"

"There's only Jesse's Hollow and Boswell left."

"That's crazy. Now I know you're lying. I've seen the other towns. At least seven of them."

"The people in the other towns were already taken away."

Sam felt his chest cave in with the blow. He thought of the hundreds of people in those other towns. People he'd taken photographs of and traded with on Market Days.

"Do you understand now? No one knows you're here except the Corsairs. No one is coming to save you! And your execution date is set. But the children will be taken first, so we have to work fast."

Sam put his hand to his throbbing head, hot despite the chill, but nodded in agreement. "I don't understand," he finally spoke. "Why are we in prison? Why even the children?"

"Revolutionaries and children of revolutionaries. All who fought in the revolutions or were descended from them were sent here."

"But we came here ourselves. Zacharias found and renamed Jesse's Hollow when they first settled here."

"That's what the Triumvirate would have you believe. Fires and battles were strategically placed to move you all to this place. Then the Border went up. It was as simple as that."

"It still doesn't explain why. Why not just kill us? Why continue this ridiculous charade?"

"We have no time for this. The soldiers are on the move as we speak. They will take the children to the old lumber mill in the Forbidden Grounds. This is where the bodies have been disposed of in the incinerator before this. But my men will be there with orders to hold the children in the facility and to burn slaughtered deer in their place to fool General Drape—he's always eager to watch the sky for the smoke of the incinerator. You must warn as many people as you can before the children are taken, but for those you can't reach in time, you must bring a group from the Watch to rescue the rest. Tomorrow only, there will be no guard at the guard station nearest the lumber mill. If you don't make the rescue tomorrow, there's nothing else I can do for you. I worry about how long we can safely keep them in the facility. Do you understand?"

"Yes."

"Alright, then, be on your way. We've spoken too long already." Mark looked around in a 360 loop again.

"One thing, Colonel. Why are you doing this?"

"You're the second person to ask me that. I suppose I should have an answer. But to fully understand my reasons, you'd have to know more of my life than I have time to tell you. You would have to understand all of the things I've experienced, all the people I've encountered. But for now, let it be enough for me to say I loved someone once who was lost to the Corsairs. It made me realize I'd been on the wrong side all along and the odds had always been stacked against the survival of the citizens. I'm just trying to even the playing field, I guess."

"Very well."

"Go now. And move quickly."

For the first time in his life, Sam willingly held out his hand to a Corsair. Mark took it, giving it a hearty shake.

"Thank you, Colonel."

* * * * *

"You're up early, my girl." Mrs. O'Dell's voice from the back doorway startled Sophie. She'd been standing at the sink, staring out the window, but not seeing the sun rise across the beach.

331

"I haven't really slept. Can I make you some coffee? What are you doing here so early?"

"I saw your lantern in the window. Thought there might be sickness in the house."

"No sickness. Just insomnia."

"If you don't mind my saying so, dearie, you don't look all that well."

"Perhaps not."

"What's the matter, then?"

"I don't even know. I guess I just feel like the ground's been ripped out from under me."

"Something the matter with you and that young man? Sure, we all have little spats from time to time. It'll pass."

Sophie set the coffee down in front of Mrs. O'Dell, who had made herself comfortable at the kitchen table.

"I wish it were that simple."

"Won't you be joining me?"

"No, I don't have much of an appetite for anything lately."

"You are looking a little green around the gills. And don't tell me it's nothin'. I know what I'm seein'."

"I don't know what you mean."

"No appetite. Fightin' with yer husband. And the worry's written all over your face. You'll be havin' a babe, sure as the sun's risin'."

"What? No, that can't be it . . ."

"Come on, now. You've had a child before. Think back. You missed your monthly, didn't ya?"

Sophie gripped the back of Mrs. O'Dell's chair, trying desperately to force the idea out of her mind. But she knew the old lady was right. Knew it as soon as she'd said it, though she had tried to force herself not to believe it. She was pregnant. Illegally. The quick-changing emotions played like light and shadows across her face. Joy and sorrow. Excitement and fear. Her legs would no longer support her, so she sat at the table across from Mrs. O'Dell.

"Don't worry, child. I'll be here with you."

"But you don't understand. I had no permit to have this baby. They're going to take her away."

"We don't know that. A lot's changin' these days."

"Yes, it's all getting worse."

"Sometimes things have to get worse before they get better. Like a fever, burning the disease out."

"If you survive the fever."

"Sure enough. Sure enough."

"Oh, Mrs. O'Dell, what am I going to do?"

"My granny used to say, 'Sufficient unto the day is the evil thereof.'"

"And what does that even mean?"

"No need to borrow trouble because today's got plenty, I'm thinkin'. All we can do is go one step at a time into the darkness, and maybe the light will follow."

Taking the old woman's wrinkled hands in her trembling ones, Sophie was grateful for the friendship she had found there. Her tears splashed on the weathered wood of the table.

* * * * *

Sophie didn't want to go to the barn. She knew the smells would send her stomach pitching. But she also knew that was where she would find Ethan. He adored Pip, and she had often found him there stroking the horse's mane or giving him carrots from the garden. When she walked into the dimness of the barn, she tried to hold her breath. She rubbed her arm gingerly, still sore from where she'd been shot, and the bruises on her neck more sore now than they had been the day before. In the dust lit from the open window, she saw Ethan with his nose pressed against Pip's. Both were very still. If Ethan hadn't been standing on his toes, she would have thought they were both sleeping like that.

"I knew I'd find you here," she spoke quietly.

"You know a lot of things."

"And there are a lot of things I don't know, too."

"Have you come to give me news about Toby?" Ethan turned to face her, standing with his shoulders squared, jaw clenched, ready to receive a blow.

"No, sweetie. We still don't know where the Corsairs have taken him."

"No one is safe, are we? They can just take anyone."

"That's partly true."

"What's the other part?"

"That we have each other. That we can try to be happy as long as that's true." Stepping forward, Sophie ran her fingers through the boy's thick hair, lighter these days than when he had arrived. "You know, eventually, everything seems like a dream. The pain passes. Even the joy passes. You look back and all you have are memories. Memories that feel like dreams, no more tangible than the mist in the night."

"Is that supposed to make me feel better?"

"I don't know. It's just something I've been thinking about."

"Where's Sam?"

She turned and busied her hands, closing Pip's feed bag. "Oh, I guess I could lie and make something up, but I'm not sure that would comfort you."

"So, where is he?"

"I honestly don't know."

"Has he left us?"

"No, of course not. He wouldn't do that."

"How do you know?"

She looked in Ethan's eyes, which mirrored her own fear. "Because I know him."

"What if he's been taken by the Corsairs too?"

"Then we'll find him. That's what family does. We look out for each other. I thought I had lost my sister. But she found me at the Border, and we're going to try to get her across. So I think anything is possible."

"I think anything bad is possible. The good things, maybe not."

"You're too young to be this cynical."

"What's cynical?"

"Believing only bad things will happen."

"Well, it's true."

"*Whatever causes night in our souls may leave stars.* What about Sam, us, this farm?"

"What about them?"

"Those are some of the good things that have happened to you, aren't they?"

"What's the use of finding good things if they can always be taken away?"

"That doesn't diminish their value. Maybe it even increases it. If we knew that nothing could ever be taken away from us, would we treasure them in the same way?"

"I don't know."

"I look forward to every single day I have with you because I know—maybe better than anyone—that nothing is guaranteed. And I know my time with you makes up some of my happiest memories and dreams."

"Me too."

"Come on, now. Pip has had his breakfast. It's time for you to have yours. Alright?" Sophie held her hand out to the boy. But instead of taking it, he wrapped his arm around her waist. They walked toward the house, arms linked behind their backs.

Sophie heard horses neighing and stomping their feet. At least a dozen. As she and Ethan got closer to the house, she saw the squad of Corsairs with a wagon among them. They had come for something. Perhaps it was to look for more weapons as they'd said in the town meeting. They would find nothing in the house. Ethan held her waist more tightly. She wouldn't show him her fear. She had meant what she said to him: They had each other.

The captain of the group approached her, pulling an official-looking document from his pouch. "By order of General Drape and the Triumvirate, all children are to be taken to a new job training academy. Room and board will be provided. Your government takes the care of your children very seriously." The captain folded his paper crisply.

Leaning down, Sophie whispered into Ethan's ear, "The beach. Run!" Without waiting even an instant, he was whipping through the field toward the beach. "Run!" she called hoarsely after him.

"After him!" the captain ordered the mounted soldiers to follow. "You're not making this any easier, citizen. The boy will be caught and taken."

Two of the soldiers, now dismounted, dragged Ethan between them, kicking and screaming. Joining in the fray, Sophie punched one of them square in the jaw before being pulled away by his comrades.

"Please don't take our son. Please don't take him. He's done nothing wrong!"

"I should arrest you for striking one of my men," the captain barked.

Soldiers flanking Sophie on either side held her before their captain.

"Please, Captain. Please. When can I see him again?"

"That is no longer your concern. He is now the responsibility of the

Triumvirate."

Sophie dropped to her knees before the captain, grasping his boots now shiny with her tears. "Please just let me say goodbye. I have to say goodbye."

The captain hesitated, looking first to his soldiers, then to the woman at his feet. "Very well." He nodded toward a sergeant to bring the boy forward.

Holding Ethan close to her, she tried to slow her breathing so she could speak. She took his face in her hands and looked into his tear-filled eyes.

"I don't want to go. I want to stay here with you," he cried.

"I know. I know. Here, I want you to have this." She took the butterfly necklace from her own neck and placed it carefully in his hand. "Listen to me carefully, my sweet boy. You are our son. Mine and Sam's. You are part of this family. I want you to know you are not a Lost Boy anymore. You'll never be lost again. Do you hear me? We will come for you. You will always be our boy." She clutched him again to her chest, crying into his neck, not knowing if the shaking she felt in her bones was hers or his.

In moments, the soldiers had pulled him away, placing him roughly in the wagon, which she only now saw held three other crying children.

"Sophie!" he called from the wagon as it drove quickly away, the soldiers riding behind in a four-by-four formation.

Sophie lay on the ground in the dust left behind, her arms wrapped around her head.

* * * * *

The house was empty, and it sent Sam into a panic. Colonel Goodson's words swam in his ears. The Corsairs had been to the farm already that morning, he could tell by the ground outside. But where was Sophie? He knew her well enough to know she wouldn't let Ethan go without a fight. Had she gotten herself arrested? Or worse? Calling her name throughout the house, his voice echoed in the cavernous emptiness. He had never thought about what this farm would be like without Sophie and without Ethan; it was a thought he found unbearable.

"Sophie!"

The empty room answered back with silence. How could he have left her like he did? She must have been so frightened to face the Corsairs alone. And yet again, Sam felt the blame and guilt weighing on his own tired shoulders.

He walked out to the porch, the midmorning sun stinging his eyes. Up above, he heard and barely saw seagulls circling. Their cries drew him out of his own thoughts. Ragged, troubled cries, they seemed. The birds dived among the sand dunes behind the house, leading down to the beach. The beach. He hadn't checked there.

As he made his way out past the house, he quickened his step. The gulls were joined now by the thrush, the warbler, and the harsh cackle of the blue jay. They all seemed to join an urgent chorus, pulling him onward. He even saw some of the birds, tucked away behind the sand dunes, seeking their breakfasts.

From the top of one of the dunes, Sam saw her. Sophie's hair, which was often held back in some kind of braid or other, was now hanging around her shoulders, flowing down her back, and being lifted in fiery tendrils by the sea wind. Sam heard the crashing waves, churning and spitting into the air. He heard the seagulls crying as they dipped low in the sky. And above it all, he heard Sophie screaming into the wind and the waves whipping around her. She would stand, sucking in all the air around her, then over and over would bend at the waist, expelling all within her into an anguished cry which even the waves couldn't muffle. She stood, and though fully clothed, Sam imagined he saw her stripped to the bone so he could see what made her heart beat and could almost see the great muscle convulsing in her chest. He made his way down to her as quickly as he could, but he knew before she spoke that Ethan was gone.

Sensing him beside her, she spoke hoarsely toward the ocean. "It's happening again. You remember after the First Revolution, they were rounding people up, taking them away to God knows where, without any way of knowing what happened to them. We can't let this happen again."

"We won't. Not this time. This time we know how to fight. You know I'll go after Ethan no matter what."

"I don't know anything. You said we didn't know each other or where we came from. You were right."

Sam held Sophie by the shoulders and gently turned her to face him, the waves churning around their feet. "No, Sophie. No. I wasn't. I was completely wrong. You know me, and I know you. We can do this. But we have to do it together."

337

"Do you mean that?"

His kiss was his answer. As he held her, he told her all that had transpired with Colonel Goodson.

"Prison? So, then, what will we do once we get the children away from that facility? We can't just come back here."

"We'll have to face that when it happens. Now, time to gather your people in the Watch. We only have one day to get the children out."

* * * * *

The blackened timbers and gray ash covered the site of where the ancient dwelling used to stand. It seemed to Kyle as if some great giant had just come along and blown it down with one puff. But he had seen it burn. He couldn't understand why this place had meant so much to him. It wasn't even his real home and served no logical purpose. He wanted to walk away and put his self-indulgence behind him, but somehow was still being pulled as if by some outside force to this spot. The spot where he'd last seen Mark. The spot where he'd watched his independence go up in the smoke from the house. The spot where he'd last felt like himself. But he didn't even know who he was anymore.

"You know I hate waste," a voice came from among the trees. The blue uniform materialized into Simeon. "And this . . . this is just symbolic of all the waste I see happening around here."

"Good morning, sir."

"Good morning, my son. Why are you here?"

"I was on my way back to Gemma's house from the town square. I've tried to talk to some of the people at the G.O., calm their fears as you instructed."

"Excellent. I'm glad you've remembered how to follow orders."

"Sir?"

"You know what happened here, don't you?"

"No, sir. I saw this place burning a few days ago. I was just curious about it. I'd never known there was a house back here before," Kyle lied easily.

"Really, now?"

"No, sir."

"Now, isn't that interesting?" Simeon walked around Kyle, not looking at him. He held a short whip in his hand, occasionally hitting his boot with it, occasionally tapping Kyle on the shoulder with it. "Then it doesn't make sense, does it?" he continued.

"What doesn't make sense, sir?" Kyle stood at attention while Simeon circled him, shark-like.

"Well, it just doesn't make sense why Mark did what he did. I thought he'd had some reason to burn this place down. But maybe I misunderstood. Maybe it had something to do with him punishing the citizens. Anyway, a sad waste, though."

"Mark burned it down?"

"Didn't you know? He said he'd seen you here that day. So I assumed you knew something about it."

"No, sir." Kyle's jaw clenched, but his voice was calm in his responses.

"Moving on. Now that Phase Two is underway, what information have you to give me about the Watch's response?"

"It does seem they're planning some kind of retaliation. There will be a meeting in one of the caves tonight."

"Excellent. I expect a full report."

"I do worry that if pushed too far, especially in regard to their children, the people's reaction may be . . . unpredictable."

"Do you really think their tiny force can make even a scratch in the mountain that is the Corsair army?"

"There are things that can wear down a mountain, even a tiny stream. Something as soft as water can cut straight through stone, given time."

Simeon stopped walking and faced Kyle head-on. "Well, time is something they're quickly running out of."

As Kyle heard the diminishing sound of Simeon's horse's hooves, he calmly reached down and picked up a piece of a charred timber, still hot days after the fire. His fingers dug into the black ash, fingernails sinking into the fibers. Then, with unknown emotions and force, he struck everything in his path with his timber. He had no connection with what he was feeling but could not stop himself from swinging the board haphazardly among the ruins. A cry ripped its way out of his chest. The birds in the forest went silent.

20
WHO AMONG US

An oppressive gray settles over the earth with the dawn drowning in rain and sleet. Smudges of clouds skid across a paler sky, but Sophie is stuck. Children in cages all around her, yet she is the one who can't escape. Walls, bars, and gray smoke closing in, trapping her. Trapping them. She looks for the keys that will free them, but there are no locks. Over the cries of the children, she hears her old song. Familiar, but different.

"So when my thoughts begin to stray . . ."

Who is singing? She feels around on the floor, crawling under the billowing smoke. Her fingers in a thick liquid, touching something warm. A body. Thin arms sticky with blood. Her sister Laurie is crying. She looks like she wants to say something, but Sophie can hear nothing over the music growing louder by the second.

". . . I know you're not far away . . ."

The music shifts into a minor key. Sophie can now see nothing but the smoke. Smoke blending into the rush of water of the falls. Laurie is gone. The children are gone. She's swinging her arms, trying to fight and hit at an adversary just out of her line of sight. She knows she's fighting shadows but can't stop hitting into the nothingness.

"I'll see you always near me, or so it seems . . ."

Sophie feels herself losing her balance. A shift in the ground being pulled from under her feet. Her quick breathing is loud in her ears, louder than the rushing waters. As she leaves the ground behind and feels only the air around her, her breath stops completely. She's falling with the water down into the gray void. An oppressive gray settles over her drowning. Falling up, falling down in empty space. Gray.

"For you will always be here somewhere in my dreams."

Sophie jumped, waking herself up, and felt her sore fingers clinging to the edge of the bed. She wasn't in her own bed, but Ethan's. Her stiff muscles, molding her into a ball on the single mattress, fought her as she tried to raise herself. Muscle spasms shot electric jabs through her feet and legs. The dim gray dawn seeped into the room like condensation on the walls, dripping with a weight of what the day would bring. The drizzling rain outside slapped at the window.

Ethan hadn't been gone twenty-four hours, but she couldn't seem to bring herself to leave his room, still fraught with his essence. He'd hung some of his photographs around the room and had stacks of them in messy piles on a tiny desk in the corner. Butterflies, lizards, flowers, a photograph of a little girl. Sophie assumed that was Daisy. There was an art and an innocence to the pictures he captured. Nothing faked or planned, but as if you had just stumbled upon something, and Ethan was pointing it out to you with his air of excitement and wonder. There were smooth rocks, picked flowers, and homemade slingshots strewn about the room as well. Sophie wondered what he shot at, since she'd never seen him show anything but affection for living creatures. His *Peter Pan* book lay open on the nightstand to a page where Captain Hook had captured Wendy and was using her to lure Peter Pan to him. The illustration on the page showed Wendy tied up, but with a look of defiance on her face, chin raised.

Sitting up in bed, Sophie waited for the nausea she knew was to come, but it didn't come. She placed her hand on her belly, more round than it had been a few weeks before. A roundness seemed to be settling over her whole body, and she wondered if Sam had noticed yet. She thought for the thousandth time about her unborn child in just as much danger as Ethan, trying to live in a world where there were more atrocities than children, more poisons than cures. If she had been a different person, she maybe would have wished for a miscarriage, an accident to rid her of the responsibility and terror of trying to raise another illegal child. But nothing—not even the Corsairs and their punishments—could make Sophie wish away the existence of any child. The children would just have to be protected at any cost.

"Sophie! I'm back!" she heard Sam calling from downstairs.

"Up here!" she answered.

341

Entering the room, Sam landed on the bed as if his legs couldn't hold him anymore, bouncing on the mattress next to Sophie. "Did you sleep at all? What are you doing in here?"

"I slept a couple of hours, I think. Nightmares."

"I'm sorry, Soph."

"Where were you?"

"I got the messages out about the meeting later. We're going to meet in the cave at low tide. Hopefully more than just the Watch will come. We need all the help we can get. Are you going to be okay?"

"I needed to be near his things. Smell his pillow." She took a deep breath as if the pillow were in front of her face and she was trying to breathe him back into their home through his scent.

Watching her, Sam remembered similar rituals she had performed with Bridget's things when he and Ethan had first met her.

"We have to find him, Sam."

"We will."

"I didn't fight hard enough for Bridget."

It was the first time Sam had heard Sophie say her daughter's name in months. He slowly laced his fingers through hers. "I don't think that's true . . ." he started to say.

"I can't . . . I can't lose another . . ."

"Shh . . . Sophie, I know. You don't have to say it. Everything you feel, I feel. Everything you go through, I go through. And we will find him. Together. I promise."

"What if we don't?"

"We will."

Since Sam and Ethan had come to stay at the farm by the sea, Sophie had never mentioned her feelings over losing Bridget. She knew they had seen the nightmares, the cries in the night, the sleepwalking, and soul-crushing depression. They'd seen it all and walked the dark road with her. And that was enough.

"Will you tell me if you're really alright, Sophie? You're pale. This is more than just not having slept well or worrying about the boy. What is it?"

She had imagined a hundred different scenarios of how she would tell Sam he was going to be a father. She could see the joy and the fear wash over his face. Standing by the river. Telling him over a morning cup of coffee. Lying in bed in the middle of the night. In every scenario, he was happy and scared. She wondered if she could wait for a time when he would just be happy, when the pure joy would not be soiled with the stain of fear. She wondered if that would ever be possible for any of them. Sophie knew this was not the time to have Sam worried about her. There were difficult tasks ahead to bring the children to safety, and she knew he'd never let her do what needed to be done if he knew she was pregnant.

Her brow furrowed slightly, and she looked out the window and around the room. Anywhere but in his eyes. "I'm fine, Sam. Really. I'm naturally pale. You know that. The curse of the redheads." She tried to laugh it off.

"I'm not at all sure you're telling me the whole truth, woman. But I trust you that you'll tell me whatever it is when you're ready."

"I'll tell you when I can. I promise."

Sam looked down, and Sophie thought she saw a tear fall from his eye. "Sam, what is it?"

"All the way home, walking back here to you, I was thinking about choices. We have choices. Humans shouldn't be compelled by outside forces to do things or go certain ways, at least that's the way it used to be or was supposed to be. The people of Before had their Bill of Rights and Declaration of Independence. But that's not the world we were born into, is it? We were born into a world of one choice. The choice between death or survival."

"I don't know that it's that simple."

"*There are no creatures that walk the earth . . . which will not show courage when required to defend themselves.* You know I am not a violent man, Sophie. And you know that I don't believe having a gun gives you courage. But sometimes to show courage and loyalty and love, sometimes merely for survival, we have to pick up a gun. I just don't know what it all means. My mind is spinning with all the shoulds and should-nots."

"We *have* been left with a choice, Sam. Perhaps the most important one—the choice between *living* and surviving. If we stayed here and did nothing, we would survive—possibly. But we wouldn't be living. Any more than other animals in cages. Asserting our humanity and our right to choose, that's the only way we'll ever really live."

"Maybe."

"The only way we'll be successful is if we believe what we're doing is right."

"I think it is. I hope it is."

"And as for courage—of course courage is more than holding a gun or even fighting. It's getting up in the morning when your body is begging you to just stop. It's staying with someone when it would be easier to walk away. Courage is believing in and hoping for the future. Those are choices we still have. They haven't found a way to control our minds yet. I don't have all the answers, but I do believe we're making the right choice because we *are* making a choice and not allowing the choice to be made for us."

Sophie took his face in in her hands and waited for his eyes to drift up to hers. "And courage is loving, giving yourself to another human being. You've done all of that. Hold on to those things for dear life, Sam. They're the only things that will get us through this."

"I don't know what 'this' is. There's no way for us to know what waits for us across the Border, but I promise you again, Sophie, I am here for you. I'm here for Ethan. And I will make sure we're a family again. And if that is the only choice that's been left to me to make, I choose you."

Sophie placed his head on her shoulder, holding tight to him, knowing that whatever courage she had that pushed her forward—his made it possible. With the same intensity she had tried to breathe in her children, she buried her face in his hair, breathing him in. She believed in his earnestness. She knew she could believe him that he felt everything she was feeling because she felt everything he was feeling as well. Their fears and their love were compounded, joined in an inseparable whole as impossible to separate as the sand on the beach moving as one entity. She hadn't been telling Ethan a comforting lie when she said he was their son. Sitting on Ethan's bed with Sam, she knew he was their son just as much as the tiny life now growing inside her. No amount of blood flowing in their veins could have bound them stronger.

* * * * *

Z's house was ringing with a song Gemma had never heard. She was relieved to hear the children playing out back and trying to sing along with Jesse's clear voice. The Corsairs had not yet come for them. There was still time for escape. With Jesse there, the house seemed brighter than it had ever been, even with the new threats hanging over them. How was it that the very light in the house was changed?

Jesse was moving about the kitchen as if she'd always lived there. She went up and down the cellar steps with more ease and vigor than one would have expected in someone her age. She brought up sweet potatoes, beans, and had gathered herbs from the garden, throwing them all in a large pot, singing as she went. It was like watching a performance, her hands moving with the grace of a dancer. She was as invincible as the woman she was singing about.

"I've never heard that before. What song is it?" Gemma spoke quietly from the doorway.

"Gemma, love. Come in, come in. Just an old song I used to listen to from Before. I always used to sing it when I cooked in my kitchen for my own children. Habits dies hard, I guess."

"I don't want to intrude. I just needed to talk to Z for a few minutes."

"Z? Is that what you call him? I always called him Zack. A younger man's name."

"He seems like a younger man since you've been back."

"I feel younger too, truth be told. He'll be down directly. Can I offer you something to eat?"

"No thanks, I can't stay. There's a meeting I have to get to. I just needed to talk to the two of you, I suppose."

"About this business with the children, I'm sure."

"Well, yes."

Zacharias came bounding down the stairs, not with his normal labored gait, but with the energy of a teenager. "Gemma! I'm glad you're here, sweetheart."

Gemma gave him a kiss on the cheek he offered. "Z, we've got to talk."

"Yes, I know."

"It's only a matter of time, maybe hours, maybe minutes before the Corsairs come for the rest of the kids. Honestly, I'm surprised they haven't been taken yet."

"Here, come sit at the table. Let's talk."

Zacharias pulled out a chair for her, then walked around and pulled out another for Jesse, kissing her on the top of the head before he sat down himself.

"So what does the Watch propose to do?"

"I'm the last surviving leader of the Watch, Z. Our numbers are dwindling. The meeting is meant to rally the rest of the citizens to help us.

Sam has been delivering messages to everyone left in Boswell and Jesse's Hollow."

Z's eyebrows went up in happy surprise that Sam was finally getting himself involved.

"But I want you to take Daisy and the twins back to the cabin, if you would."

"What cabin?" Jesse asked.

"Our old cabin, honey."

Emotion flooded her eyes. "That haunted place . . ."

"It's where the kids lived for a long while before we brought them here," Zacharias offered.

"It's still within the borders, but the Corsairs may not know about it yet," Gemma continued. "It's pretty far off the beaten path. At least they won't check there right away. I think it's the safest place for them for now."

"They can't stay there alone, these little 'uns," Jesse insisted.

"They've done it before. They'll be alright. And when we get the other children out of the facility, we'll bring them there too."

"No, Jesse's right," Zacharias responded. "I'll have to stay with them."

"You mean we'll have to stay with them." Jesse took his hand. "I have no intention of letting you go alone."

"Would you?" Gemma hadn't wanted to ask it of them but was grateful for the offer.

"Of course." Jesse took Gemma's hand as well, holding their little group in a circle.

"There's no telling how long you'll have to stay there, so bring plenty of food. I'll join you as soon as I can."

Concern showed itself in the deepened creases of Z's forehead. "What do you plan to tell Kyle?"

"I have no idea."

"Do you think he could be trusted with the information?"

"I'm sad to say, I don't think so. There's something wrong with him, and I haven't been able to figure out what is bothering him. But I won't be giving him anything else to worry about or be suspicious of."

"You don't think he's the spy, do you?"

"I honestly don't know what to think anymore, Z. I can only handle one crisis at a time, though. And right now, that's saving the children."

"Very well. We'll get things packed quickly and be gone within the hour."

"I wish you could come to the meeting with me. We could use your help convincing the citizens to help us."

Jesse was surprised the citizens needed to be talked into the fight that lay ahead. "You don't think saving their children will be enough of an incentive for them?"

"For some, maybe. They're just all so frightened of the Corsairs."

"With good reason." Jesse held tighter to Zack's hand.

"But if we have any chance of succeeding, we'll all be needed to fight as one. Now, where's Daisy? I want to say goodbye to her and explain things."

"She's up in your old room. The twins are out back."

"I'll go up to her first. Thanks, Z. And Jesse, thank you for everything."

"I've done nothin' much, love."

"More than you know."

"You take care, now, and come back to us and these children. Safe."

"I will."

Sprawled on the floor of her old bedroom, Gemma found Daisy among scattered drawings and what few books they had left after the Corsair raid. Her blonde hair was pulled back from her face in a loose braid that kept falling over her shoulder. She was working on what seemed to be a picture of a boy with a butterfly. She bent over her work in deep concentration, not hearing Gemma enter the room.

"Hey, kid."

"Gemma!" Daisy was up in a second, flinging her arms around Gemma's neck. "I'm glad you're here! I wanted to show you my new drawings."

"They're great!"

"Do you want to take one home with you?"

"Maybe another time. Right now, we've got to get you packed, and I'm going to need you to help Z and Jesse with the twins."

"Where are we going?"

"You've got to go back to the cabin for a little while until we can figure things out with the Corsairs."

"Aren't you coming too?"

"I'll meet you there in a couple of days."

"You promise?"

"Promise."

"Are the Corsairs coming after the kids like you said?"

"Yes, sweetie. They've already taken some to a government facility."

"Ethan?!"

"Yes, I'm afraid." Gemma thought Daisy would cry at this news. But she started to head for the door instead, ready to take on anyone in order to save a friend.

"We have to go after him!"

"Hang on now. That's not your job. That's my job. Your job is to go help Z and Jesse, alright?"

"But I want to help! He's my friend."

"You will be helping. You'll help me because I won't have to worry about rescuing you, too. While you're safe, I can focus better on saving Ethan and the others. Maybe even Toby, too. Alright?"

"It's not fair. I can fight." Daisy turned toward the window, the sun catching the silent tears on her cheek, her lips a fine line of defiance. She shoved her hands roughly into her pockets.

"I know you can. That's why I need you to help protect the twins. Zacharias and Jesse are old. They're smarter than me, but I don't know how they would be in a fight. I'm counting on you to protect the twins and run for help if you need it. Can you do that?"

"I guess I can."

"You guess?"

Daisy turned back toward Gemma, grabbing one of her hands in her own. "I will. But Gemma, promise me you'll save Ethan. He's my best friend. My best friend besides you, I mean."

"Daisy, you are *my* best friend. And I'm making you a promise that I will do everything in my power to bring Ethan back. Now, give me a hug before I go."

Daisy laid her head on Gemma's chest, her arms around her waist tightly. "Gemma?"

"Yes, sweetie?"

"I love you. I never told you this, but I wish you were my mother."

"So do I. I've never been prouder of anyone in my life."

"Be safe. Here, take this picture with you." Rummaging among the pile, she pulled out the desired paper covered in brightly colored trees with a house and two people front and center.

"What's this?"

"It's you and me in a new house outside the borders. So you won't forget me."

"I can never forget you, Daisy. Never." Gemma kissed the child on top of her head, breathing in her scent, and rushed out before Daisy could see her tears.

* * * * *

The ocean was larger and louder than Jesse remembered. And yet in its deafening roar, waves crashing on land that hadn't felt a salt bath in centuries, she could hear her deeper thoughts that often ran away from silence. She was overwhelmed by her senses, feeling the cool spray of the saltwater in her face, smelling the ocean's perfume. The gulls circled overhead. She let it all consume her as she imagined the sea had consumed her old home in Australia. She remembered her mother, the time they'd spent together on the beach. What was it she used to say? "We always get the miracles we don't need."

Jesse thought of the water making its way further and further inland and knew her mother was right. Strange things occurred on almost a daily basis these days, but it never seemed to be the miracle she needed.

All the songs left in Jesse's mind seemed to be ones her mother used to sing to her, and by extension were songs she'd sung to her own children. They played in her mind, co-mingled with the cries of gulls and the sounds of the beach. She held her hands to her face, breathing in, imagining Jill's and Max's hair in her hands, breathing her children in. But it was only the sea wind that entered her lungs.

As she stood with her toes sinking into the freezing sand, the sound of the wind and the waves was her mother's voice cooing in her ear, hushing her to sleep after a nightmare. "It's alright, Jesse. Mummy's here. I won't leave you. I'll not be goin' on walkabout." And she hadn't.

But Jesse had been the one to leave her. She'd been so sure she would get back for another visit. And then the Disaster. No word anywhere to anyone. Then wars. Lost children of her own. Prison. Exile. But somehow, she came back to the sea, the waters connecting the whole earth. And maybe this wave lapping over her feet right now came from Australia, from

Brighton Beach. Maybe they weren't so far away after all. Jesse wished she was a sailor on a ship that would take her and Zack across the vast ocean to Australia. Even living in a world littered by natural disasters would be better than trying to piece together a life from the ruins the Corsairs had left them on these desolate shores.

She sensed movement behind her. The waves had receded. Low tide. The meeting was beginning. She had to get to the cave. It wouldn't do to be seen out here on the beach.

The citizens of Jesse's Hollow and Boswell crammed themselves into one of the deeper caves. In the cold air, they were grateful for having other warm bodies close. As they'd traveled from their homes in the changing shades of leaves, the strands of summer unraveled and frayed, leaving the citizens to piece together autumn as they could with what was left them while the dying year limped toward its inevitable close. The cold hand of its dying lingered on their shoulders, prompting them to pull their coats tighter, raising their shoulders around their ears.

Sam stood at the back of the crowd with Sophie, looking anxiously for Gemma. He knew she would be running the meeting as the highest-ranking member of the Watch left. Her superior officers had been taken by the Corsairs. The net was closing.

He heard her voice over his shoulder from the side of the cave. Gemma was making her way toward them, talking to other citizens along the way. As he turned to face her, he noticed Sophie looking at her with recognition.

"That's my Captain Foxglove. I'll introduce you before the meeting begins," Sophie whispered in his ear.

"Aishe, hello." Gemma held her hand out to Sophie. Her eyes turned to Sam, and his eyes in turn begged her not to say anything. He didn't want Sophie to know of their connection. She needed to stay focused on the mission to come.

"Captain Foxglove, this is my husband, Sam. He's decided to join us."

"It's nice to meet you, Sam. We can use all the help we can get." Gemma shook his hand briefly. Sam was impressed with her performance. He knew now why she'd done so well in the Watch.

Suddenly, she looked past him to the mouth of the cave where she seemed to recognize someone. Sam and Sophie followed her gaze to rest their eyes on Jesse, the autumn sun pouring in and lighting her white hair on fire.

"Jesse? Why aren't you with Z?" Gemma asked straight to the point, worried that something had gone wrong with the children.

"He asked me to come here. Said you needed moral support. I'd say he's right. I'll meet him at the cabin shortly."

Sophie wrapped her arms around the woman she knew as Gran. "What about the ripples?" she asked with a smile on her face.

"Ripples? Hell, it was time to make waves," Jesse laughed quietly.

"Shall we get started?" Gemma asked as she walked to the front of the gathering crowd. Most of the remaining members of the Watch stood behind her as she faced the crowd with Sam and Sophie on either side of her. There were no more than twenty total members left. Two stood guard at the mouth of the cave, hidden behind two large boulders, but where they could still see anyone approaching.

"Welcome, friends!" Gemma shouted over the din to get their attention. "We don't have much time. Settle down, please. As many of you may already know, the Corsairs are now targeting the children. Their plan is to take them to a government facility outside the borders, for what purpose we don't know. We have obtained intelligence about the location and will have a short window of access to rescue them. We must call for volunteers to help us in the rescue."

A low mumble went through the crowd. Citizens looked at each other and at the ground.

"I know this is a lot to ask. But we have no choice if the children are to be saved. We must also hide those children who have not already been taken. Now, please raise your hand if you're willing to go with us."

The sound of the waves outside the cave was her only answer.

"Come, now. Will not one of you join us? The Watch has been looking after all of us for many years. And now that their numbers have dwindled, it's up to all citizens to protect themselves and their children, to join together as one."

A shout from the back of the crowd caused the citizens to turn around. "Who among us thanks the founders of the Watch, the fighters of the First Revolution for their actions?" A man roughly Sam's age stood with his hands shoved in his pockets, a frown on his forehead, and fear in his eyes.

"Truthfully, who?" No answer was to be had for his question. "Isn't it the Watch who got us into this mess in the first place? We talk about them," he continued, "We have daily reminders of their actions and the results. Most of us were robbed of parents, siblings, homes. But do we thank them for their sacrifices and for the residual payments we're forced to make in terms of the way we live . . . to pay for their choices? Or do we hate them for the burdens they saddled us with? Do we wish and pray to their gods that they'd kept their damn mouths shut and just waited for things to settle down and get better?"

The word "hate" echoed and rang against the walls of the cave, striking like a bell.

"And how has that strategy worked out for you, sir?" Sam responded when no one else would. "No, I mean it. Has your life gotten better for all of your silence and keeping your head down? You see, I used to be like you. Don't fight, I'd say. Just keep your head down. Try to keep them from noticing you. Don't do anything to stand out. Fall in line. But with every blow, my face got closer to the ground until I realized that looking at and eating dirt is no way to live."

"What other choice do we have? Death? Because that's all that waits for us if we fight them," said the man, not backing down.

"Sam is right!" It was Sophie's turn to speak up. "They've pushed us and moved us, fought us, abused us, and we've always retreated, always fallen back. Well, now they've pushed us all the way to the sea. They've taken our children, just as we were taken. There's nothing else they could take from me but my life, and I will gladly give that if it will make someone else's life better. We have no choice but to stand and fight. And any fight that doesn't take down the corrupt oppressors is no fight at all. This is more than just saving the children. It's to stop them once and for all."

Sophie was shocked when the crowd was still not responding. She couldn't believe how deeply the fear had sunk into their hearts, how completely conditioned they were to not respond. She took a deep breath before speaking again, trying to calm her heightened emotions. She knew shouting would never convince them. "There are things that are still right and things that are still wrong. To just sit by and watch as the wrongs continue to pile up, drowning us in the ashes of our consciences, that's not surviving. It's just dying more slowly. That kind of life will leave you incomplete, empty."

"We'll never take them down. Our numbers are too few!" The man shouted from the back.

Gemma regained her voice, "Sir, do you have children?"

"No."

"Then I'm sorry, but I believe that makes your opinion somewhat irrelevant. I'd like to hear from those of you who have children. How many here are parents?"

Fifty or so hands reached slowly into the chill air.

"I still say losing is inevitable, whether you're a parent or not." The man refused to give up his argument but spoke more quietly.

"It doesn't matter if we lose!" Gemma finally shouted. "It only matters that we fight. They're counting on us not fighting. They're counting on the fear they've sown being enough to hold us back. All this time, all the horrors we've seen, have been orchestrated to convince us that fighting was useless. They were constantly testing us to see if we'd react. So if they expect us not to fight, we just might win if we do. But isn't it worth the risk? Aren't our children worth the risk?"

"How do we even know if any of this is true? It could be a trap," another citizen finally spoke.

Jesse's aged voice came from the back of the crowd this time. "Oh, it's true."

Gemma, Sophie, and Sam were happy to see Jesse walking forward through the crowd parting before her.

"I heard the plans from the Triumvirate's very own mouths. Look, I know you've all seen horrible things in your lives. But none of you are old enough to have lived through the Disaster. The days of panic and mass casualties. It wasn't a natural disaster, my friends. There was nothing natural about it. All orchestrated for sick government purposes. A cleansing, they called it. Nothing clean, though. The world became more filthy than ever. And now here we are again. Being moved and manipulated like pawns on a chessboard. The only thing we can still call our own? Free will. The will to decide not to lay down and die. The will to say, 'No! You've taken our homes and our food, but you will not take our children.'" As she reached the front, she placed her withered hand on Sophie's shaking shoulder. "This young woman has lost her son in this attack from the Corsairs. She could have taken this information and gone straight to him, concerned only for her own family's well-being. But she came here to warn you, to help you save your children as well. Now who among you is still possessed of your free will? Who among you with stand with an old woman and these young parents to fight evil?"

Jesse's heart was beating loudly in her ears. She let the gathering silence weigh heavily on the citizens before her. But soon she knew it was not just her heartbeat she heard. Muffled hoofbeats echoed the blood beating in her ears. Horses. Horses getting closer.

The two guards ran into the cave. "We have to get out of here! Corsairs are coming. Run!"

"Scatter, everyone!" Gemma called over the commotion. "Don't all go the same direction. They won't be able to follow all of us."

The mass of bodies crushed to escape the cave, seeing Corsairs on horseback riding down the beach, sand flying in their wake. The low tide made access to the cave easy for them. Guns pulled out of holsters, they raised their rifles, holding the reins of the horses in clenched teeth. Bullets flew down the beach as swiftly as the sand behind the riders. No shots were heard from the guns bearing silencers. But as the citizens ran and scattered like tiny bugs, they heard the dull thumps and groans next to them as their neighbors were struck and fell in sprawling motion over themselves.

Thuds. Bullets ripping through clothing and flesh. Ringing ears from whizzing near misses. Blood and saltwater blending in a swirling red cocktail. Twisted limbs in strange shapes. People lying still on the sand but looking as if they were still running. No one stopped to calculate the number of Corsairs versus the numbers of citizens or the odds of their escaping. The bullets kept coming. One after another. Five citizens down. Ten.

The soldiers fanned out from a column to a follow after the fastest runners scrambling over the dunes toward the forest. If they reached the tree line, they'd be lost. And still more people ran out of the cave. The leaders were the last.

Jesse turned to Gemma. "Go! I'll get back to Zack and the children in the cabin."

"We'll draw the soldiers' fire first, then you run out in the opposite direction."

"I'll be fine."

"Jesse, take care of Daisy. Please."

"I will. Now go!"

Gemma turned to Sam and Sophie. "Three different directions. Meet me at the abandoned guard station. We'll cross the Border together. One hour."

Sophie kissed Sam quickly, and they all ran. North, south, and west.

21
WHERE THE TRAIL RUNS OUT

Although Kyle was expecting him, the sight of Mark in uniform on his horse hit him behind the eyes and in the pit of his stomach. Broad shoulders covered in the tight blue uniform, head held high, almost arrogant, but he'd lost the old twinkle in his eyes. Riding to the Border, Kyle had felt his resolve like a wall around him, protecting a vulnerable core. But when he saw Mark on his horse, his wall began to crumble. Kyle breathed in the rain-washed air deeply yet felt as if he were filling his lungs with hot, choking ash, burning him from the inside out. Spontaneous combustion.

Mark approached the Border fence slowly, cautiously. He absently saluted the guard in the shack as he passed through the gate. He was surprised, yet somehow not surprised, to see Kyle in his old Corsair uniform on the other side of the fence. The two men sat, shuffling slightly with the movement of their standing mounts, looking each other squarely in the eye. "I got your message. Why are we here?" Mark asked stiffly.

"Let's not talk here. There's a spot near the Northern Border where the trail runs out."

"Fine."

They rode in silence along the Border for a while before Mark spoke again. "Why the uniform? Back to your true colors?"

"I thought it would be less conspicuous for us to be seen talking if we were both in uniform."

As they rode, Mark held the reins gently, often reaching down to stroke the mane or pat the neck of his horse. Kyle felt a sense of indulgence watching Mark's gentleness, a quenching of a thirst he didn't know he had.

He reined his mount in sharply. "We're here." Dismounting, each man drew his horse further into the trees, tying the reins to nearby branches.

Mark hesitated, looking around intently, seemingly expecting an ambush. Light cut through tall, straight trees as if it were coming through bars. But he saw no one else about. "So why did you summon me?" The edge of his voice cut Kyle more than a sword could have.

"I didn't like the way we left things." Kyle moved toward Mark, reaching for his hand. But Mark pulled away, taking a step back.

"Is there any other way we could have left it? I mean, I don't even know who you are anymore."

"But you came anyway. That must mean something."

"Kyle, I've watched Simeon take you away from me a piece at a time. Like you're dying in front of my eyes. I don't think I can continue to watch it."

"I'm not dying. I'm still here."

"Are you? Because the Kyle I knew would not be working against the rebels, but with them."

"We gave them a choice. They chose wrong."

"It's not an either/or choice. How can we make them choose from the catalogue of horrors that could be visited upon them?" Mark took a deep breath and a step forward before he continued, steeling himself for the reaction he thought was to come. "To conquer the monster, we first have to face it. Kyle, what do you remember about the last fifteen years? Do you even remember the things Simeon has done to you? To other people?"

"I remember you."

"I'm serious. Think hard."

"I'm serious too. Of course I remember. He made the soldiers strip off my clothes first. But it went deeper than that. It felt as if they were stripping away my skin, getting into places inside me I didn't know existed. We were children, he said. And we hadn't yet earned the dignity of clothing."

"I remember."

"We were treated like less than dogs, marching, digging, training, eating, shitting, bathing so close to other men I didn't know where I left off and they began. Nothing left that signified . . . me. After a while of living like that, I finally started to feel like a part of something. More connected than I'd ever felt with the rebels. Sure, it was all hard to go through, but I felt like there was a greater purpose."

"But Simeon. What of Simeon? Living in his house, being his son?"

"I'm getting to that. By the time he put the uniform on me, he told me that's all I was. That's all I was ever meant to be. And without the uniform, without the Corsairs, I was nothing. That month after I helped the old woman escape, when he had me in solitary confinement . . ." Kyle's voice broke off like a twig snapping. He felt his breakfast rising in his throat and hot tears behind his eyes. "It was so dark in the Box. Took me weeks to get used to light again when I got out. I lost all sense of space or shape. Sometimes it felt like I was falling. I had to walk the couple of steps along each wall to just keep my balance. But yes, to answer your question, I remember everything about Simeon. Every slap, kick, punishment. Every kind word, every caress. But more than anything, I remember you. Through all of it, you were there with me. In that pitch-black box for a solid month, you were there next to me, the only light in that room."

"And how do you feel about me?"

"You have to ask?"

"I need to hear you say it."

"If I start getting into all that now, I'll never stop."

"So why do you have to stop? We're both still here, and we have a chance to make all of this right. Maybe even bring some justice to Simeon and the rest of the Triumvirate, to heal ourselves from all that happened to us." Mark's hand was on Kyle's face.

"Justice." Kyle thought of the old abandoned house, his one refuge burning, and saw in his mind's eye Mark lighting the match, and he pulled away. "Did you do it?"

"Do what? Kyle, what are you talking about?"

"Nothing. So much has happened in the last few days. It's all just getting to me, I suppose."

"These uniforms, these guns, this is not who we are, Kyle. Not you and me. We never wanted to join the army, never wanted to fight this fight on the other side. Half the time, I feel like I'm playing dress-up or something. Just pretending. Play acting."

"But it's not a game! It's reality, and we've both chosen sides."

"We haven't! They were chosen for us. God, Kyle, it's not for us to dole out the punishments, judgments."

"So why don't you go? You could leave, get away. There are a million places you could go. Just get on your horse and ride."

"You know why I stay."

"Because of me? Well, don't. I'm not worth it."

"I would go. But only on one condition . . . if you came with me. Right now."

"What about all the rebels you have to help?"

"I'll say it again. I will leave if you'll come with me. We can both stop fighting. Those are my terms."

Kyle turned away from Mark, walking to a nearby tree. It was an ancient red cedar, its branches high above his head, sheltering, engulfing. Green moss grew along the trunk. Kyle ran his hand along it. Mark's suggestion was tempting. As tempting as a cool drink from a river after a day of running from . . . from what? From the Corsairs. He looked down at his uniform and could have almost laughed at the irony of that memory coming to him just at that moment.

A stick snapped nearby, reminding him where he was and why he'd come here in the first place. A flash of blue behind another tree trunk let him know where Simeon was hiding. But as surely as he knew anything, he knew he couldn't go through with the plan. He had to work fast.

Kyle turned back to face Mark, stepping closer to him, placing his body between him and Simeon. "Listen, Mark. You'd better go now. Any further conversation is useless. We'll never be in the same place again."

"Why the hell did you bring me here?"

"To try to talk some sense into you? To say goodbye? Who knows?"

"I don't believe that. Something's wrong, isn't there? I know you."

"You don't know anything! Least of all me! Now, I mean it. Just go now before I have to do something we'll both regret."

"Kyle . . ."

"What do I have to do to make you leave me?"

"I'll never leave you."

Kyle sensed movement from behind him. Mark began to reach for his face again, forcing Kyle to act quickly. He threw his fist, catching Mark across the jaw, landing him flat on his back.

"Now do you believe me that I want you to go?!"

Mark lifted himself on one elbow, still lying in the leaves at Kyle's feet.

He rubbed his jaw tenderly.

"Fine, then. Have it your way. But this is it. I won't come to you again if you send for me. This is where we part ways for good." He stood in front of Kyle, internally begging him to change his mind.

"Just go."

"Goodbye, Kyle."

The brown and gray tumble of leaves swirled around the horse's hooves as Mark rode away.

After he'd gone, Simeon came up behind Kyle, pulling at his shoulder, forcing him to face him. He jammed the barrel of his pistol under Kyle's chin. "What the hell did you do?"

"We just got in an argument, and he left before I could stop him."

"You were blocking my shot. If I didn't know better, I'd say you intentionally sabotaged our plan."

"No, Father."

Lowering the pistol, he placed it in his holster. "Well, I suppose I can clean up the mess of your screw-up, like I've cleaned up all your other screw-ups. We'll give him a little rope to hang himself." Simeon cracked the knuckles of his gloved hands. "In the meantime, what's your next objective?"

"Find Foxglove."

"Exactly."

"There's a Watch mission plan to cross the Border and get to the lumber mill. Foxglove will most likely be there. She wasn't among the dead on the beach after the raid."

"I want you to go there and find her. Do not come back empty handed. And then you will meet me at the bunker. We obviously have some work to do with you."

* * * * *

Sam came through the silver mist to find the cabin. He'd run all the way from the cave, not even stopping for breath. He caught it now on the doorstep of the cabin, gulping in the chill air before going in.

"Z! Jesse!" he called as he entered. It took his eyes a moment to adjust to the dim light. But very soon he saw the two of them huddled with Daisy and the twins in front of the fire. "Oh, good, I'm glad you're here. I wanted to make sure y'all were safe before I left. I'm meeting Sophie and Gemma at the Border."

Zacharias and Jesse slowly raised themselves from the wooden floor, their bones creaking with the wood. "Yes, we're here. And we're safe." Z reached out to fold Sam into a quick embrace. "Who else is going with you to the government facility?"

"Just the three of us. Maybe it will be better that way. Less conspicuous than a squad crossing the Border. Now, look, did you bring any guns with you?"

"I have a rifle and a pistol."

"Plenty of ammo?"

"I have done this before, Sam."

"I know. I know. Alright, I guess I should go. Sophie and Gemma will be waiting."

"I'm proud of you, son. You're doing the right thing."

"It's not about doing what's right. They took my son. I'm going after him. It's that simple."

"Exactly."

Sam looked down at the floor and shuffled uncomfortably. "Look, Z. I don't know if I'll see you again. I wanted to thank you . . ."

"Now, now. Stop that. You're coming back."

Jesse spoke up, placing her hand on Z's arm. "Zack, let the boy say what he needs to say. We all know we're never guaranteed tomorrow."

Sam smiled shyly at her, this woman who had such sway over the man who'd been the greatest influence in his life. "I just wanted to say thanks, Z. You saved my life. More than once. You've been the best father a man could have. I'll do everything I can to do the things you taught me and to get back here." He cleared his throat. "I love you, Z."

"Come here, boy. *Life is made of so many partings welded together.*" Zacharias held Sam tightly in his thin arms. He thought how different it felt to hug him as a man than when he was a small boy. He remembered the grubby little kids he and Gemma were that he'd found in this very cabin and struggled to hold back his tears. Jesse wrapped her arms around them both for a moment before the spell was broken.

"Alright, then. I won't say goodbye. Just see you later," Sam said gruffly as he left the cabin as quickly as he'd entered.

* * * * *

"It won't do for all three of us to waltz in there. It could be a trap. Let me go first and check it out." Sam looked earnestly at Sophie, hoping she'd back him up. The three of them sat huddled in a tight stand of trees just across the Border fence. There had been no guards at the guard station, just as Colonel Goodson had said. Sam hoped this meant they could trust the rest of his information.

"Sam, is it?" Gemma asked as if they'd just met, keeping up the pretense for Sophie. "We'll be fine. Aishe and I have trained for just these sorts of situations. We don't need you to protect us."

"Foxglove," Sophie stepped in, "it may not be a bad idea to have some reconnaissance."

"We're running out of time."

Sam was becoming annoyed. "Exactly. The longer we argue, the more time we're wasting. I can go on ahead and give you an owl call if it's safe."

"Fine. Just hurry," Gemma responded. She didn't like letting him take charge, but she knew Sam and Sophie were right.

The old sawmill sat like a dark gray monster deep within the forest of the Forbidden Grounds. No road led to it anymore. Almost all mark of humanity had been wiped from the surrounding grounds, giving it the appearance of having grown up out of the earth itself, a great beast upon the land. A soft white ash like fresh winter snow covered everything surrounding the lumber mill. All the trees and ground were within a light shroud of feathery non-substance that was just as likely to fly in your face as lie still. Ghost-like feather fingers borne on the breeze, falling from the smoke-filled air being pumped out of the cylindrical brick incinerator attached to the old sawmill.

Sam made his way quickly toward the mill, hoping the Corsairs weren't burning what he thought they were. He pulled his tunic up, breathing through the fabric to protect his lungs from the smoke. A movement in the air caught his eye as a bright-red leaf fell from an empty sky.

A blanket of leaves swelled and moved to his right like a wave. Before he could step away from it, a hand reached out and grabbed his leg, pulling him to the ground. Scuffling among the ash-soaked leaves, Sam saw only gray and movement all around him. Hands moving faster than him, blocking every defensive move he tried to make. In a moment, he was pinned to the ground, a gray form sitting on top of him, his arms unable to move at his sides.

"Sam! Sam, it's me, Kyle. Stop fighting me, will ya?"

"Kyle! Get the hell off me!"

"Not until you promise not to run. I need to talk to you."

"Well, you've got a funny way of getting someone's attention. Why the hell were you hiding in the leaves?"

"I didn't know who would be coming along this way. I couldn't take a chance on being seen."

"Let me up!"

"Promise not to run?"

"Yes, just get off me!"

Kyle stood up slowly, brushing ash, dirt, and leaves off of his clothes as best he could. He ran his hands through his hair, shaking his head.

Sam sat up without taking his eyes off Kyle. He saw the pistol in his holster but also noticed Kyle was in no hurry to pull it out. Sam's own gun had fallen to the ground with him. He saw the rifle on the ground a few feet away.

Kyle followed Sam's eyes to the gun. "Let's just leave that there for now, okay?"

"Fine. What do you want?"

"I want to keep you from making a tragically stupid mistake."

"I don't want to play this game with you anymore, Kyle. You always stepping in to save me from myself as if we're still friends."

"I am still your friend."

"And yet you're in a Corsair uniform. I knew you hadn't really left them."

"You're right about that. But it doesn't mean I want to see you get hurt."

"Not really your call anymore."

"If you'd just listen to me. Sam, please don't go through with whatever plan you've got. It's bad enough that you crossed the Border. You could be shot on sight."

"That's why I plan to stay out of sight."

"Whatever it is you're planning. It's too late anyway."

"What do you mean?"

"You can smell it as well as I can. That's not wood burning. If you're here, you know what this facility is and what it's for. The fact that the fire has already started proves you're too late."

"Well, I need to see for myself."

"Don't be an idiot. There will be at least a squad of Corsairs in there."

"Why are you here, Kyle? You said you didn't know who you'd come across."

"I'm on a mission."

"Now we get to it."

"Tell me who Foxglove is. I have intel that says she'll be here too."

Sam kept a stone face while internally he felt relief that Kyle didn't know he was looking for Gemma. "I'm not in the Watch, and I don't know their code names."

"But you know they have code names, and you're obviously here with them somewhere. Is she on her way?"

Sam was silent.

"This will go better for everyone if you just tell me. You know I'll find out anyway. What's the signal to tell her to follow?"

"I don't know, and I wouldn't tell you if I did."

"Sam, how do you think the Corsairs found out about your meeting in the cave and your plan to come here to rescue the children? Do you think I haven't had you followed? Now, I can only protect you for so long. Please! Please just stay out of it like you've been doing. This isn't going to turn out like you want it to. Believe me."

Sam had never heard Kyle beg for anything before. He could hear the sincerity in his voice behind the emotion. He knew Kyle truly wanted to keep him safe. But how much else of what he was saying could he trust?

After a few silent moments, Kyle finally sat next to Sam on the ground, pulling his knees up and holding them tight to his chest. His knee-high boots were no longer shiny but scuffed and covered in dirt and ash. "Nothing has turned out like we thought it would, has it?" He spoke to Sam as if they were just two old friends reminiscing. "You remember our plan? We were going to find an old farm across the Border. I'd clear the land, you'd farm it, Gemma would do the cooking."

"You know she hated that plan."

"Yeah, she wouldn't agree to it unless we told her she could go hunting with us."

"She was always the better shot."

"But nothing turned out that way. We couldn't manage to get away from the war."

"It always followed us."

"Sam, can you do me a favor?"

"I don't know."

"It's the last favor I'll ever ask you."

"Maybe."

"What did we say we'd do if we were caught?"

"We'd shoot each other because neither one of us ever wanted to fight for the Corsairs."

"But when it came down to it, I didn't let you do that, did I? I let them take me."

"I never could figure out why."

"Because deep down, I knew I couldn't shoot you. So all I could do was keep you away from them. But now . . . after everything that's happened. I need you to follow through on our original bargain. I need you to shoot me." Kyle pulled out his pistol, handing it to Sam handle first.

"You're talking crazy, Kyle. I don't know what it is that they've done to you, but I can't . . ."

"We're all dead anyway! None of us is getting out of here alive. You have to know that."

"I don't know that."

"You were never realistic. Always a dreamer."

"I just believe we still have a chance."

"Well, I know. I know we're playing a rigged game. There's no way for any of us to win."

"Even if you're on the winning side?"

"There is no winning side. There are only losers and the dead. But I'd rather be dead now than see what's going on in that mill. To see all the horrors that are coming. Please, just do it, Sam. Take the gun!"

"You don't have to go back to the Corsairs. Come with me."

"It's too late."

* * * * *

"He's taking too long," Gemma breathed in frustration. "Come on, Aishe. We have to go after him."

365

"I think we should give him a few more minutes. I've never known Sam to not follow through on something he said he would do."

I have. Gemma was thinking of the seven years without him. But knew she couldn't say anything about that. "There's no telling what he walked into. He could be in trouble."

"And what if he's trying to protect us by not signaling, and we just make it worse by rushing in there headlong?"

"I'll give him five minutes. We're going to lose the light soon, and we still have to get the kids back across the Border and to the cabin."

The two women sat with their backs to one tree trunk, shoulder to shoulder.

"So you and Sam haven't been married very long, have you?"

"No, not very. Feels like longer."

"How did you meet?"

"It's a long story."

"And now you're going to have a baby?"

"How did you know?"

Gemma cocked her head to one side and let a sad smile fall across her lips. "Aishe. A pregnant woman moves differently. Holds herself more carefully. Even subconsciously protecting the unborn."

"I suppose so. I haven't told Sam yet."

"And he hasn't guessed?"

"We've been sort of busy with other things."

"When will you tell him?"

"After we get the kids back, I guess. I knew he'd be worried about me coming on this mission."

"As am I."

"I'll be alright. Really. You know, there are people who can fill the spaces you never knew were empty. Sam was that for me. I just have to make sure the time is right when I tell him."

"I'm happy for you, Aishe. Truly, I am." Gemma took Sophie's hand in hers, allowing herself a moment only to feel all of her feelings. Envy that another woman was having a child, Sam's child. Joy that there would be a tiny piece of Sam and Aishe left in the world. Fear of what would happen to her friend if the Corsairs found out. Too many things to fully process in so short a time, she took only a glimpse of her inner heart as if she were seeing herself from a great height, only getting a general idea of what was there.

She took a deep breath, pulling herself in before the first tear fell. "Right, then. No signal yet. It's time to go."

Sophie and Gemma entered the lumber mill only lit from what little sun came through the smoke-streaked windows. They'd found no sign of Sam or anyone as they approached the building. No soldiers standing guard. No one on the inside. The lack of force was eerie to them, the silent void that fell over the earth before a storm.

There was a large main room with conveyor belts along the walls. Stacks of unused lumber had been left years ago. A creeping, gloomy decay settled over everything within their immediate sight. Decades of grit and cinders lay over slabs of bark and piles of sawdust, and a smell of rotting wood hung limply under the burnt air.

Heat was coming at them in suffocating waves from the large brick incinerator on the right side of the building, a large circular oven as big as the cabin if it had stood on its side. They could see drag marks through the sawdust leading toward the incinerator, and the smell was unmistakable. Sophie felt her stomach hitting her throat, the nausea rising at the thought that they were too late. Covering her mouth tightly with one hand, she physically held down her choking sobs. But in the silence of a gathering breath, she heard it. Someone else was crying. More than one person. Children.

"Foxglove, listen," she whispered, grasping for her captain's hand.

"I hear it. Where are they?"

Sophie looked frantically around. "Back there!" Behind some stacks of lumber, she could see the tops of cages. She and Gemma ran to them to find at least a dozen children huddled together, dirty faces streaked with tears. Sophie excitedly scanned the faces for Ethan while Gemma looked for something to break the one lock that held them in. A series of cages had been strung together almost like a tunnel, barely tall enough for the tallest child to stand, and with only one door that would let them out.

"Stand back." Foxglove swung a large piece of wood, easily breaking the rusted lock.

"Ethan!" Sophie cried, still not seeing him among the crying children.

"Sophie? I'm back here." At the far end of the row of cages she saw him, sitting in a corner with someone in his lap. She crawled quickly to him, the other children filing out around her at Gemma's gentle command.

She was next to him in a second, sitting on the sticky floor, not allowing her mind to venture to what would make it so. Her hands were on his face. "Oh, sweetie, what have they done to you?" She had him in her arms, finally feeling complete again.

"Sophie, Sophie, look," he was saying through sobs. What was he trying to show her? Words were tumbling out of their mouths, both trying to speak and listen at the same time.

"What is it?"

"Sophie, this is my mother. She's been shot. She needs help."

For the first time, Sophie looked down and noticed it was a woman lying in Ethan's lap. There was blood coming through a hole in the shoulder of her tattered shirt. Her eyes were starting to flutter open. "Laurie?!"

"Sophie, is that you?" the woman whispered.

"Ethan, this is my sister, Laurie. She's your mother? How can that . . ."

"Aishe! It's time to go! Come on. We have to hurry before the guards get back to the station."

Sophie's head was spinning. "Laurie, can you walk?"

"I can try." Laurie raised herself enough to half-crawl and be half-dragged out of the cages by Sophie and Ethan. They rested for a moment on the side of the bars.

Ethan rushed through what he knew. "The soldiers picked her up in the woods, Sophie. Some colonel told them to bring her here with us. Then he ordered them to throw deer into the incinerator. What's happening?"

"I'm not sure, Ethan. All I am sure of is that we're getting you out of here. Laurie, let me look at your shoulder."

"Not here, Soph. It's been too long since I was shot. The fabric is deep into the wound. I'm gonna need a doctor."

"Alright. Alright, we're going to get you to a doctor. I swear." Sophie kissed the top of her sister's head.

Two shots pierced the air from outside the building. Rifle shots. Within seconds, Sam was in the doorway.

"Sophie! Ge . . . Foxglove!"

"Sam, we're back here."

Sam made his way through the throng of sobbing children to find Sophie, Gemma, and Ethan all huddled around a woman on the floor.

"We've got to get out of here. Quick! Two squads are headed this way, one from the north, and one from the south. I just shot their scouts. They'll be here in minutes. If we head straight east to the Border, we may just miss them. We've got to make a run for it."

"Right. Sam, you help Aishe with her sister. I'll herd the kids to the Border." Gemma was back in control.

Gemma and the children moved quickly among the trees, their fear quickening their feet. Sophie and Sam struggled along with Laurie between them, Ethan bringing up the rear. He wouldn't let his mother or Sophie out of his sight.

Only yards away from the mill, Laurie stopped walking.

"What is it?" Sophie asked.

"Soph, I'm not going to be able to make it with y'all."

"Don't be ridiculous. We'll carry you."

"Mother, come on. Please!" Ethan begged, tugging at her clothes.

"Ethan, honey. I think the little kids need your help. Can you run on and help them?"

"I won't leave you!"

"Come here." Standing on her own feet, she held her son in her arms, arms that hadn't held him since he was half his height. "I want you to know that I love you, and I'm so proud of the young man you've become. I need you to be brave and go with Sophie and Sam."

"I won't leave you like I did before. It was all my fault. I'm sorry, Mother. I'm so sorry." Ethan buried his face in his mother's chest, his tears blending with her blood.

"Nothing has been your fault, my boy. I'm so happy I got to see you again. Now, I need you to go. Do this for me. Please, my love. Sam, take him."

Sam looked to Sophie to see what she wanted him to do. He could tell by Laurie's pallor and breathing that she wasn't going to make it. He'd been close enough to death in his life to recognize it now. But was it right to leave her?

"Go on, Sam. I'll be there in a minute," Sophie whispered.

He gently pulled Ethan into his arms and carried the boy to catch up with Gemma and the other children.

Laurie was leaning on her sister's arm for stability. "I'm slowing you down, Sophie. I've got enough strength in me to lead the Corsairs in the

369

opposite direction. With any luck, they'll follow my trail and not yours. And if they catch sight of me, we look enough alike that they won't know it's not you they're chasing until it's too late."

"I can't let you do this, Laurie. I agree with Ethan. I can't leave you like I did before."

"We're running out of time. As long as they're looking for me, maybe they won't be hurting anyone else. I'm finished anyway, Soph. You know that. My life hasn't meant much of anything up until now. At least let my death mean something."

Looking into her sister's eyes, Sophie saw so many things she couldn't explain or even have words for. She saw herself in the facial expressions, the crinkle of the eyes. She saw their mother in the warmth mixed with fierce determination. And now for the first time, she saw Ethan, his kindness and strength, but also his fear. She saw all the moments he hadn't been able to share with his mother and would never share. Seeing Laurie's pale skin, losing color and life before her eyes, Sophie felt the weight of motherhood shifting from her sister's shoulders to her own, and she welcomed the burden. She didn't have to tell Laurie that she would take care of Ethan as her own. Laurie would know just how well cared for Ethan would always be with Sophie.

Sophie held her sister one last time. "I love you, Laurie."

"I love you. Now go."

Without looking back, Sophie ran to catch up with the others.

Following the river, Sophie's breathing quickened as she neared the waterfall. They'd gone farther north than they should have. It would take longer to get back to the guard station now. Branches, twigs, and underbrush slapped at her legs and tripped her up as she pushed to speed up her pace. She could see Sam, Foxglove, and the children pausing for a drink at the head of the falls, the quick rush of water pulsing in her ears.

"Sam, Foxglove, time to go. A couple of Corsairs broke off from the group. I think they saw me. I doubled back and around a couple of times, but they can't be far behind."

Gemma didn't hesitate but rounded the children up and began running again for the Border. Sam waited for Sophie.

"I'm not coming with you right now, Sam."

"Don't talk crazy. Come on, let's go."

"They saw me, Sam. So even if we get away now, they won't give up until they find me. You, Ethan, and the other kids won't ever be safe."

"We'll figure it out."

"No, I've got to make them think I'm dead."

"Don't do this."

"You saved me once. Ethan, too. Now let me do this. Take the children. Take care of them. I'll come to you when I can."

"It's not bravery to sacrifice yourself for nothing. Sometimes bravery is knowing when to live to fight another day."

"Bravery is fighting for the greater good despite the odds and despite fear. I am terrified, but when are you going to realize that you are the greater good? You're *my* greater good."

"I need you to come back!"

Sophie held and kissed him for as long as she dared. She stood listening to his steps through the forest grow quieter, all the while her breathing and heartbeat grew louder. And still she waited, listening to the sound of Corsairs on horseback grow closer. She had to wait for them to see her before she could make the plunge. She peered over the edge of the waterfall, at least fifty feet to the swirling pool below, and felt herself start to hyperventilate. The waterfall was spraying water into her face.

Horses plunged through trees and underbrush. She heard the commotion stop and turned to face her pursuers. With one graceful leap, she abandoned the ground under her feet and was over the cliff, falling with the water. Her breathing stopped, and all went silent with the release.

22

LEFT BEHIND

Once they'd gone back across the Border, with still no guards at the station, Gemma stopped under a stand of trees, letting all of the children and Sam catch up with her. Dusk was descending, light draining from the sky, leaving an empty yet encroaching darkness behind. It was becoming harder to see, even as their eyes adjusted to the dimming light.

Sam was sweating despite the chill in the air. He worried how they were going to get all of the children home without being caught by Corsairs for being out after curfew. The group was large and conspicuous, and no matter how many times he and Gemma had begged the children to stay quiet, there were still one or two whimpering to themselves. Ethan, on the other hand, had not said a word since they left Laurie outside the mill. Sam kept having to look for him to make sure he was still with the group.

"Why have we stopped, Gemma?"

"Let the children rest a minute." She wiped her forehead. Sam could see what this day had taken out of her. Not much had happened as they had planned or hoped.

"We're losing the light. Look, while I'm thinking about it, I need to tell you something about Kyle."

Gemma sighed heavily with exasperation. "Oh, for the love of . . . please don't start all of that again, Sam."

"No, this is important. You need to listen to me."

"No, *you* need to listen. Sam, I'm going back for Sophie."

"Like hell you are!"

"Calm down. You'll upset the kids. Come over here." Gemma pulled him away out of earshot of the children.

"I'm her husband. I should go," he pushed on.

"That's exactly why you shouldn't go. You won't be thinking clearly, Sam. You'll make risky choices and get both of you killed."

"I have to do this for her. I promised to protect her."

"If she wanted you to protect her, she wouldn't have jumped off that cliff!"

"I don't care. I'm going. You take the kids back."

"And what about Ethan? What would he do if he lost you and Sophie and his mother all in one day? You have to let me do this for you, Sam. You have more to lose here than you think. Let someone save you for once. I'm just trying to live the code too. Until you can stand on your own. Right?"

She was right. He knew it, and he didn't want to know it. He felt useless, weak, as if he couldn't live up to some version of manhood in his head. Kyle had always called him a coward. Maybe he was right. Sam tried to hold onto what Sophie had said about courage. Had it only been that morning? It felt like at least a week had passed since then. *Courage is giving yourself to another human being. Courage is believing in and hoping for the future.* Sitting on the edge of the bed, her skin so pale in the morning light. Her hand on her . . .

Her hand on her belly. Pale skin. Nausea every morning. *Courage is giving yourself to another human being.* It couldn't be. Sam wrestled with his feelings, vacillating between elation and terror.

"Gemma, what do you mean by saying I have more to lose than I think?"

"Just that you'd be fighting for your family . . . it would make it harder to be objective. You know what I mean," Gemma stammered through her words.

"Tell me the truth. Is Sophie pregnant?"

"Sam, this is not the time to have this conversation . . ."

"Tell me!"

The words came out before she could stop them or think of the consequences. "Yes, she is. She told me just before we went into the mill."

"Why didn't she tell me?"

"Look around, Sam. There hasn't really been a good time for that kind of revelation lately."

"Did she think I wouldn't be happy about it?"

"I'm sure she was trying to deal with her own feelings about it first. This child is illegal. And we've been racking up the crimes against the government today. It's only a matter of time until we're all caught. She's terrified about the world your child will be born into and whether or not any of us will survive."

"And she's been trying to handle it all on her own . . ." Sam's face fell into his hands.

"Focus, Sam. Stay on mission. Get the kids back to the cabin, let me go after Sophie."

Taking a deep breath, squaring his shoulders, "I still say it should be me."

"And what if she's hurt or had a miscarriage, would you know how to help her? Because I would. Sometimes it takes a woman to help a woman. Alright? Now, let me do this. We're running out of time." Gemma placed her hand on his arm, the first time she'd allowed herself to touch him since the day he'd returned from the work camp. Sam hated her logic, her complete objectiveness about everything. But he let her go all the same.

* * * * *

Jesse found Sam sitting at the table in the cabin. The same old wooden table where she had sat waiting for Zack after she had come to the cabin with her children and Aabirah that first horrific night that changed all their lives. It had been several days since his return. Days since he'd brought all of the children back to their grateful parents, not one child lost or left behind. And days since they had last seen Sophie or Gemma. Ethan had not yet spoken a word, and Sam just paced around the cabin and outside along the stream. Always looking, always waiting, the tension and anxiety working dark circles under his eyes and lines into his gaunt cheeks. Jesse wondered if he'd even slept since that day.

Zack didn't know how to help Sam through this. "Because you've lived through it yourself," Jesse had pleaded. "My God, Zack, the boy's in pain!"

"Exactly," he had responded. "That's why I know there's nothing I can say that will help." He told her to give it time, but she knew from her own experiences with loss and grief this could not continue. He would worry himself into an early grave. And she worried Ethan would stay shut away inside himself if they couldn't draw him out enough to process his grief over losing his mother a second time.

Standing at the sink and watching Sam over the bar, she tried to busy her hands with the dishes, while his hands continually ran through his rumpled hair, pulling at it as if he could rip out the memories of the trauma he'd lived through.

"Sam, can I make you some tea, son?"

"Nah, thanks," he grumbled under his breath.

"You need to get something into you. When's the last time you ate?"

"I don't know."

"What are you thinking about?"

"What?" The question caught him off guard. Sophie was the only person who ever asked him that.

"You're sitting there staring at the grains in the wood as if they're trying to attack you. You must be thinking *something*."

"I was wondering why they went after the children, and why did they go to our house first."

"You think there was a plan beyond what I heard from the Triumvirate?"

He got up and started pacing around the room again. "I mean what if it's more than a general plan? What if it's something to do with me? Kyle said they'd been following me. Why me? Why not someone in the Watch?"

"Do you think they could have been baiting you . . . using the children to draw you out?"

"I don't know. I don't know! But if they were, it worked, and I played right into their hands. I've been such an idiot."

"Now, I can't let you get away with that."

"Why not? It's true. I've ruined everything I've touched since I came back a year ago. She would have been better off if I'd just stayed out of her life. She's going to have my child, and I let her jump over a cliff."

"Now, now. From what I hear, you saved that girl's life and her reason. Who's to say if she'd even still be alive today if you hadn't been there to pick up the pieces?"

Jesse had left the kitchen and stood directly in front of Sam in the middle of the room, preventing anymore pacing. The floor was scattered with the few toys and belongings the twins and Daisy had brought with them. They could hear all three of them playing out by the stream with Zacharias, all the children except Ethan, who was sleeping in the back room.

Sam bowed his head, looking as if he were about to confess a dark sin. But all he said was, "I love her, Jesse. I love her more than my own life. I have to know what happened to her."

"I know. Believe me, my boy, I know how you feel. You've lived in fear and grief for so much of your life. And the minute you think you've found something permanent, some kind of family, the Corsairs come in and take it away. Thinking about all the possibilities of what could have happened to Sophie, your child, and Gemma play over and over again in different iterations in your head until you think you'll go mad. Playing through the scenarios takes up so much of your thoughts that there's no room for anything or anyone else. Right?"

"Yes," he said with surprise and a hint of relief in his voice.

"But there's someone else you've got to make place for in your mind and heart. Ethan is in trouble. More than you, maybe, because he's only a young boy. He's feeling the loss of Sophie too, but also he had to lose his own mother again. Think back, son. I know you know what he's going through. Try to think of what you needed at that time of your life. That's what he needs now. From you."

"I can't help him. I can't even help myself."

"Yes, you can. And you must. I believe Sophie is still alive. And you've got to help him find hope in that."

"I don't know. Maybe it will be best for the boy if we go on as if she's . . ."

"You can't even say it."

"It's been days, Jesse! If she were going to come back, she'd be back by now. They're both gone. I never should have let Gemma be the one to go after her."

"You'll never heal or help Ethan heal if you keep beating yourself up for past decisions. Guilt will rip through you like wildfire, and it will destroy everything good that's left, including your son. You've heard me talk about ripples and how they spread. Just like ripples in water spread, so does fire. A fire may begin in one part of the house or town, but you'll find smoke and soon little flames farther away than you thought it could jump. You've got to control it now at its source."

"I don't know how."

"Just think of Ethan as the little boy you once were. You'll know what to do."

Sam looked toward the back-bedroom doorway to where Ethan slept. He looked back at Jesse's expectant face. In the end, he retreated to the outdoors, the place he could find a semblance of peace.

Sighing at her apparent failure, Jesse moved toward the bedroom. She thought she heard stirring inside.

"Ethan, sweetie, you awake?" she whispered from the doorway. The door itself long gone and canvas hung where the walls used to be.

No answer. She ventured in a little further, seeing him tumble and flail on the bed, grunting and crying out every few seconds. Sitting softly on the bed next to him, Jesse tried to calm without waking him. She ran the back of her fingers along his cheek, humming the tunes of her own mother's comforting. His nightmare dragged on until it had spun itself out. He woke with a start, nearly striking Jesse across the face with his thrashing arm. But she was too quick for him and caught him by the wrist.

"It's alright. It's alright, Ethan. It's only me. It's Jesse, my boy. You were having a nightmare."

He looked in horror at his arm she was still holding as if she were holding a snake before him. Realizing what he'd almost done, he broke down in tears on her lap. "I'm sorry. I'm so sorry. I didn't mean to hurt you. I'm so sorry." He repeated his stifled, sobbing apologies into the apron at her waist.

"You didn't. Ethan, there's been no harm. Hush now." She stroked his hair, whispering softly her soothing words.

When he was calmer, he sat up, looking into Jesse's open face for answers she didn't have.

"Can I get you some water or something to eat?"

He shook his head, wiping tears and running nose roughly with the back of his hand.

"Do you want to talk?"

"What about?"

"Anything. About what you're feeling or thinking?"

"What's the point?"

"What do you mean?"

"I mean everyone I talk to or get close to goes away. So if I talk to you about how I feel, maybe you'll go away too."

"That's not going to happen."

"You don't know that," he said quietly.

"You're right. I don't know that for sure. I was just saying what I hope."

"I used to hope a lot of things."

"And you don't now?"

"I've got to go check on Sam." Ethan tried to get up from the bed but was stopped by Jesse's surprisingly strong arms. She wasn't as frail as she looked.

"Hang on there. Not so fast. Sam is a grown man and can take care of himself. Maybe it's time you let someone take care of you."

"It's my job to help him."

"Not anymore."

"No, it is. You don't understand."

"Help me understand."

Ethan sighed and began slowly. "When he found out Gemma married Kyle, he went up into the mountains, and he almost died. I think he would have died if I hadn't found him. So I've been taking care of him ever since. Sophie helps. Or she did. But now it's just me and Sam again, and I have to help him. I have to be brave for him."

"Sophie may still return. But Ethan, you've been brave enough, my boy. It's his turn."

"I can't lose him, too." He was visibly trying to still his quivering lip, wiping again at his face, seemingly annoyed by the tears determined to fall. *He's such a little boy still,* Jesse thought, *trying so hard to be a man.* In her mind she saw a parade of silent children standing upright as adults, children who had lost their childhoods. Too many.

"What terrible things those young eyes must have seen." Her hand was again on his cheek, wet now with tears. "Blue eyes. I wouldn't have expected that with such dark hair."

"My mother's eyes were blue."

"So they were. So they were. Did you know I met your mother once?"

Ethan sat up, interested. "Really?"

"It's true. We were both in the Forbidden Grounds. She said she had a boy."

"What did she say about me?" Ethan leaned forward, hungry for any scrap of information about his mother.

"She said she was proud of you and hoped you had found another family to take care of you."

Ethan looked down at his hands.

"I'll tell you a story, shall I?"

He nodded.

"There was one day in particular in the Forbidden Grounds that was extremely hard for me. I remember it was about the time of year of my own little boy's birthday. Max. I was out in the forest walking along these old railroad tracks. Do you know what those are?"

"Sam and I have seen them."

"Yes, well, these old tracks were covered with moss and underbrush. Ferns and things seemed to be sprouting from the railroad ties themselves. And they just went on and on. It seemed like there was no end. And I was thinking that's how my life felt. Just this endless monotony of days blending into days, all looking the same without my children there to brighten even a moment. Always wondering what happened to them. I was feeling pretty sorry for myself. But coming over a hill along this track was a woman with bright-red hair."

"My mother."

"Your mother. She came and talked to me for a while. Spent the day. She made that day stand out. A bright spot among all the other days that had just looked the same. She saved me, I think. At least made me a little less sad."

"I'm not just sad."

"Oh?"

"I'm angry."

"At what?"

"Angry at the Corsairs for shooting her. Angry at myself for not being able to save her. Angry at her for not being able to find me." He lowered his voice to almost a whisper, barely able to get the words out. "Even a little angry at you and anyone else who got to spend time with her."

"It makes sense. And I felt the same way after I lost my babies."

"Will it always hurt like this?"

"You will always have the pain with you like a stone you carry in your pocket. But you will gain strength from the carrying. And eventually, it will get easier. I will say this, though, my boy. And mind me well. Soon you will learn that love is the only thing that will truly help you heal."

Ethan reached out his young hand to take Jesse's wrinkled one. In that moment, there was no difference between their souls. Old and young alike met each other, making no other words necessary.

"Come on, then," she said more lightly than she felt. "Let's go outside with the other kids. I think Sam's out there too."

Sam sat on an old tree stump just outside the cabin door, whittling sticks on each end with his pocketknife. A pile of shavings swirled around his feet. His knife was sharp enough that each swipe along the stick flowed smoothly down and away from him, no breaks, no stops until he'd come to the end of the stick.

"What'cha doing?" Ethan asked, placing his hand on Sam's shoulder as he looked on. It was the first time they'd spoken since they had returned from the mill.

"I'm going to set some bear traps around the cabin."

"Bears?! I thought you said they were extinct."

"We believe they are extinct, yes."

"Then why the traps?"

"Well, we might catch other things with the traps. And you sometimes have to be prepared for the things you don't see coming."

"How can you know how to be prepared for something if you don't see it coming?"

Another swipe of the knife. "Honestly, I don't know, son."

"How will it work?"

"We'll dig a shallow hole about the size of a bear's paw and jab these sticks in a circle around the sides of the hole kind of like spokes, see?" Sam demonstrated on the ground, placing the sticks in a circle. "The bear or moose comes along, steps in the hole, and the sticks catch on its paw, and he can't get out."

"Why the traps, Sam? You don't kill animals. Not even squirrels."

"Like I said, maybe we'll catch something besides a bear." Sam didn't look up from his whittling.

Ethan knew then the only animals Sam wanted to catch were Corsairs. But he didn't say what he knew. "Well, I think it will be a great trap."

"Thanks. Why don't you run on and find Daisy?"

"The twins said she went out to find a blackberry bush."

Petal called from the stream, "Ethan, that was supposed to be a surprise!"

"We'll pretend to be surprised, eh?" Sam winked at Ethan. "Meanwhile, you can come with me to set these traps, if you want. Maybe bring the camera. Take some pictures?"

Ethan's tentative smile was answer enough.

* * * * *

Daisy could see the low, creeping bushes spreading out from the bank of the river. She picked her way carefully to avoid the jagged thorns. She couldn't believe the birds had left so many berries on the bushes this late in the year. Usually, they'd all be gone. But here she gazed at a mass of ripe blackberries dripping from the gray-green vines, almost touching the ground with their heavy load. There would be a feast in the cabin tonight. After all that had happened in the past few days, Daisy was happy to find a little pocket of joy to bring her friends. Ethan, especially, needed to have his spirits lifted.

Still not knowing where Gemma was, Daisy was worried herself. But she had complete faith in Gemma's ability to get through any trouble or danger. Hadn't she taught her all the self-defense moves and means of escape? It was maybe taking longer to get back this time, but if Gemma said she'd come back, she would. Daisy was sure. She just had to be patient and distract herself with the little tasks around the cabin and finding special surprises like these blackberries.

"Hey, kid."

Daisy whirled around. Hearing Gemma's familiar greeting come from a male voice startled her. Kyle stood before her in his old citizen's garb of gray tunic and gray coat, but still wore the black Corsair boots over his trousers. She hadn't heard him approach.

"Hello, sir."

"Now, you don't have to call me sir. We're old friends. I'm Gemma's husband, remember? You came to my house one day. So you can call me Kyle."

"Yes, sir . . . Kyle."

"That's right. Looks like you've got quite a lot of berries there. Need any help?"

Daisy held the berries in an upturned apron around her waist. "I don't think so. But thanks. I was just picking them for some friends. What are you doing out here?" She turned the conversation around, putting Kyle on the defensive. *Always keep your enemy guessing, don't let them anticipate your next move. If you can, get them talking about themselves,* Gemma had said.

"Well, you know, I was hoping you could help me find another friend of yours from the Watch. Foxglove? I really need to talk to her."

"Sounds like a silly name to me. I don't know any Foxglove."

"No? I thought sure you did. At least that's what Sam told me."

"You know Sam?"

Kyle began picking berries from the bushes, popping them into his mouth one after another as he talked. "Oh, sure. We were kids together. Best friends, really. So, what do you say? Can you help me find Foxglove?"

"I don't know Foxglove. Sure is a silly name, though. And I should really be getting back."

"Come on, now. Lots of people in the Watch have silly names, don't they? I bet you've seen them on the notes you deliver to Cypress, Oak, Tower." He took a step closer to Daisy, reaching behind her for some hard to reach berries.

Daisy started to shake, recognizing the names of the members of the Watch who had been killed recently.

"It's alright, Daisy. You have nothing to fear from me. I won't hurt you, I promise. I just need to give Foxglove a message."

Daisy's head was spinning. She always tried to follow her instincts about people. His voice sounded sincere. And he was Gemma's husband, after all. But all of the leaders of the Watch were dead, and now Kyle was looking for Foxglove, her Gemma. It couldn't be a coincidence. "Well, if you give me the message, maybe I could find someone who knows this Foxglove." *Let them think you're playing into their hands. Let them think you'll help them until you can get away.*

"No, I really must give it to Foxglove personally. It's really important."

"I'm sorry, Kyle. I don't know who or where she is, but I've got to get back for dinner now. Z will be looking for me."

Another step forward. Kyle was now only inches away from her. "She . . . so you know it's a woman. You really do know who she is, don't you?"

"You said 'her' earlier. Goodbye, now." Daisy started making her way along the riverbank again, pushing past Kyle as he was trying to block her way. She'd go in the river if she had to, no matter how cold it was.

Kyle grabbed at her, his fingers curling around her thin arm. "No, wait!"

* * * * *

As Sam and Ethan made a wide circle around the cabin setting the traps Sam had prepared, a thick gray fog was rolling down from the mountains, settling over the river. The wind poured in with it, rustling fallen leaves in the mist in a red, orange, and brown soup as high as Ethan's shoulders. A silence settled over the forest as thick as the fog, and as disconcerting. Sam worried when the birds stopped singing their evening melodies.

"It feels strange out here," Ethan ventured. "How far are we from the cabin? I can't see it anymore." He was looking around him, obviously disoriented.

"Not far."

"Do you feel it, Sam?"

"I'm not sure what it is I feel."

Ethan thought of the weeks Sam had spent in the mountains. He thought of the days they spent not speaking since they'd returned from across the Border. Sam didn't need words to convey his fears about Sophie's and Gemma's fates. Ethan just knew. "They're coming back, Sam. Sophie is going to come back."

"We don't know that for sure. It's not helpful for us to believe in stories and fairy-tales."

"It's not a fairy-tale. I know it."

"How do you know?"

"How do you know the sun will come up in the morning?" Ethan countered.

"Because it always has."

"Right. Sophie's always been there for me. She hasn't let me down once since I met her. When the Corsairs took me from the farm, she punched one of them in the face. Did you know that?"

Sam smiled. "No, I didn't. But I believe it."

"She told me I wasn't a Lost Boy anymore and she would come for me. And she did. She said we'd always be a family. And I believe her."

"Alright, son. I'll try to believe her too."

"Maybe we should head back now."

"Perhaps you're right."

Sticks cracking in the underbrush were as loud as gunfire in the silence, drawing Sam's quick attention. His eyes shot to the left where he'd seen something out of the corner of his eye. He placed his arm in front of Ethan, gently moving the boy. "Stay behind me."

"What is it?"

Sam saw the fog moving in swirls ahead of them, as if a creature at least the size of a man was moving through the haze. Another swirl moved to his right. Something was closing in on them. Sam knew he didn't believe in ghosts, but there was something uncanny in the forest this evening.

So when my thoughts begin to stray . . . An echo of a song hung in the air just out of hearing in mist ahead. Not a true sound, but something like the memory of a sound when someone has stopped singing. Just the slightest suggestion that the air had reverberated with sound only seconds before.

"Did you hear that?" he asked Ethan anxiously.

"What? The leaves moving?"

"No, the song."

"I didn't hear a song."

"Listen."

Their breathing stopped, willing the very machinations of their bodies to silence themselves as they strained to listen.

For you will always be here . . .

"That! Did you hear it?"

"No, Sam."

Somewhere in my dreams.

"It's right there, I can almost hear it, but not quite."

"Hear what?"

"Sophie's song."

Ethan took Sam's hand in his as they walked slowly into the gathering mist. "Let's go back, Sam."

"Just a minute."

More sticks cracking in the fog ahead of them. They both stopped, feeling the moist leaves and every vibration beneath their feet. Something was walking toward them. Something large.

At first, Sam and Ethan each thought they were imagining things. But in seconds, a large white stag began to materialize before them out of the mist, head and antlers towering over them both. Sam wondered if he was hallucinating from lack of sleep. He remembered the white deer on the mountain but knew this couldn't be the same one because he'd had to kill the other for his own survival. No one could take away his belief that the buck had offered itself to him on that day for that very purpose. Yet here stood another. One of the rarest animals in the forest, and he had seen two within the course of a year.

"Ethan, tell me you see it too."

"I see it. It's a white deer."

In the dwindling light, and with the fog playing with their senses, the stag almost appeared to be made of dew and mist, its every movement, every breath, courting a graceful dance with the bank of haze surrounding it.

"Hand me the camera. Slowly. I'm going to try to get a picture of it," Sam whispered.

Ethan reached for the camera in mini-movements as if he were a set of still pictures taken one after another, trying not to startle the animal. But as he placed the camera in Sam's outstretched hand, the buck turned to walk back into the mist. It didn't run or leap away. In fact, it turned back to look Sam in the eyes, seemingly as if he wanted him to follow.

Follow they did, one tentative step after another until they were finally in a clearing of trees nearer the river. They could hear the gurgling waters, though at this part of the forest, the riverbed hid behind many berry bushes for at least half a mile. The deer stood and began nibbling among the leaves just as if he were all alone. Sam got into a good position, lining the great white deer in the sights of his camera, clicking the shutter button, turning the film crank, and clicking again. He took several photos before the fog began to thicken and it became impossible to see the white deer in its camouflage.

"We can go home, now, Ethan. We got what we came for. And, I believe, what we were meant to see."

"What do you mean?"

"Long ago, the Native Americans believed the white deer was a good omen, a symbol of change and good things to come. I saw one in the mountains last year just before you found me and just before we met Sophie. And now we saw one again today. So maybe you were right after all."

Ethan smiled to himself as they walked in sacred silence back to the cabin.

23

A STILL HEART

Sam and Ethan left the cabin while it was still light enough to see the road to Jesse's Hollow. In the shadowed starlight now freed from the fog as winter stabbed the air, they made their way to the shed at Z's house. Ethan didn't want to wait to develop the pictures.

It was cold in the little shed. Sam wished he would have started a fire inside the house to warm it for when they went inside. But he was now involved in developing the pictures and didn't want to stop until the task was complete. He moved the paper from the chemicals to the fixer to the water, the liquid cold on his fingers as he watched the image start to slowly appear in the dim light. His mind wandered in the silence, finding dark and hidden paths that frightened him to consider. Paths that led to terrible endings where Sophie or Gemma was dead, or both.

"What are you thinking about, Sam?" Ethan startled him out of his thoughts.

"Huh? Oh, I was just thinking about shifting focus, I guess."

"Shifting focus?"

"Yes. You know, when you take a photograph, depending on where your focus is, sometimes what's in the foreground is in perfect clarity, and sometimes it's what's in the background. Regardless, though, once you find your focus, everything else fades away."

"Do the pictures always show you the truth, Sam?"

"Not always. The truth is different, depending on who's looking at it and where their focus is. Sometimes pictures show you things you never thought were there. Sometimes they show you only what you wanted to see."

"You say 'sometimes' a lot."

"I guess that's because things always change. Very little in this life is sure. Now let's see what these photos have to tell us."

Sam hung the dripping pieces of paper up on a line to let them dry.

He picked up his pack to go into the house to make a fire, but his copy of *Great Expectations* fell out on the dirt floor of the shed, splayed on the ground like a bird with wings outstretched. Picking it up and brushing the dirt from its leaves, he noticed a page dog-eared. It was not his habit to mark pages that way, so he turned to look at the page.

Scanning the page, he saw a few lines underlined: *Heaven knows we need never be ashamed of our tears, for they are rain upon the blinding dust of earth overlying our hard hearts. I was better after I had cried, than before—more sorry, more aware of my own ingratitude, more gentle.* In the margin, he recognized in Sophie's handwriting a short note: *I am more grateful and more gentle because of you.*

"Oh, Sophie," he whispered, sitting down on the one short wooden bench in the shed. There was dust on the floor and on all the bottles and equipment in the shed. In the diffused light from the lantern, it was hard for him to focus his vision. Or maybe it was the tears in his eyes.

"What is it, Sam?" Ethan's hand was on his shoulder, ever mindful of Sam's well-being.

"I just miss her, boy. I wish I knew where to find her."

"Should we go look for her and Gemma?"

"Gemma would kill me if she knew. Sophie too, probably. And they would tell me they can take care of themselves."

"What do you want to do?"

"I want to look for them."

"Then that's what we should do."

"You're right, boy. If they're not back by tomorrow, we'll go after them."

Ethan picked up the book lying loosely in Sam's open hands. "Why do you love this particular book so much?"

Sam wiped his hands over his face, putting his dark thoughts away for later. "It's a study of what it means to be human. And because it's equal parts good and evil, as I imagine the world to be."

"Seems like there's more evil in the world than good."

"That's here. The result of the prison we're living in. But if there's more evil here, that means there must be more good somewhere else in the world."

"How do you know?"

"It's just a feeling, a sense, like an animal sniffing the air. There's more good out there, son. We just have to find it."

"Well, I guess we found Sophie once, so that's a start."

"So it is."

Outside the shed, moonlight cut through the trees in sharp shafts of reflected and filtered light. Some aspects of the trees and ground revealed, some hidden. *Focus and light,* Sam thought. *So much can change with focus and light.*

* * * * *

Morning sun shone across the barren yard, its ugliness covered by a fresh but thin layer of snow. The ice crystals reflecting and magnifying the sun made Zacharias feel surrounded in light, yet not warmed by it. Even the warmth of the horse beneath him wasn't enough to soothe the chill in his bones. One of the villagers who brought him the message he was delivering had also allowed him to use one of the Corsairs' stolen horses so he could be quick. But he walked the horse slowly toward Gemma's house. The animal blew out plumes of visible breath in the cold morning air. The metal of halter and reins clinking and echoing around him. Its hooves crunched in the snow. Every sound like fingernails on chalkboard in the old man's ears.

Zacharias found himself hoping she wouldn't be there. They hadn't heard anything from her or Sophie since they'd gone to the lumber mill. But his loyalty to Gemma made Zacharias take the trip to her house to tell her the news he bore on his weary shoulders. He kept thinking it would be better, though, if she were still out on her mission with Sophie.

He dismounted and dragged himself up the slick porch steps. His knobby knuckles rapped on the door, five quick taps. He turned away from the door, surveying the front yard. No other footsteps in the snow besides his. Maybe she wasn't back yet. His boot was down the second step when he heard the door open behind him.

"Z? What are you doing here?" Gemma's voice was weary, hoarse with sleep.

"I didn't think you'd be back," he said over his shoulder, taking a deep breath before he turned to face her.

"Just got back the middle of last night. So why are you here if you didn't think I'd be here?"

"I had to check."

Gemma wrapped her arms around herself against the cold. She hadn't even changed her clothes when she got home. Just fell asleep on the couch, not wanting to wake Kyle. "I can tell something's the matter, Z. Please just tell me what it is. Is it Sam? Did something happen to him?"

"No, Sam is fine. He's at the cabin with . . . He's at the cabin."

"Then what? My God, you're white as a sheet."

"I have to tell you something."

"Come inside. Sit down. I'll make some coffee."

"No. Gemma." Another breath to steady his voice. "Gemma, I don't know how to . . ."

"Just say it."

"A young girl has been found in the woods."

Gemma's eyes asked the question she couldn't voice.

"We aren't sure who it is yet. But Daisy has been missing since last night."

Gemma ran as if she was physically pulled from the porch.

"Gemma! Gemma, wait!" he called after her. But she was gone.

She didn't feel the ground under her feet or the dry branches lashing her legs, arms, and face. She ran almost without breath, no sense of time. All the way to where a small group was gathered. They parted for her as the wind parts the leaves in the trees. A form lay motionless on the dank earth, too cold to receive her. She had known as soon as Zacharias had said the words. Daisy.

Gemma knelt beside the girl whose head bore the wound of the jagged rock beside her. Blood, melted snow, and mud beneath her. Her white apron stained with berries.

"A fall, must have been," the people whispered.

Gemma gently lifted Daisy's head and shoulders, holding her in her lap. She softly pulled leaves and dead grass out of the girl's hair, piece by piece. Then slowly pushed her blonde hair out of her face. Gemma began to rock gently as she would have rocked her children, yet unborn.

No one neared her, no one moved, but held a circle around her. Gemma's beating heart pressed against the still one in her arms. What little space there was between them began to pull an almost feral whimper from her chest, her heart unwinding in a long string of sound. Rocking, unable to think or speak or hear anything but the rush of blood in her own ears, Gemma's cry grew into a wail which would never leave the ears of the circle of witnesses.

Zacharias had ridden up in time to hear the scream and tried to hold Gemma, his adopted daughter, and comfort her as he used to. But she would not allow him to touch her.

"Where were you?" she whispered hoarsely. "How did she end up out here in the woods alone? Why weren't you with her?" Her voice broke, and the cries continued unbidden. She was not pushing out her screams, they were being wrenched from her.

Zacharias retreated as if he'd been struck. He knew her pain was responsible for her words. But he also knew the truth that lay behind them. He had been responsible for the loss of another child. And that poisoned truth bled into his veins, into his very breath, into the tears on his face.

After what seemed like hours, the villagers brought Kyle to Gemma. Some wondered if they should try to get a tranquilizing medicine from the Council of Doctors. But Kyle, with tears in his own eyes, said he would tend to her. He gently removed the stricken Daisy from Gemma's arms to be buried by the others, then helped his wife, leading her like a child through the trees and back to their home.

With stooped shoulders, Zacharias returned to the cabin. When Jesse saw him walking up the path, she wondered how it was possible he had aged ten years in a couple of hours.

* * * * *

Mark Goodson was in command of a regiment of one thousand Corsairs. But standing at attention before him in a small clearing just west of the Border were his personal security force, a company of one hundred and fifty men under the command of his Lieutenant Colonel Taylor.

Colonel Taylor stood at his elbow as Mark hesitated. "The men are ready for you, sir."

"Yes, Taylor, I know."

"Is everything alright, sir?"

"Nothing is alright, Taylor. Not a damn thing."

Mark stepped forward to address his men, wondering for the thousandth time if he was doing the right thing, coming again to the inevitable conclusion that there was nothing else to be done.

"As I speak to you, men, General Drape is instructing the Fire Brigade of Corsairs to set fire to the Forbidden Grounds." He saw the ripple his words cast over the company, though they all remained at attention as they'd been trained to do. "I know this comes as a surprise to you. But this is only the first step of his final plan, which I have learned is to exterminate everyone within the borders of this prison. He does this of his own accord without the sanction of the rest of the Triumvirate. Now, I don't know about you, but I've never thought of myself as an assassin or an executioner. But that is what we've all become over the years under the command of General Drape. And I say no more!"

Another ripple through the group.

"I make a vow here and now to stop him, whatever the cost. You are my most trusted soldiers. And I hold you in the highest esteem. I've learned to rely on you. So I invite you all to join me in this endeavor. However, those of you who want to leave may leave without repercussion. If you stay, you need to know from this moment on, we are no longer Corsairs." His voice was growing in intensity with each word. "From now on, we are rebels! So, what say you?"

After a few moments of loud silence, a sergeant stepped out from the center of the group. "If I may, sir?"

"You may speak, Sergeant."

"I say better a rebel with you than a Corsair with General Drape."

The men behind him cheered in unison.

"Very well, then," Mark responded. "We'll have to change these uniforms. Taylor, bring out the coats." Colonel Taylor, with the help of some of the other men, started unloading citizen-gray coats taken from the Government Office.

"Take off your army blue and put these on."

The sleeves just under the shoulders of each of the coats had been marked with a thick streak of black ash to distinguish them from the other citizens. Mark needed to know who his men were. He was more relieved than he could express that they'd all decided to stay with him. He hadn't been altogether sure how they would protect themselves from Simeon if one of the soldiers had decided to go back. Now they at least had a chance.

The men stood again before Mark in their new uniforms, looking brighter in their ashed gray than they had in the bright-blue Corsair uniforms.

"Alright, soldiers. We'll spread ourselves out along the Border at the guard stations. Five per station. You will relieve the current guards of their posts by whatever means necessary. Your primary objective after that is to prevent fire in the Forbidden Grounds, preferably before it starts. That will require you to stop the Fire Brigade from getting through. They will be coming down from the north, from the Wash District. Take plenty of ammunition and use the guard stations to your advantage. Don't come out in the open unless you absolutely have to. Your secondary objective will be to allow the rebels and citizens to pass as they need to across the Border from either side. The Fire Brigade will be attempting to trap people within the Forbidden Grounds before they set the fires. We can't allow this to happen. Understood?"

"Yes, sir!" they shouted in resounding unison.

"Very well. Live free or die!"

"Live free or die!"

"Let's move out!"

* * * * *

Zacharias had been sitting in front of the fire for more than an hour. After Jesse's attempts to comfort him had been rebuffed, she had decided to leave him to himself for a while. The twins were still sleeping in the back bedroom. She let the children sleep as much as they cared to. It seemed to be easier on all of them.

But now she saw her husband slouched in front of the fire in a rocking chair. He was an old man. Of course she'd noticed his white hair when she returned, and the toll that forty difficult years had taken on him. Surely he had noticed her aged body as well. But it hadn't hit her until this moment that he was, in fact, an old man. All the life seemed to have been drained out of him, leaving a wrinkled and sagging shell. It frightened her. This would not do. She felt as if she saw him careening toward death as surely as if he were sliding toward the edge of a cliff. She knew she had to do something to stop it.

"*Restless and lost on a road that you know*, eh?" She walked up behind him and put her hands on his shoulders, so much thinner than she remembered, and hard of bone.

"What's that mean?" he grumbled.

"Old Lawson poem. I just mean we've been here before. You've always been your own worst enemy."

"I'm not the enemy."

Jesse walked around to face him, blocking the fire, throwing a shadow over his lined face, then knelt with difficulty before him. "You know, I learned a lot of hard lessons when I was in prison, and after—when I was in the Forbidden Grounds."

"You haven't told me much about that."

She laid her head in his lap. His hand naturally began stroking her hair. "There's no reason for you to know things that will only hurt you. But one of the most important things I learned—I would have gone crazy without it. Completely mad, I would have been."

"Tell me."

"Happiness, contentment, glory, whatever you're looking for, is not something that will come from the outside. It's something that grows from within. That feeling when you see the sun shine through autumn leaves or you hear that perfect piece of music or a baby laugh. When a simple kiss shows you all that's beautiful in the whole world—these are the glories or part of a larger glory, and it fills you with a kind of light, a spark that can't be doused like a fire. It can only be put out by our own self-doubt and fear. It's within our own hearts and souls that we hold the seeds of the fire and the means to kill it. Everything good and everything that stops the good."

"Jesse, you don't understand. I did it. I killed that child by not taking care of her, just as I was responsible for our own children and your capture. It's my fault. Everything that was ever good in me came from you."

She sat up to look in his eyes. "Now 'ang on. If you believe that, then you'll lose yourself when you lose someone else. Everything good in you was already there, love. I maybe just helped you to see it. Those things we love and the things we fight against—none of it comes to us from the outside, but from within. It's all within us. These young ones, they don't know that yet. But they will."

"If they survive."

"They will survive. And you will survive, my love, because I need you
to. But more than that, they will live because of the love and strength they
give each other. Because of the love and strength they already have inside."

* * * * *

Mark took position at one of the center guard stations with five of his
new rebels. He'd sent Lieutenant Colonel Taylor north, and his second in
command, Captain Peck, south. He spread out his high command along
the Border. He was hot in his gray coat in the guard station and thought
about removing it. The men with him weren't men at all, really. The oldest
couldn't have been more than twenty-five. He thought of how many
battles he'd already seen by the time he was twenty-five. More than one
for every year of his life. Fighting was all he'd ever known, and it was all
he wanted to leave behind.

"Look!" one of the soldiers shouted, peeking through a crack in the
wood slats of the guard station. Looking north into the blaring blue sky
above the trees, Mark could see a string of smoke curling up like a giant
hand pulling apart a swab of cotton. A few minutes later, another string of
smoke closer to them appeared. The first was larger now and turning gray.

"That's two stations down," the young soldier's voice was valiantly
trying not to quiver.

"Steady, men. Focus on what's right in front and around you. Your
fight is here at this station."

Mark felt like he had the advantage over the enemy, knowing their exact
methods. General Drape was always somewhat predictable in his
ruthlessness. He knew he'd order his Fire Brigade to light up the stations
regardless of the men inside. The key was to shoot them before they had
a chance to get close enough. He just wished there wasn't so much blasted
fuel for the fire all around them.

"Rogers, take that bucket in the corner, bring water from the stream.
Douse this shack with it. Stratton, you go with him."

At least that would slow down the fire a little, if it hit. Another station
had thrown smoke in the air. And another. The brigade was getting closer.

* * * * *

Sam held three pieces of photographic paper tightly in his hand as he shuffled through the morning snow. He checked his belt again to make sure the pistol was there, even though he knew it was. He ran his fingers through his hair and tried to keep the anger high in his chest. He couldn't afford to let the adrenaline that was fueling him wane. He couldn't let the anger turn to sadness.

He'd spent the entire night blowing the photographs up to get a closer look at what he didn't want to see. Somehow, in the pictures of the white stag in the misty woods of the night before, he'd managed to capture something in the distance, something he and Ethan hadn't even seen with their own eyes. He had to make sure he was right. But the evidence was there in his hands. Kyle had been with Daisy in the woods and had knocked her to the ground, leaving her there. Sam had sent Ethan back to the cabin to let them know where Daisy was and to see if anything could be done for her. But the responsibility of facing Kyle was his. He'd gone too far this time in attacking a child. A child!

"Kyle!" Sam burst through the back door without knocking. He wanted to catch Kyle off guard. He didn't want him to have any time to prepare for their confrontation.

Gemma sat up from the couch. Now it was Sam who was caught off guard. She didn't say anything but sat staring at him as if she were still half asleep.

"Gemma! What the . . . I thought you were still out looking for Sophie or . . . worse. God, I'm so glad you're okay." Sam was across the room, holding her by the shoulders. "Is Sophie . . ."

He cut himself short. Something wasn't right. Gemma wasn't herself. She held a piece of paper crumpled in her hands. It looked like a child's drawing. She hadn't spoken a word since he came in. She would never normally let him burst in her house without giving him hell for it.

"What's wrong? Where's Sophie? Where's Kyle?"

She stared at him, barely seeing him.

"Gemma. Gemma!" He tried to shake her a little. But when he stood back and looked at her again, he noticed for the first time there was blood on the front of her clothes.

"Gemma, whose blood is it?"

"They found Daisy," she whispered.

"Oh, Gemma. I know. I'm sorry."

"She's dead."

"Dead?" Sam gripped the photos tighter in his hand.

"Just like that."

"Do you know what happened?"

"No, they just found her this morning out in the woods. All alone."

Gemma hadn't moved from the couch. Sam pulled up a chair to face her.

"So no one told you what happened?"

"Nobody knows."

"Where's Kyle?"

"Market Day. He wanted to get me something from the G.O. to help me sleep. I haven't slept."

"I don't think you should take anything that he gives you."

Gemma dropped the drawing, covered her face with her hands, and spoke through her fingers. "Don't, Sam. Not now. What are you even doing here?"

"Um, well, I came to talk to him, actually. I should probably go find him. But first I want to make sure you're okay."

"Nothing's okay. Nothing can be."

"Have you eaten?"

"No. I can't."

"I'm going to fix you something, alright?"

"Just go, Sam."

"Nope. Lunch first."

Sam started moving around the kitchen, putting a light lunch together. Some smoked ham from the cool box in the cellar, a few sautéed vegetables. The house had been freezing when he walked in. So he stoked the fires in the kitchen stove and in the fireplace. Every few minutes, he looked over his shoulder toward Gemma. She sat on the couch staring straight ahead, not speaking. He tried talking to her but ended up just talking to himself. Silly things about what he was doing in the kitchen. Still not a word in response from her.

"Okay, you think you can come to the table, or should I bring your food to you?" he called to her. She still didn't speak but stood up and walked over to the table.

"Maybe we should change your tunic first, huh?"

397

"Don't touch it."

"Alright. Alright. Suit yourself. Just eat, okay?"

Gemma sat and started moving the food around her plate. Sam set a cup of water before her, splashing lightly on the photographs that lay facedown on the table. He quickly snatched them up and brushed them off with a dish towel.

"What are those?" Gemma asked as if she were hypnotized or sleepwalking.

"Nothing. Something I wanted to talk to Kyle about, that's all."

"Let me see."

"No, I don't think that's a good idea."

"I'm not a damn child, Sam! Give me the papers."

"They're photographs."

"Of what? Don't make me pull it out of you. I don't have the energy."

"Well, Ethan and I were out setting traps last night. I took some photos of a white stag."

"What does that have to do with Kyle?"

"It's what I didn't realize I'd caught in the background of the pictures."

"And?"

"It's what happened to Daisy."

"Show me."

"Gemma . . ."

"Show me, damn it!" She ripped the photographs out of Sam's hand before he could stop her, laying them out one by one on the table. In the first photograph, Kyle was talking to Daisy. In the second, he was stepping toward her with his hand outstretched. In the final picture, Daisy was on the ground and Kyle was leaning over her.

"What does it mean?" she asked, staring at the pictures, willing them to give her answers she didn't have and wasn't sure she wanted.

"Well, it looks like he might have been there when she fell. He must at least know something about it."

"He killed her. That's what you mean."

"That's what I intend to find out."

"He did it. He's been so strange and cold. Then today, all of a sudden, trying to take care of me. It's guilt. He feels guilty because he's the one who killed her."

"We don't know for sure."

"Don't we?" Gemma collapsed in the chair behind her, her head in her hands. "Oh, God, Sam. What have we come to?"

"We've been in situations like this before, only we were the children."

"I didn't think it could happen again. Not like before."

"Humans have found ways to do terrible things to each other."

"So many terrible things. It's exhausting trying to fight them all."

"Come on, Gemma. Let's get you changed and into bed. You need rest more than anything."

"Actually, can you go out to the pump and get me a fresh cup of water? This pump in the kitchen has had some silt in the water."

"Sure, I can do that. Wait here."

While he was gone, Gemma went quickly to the desk in the main room where she had started writing a letter to him before they went across the Border. She scribbled a few more lines, signed it, and put it in her pocket just as he was coming back in the house.

As Sam handed her the glass of frigidly cold water from the outside pump, she looked at him over the top of the glass.

"Can I ask you another favor?" Her voice was a whisper, something you'd catch on a breeze from far away.

"Anything."

"She's out there alone, Sam. With strangers. My Daisy with strangers . . ." Her voice started to trail off. She took a gulp of water and forged on. "I need you to be the one to bury her. Bring her back home and bury her. Don't leave her with strangers. Bring her home for me."

"Of course I will."

"Go now, Sam. It can't wait."

"Gemma, I need to make sure . . . I mean, are you going to be alright?"

"You've kept the code here, Sam. I'll be fine."

"I don't believe you."

"I need you to do this for me. Please, Sam. Before it's too late."

"What does that mean?"

"Just go. I'll be fine."

Sam tried to see into her eyes, tried to read what was hiding there. But Gemma could be inscrutable when she wanted to be. He wasn't at all sure he should leave her alone. Then he thought of Sophie. If Gemma had come back, maybe Sophie was waiting for him back at their house. Maybe she needed him too. He couldn't bring himself to ask Gemma the unspoken question. Was Sophie still alive? He needed to hold on a little longer to the belief that she was, and that she'd be waiting for him at home.

Gemma threw her arms around Sam's neck, pulling him out of his thoughts. She held tight for a few moments before releasing him. "Now go. Hurry."

"I'll come back later."

"Fine."

"We'll get through this."

"Of course we will."

She sounded sure. Sam held onto that surety as he forced himself to walk away from the house.

* * * * *

Smoke was filling the woods around them. Mark didn't know how many guard stations had been taken. He still had his five men in the guard station with him, and they hadn't seen a Corsair yet. He started to wonder if his plan had been faulty from the start. Maybe they were avoiding the guard stations altogether.

"Rogers, Stratton. You're with me. We're going to scout out the perimeter. The rest of you hold this station. If you see a Corsair, fire at will. Do you understand? You are to shoot first and ask questions later."

"Yes, sir!" the three remaining soldiers shouted.

Rogers and Stratton flanked Colonel Goodson on either side as they started to make a wide sweep of the area around the guard station. It was hard to see anything through the thick smoke, but they could not tell where it was coming from. They saw no fire.

"Stay close, men," Mark found himself whispering.

"What if it's a trap, sir, to draw us out?" Rogers asked as they crunched and slipped through the snow.

"Tell me what you're thinking."

"It may not be fire at all. It could be smoke bombs."

"Maybe. But we'll soon find out." Mark began coughing. The smoke was getting thicker. He turned to look at Rogers just in time to see three Corsairs running up behind them. "Look out! Down!"

Rogers and Stratton dropped to the ground, barely missing the swing of a rifle butt. Mark fired on the first Corsair. One down.

Rogers was back on his feet, giving the next Corsair a bayonet in the belly. Two down.

Stratton and another Corsair were going hand to hand. Mark and Rogers started to assist, but Mark caught a glimmer of orange out of the corner of his eye. One, two, three torches that seemed to be floating in the air, coming closer. He and Rogers ran toward them, pistols drawn. The other Corsairs were on horseback going for the guard shack, while another was on the ground pouring fuel on every stick and blade of grass in sight. It was too late to stop him adding fuel to the fire. They had to get to the men with the torches.

"Rogers, if we shoot them from here, the torches will fall in the fuel and it will all be useless after that."

"What should we do, sir?"

"We've got to get those torches out of their hands."

"There's three of them, sir."

"We'll give the others the signal to come out. Are you ready?"

"Ready, sir."

"When I give the signal from over here, you run in the other direction and get that first Corsair on horseback. We'll take them one at a time and hope the smoke disorients them."

"Right."

"One, two . . . Live free or die!" Mark gave the signal, then ran toward the second Corsair. Three of his rebels came running out of the guard station, guns drawn. They saw the situation and didn't start shooting right away. Seeing their colonel and other comrade going hand to hand with the men on horseback, they did the same.

One Corsair went down hard from his horse, Mark wrenching the torch from his hand as he fell. He kicked the soldier in the head and threw the torch into the nearby stream. Another down.

He looked to his men and seemed to see it all moving in slow motion, every second drawn out into minutes. Gray tunics blending with smoke and snow. Blue uniforms illuminated by fire, eyes wide and shining all around him.

The second Corsair was off his horse on the ground. Two of his men subdued him and threw the torch into the stream. One left.

Mark looked up and saw the Corsair on his black horse looming above him. He swung hard with his rifle, just missing the Corsair's head. The man held the torch miles high above Mark's head, it seemed. He suddenly felt like a little boy again, trying to grasp for a toy his older brother held just out of reach. He knew, somehow, he never would reach it. Where were the others? Still on the ground, wrestling the other Corsair. Why didn't they fire? He'd ordered them to fire. They didn't want to shoot their old comrades. Too many confused thoughts and feelings. The smoke was filling his lungs. If he could just reach higher to get the torch.

The young Corsair seemed to be grinning at him, knowing he had the advantage. Mark pulled his knife from his right boot, stabbing the Corsair's foot with full force. Everything slowed. Blood began to drip in the snow. The Corsair cried out. His voice carried from far away on a sea of smoke. The torch fell, spinning in the air, hurtling toward a shining bush of dead and brown twigs. With a burst of flames, Mark could no longer see anything but the fire before him.

24

STANDING ON THEIR OWN

The wind cried with the shrill voice of a wounded animal. The few brown leaves still clinging to the branches pushed and rustled against each other like children fighting for space. Empty branches scratched against the closed windows of Sophie's house by the sea, the waves breaking in the background.

As Sam walked slowly into the house, he heard the echoes of silence and emptiness. The house smelled musty after being closed up for over a week. The cold inside the house was almost more piercing than the open cold he'd left outside. Shadows played in the dusty light through the curtains.

"Sophie?" Sam didn't need to call for her to know she wasn't there. But he called anyway. He went from room to room, willing her to appear, desperate for his hope to take shape in her lithe form. Only empty rooms and clouds of dust greeted him. This would be his life from now on, he thought. Empty rooms.

He went to the pump in the kitchen to wash the dirt from his hands from digging Daisy's grave. He wished he would never have to dig another. There had been too many graves. Too many buried. How could it continue? Who would even be left in the coming days to dig the graves? Simeon? The Corsairs? He'd seen how they had treated the dead, left to rot in the sun. And where was Sophie? Would he have to find her and bury her as well?

As he looked for a towel to dry his cold, chapped hands, he started thinking of how he would get back across the Border to retrieve Sophie. There wasn't a towel in the kitchen. Everything was in disarray with Sophie gone. It always would be.

Sam brushed his hands along his coat and felt something in his pocket he hadn't realized was there. He pulled out the letter and recognized Gemma's handwriting. When had she given him this, he wondered.

Dear Sam,

You will find this after I have gone. It's the way I wanted it. I almost don't have the words to write here. You were always better in that area. I always thought so much more could be said with a look or a touch of the hand. In those days when we had no one else but each other, how much the touch of your hand could comfort me.

"Don't you dare," he said aloud to the empty room. His mind started to race before even finishing the letter. Where would she go? What would Gemma do in her present state? Kyle was in the town square. Would she go after him there?

Our lives have gone on in different directions, ways that no one could have predicted. All I can hope now is that you don't hate me. Because I have loved you. Always.

"No, no! Damn it! You're not going out this way. I won't let you."

* * * * *

Kyle walked out into the brisk air outside the Government Office. The blood in his ears was beating like a drum calling for a charge. He stood perfectly still under the office porch, breathing in and breathing out, willing his heart to stop beating. He held the medicine for Gemma. She needed a tranquilizer to help her sleep. He had underestimated how much the child Daisy had meant to her. He had suspected for some time they worked together with the Watch, but he hadn't fully realized their connection. He should have listened more carefully when she kept asking him to apply to have a child. He should have listened. And now all he could hear were her screams in his ears, pushing his nerves and his guilt to the breaking point. She had to be sedated not just for her own sake, but for his. Perhaps he could explain to her in time. Perhaps she'd even come to understand. He'd only meant to frighten the girl to get the information about Foxglove he needed. He was only trying to complete his mission. She wasn't supposed to die.

"Kyle!" The voice was familiar, yet strange. He opened his eyes to see Gemma's haggard face dangerously close to his.

"What are you doing here? I was just on my way back."

"I needed to walk," she said quietly. "So I thought I'd come meet you."

"Honey, you need to rest. Let's get you home. I've got the medication for you. It will help."

"What happened to Daisy?" she asked him in her strange other voice that was hers, yet not hers. It was layered with something Kyle couldn't place. It sat in the back of her throat like bile. An edge. Fear mixed with accusation and anger. But behind it all was a kind of resignation.

"Let's not do this here." Kyle looked around to see if anyone had heard her.

"Tell me what happened." The volume of her voice was rising like boiling water.

"Sweetheart, I told you what happened, remember? I know this has been hard for you. I know how much she meant to you." Kyle attempted to put his arm around her shoulder, but she shrugged him away, taking a step back.

"I know what you told me. Tell me again."

"Gemma, I don't think that's a good idea. Why don't we get you home to rest and later . . ."

"Tell me!"

He looked over his shoulders again and saw people coming out of the Government Office, others looking up from their booths in the market. "Keep your voice down, alright? I don't know much more than you do. Some villagers found her early this morning. She'd gone out to pick some blackberries and must have slipped and fell. She hit her head."

"Is that what happened?" The tears started to form in her red eyes.

"Yes, that's what happened."

"Then how do you explain these?" Gemma shoved the three photographs hard into Kyle's chest, making him catch his breath. He gathered them up before they fell to the ground.

"What are these?"

"You tell me."

He looked slowly at each individual picture in silence. Gemma watched the color drain from his face, then his ears turned red, followed by his cold cheeks. "Where did you get these?" he asked.

405

"Does it matter?"

Kyle stood up straighter, almost at attention. "Yes, as a matter of fact, it does. Did you get them from the Watch, Gemma?"

"You can call me Foxglove."

* * * * *

Sam couldn't remember the last time he'd run this fast. The winter air was burning his lungs as he gasped for breath. But he couldn't stop. He had to get back to Jesse's Hollow before Gemma did something stupid. He wondered if he should have taken the time to saddle Pip and ride into town. Too late for that now. He took every shortcut he knew. Through fields, splashing across the stream as it changed course and zigzagged through the woods, crossing his path in several places. He still had the pistol in his belt. He was prepared as he was going to be, if he could only get his legs to move faster.

Through time and distance, pleasure and pain, my love for you will live on, even when all else is dust. I loved you in the sunlight and the firelight, in the moonlight and the starlight. I loved you when the dark was blinding and when the light was too bright for us to see. And despite all that love I had for you, I let you go. As I now ask you to let me go. You are with Sophie. And it's the way it should be. Sophie is stronger than me. Always has been.

* * * * *

Sophie sat at the small wooden table in the cabin, allowing Jesse to fuss over her, bring her food and water, wiping her face down with a warm cloth.

"You've been through quite the ordeal, love. But we'll soon set you to rights."

"We don't have much time, Jesse."

"Now, what are you going on about?" Jesse was bustling through the kitchen and into the bedroom, bringing Sophie a clean tunic.

"A war is coming, Jesse. I saw the smoke from the Forbidden Grounds. It's already begun."

Zacharias joined them, finally leaving his rocking chair. "But Colonel Goodson . . ."

"Yes," Sophie interrupted, "the colonel said there is no war and we're in prison. But call it what you will, there will be a fight. You can feel it coming, can't you?"

Jesse stilled her movements and looked into Sophie's eyes, mirroring her own fear. "You know we can."

"Yes, and it worries me," Zacharias added. "We have limited supplies of food and necessities. As soon as the fight begins, that's all we'll have. There will be no more government supplies. They've got us completely dependent on them and they know it. I don't know what kind of a war this is going to be. In fact, I don't know why they haven't just cut off our supplies before this."

Jesse, ever hopeful, offered, "Maybe that shows a little bit of humanity left in them."

"Not likely," Sophie responded. "Just look at what they did to that poor child Daisy."

"You think that was the Corsairs?" Z asked, astonished at the cruelty he couldn't even imagine.

"I don't know for sure. But I do worry that Foxglove will try to punish whoever did this to her. She was very attached to Daisy."

Ethan walked in the door just as Sophie was speaking. "It's Kyle. Kyle did it."

Sophie was up in a second, taking Ethan in her arms. They each took a moment to breathe and let it sink in that they hadn't lost each other. She held him for a few moments before she asked him the question burning in her mind. "Now, what is this you're saying?"

"Kyle killed my friend Daisy. Sophie, Daisy's dead." Ethan crumpled in her arms like a rag doll under the weight of the past few days. Sophie brought him to the chair in front of the fire, rocking him as she should have a much younger child.

"I know. I know, sweetie. It's terrible. You can cry."

"I don't want to cry. I want to do something."

"Where's Sam?"

"We had a photograph of what Kyle did. That's where Sam is. He went to accuse Kyle. But if Gemma is still alive, she'll go after him too. She'll never forgive him for what he did to Daisy."

"Gemma?" Sophie blinked, shaking her head, trying to register what Ethan was saying.

Jesse walked up behind her, placing her hand on Sophie's shaking shoulder. "You didn't know, did you, that Gemma is Foxglove."

"Gemma as in Sam's . . ."

"Yes, my dear," Zacharias confirmed.

Sophie's face showed her pain, but she didn't hesitate. "She's going to go after Kyle. Whether she's in her right mind or not. I know exactly what she's feeling. She wants to kill whoever killed her child. I have to go to her. She needs me. Ethan, you say Sam's gone to their house? But it's Market Day. They'll be in the square. That's where I have to go."

"You can't go alone, my girl. Zack and I will go with you."

"I can't ask you to do that, Jesse. It'll be dangerous, especially if Kyle is actually working with the Corsairs. We have no idea what we'll be walking into."

"Exactly. Now, we're not as frail as all that. No arguments. Ethan will stay here with the twins and the rest of us will go."

Sophie smiled in resignation. "Alright. Do you have any weapons here?"

* * * * *

Kyle placed his face within a whisper distance of Gemma's. "You don't know what you're saying. I want you to think very carefully about the consequences of your actions. I don't want to have to . . ."

"The consequences?! She was just a child! What consequences did she deserve, you bastard?! What could ever justify what I'm seeing in these pictures? You murdered a child!"

Kyle looked down at his Corsair boots. He couldn't see a clear path to his mission. He felt the air closing in around him. Gemma's fist across his face took him by surprise, and before he could catch his balance, she'd jumped on him, hitting, gnashing, and tearing at him like a wildcat.

"You must think, boy! Think about the consequences of your actions." Simeon's voice is in his ear, the underlying music of the blows being rained down upon him. One fist, a boot, another fist in the stomach, another fist to his face. He sees a blend of colors more convoluted than a rainbow. There are hideous streaks of red, blue, green, and brown all around him, tying him into a ball.

"Think about the consequences!"

"You must think about the consequences!" Kyle shouted at the balled-up form on the ground before him. "I've been ordered to kill Foxglove. We must stay the course and complete the mission." His fists moved on their own without any direction from his mind.

Gemma tried to see through her hands covering her face. A crowd had gathered around them but made no move to intervene. In the monochrome din of gray and empty faces, Gemma looked for help that would not come. But she didn't really want help. If she had, she wouldn't have confronted Kyle alone. Who is to say when we really die? Somewhere along the way, a string is pulled that will unravel the rest of our lives. Daisy was that string for Gemma. The thread that had kept her life together. In a way, Gemma knew she was already dead. She had known it since she held Daisy's lifeless body in her arms. She had felt herself draw her last real breath and known that every moment of her life after that was a stolen one. She was no longer meant to be here.

Suddenly the blows stopped. There was a moment of peace as her brain began to feel the places of pain all over her body. She heard a voice in her ear, "Gemma, stay down. Please stay down. I'll try to get you out later. Don't get up. Stay down."

Gemma struggled to match that voice with the voice of Kyle screaming about consequences, but it was the same.

* * * * *

Sam's body had forced him to slow to a jog for the past mile. But as he came to the road that led into the square at Jesse's Hollow, he pushed again into a sprint. The empty branches of the trees along the road blurred together into jagged lines. The smell of smoke was sharp in his nostrils. Heat and cold blended into a confusing soup of temperature coursing through his body. He ignored the burning in his muscles, lungs, and face.

The light is gone now, Sam. There's nothing left but this one last fight, and I have to do it on my own. It's my enemy to kill. And I will do it, even if it takes my last breath. Hold on to the ones you love, Sam. And hold out for a better life. You deserve it. Live free or die. Love, Gemma

* * * * *

409

From his vantage point on the wooden stage in the middle of the square, Simeon stood at ease, his legs parted into a triangle, his hands behind his back, surveying the citizens of Boswell going through their last Market Day, though none of them knew it would be their last. He watched with pleasure as the smoke continued to rise out of the Forbidden Grounds, and all of these little ants just continued to go about their days as they were expected to do. So predictable.

"Sir," a young lieutenant interrupted his thoughts.

"Have my orders been fulfilled, Lieutenant?"

"Yes, sir. The fire has begun."

"Excellent. You are dismissed. Go and avail yourself of some of the delicious concoctions these citizens can come up with out of limited rations. They really are quite inventive."

"But sir . . ."

"Yes, what is it?"

"There's news from Jesse's Hollow."

"Well?"

"Your son has found Foxglove. He has her in the town square there. Apparently, a crowd is forming. There may be some trouble."

"Nonsense. Look at the little busy ants here. Jesse's Hollow is the same. But I will go be with my son in his hour of triumph. Bring me my horse, Lieutenant."

"Yes, sir."

* * * * *

"Sophie Bryan," the young soldier read her ID card. "You are a citizen of Boswell, not Jesse's Hollow. You must attend Market Day there. Please step back."

"But sir, I've come to trade."

"All trade has been suspended until further notice. Please return to your own village."

"Sir . . ."

"Silence, or I will have you arrested. You, old man, old woman. You may pass. Your ID cards are in order. Move along."

Sophie turned, whispering to Jesse and Zacharias as they passed by her.

410

"Get to Gemma if you can. I'll find another way."

Jesse looked at Zack, trying to think of something they could do to get Sophie past the guards. She wasn't at all sure there was anything the two of them could do alone to help Gemma if she had gotten herself in trouble.

* * * * *

Gemma stood slowly, her legs shaky beneath her. One eye was swollen shut, and she winced as the slightest movement brushed against her wounds. Kyle seemed surprised to see her standing, and he hesitated. She stole his moment of hesitation to touch his hand. "We never really knew each other, did we?" she said softly, speaking to him as easily as if they were in their own living room having a normal conversation. "I've only done what I had to do. But you should know, for every time you knock me down, I'll still rise. You know what you'll have to do to stop me."

Kyle clenched the fist of the hand she had touched, but still waited, looking into her face and the evidence of his actions.

"Do it!" Simeon's voice traveled over the heads of the gathered citizens.

Kyle saw him sitting atop his horse at the edge of the square, looking with a broad smile at the scene before him. Kyle felt a click in his brain, a flow of violence and anger unbidden rushed and pounded at his temples. He struck Gemma with his left hand this time, a little less forcefully, leaving his bloody right hand limp at his side. He heard a gasp from the crowd that had been silent before this. As he looked for the source of the sound, Kyle's eyes fell upon Zacharias. He had his arm around the shoulders of an old woman standing next to him. He'd never known Zacharias to have a wife. He squinted his eyes to look harder at the pair while everything around him seemed to stop. There was no sound. No color over the earth. He alone stood with the old woman in a sea of gray. She seemed to float nearer to him, and as she did, he saw the years being peeled away from her. Her hair went from white to gray to auburn, the color returned to her cheeks. She stopped midair before him, and he saw bars separating them. Walls closing in. Her strange accented voice was in his ears as he opened the barred door. "Thank you," she whispered.

This old woman staring in horror at him from across the square was the same woman he had saved from prison so many years ago. This woman had thanked him and made him feel like he was still a human being. This

411

woman, the reason he'd gladly spent a month in solitary confinement, had come back to haunt him and remind him again of the boy he once was.

He looked down in horror at himself and what he had done to his wife on the ground before him. He started to reach for her to help her up, but she winced and moved back as she saw his hand come nearer.

Simeon was at his elbow now, holding the whip just within his line of sight. "What are you doing, boy? Think about the consequences of your actions. Finish it!" His voice was a jagged rock cutting Kyle's ears.

Sophie moved easily through the still and silent crowd before her. As she came through the circle, she saw Gemma on the ground and went to her without thinking. She took a cloth from her pocket, gently wiping dirt and blood from Gemma's swollen face.

"No, don't try to move," Sophie whispered.

But Gemma stared at her with a pleading in her eyes that Sophie recognized.

"You don't have to do this," Sophie entreated.

"Yes, I do," Gemma coughed out.

"Can you stand?"

"I think so."

"Then I'll stand with you." Sophie gently lifted Gemma to her feet. The two of them stood before an astonished Kyle and Simeon, both men shocked, motionless and silent.

Gemma struggled to reach her hand up to touch Kyle's face. Her words were barely discernible, and he wasn't even sure he had heard them. "I know there is good in you. I know you are more the man I've lived with all these years than you are like him." She coughed, struggling for breath. "I know you."

Kyle's eyes held his unshed tears and began to reflect the man he'd always wanted to be. The man she had needed him to be.

"Finish it!" Simeon hissed again.

Kyle turned to face him, hands helpless at his sides. "Father . . ." he pleaded.

"I've always suspected you were just a coward. And now, to be cowed by a woman." He almost spit the words in his face. He pushed Kyle easily out of the way as he turned his attention toward Gemma. Simeon struck a precise blow to Gemma's right temple, nothing haphazard about him, every move calculated. As Gemma was struck, she crumpled in a heap, bringing Sophie to the ground with her.

Movement in the crowd. Mark pushed his way through, still coughing smoke from his lungs. He saw Simeon beating Kyle with the full force of his whip. Gemma and Sophie still lay on the ground before them. Mark was shocked again at the lack of response of the citizens when they saw this kind of violence. His face was streaked with sweat and ash. The crowd moved away from him like leaves before a wind as he came through.

"Simeon!" he shouted, raising his pistol.

"I always knew what the two of you were," Simeon hissed. "Always knew I'd have this moment of retribution. Now here it is."

Kyle heard Mark's voice, and in a second of clarity, he could see what was going to happen. He saw Simeon's hand moving toward his gun, saw Mark looking at him on the ground. Kyle jumped up more quickly than he should have been able, placing himself directly before Simeon. He saw the pure hatred on his face as a shot pierced the still air. The barrel of the fired weapon burned on his stomach as he fell forward into Simeon.

Looking up into Simeon's face, the truth fell upon him like dew. "You were never my father," he gasped out. In the distance from somewhere far away, he heard Mark's screams.

Just as the gun had fired, the crowd finally broke into a fury of chaos and reckoning. They turned on Simeon, sending him scrambling for his horse. They descended on the Government Office with sticks and anything else they could find. Furniture began flying out of windows, supplies looted. All in a frenzy.

Mark was at Kyle's side, falling down next to him, trying to lift him to take him to the nearby doctors. But they both knew it was too late.

"Stop. Mark, listen."

"Why did you do it? Why?"

"You know why," Kyle coughed out.

"I need to hear you say it."

"You'll never believe me." Kyle was gasping for breath.

"I will."

"I love you."

Mark buried his face in Kyle's chest, screaming into him.

"Take off my coat," Kyle whispered. "I won't die a Corsair."

As gently as he could, Mark removed the blue coat, rolling it into a pillow under Kyle's head. His white shirt now soaked with blood.

"Go now. Danger."
"I won't leave you."

Sam had heard the gunshot and pushed his way through the crowd of crazed citizens, now venting all of their repressed anger and revenge on the few remaining Corsairs. He saw Mark and Kyle in the middle of the square. Neither seemed to be moving. Only feet away, Zacharias and Jesse were standing over two women also on the ground. Sam ran to them. He couldn't quite piece together the scene that lay before him or what had happened. Sophie was sitting, holding Gemma's bruised and beaten body in her arms.

Gemma seemed to be struggling in and out of consciousness. She would turn and reach out for something or someone who wasn't there. "The river and the rocks. I have to find him. Sam. Where's Sam?"

"I'm here." Sam appeared next to her.

"I couldn't save them. Couldn't move. The little boy. Daisy. Sam. Couldn't save them." She was beginning to thrash with what little energy was left her and tried to get up.

"Gemma," Sophie whispered.

Gemma looked at her friend, coming back to the present. She knew then that they both truly knew each other and took her hand and held it tight.

Sophie whispered, "Remember what you said in the letter you wrote me? *One equal temper of heroic hearts, made weak by time and fate, but strong in will to strive, to seek, to find, and not to yield.* You did it, Gemma. You saved us, and you didn't yield."

A peaceful smile passed over Gemma's face. Sophie pressed her lips to Gemma's forehead. And she was gone. Sophie now saw her without the mask of code names for everything she had been in her life. Not only had Gemma saved her life, but she had given Sophie her reason for living by giving Sam to her. Everything she had now and loved in her life was because of Gemma. She held her tighter, the blood on Gemma's face washing off in Sophie's tears.

Sam still struggled to piece everything together in the chaos around him. He looked at Sophie, not knowing if she were real or an angel until she touched his hand, his wife who was dead, brought back to life. And though he mourned the loss of his childhood friend and sweetheart, he knew he couldn't have borne the reverse.

He raised Sophie up, taking her in his arms. "I knew you'd still be alive. Some deeper instinct beyond the fear, beyond what my mind told me was true—that deeper instinct led me and told me to trust."

"We lost her, Sam. We lost Gemma."

"I know."

"There will be time later for mourning." Mark had walked up to the saddened group, wiping the tears from his own cheeks. "Right now, we have to move quickly. Simeon will be heading for his bunker to alert more Corsairs. We have to get to him before the fire spreads."

"Where is it now?"

"They've lit up the entire Forbidden Grounds from the fence to the wall. He'll take the one path left on the other side of the stream, but he will have ordered his men to light it up behind him. We've got to go now. There are horses in the barn behind the Government Office. Let's organize these people and move out."

Zacharias stepped forward. "I'll stay behind to try to help fight the fire. People will be trying to escape the Forbidden Grounds. Someone has to cut the fence."

"I'll stay with him," Jesse added.

"Do you know what you're doing?" Sam asked.

"Of course we do. This is your fight now, son. I know you can do it. Live free or die."

"We love you both."

Sophie and Sam embraced the elderly couple before following Mark to gather the horses. "Live free or die!" they called over their shoulders.

In one clear patch of sky, the smoke parted, freeing a shaft of sunlight amid the blue.

25

ASHES AND LIGHT

In what should have been the long, cool twilight, heat rose up all around the diminished remainder of rebels, no more than twenty. In the glow of fire, their shadows pressed together in one long jagged blackness on the ground behind. Horses jostled old and young bones unaccustomed to riding. Mark, Sam, and Sophie were leading the charge. Mr. and Mrs. O'Dell, other friends and neighbors, and Mark's few remaining soldiers all made their way through the Forbidden Grounds at a breakneck pace.

"We've got to get to the tunnel. He'll be in his bunker. Dead certain," Mark called out in the roar of the fire.

"We'll make it," Sam replied. He tried to sound confident, but he wasn't at all sure. He was beginning to lose his bearings with the fire closing in around them. He wasn't even sure they were going the right direction anymore. He had to trust that Mark knew the way better than he did.

There were no more trees or broken cities around them in the Forbidden Grounds, only kindling for the fire. Every living thing had taken flight in the opposite direction of the mob of rebels, and they were left to battle the fire and the ride alone. Branches descended in a rain of sparks. The horses reared and froze in their tracks.

"We can't stay here, and we can't go back!" yelled Sophie.

"We have to keep heading for the wall." Sam's voice was almost lost in the inferno.

Mark took charge. "Cover the horses' eyes with anything you've got. We keep going. The stream's just ahead. We'll ride in it 'til we reach the tunnel. Let's move!"

* * * * *

The regiment of Corsairs known as the Fire Brigade spread themselves out along the Border fence. "Our orders from General Drape are clear, gentleman," the colonel shouted above the roar of the approaching flames. "Burn them all and shoot the survivors. Anyone nearing this fence will be shot on sight. Understood?"

"Yes, sir!" his men robotically responded.

"Stay the course!"

"Stay the course!" came the automatic reply.

* * * * *

The cabin was the nearest dwelling to the Border fence. Zacharias and Jesse took horses to get there quickly for Ethan and the twins. Ethan had Petal and Hughie packed with what food and few belongings they could carry, with canteens of water for whatever journey lay ahead. He had trusted that someone would come for them, and they had.

Jesse and Zacharias went through the cabin, gathering their own supplies and meager tools to cut the fence.

"Ethan, there's a horse for you, son. Put your things in the saddlebags. The twins will ride behind Zack and me. Hop, now," Jesse kindly commanded.

Ethan quickly did as he was told, not stopping to ask where Sam and Sophie were. He had learned through hardships how to trust his new parents. They would come for him when they could.

"One last look around, then we can go," Zacharias said, walking toward the kitchen.

Jesse held his hand for a moment, bringing peace into the tumultuous situation. She gently placed her fingers in the lines on his forehead. "Pain wrote those across your face."

"You have a story of pain on yours as well. You should go with the children before the fire spreads. Head for the Southern Border where the fire isn't as strong. It won't be safe. I'll come to you when I've gotten everyone through."

"I'm not leaving you ever again." The tears ran in the rivulets of time on her face. "This time, we're walking out of this cabin together."

Jesse took her husband in her arms and began to sing quietly in his ear. *"Keep smiling through the day, keep smiling through the night. The shadows fly away when they can see your light."*

Zack had missed this about his Jesse, and he wished he had time to continue to be reminded of their love day by day.

She went right on singing her tune of comfort. *"If I can keep you with me in day and nighttime too, I know the dark won't find me because my light is you."*

With the end of the song, she kissed his cheek and said, "Come on, love. We can do this. Let's go." Jesse took his hand as they walked through the door of the cabin together.

* * * * *

The small band of children and old rode along the fence cutting holes in the Border, helping people through as they could. Many had already suffered at the hands of the Corsairs and the fire, caught in the barbed wire, hanging like scarecrows. And still the group rode on, pushing horrific images behind them. As they rode farther south, Jesse and Zacharias watched in horror as the fire jumped the fence and began to consume the encroaching trees ahead and around them.

Zacharias stood at the fence, cutting barbed wire as fast as his old hands would allow him, stragglers from the Forbidden Grounds wriggling through like wild animals escaping the fire.

From her place next to Zacharias, Jesse looked up into the frightened face of the boy on the horse. "Ethan, you know the way to the beach, son?"

"Yes," he said hesitantly.

"Take Petal and Hughie and head for one of the caves. We'll find you there."

"But Jesse . . ."

"Go on now, son. I haven't broken a promise to you yet, have I?"

"No."

"Alright, then. Remember what I told you. Your mother was proud of you, and so am I. I'll see you soon, my boy." She could see the fire shining in the tears in his eyes.

Zacharias called to her from the fence, "Jesse, take the children and ride for the coast. You'll be safe on the beach. Go now!"

She stood next to him, placing her hands on each side of his dirtied face. "I told you, I'm not leaving." The tears ran in streaks with the sweat on their faces. As they watched the children ride away, the trailing smoke and flames leapt behind them.

"There's a road out there that will lead us all back," Jesse said through the smoke.

* * * * *

"We'll have to leave the horses here," Mark called from the edge of the tunnel. He was amazed they had made it this far.

Cut into a concrete wall more than fifty feet high, a dark hole emerged, blocked with iron gates. The gray of the wall blended with the smoke, so the group hadn't seen it until they almost ran into it. There were no other openings, ladders, or any means of penetrating the wall as far as the eyes could see in either direction.

"How do we get through?" Sam asked.

"I have a passkey, if they haven't deactivated it. Now listen, I've sent a distress signal through their communication system on the other side of the wall."

"How?" Sophie asked.

"It would take too long to explain. It's called the Internet, and the message is going out to every citizen's personal device via an emergency system. Maybe someone will come help, but we can't be sure. We may be on our own. You two take the citizens with you to get to Simeon's bunker. Follow the tunnel until it comes to a T. Turn right down that tunnel and go about fifty yards. There will be a bunker on your left. Take my passkey. Simeon will most likely be there if he's anywhere."

Sam didn't like the idea of walking into the lion's den alone. "Where will you be?"

"I'm going to stop more Corsairs from getting through. I'll take my men with me. We'll meet you in the bunker."

Sam fought the urge to think of this as a trap, reminding himself of all that Mark had done for them up to this point at his own peril.

"Alright, we'll meet you there."

Mark held a small rectangular card up to a black box on the side of the tunnel. They heard a beep, then a cranking of gears, pulling the gates up. The group of citizens tried not to stand too long in amazement at what they'd just seen. Something told them there were many wonders awaiting them on the other side of this wall.

Entering the darkened tunnel, the shadows of the closing gate cut diamonds into the light on the wall. Mark handed Sam a short circular gray tube.

"What's this?"

"A flashlight. It'll be dark down there. Here, hit this button to turn it on." As Mark touched the button, a bright beam shone from the tube, surprising Sam again.

Mark took his men in first. As they came to the T in tunnel, their group went left while Sam's group went right.

As they made their way carefully through the darkened tunnel, Sophie winced and stopped walking.

"You alright?" Sam grabbed her arm, and Mrs. O'Dell came to her other side.

"What is it, dearie?"

"Nothing, I'm fine. Let's keep going."

"Sophie, is it the baby?" Sam's concerned furrowed his brow.

"You know?"

"Yes," he smiled, despite the circumstances.

Sophie tried to control her emotions. She'd been so worried to tell him, worried how they'd face it together. Now, in the midst of a fight, she found out he knew all along. She couldn't believe how much she had underestimated him and his ability to handle whatever was thrown at him.

"Maybe you and Mrs. O'Dell should wait at the mouth of the tunnel."

"Not on your life. The baby was just kicking. Now, you listen to me, Sam. They may kill me, but they'll never stop me. You understand? We're going into this together." She took his hand slowly as if they had forever. "If we die tonight, we will die fighting and together. No matter what, you and I together. In the end, isn't that what matters?"

"Of course it is. Let's keep moving."

As they came to the door of the bunker, Sam came to a decision.

"Alright," he whispered, sound barely carrying because of the impenetrable walls. "Sophie and I will go in. The rest of you stay out here. If you hear a scuffle, come in guns blazing. Got it?"

The group behind him nodded in agreement.

Sam took Mark's passkey from his pocket and held it to the black box as he'd seen Mark do. The heavy metal door clicked open. He pulled his pistol, throwing the door open as they entered.

Simeon sat at a gray metal desk on the opposite side of a long rectangular room. His face was lit grotesquely under his white hair by one single desk lamp. He appeared as a skeleton staring back at them.

"Well, hello there, Sam. I've been expecting you. And you've brought your wife. How lovely."

"This isn't a game, Simeon!" Sam held up his pistol so it could be seen.

"Of course not. It's most serious." Simeon stepped out from behind his desk and walked slowly toward them.

"How did you know I'd be here?"

"Because, Sam, you are like me, and I am like you."

"That's the second time you've compared us, and I find it offensive."

Simeon laughed an echoed laugh more frightening than if he'd growled at them. "My boy, you're so angry. But this isn't my fight any more than it is yours. I inherited it from the ones who came before. We're the same, you and I. We both want peace."

Sophie found her voice but was amazed at how difficult she found it to force sound from her lips in the room that felt like a vacuum, a void of space, feeling, or sound. "So why not just let us live in peace?"

"Because, my dear, peace like that requires a sacrifice. A blood sacrifice." He savored the words. "History teaches us that. Look at all the countries of the world. But then, of course, you wouldn't know about that. You'll just have to trust me. But history was full of assassinations, plots, coups, violence. A terrible business. How can I explain this in terms you'll understand?" Simeon took a step forward and looked to the ceiling as if his answers were there. "A mosquito is going to bite you. It's in his nature. Inevitable. You can either wait for it to happen—the little parasite draining your blood and spreading disease—or you can kill it. Better yet, you can exterminate all the mosquitoes. That's what this is—an extermination to prevent the spread of disease. Kill off all the troublemakers and what's left? Peace."

421

"Promising peace at the cost of freedoms is a clever lie, but a lie all the same," Sam responded.

"Lies. So many lies from so many places. Religions used to lie to the people. The churches and religions were behind so-called holy wars. So we got rid of those. With books and then the Internet, the flow of information was too free and easy. People were drowning in information, so we saved them from that burden. The books you're so fond of, Sam, they told lies too. I allowed you to find them in the Forbidden Grounds to prove to you what lies they all were. I knew you wouldn't believe me. They taught you to fight for things, to stand up to the oppressor. But where has it gotten you? Death and destruction. You see, this was a test. If you had just done what you were told, you could be free now. But you ignorant, predictable fools had to always fight, always buck the system. And now you have nothing. You've failed the test miserably but proven what I've said all along: Once a rebel, always a rebel."

Sam felt his veins pounding in his temples. The room was hot. His sweat was dripping down his back, wetting his tunic. "You took the books, the beauty, the things that make people human. You made us live like animals!"

"Oh, Samuel, we took nothing they didn't happily give away," Simeon laughed again. Sophie stepped closer to Sam. "We never could have taken the books away from them if they'd actually still been reading them. No, you see, they wanted nothing more than for someone to tell them what to do and how to think. They practically begged for it. First, it was the talking head celebrities, but it was easy enough for us to step in and fill that role. We've only given the people what they always wanted: simplicity, security, consistency. We give them security, and they give us authority. We stay the course. The government took it on ourselves to protect our citizens. And they were happier. Believe me."

"*You* did all that. You admit it."

"You're not listening again. I inherited all this. The government made decisions before me. They needed a hard reset. The weather wars compromised the electrical grid. We were running out of food. Drought, riots, not enough resources for more food. Nearly ten billion people on the planet, and only enough food for maybe a quarter of them. It was only a matter of time before everyone found out, and there would have been utter chaos. So we knew we had to do something drastic. The leaders of the different countries got together and decided this was the best way. Basically, just turn off the lights and start over. We pulled in all of our armies and navies, called truce on every war, and agreed to each take care of our own people. What else could we have done? And is this not better? A simpler way of life? No more of the ancient distractions."

"No, because now we're just fighting to survive," Sophie shouted at his complacency. "You tried to destroy the beauty of what we stayed alive for."

Sam couldn't believe what he was hearing. "Are you telling us you intentionally killed all of those people with the Disaster?"

"Not at all. We just turned up the volume on natural selection, so to speak. We let nature take care of herself, and we took care of the leftovers."

"The leftovers. Is that what we are?"

"Most of the fighting began to dissipate. But there were always those rebellious few. The troublemakers. So the Triumvirate came up with an experiment. I will take credit for that one. I wanted to see if we put all the rebels in one place, in a completely controlled environment, and gave them one generation, could we breed the rebelliousness out of them?"

"Why the lies? Why not just tell us we were in prison?" Sam was becoming angrier by the second.

"Everything in this plan depended on you believing you had at least some freedom. But sadly, the experiment was a failure. The only thing left was to remove the undesirable element."

"But those weren't your orders!" Mark shouted from the doorway.

"Ah, Colonel Goodson. The prodigal son returns."

"The orders were to reprogram and reintegrate."

"That never would have worked! You're proof enough of that fact, my boy. You and that fairy Kyle I adopted. Never could reprogram either one of you. No, the rebels had to be killed off. Yes, and all their children, too. Completely cleanse the gene pool."

"What about you, then?" Mark stepped forward, pointing his own pistol at Simeon.

"What about me?"

"You're the child of rebels too."

"You're missing the point! All of you could have been so much more than you are. If you'd listened to us, if you'd let us help you, you could have been a leader. You had so much potential. Such a waste."

An understanding began to come over Sam. A realization of why Simeon had been targeting him and all the rest. "I've tried to figure out what you hate so much about the rebels. And now I think I know. You hate that we continue to fight for freedom where you retreated and turned your back. You hate your own cowardice and want to punish us for it. Well, you'll never beat it that way. The cowardice and fear and loathing will still be with you long after we're all dead."

Simeon's cool facade started to disintegrate. "You want to know what I hate? I hate your damned arrogance. Always believing you're right. How do you know? How can you really know? Maybe all those people you killed in the war and the ones since then—maybe their deaths were all pointless and meaningless. How can you even live with yourselves?"

Mark had to laugh at this. "You ask *us* that?"

"You people thought your 'great revolution' was going to make a difference. How could it? No one even knows you're here. And now my Corsairs are coming to finish the extermination. Truly, it's as if you're already dead. We've killed all of your leaders, ending with Foxglove. Now there is no one left to lead you."

Sophie stepped up. "You're not as smart as you think. I was Foxglove all along."

"Don't be ridiculous."

Mrs. O'Dell stepped into the room behind Sophie. "No, I was Foxglove."

"I was Foxglove," Mark added.

The entire group of rebels and Mark's men filed into the bunker. "I was Foxglove," they said in scattered voices, hitting like bullets on the concrete walls. For the first time in years, the citizens stepped forward, no longer cowed by Simeon or the fear he sowed.

"No Corsairs are coming," Mark grinned.

"What are you talking about? I've already set off the alarm."

"And I let them know you are dead. Executed at the orders of the president and vice president for high treason. No one is coming to help you."

Simeon's calm facade finally cracked under his skin. His eyes darted around the room, his hands shaky. In one last desperate attempt to inflict pain, he lunged for Sophie's throat, the closest to him. But before his foot had fallen on the floor before him, twenty bullets from twenty guns had pierced his angry shell. Simeon fell in a heap, leaving a peace behind the echo of gunfire. A peace he had claimed to want so badly.

The group stood in dazed silence for a few minutes, trying to realize the truth that their enemy was in fact dead.

"You know this isn't the end, don't you?" Mark finally spoke. "Yes, Simeon went against the Triumvirate, but they were part of the same body. The same problem."

"So, what's the answer?" Sam asked.

"Remove the Triumvirate. Find a new kind of democracy or republic. Return people's freedoms and natural rights."

"But how?" Sophie asked.

"It will take a long time, but we have to wake up the people. They've been asleep, anesthetized for decades. Fed solely on a diet of entertainment and pleasure. Pleasures handed to them at the cost of their freedom and yours. The work camps supplied everything. Now that those are gone, the Triumvirate will try to create another slave class. They'll begin by villainizing people, those who are different. And we can't let that happen."

"What can we do about it?" Sam asked. "There are so few of us left. And we have no idea how to live in the world on the other side of the wall."

"You'll learn what you need to know. A movement starts with one idea. One spark. One person. We have enough. We have the idea."

EPILOGUE: OVER THE WALL

Sophie followed Sam out of the tunnel. The light from the other side of the wall was almost blinding after the dimness they'd left.

"The world looks almost brighter here," she said. "Is that possible?"

"It is. You're looking through freedom." Sam took her hand in his. Stretching out before them in a valley, they saw a sprawling city with speeding cars and trains. Machines flew overhead, silently zipping across the sky. Mark called them airplanes. As they made their way into the city, they saw people walking in a kind of daze. Each person had a tiny transparent screen in front of one eye. Occasionally, a person would smile or speak to no one in particular. Mark tried to explain their personal communication devices. But everything seemed strange to Sophie and Sam. Foreign. Although the citizens looked clean and even radiant in their colorful clothing and fast-moving vehicles, they also seemed disconnected from each other.

"Why didn't someone try to get over the wall before this?" Sam asked, concern on his face.

"They were told there was nothing but destruction on the other side of the wall," Mark answered, "and they believed it. If anyone had tried to get through—and the tunnel was the only way—they would have seen nothing but the evidence to support that lie. Twenty miles is a long way to travel through a lie to reach a truth they didn't know was there."

"We've read so much about this place, Sam, and yet it's nothing like we imagined. I'm not sure it's better," Sophie said, gripping his hand to still her fear and discomfort.

"I think they think it is. Look at their faces. But it's been handed to them under a blanket of lies."

"Not exactly a paradise."

"I don't think paradise is a real place to be found. I think it's within us. One day they'll see, like we did, how much they're in the dark."

"But how can they, without someone from the outside shining a light?"

Sam lifted up the flashlight he still held in his hand, pressing the circular button as he'd seen Mark do.

Sophie smiled.

* * * * *

Months Later
A Hospital in Virginia

The wall had fallen at the hands of a group of rebels, grown stronger. Piece by piece they'd struck it down with hammers and words and ideas. Sophie looked out from her hospital window ten stories high, overlooking the valley all the way to the decimated wall. She couldn't quite see all the way to the ocean but wished she could. She sometimes missed the sound of the waves at night.

Her door beeped and then opened, Sam, Ethan, Petal, Hughie, Zacharias, and Jesse all filing into the large suite. Jesse went straight to the bed to kiss Sophie's cheek and see how she was doing. Sam walked over to the tiny incubating crib, lifting the little baby who was only slightly bigger than his hand. The other children smiled to see her squirming and grunting. They'd never seen a baby before. It was truly a wonder. Zacharias and Jesse remembered back to their own small babies more than a lifetime ago.

Sam proudly placed the baby girl into Sophie's waiting arms. The tiny one opened her eyes, trying to take in all around her. "Can you turn off the overhead light?" Sophie asked. "I'm still not quite used to artificial light."

From the dimmed hospital room, the baby girl shot her tiny fist in the air, a silhouette against the sunset from the window. As the sun peaked across the river, unmuted through air no longer filled with ash, the light winked. The river twinkled with quivering movement.

"She has red hair," Jesse observed.

Sam smiled. He couldn't have been happier about that. "What should we call her?" he asked, taking Sophie's hand in his.

Sophie thought for a moment, looking into the deep-blue eyes of her daughter. "Hope."

ACKNOWLEDGMENTS

Writing a book is an all-consuming and sometimes solitary endeavor, but no one writes in a vacuum. All writers are influenced in some way by the people around them. So, I must acknowledge the people in my sphere who contributed to this novel.

First and foremost, I need to thank Jen and Steven. You are my truest, most loyal friends, my sounding boards, first readers, most valued critics, keepers of all the secrets, and first-aid team for my heart. I adore you both and could not survive any of this without you.

I want to thank my dear, sweet nieces and nephews. Y'all are the inspiration for all the children in this book and some of the most important people in my life. Thank you for being "my kids." I love you to the moon and back!

Thank you to my sisters, who encouraged me to think outside of the box, and my parents, who pushed me to follow my dreams no matter the cost.

Kristi, my counselor, friend, and encourager, a simple thank-you will never be enough.

Loralee, words are not enough to express my love and appreciation for you. I am a better person for having you as my friend. I will always be your "Clyde Frog."

Courtney, Candi, and Aubrey, thank you for being kind and honest beta readers.

Colleen, Nicole, and Megan, thank you so much for being my daily cheerleaders and always believing in me.

Jen R., you keep me looking sharp, keep me on my toes, and bring laughter to my life.

I must thank Vince Font of Glass Spider Publishing and Judith Nicolas, the most awesome cover designer. Your work strengthened my own.

Jennifer Perry, you are the best publicist on the planet and the cheerleader I never knew I needed. Thank you for everything.

Last, but definitely not least, thank you to my writing mentors: Judy, Vicki, Merlin, Sally, Gary, Christy, and "Gibs." You helped me begin and taught me how to improve my writing. You each, in your own ways, encouraged me to believe in myself, build self-confidence, and never give up on this crazy writing dream. Thank you for all the things!

ABOUT THE AUTHOR

Photo courtesy Kacy Peckenpaugh.

Rachel Anne Cox is an English instructor at Weber State University and author of the new novel *A Light from the Ashes*. She made the trek from Louisiana to Utah thirteen years ago to pursue her studies in theater, literature, and creative writing. Rachel loved university life so much that she decided to teach college English. Rachel has always been fascinated by the stories of underdogs, scrappy rebels, and seekers of truth. When she isn't pursuing her lifelong passion of writing, you might find her looking for her newest elephant figurine, painting at her favorite pond, or exploring the trails in northern Utah, always with a camera in hand. You can visit her online at www.rachelannecoxwriter.com, find her on Facebook at www.facebook.com/rachelannecoxwriter, or find her on Instagram at www.instagram.com/rachel_anne_cox_writer.

Discussion Questions

1. *A Light from the Ashes* relies heavily on allusions to other literary works. What meaning did they add to the story? How so?

2. Sophie exhibits extreme resilience in the face of sometimes impossible odds. What gives her strength and helps her push through the obstacles?

3. Many of the characters in the *A Light from the Ashes* are passionate about their cause and believe they are right, even when they fight on different sides. How can we know if our cause or things we are passionate about are right and just?

4. Zacharias is a father figure and mentor to several characters in the book. Think of someone in your life who has been a mentor. How did he/she inspire or guide you?

5. What is a metaphor that stood out to you in the book? Why?

6. What themes within the book relate to current issues in our society?

7. Share a favorite quote from the book. Why did this quote stand out?

8. There are several generations portrayed within *A Light from the Ashes*. How do they handle the problems with the government differently? How are they the same?

Made in the USA
San Bernardino,
CA